GOLD
is the lure, and death is the trap, in Steve Frazee's chilling, "The Singing Sands"

GREED
twists the passions of a town into a lynching noose in Dorothy Johnson's rope taut "The Hanging Tree"

GUNPLAY
waits for a traveling judge riding into the sights of a quartet of killers in John M. Cunningham's pulse-pounding "Raiders Die Hard"

AND TRUE GRIT
as a troop of U.S. cavalry with a divided command unites to face an overwhelming Apache charge in James Warner Bellah's magnificent "Massacre"

Nine of the greatest Western stories ever written . . . each one made into an all-time top Western film . . . now together in—

BEST OF THE WEST III

BEST OF THE WEST III

More Stories That Inspired Classic Western Films

edited by
Bill Pronzini
and
Martin H. Greenberg

A SIGNET BOOK

SIGNET
Published by the Penguin Group
Penguin Books USA Inc., 375 Hudson Street, New York,
New York 10014, U.S.A.
Penguin Books Ltd, 27 Wrights Lane, London W8 5TZ, England
Penguin Books Australia Ltd, Ringwood, Victoria, Australia
Penguin Books Canada Ltd, 2801 John Street, Markham,
Ontario, Canada L3R 1B4
Penguin Books (N.Z.) Ltd, 182–190 Wairau Road, Auckland 10, New Zealand

Penguin Books Ltd, Registered Offices: Harmondsworth, Middlesex, England

Published by arrangement with Doubleday and Company, Inc.

First Signet Printing, December, 1990
10 9 8 7 6 5 4 3 2 1

CONTENTS

INTRODUCTION

Like the two volumes which preceded it, *Best of the West* (Signet, 1986) and *Best of the West II* (Signet, 1990), *Best of the West III* is an anthology of outstanding Western short stories which were the bases for noteworthy films. In our introductions to the first two volumes we made a point which is also applicable here: some of the tales in these pages have not been faithfully transferred to the screen, while others contributed only the basic idea to the movies they became. None is exactly like its Hollywood adaptation; some are barely recognizable as source material, after having gone through the multifarious hands of producers, directors, actors, and (especially) screenwriters. A comparison of the two versions of each entry can be educational, in that it offers an insight into the workings of the "Hollywood mind."

A brief look at the films, first:

The great John Ford's *Fort Apache* (1948), starring Henry Fonda, John Wayne, and Shirley Temple, is one of the best cavalry films ever made and the first of Ford's famous "cavalry trilogy." Based on James Warner Bellah's 1947 story "Massacre," its message was the importance of myth in the lives of a country's people; but most moviegoers responded to the tension between Fonda and Wayne (the latter in a somewhat cynical and deeply drawn role) and to the fine photography by Archie J. Stout.

Tennessee's Partner (1955) was directed by Allan Dwan, a veteran Hollywood director whose career began in 1909. Written by a team of four scriptwriters including Milton Krims, it was adapted from the famous story of the same title written by Bret Harte in 1869. John Payne starred, along with Ronald Reagan, Rhonda Fleming, and such veteran character actors as Anthony Caruso and Morris Ankrum. Angie Dickinson had a bit part.

John M. Cunningham's *Dime Western* pulp novelette "Raiders Die Hard" served as the basis for 1955's excellent *Day of the Bad Man,* directed by Harry Keller. The film stars Fred MacMurray as a circuit judge who refuses to give in to threats made by the four brothers of a convicted murderer, and is packed with the same kind of tension that makes *High Noon* (also based on a Cunningham short story) such a classic. Joan Weldon, John Ericson, Robert Middleton, Edgar Buchanan, and Lee Van Cleef had supporting roles.

The Texan (1930), directed by John Cromwell and written by Daniel N. Rubin and Oliver Garrett, is based on O. Henry's 1905 Llano Kid story "The Double-Dyed Deceiver." Gary Cooper, early in a career that would make him a Hollywood legend, portrayed the Kid whose rough ways are changed by the love of a woman. Fay Wray, of later *King Kong* fame, also appeared in this sentimental but satisfying film.

Steve Frazee's "The Singing Sands" (1954) was the basis for the 1961 film, *Gold of the Seven Saints.* Under the direction of Gordon Douglas, this feature starred Clint Walker, Roger Moore (yes, the same actor who would later portray James Bond), Chill Wills, and Robert Middleton. It is an "odd couple" story that pairs the rugged Walker with the less-than-believable-as-a-Westerner Moore and is not nearly as good as its source.

Trooper Hook (1957), directed by Charles Marquis Warren (himself a writer of Western fiction) and based on Jack Schaefer's fine 1951 short story, "Sergeant Houck," is an important and powerful film, one of Hollywood's earlier attempts to deal with racism and miscegenation. The stars are Barbara Stanwyck as a woman hated by her fellow whites because she has lived among Indians and Joel McCrea as the brave soldier who helps her.

Under a Texas Moon (1930), directed by the great Michael Curtiz, is based on Stewart Edward White's 1907 story "The Two-Gun Man." Featuring Frank Fay, a very young (and beautiful) Myrna Loy, Raquel Torres, Noah Beery, Sr., and George Stone, it is among the very few *musicals* developed from a short story (and a reasonably serious story at that). Its basic plot, of a man (Fay) caught between two women (Loy and Torres), later became a common one in motion pictures, Western and otherwise; but the film is a good one and stands up as well as can be expected of a fifty-five-year-old early talkie.

1970's *A Man Called Horse* was taken from the late Dorothy M. Johnson's superb 1949 *Collier's* story of the same title. This film is best known for the powerful scene in which star Richard Harris hangs by his chest from the top of a hut during the Sioux Sun Vow Initiation Ceremony—and is one of several extremely violent Westerns made by Harris. Its most unusual characteristic is the casting of Dame Judith Anderson as a Sioux woman, a performance that brought both praise and derision from the critics. Elliot Silverstein directed.

The Hanging Tree (1959) adapted from Dorothy M. Johnson's poignant novella of the same title, features another outstanding performance by Gary Cooper. In his next-to-last Western film Cooper portrays a doctor trying to forget his past in a mountain mining camp, until the blinded survivor of an Indian raid (played by Maria Schell) gives him a new lease on life. The supporting cast is uniformly excellent. George C. Scott (in a memorable role as a mad preacher) and Ben Piazza made their screen debuts; and Karl Malden (who doubled as emergency director when illness struck Delmer Daves) gives his usual flawless performance.

These, then, are the films; now for the stories that inspired them—stories that, like those in *Best of the West* and *Best of the West II* are among the most entertaining in the Western genre. Good reading.

—Bill Pronzini and
Martin H. Greenberg

MASSACRE

BY JAMES WARNER BELLAH
(Fort Apache)

No one has written better stories of the life of frontier soldiers or given more historical accuracy to the oft-used (and oft-misused) theme of battle between the U.S. Cavalry and the Indian nations than James Warner Bellah (1899-1976). And his 1947 story "Massacre," a fictional rendering of the Little Big Horn destruction of General George Armstrong Custer and his troops, is perhaps the most accomplished of all his works of this type. It was filmed as Fort Apache *in 1948, the first of director John Ford's cavalry trilogy starring John Wayne and adapted from Bellah stories; the other two films are* She Wore a Yellow Ribbon *(1949), from "Big Hunt" and "Command" and* Rio Grande *(1950), based on "Mission with No Record." Ford also directed yet another film taken from a Bellah work:* Sergeant Rutledge *(1960), from the* Saturday Evening Post *serial of the same title.*

The wind was out of the east, and there can be a great restlessness of soul in the east wind—a ghost shuffle of unfulfilled promise. Flintridge Cohill awakened quickly all over, and lay quite still from long habit, until it came back to him that he was safe in his own quarters at Fort Starke. He snaked out a hand to his repeater and pressed the ring-back release. The watch struck three quarters of an hour past three o'clock. And as the soft bell sang in the darkness, Flint was a little boy again, watching his father, the captain, come angrily up the path to their quarters at Sackets Harbor, seven years before Sumter, push open the door and fling his cap to the rosewood table in the hall. "Molly, they've finally got Grant. He's

10

resigned . . . for the good of the service!" Why should those things come back years later? Some friend of his father's. Some captain out at Fort Humboldt. A brother officer who had fought at Contreras and Chapultepec with his father.

Flint sat upright in bed. "Good God, I'll bet that was General Grant!" he said out loud, and he snorted. "And at a quarter before four in the morning twenty years later, what difference does it make if it was?" Then he heard the distant staccato of feet running.

Someone's boots pounding the headquarters' duck-boards. The sound bounced clearly across the parade ground to the row, on the east wind. In a moment, Fire Call would sound or someone would bawl for the corporal of the guard. Cohill flung out of bed and went out on his lean-to veranda. There was a carriage standing across the parade ground in the darkness by headquarters. A carriage with restless horses and dry axles.

It'll be twenty years more before I get within shooting distance of general officer's stars—like Grant and the Old Man—and by that time I won't care. It won't be nearly as important as making captain, in a few more years. But I'd like to be a general before I die—the best damned general in the world at the right time and the right place! It's only the middle of the month and that's a paymaster's wagon over there. I can see the glass glint silver in the starlight like a sheet of bucket-flung water.

Cohill was pulling on cold breeches and stiff boots, and his teeth were chattering in the east wind; he was running fast and silently through the living darkness of the parade ground, with somewhere in the cellars of his mind the nasty-sounding name of Custis Meacham, Indian agent at White River. What are those tricks of association?

Feet raced toward him. He pivoted with flung arms, bending down to silhouette whoever it was against the lighter darkness of the sky. "Brailey?"

Brailey came toward him. "Mr. Cohill, sir, I got orders to call you and Mr. Sitterding and Mr. Topliff. You're wanted at post headquarters, sir."

And Cohill said, "What's the paymaster's wagon got to do with it, Brailey?"

Brailey said, "The new post commander arrived in the wagon. Drove all night from Indian Wells."

Owen Thursday was a tall man, dried out to leather and bone and sinew. Whatever he was doing, he moved about incessantly, not with nerves, but with primeval restlessness; not with impatience, but with an echo of lost destiny. Brevet Major General Thursday, of Clarke's Corps—Thursday of Cumberland Station and of Sudler's Mountain, at twenty-six. Now a major of cavalry at thirty-eight, back in the slow Army runway again, with the flame of glory burning low on his horizon ("I don't know what you were in the habit of doing under similar circumstances when you commanded your division, major, but as long as you have a battalion in my regiment, you will—") for it is far worse to go up and come back again than it ever is not to go up at all. And the cities of the world should always be a vision. For few men can walk their streets and come back to live at peace with their souls in the quietude of their own villages.

"Lieutenant Cohill, sir"—the dark was alive and prowling, like a large cat. There was cool dampness in it, and the faint whisper of threat. A horse whinnied in screaming soprano. Close to, when the team moved the paymaster's wagon, its glass windows flashed black, like polished ebony in the starlight.

"You got here damned fast, Cohill. Where's the acting post commander? Do you all sleep with the covers over your heads at Fort Starke?"

There were booted feet on the veranda boards of headquarters. Inside, someone cursed persistently over the lighting of a lamp. Bitter wood smoke fanned low from a chimney lip and stained the smell of the white dawn air to gray. "Your father, General Cohill, asked me to convey his affection to you, Cohill, when I left Washington."

"Thank you, general."

"Not 'general,' " Thursday said sharply. "A man is what he's paid for. I'm paid in the rank of major."

"Yes, sir. I remembered you as General Thursday."

Then Joplyn came sprinting down the duckboards and braked himself to a quick stop. "Captain Joplyn, sir, acting in command."

"Joplyn," Thursday said, "I've come all the way in from Indian Wells on the whip and two wheels. Mr. Meacham, the agent at White River, wants a show of strength up there at once. He's afraid Stone Buffalo will get out of hand without it."

"Stone Buffalo has been out of hand for months. He is trying to see how far Meacham's religious sentiment will let him go, sir. And Meacham is the biggest fool west of Kansas City and the biggest liar. I'll get a half company off by reveille. I'll take it up myself."

"I call it to your attention that Mr. Meacham is an agent of the United States Government. You will get two companies and an escort wagon train off before reveille, Captain Joplyn. And I'll take them up to White River myself. I've had the officer of the guard send a runner to knock out Mr. Sitterding and Mr. Topliff. Mr. Cohill has already reported in. I'd like all three of them with me, for I know their names and records from department files. And I suggest you keep an officer at headquarters in future—on night duty— until I get back to take over command formally. I don't like daylight soldiers."

"Yes, sir." Joplyn turned sharp about to Flint Cohill with no change of voice, no strain in his manner. "Mr. Cohill, pass the word at once to A and B. Turn them to. Full field equipment, and three hundred rounds of carbine ammunition per man. You will take eight escort wagons, rations and forage for fifteen days, and half of C as mounted wagon guards."

"That is a lot of ammunition . . . for men who are supposed to be trained to shoot," Major Thursday said. "One hundred rounds per man should be ample for any emergency."

"One hundred rounds of carbine ammunition per man, Mr. Cohill. Fifty rounds for revolving pistols per pistol. Sitterding commands A. Topliff, B. You command the escort train. It is twenty minutes after four. How soon can you move out, Mr. Cohill?"

"Reveille is five-forty-five. We can pass the head of the column through the main gate at five-thirty, sir. When Topliff and Sitterding get here, will you tell them I shall be forming the train in the area in front of the cavalry stables? They can find me there. Their first sergeants will know everything you've told me . . . Brailey, follow me on the double as runner." Flint Cohill then turned sharp about to Thursday. "Have you anything additional, sir?"

"Yes, I've several things. I've a few ideas of my own

on how Indians should be dealt with. I shall want colors and a proper color guard, guidons and trumpeters. Have the men bring their polishing kits and button sticks and boot blacking. A little more military dignity and decorum out here, and a little less cowboy manners and dress, will engender a lot more respect for the Army. I'll meet you here to take over command, Cohill, as the column passes. You will act as adjutant, in addition to your other duties. Officers' Call in the saddle on the march for further orders as soon as the tail clears the post. Questions?"

"Nothing, sir."

"Move out."

The sun in August is a molten saber blade. It will burn the neckline and the back of a hand to blistered uselessness as you watch it. It sears the lower lip into stiff scar tissue and sweats up shirts and beltlines into noisome sogginess while you stand still. The column was headed due north to make a crossing of the upper reaches of the Paradise, girths frothed white, saddles hot damp, hat brims low, and the blue of trousers and shirts faded out to Southern gray with the dust silt that blanketed everything except eyeballs and the undersides of tongues.

Owen Thursday rode alone, off to the right of the leading files, where he could turn and look down the strung-out length with the faint echo in his eyes of larger columns he had commanded—of regiments of infantry with colors and field music; of artillery rolling inexorably in its heavy dust, hames taut and chains growling, wheels slithering in ruts with the protesting sound of cracking balk ends; of cavalry flank guards flung far out on his right and left by battalion.

All of which dissolved into a hundred and nine officers and men and eight escort wagons—as big a detachment as Mr. Cohill or Mr. Topliff or Mr. Sitterding had ever taken on the warpath in all their service.

"Mr. Cohill!"

Flint kneed out of column and put his horse to the gallop and rode in on Major Thursday's near side.

Thursday said, "Move down the column and have every man crease his hat fore and aft as a fedora. The front of the brim may be snapped downward as eye protection, but all the rest of the brim will be turned up. The hat will sit squarely on the head. Look at them, Mr. Cohill! They look like scratch farmers on market day! The hat is a uniform, not a subject for individual whimsical expression!"

Thursday had a point ahead and flankers out on either side and a tiny rear guard with a warning mission only, but somehow it seemed more like a maneuver—a problem —than it did a march into hostile territory. D'Arcy Topliff, heading up B, never knew where the thought came from. But it was there suddenly from something he'd read years before or heard someone say: The major has fewer years left to live than he has lived already, and when that knowledge hits a man's mind, he can break easily. He must hurry then, for his time is shortening. He must seek short cuts. And, seeking them, he may destroy the worth of his decisions, the power of his judgment. Only a solid character with a fine sense of balance can face the fewer years as they shrink ahead, and go on into them with complacent courage, all the way to the Door.

Flint Cohill, with the wagons and head down to the dust, thought, *Damn it, this isn't a ceremonial detail of the First City Troop turned out for a governor's funeral. He's got the men disliking him from the start, deliberately, for picayune cause.*

And then Flint remembered a name brought into conversation at a reception once, and he likewise remembered old General Malcolm Hamilton's grave bow.

"Madame, only four officers in the Army know the facts of that incident, but none of them will talk as long as the colonel's widow lives."

Three days north of Fort Starke, the detachment went into bivouac on the high ground above the headwaters of Crazy Man Creek, which is the south branch of White River, and a little under thirty miles from the agency. The commanding officer sent Clay Sitterding on ahead to scout and contact Custis Meacham, the agent.

Clay rode back in, about sundown. "Stone Buffalo is camped at the junction of White River and Crazy Man, sir, in the chevron the fork makes. His camp is about a week old. From three hundred to three hundred and fifty people, all told. Most of them warriors and dog soldiers. No women and children. It's a war camp. There are scouting parties all the way along between us."

"You contacted Meacham, Mr. Sitterding?"

"I did, sir. He professes to have Stone Buffalo's complete confidence. Stone Buffalo has attempted to have himself accepted as medicine chief as well as war chief of all his nation. Running Calf contested the claim and took the Red Hill people and left the reservation. Stone Buffalo followed him to force him back into the fold. Mr. Meacham sent for us to stop the two factions from warring, but the last four days seem to have settled the argument peaceably."

Major Thursday's lip thinned. "In other words, as soon as the Indians knew troops were on the way, they decided to behave."

"That could be it, sir. Stone Buffalo would like to smoke with you. Mr. Meacham requests it. I strongly advise against letting Indians into our camp. It will not be advisable to let them know any more about our strength than they do now."

"When I want advice from my officers, Mr. Sitterding, I ask for it. Will you remember that, please?"

The smell of an Indian is resinous and salty and rancid. It is the wood smoke of his tepee and the fetidity of his breath that comes of eating body-hot animal entrails. It is his uncured tobacco and the sweat of his unwashed body. It is animal grease in his hair and old leather and fur, tanned with bird lime and handed down unclean from ancestral bodies long since gathered to the Happy Lands.

Major Thursday saw their impassive Judaic faces, their dignity, their reserve. He felt the quiet impact of their silence but being new to the game, he had no way of knowing that they drew all of it on as they drew on their trade-goods blankets—to cover a childish curiosity and the excitability of terriers. Stone Buffalo. Black Dog. Pony that Runs. Running Calf. Eagle Claw. Chiefs of tribes in the sovereign nation of Stone Buffalo—a nation under treaty of peace with the United States. A nation, in effect, held as prisoners of war, so that it would keep that peace.

Custis Meacham was painfully nearsighted and frighteningly short of breath. It was necessary for him to gasp wide-mouthed when he spoke. His hands were damp in the palms and restless. His fingernails were concave, like the bowls of small blue spoons. He sat with the skirts of his greasy Prince Albert draped across his pendulous abdomen.

The pipe went solemnly around to the left, each man pulling it red until his cheeks ached, drawing in its raw smoke until his lungs were stifled.

Custis Meacham coughed himself redeyed and completely breathless. "Oh, dear," he said. "I can't stand to be near them when they smoke. I trust that you don't indulge in the vice for pleasure, Mr. Thursday?"

"I do, constantly," Thursday said. "And I am Major Thursday, Mr. Meacham, not Mr. Thursday."

"God bless you, I pay no attention whatever to military titles. I don't believe in titles of any kind. You can see from their faces and actions, as they pass the pipe, that they have settled all their troubles peaceably among themselves. Thanks be to God. You can take all your soldiers straight back tomorrow. What is your church, please?"

Owen Thursday looked long at Custis Meacham. He said, "You put in a request for this detachment, but that does not put you in command of it. Any further action on your part will be made through the same channel you used for the original request—direct to departmental headquarters. I am a back-slidden Presbyterian, Mr. Meacham. I intend to remain one."

"You cannot tell me what to do." Custis Meacham's voice was shrill. "I am quite used to the way the Army does things! When I was secretary of the International Bible Association, I once told General Scott—"

Flint Cohill touched the major's arm. "Stone Buffalo is going to speak, sir," and, after a moment, Stone Buffalo rose. He talked and for a great many minutes Cohill said nothing.

Then he said, "All he has said so far is that he is a very, very brave man." Thursday nodded, and Stone Buffalo talked on for many more minutes. Cohill said, "He says now that he is also a very great hunter—he and his whole tribe." Again Thursday nodded, and Stone Buffalo told how the railroads and the white hunters had killed off the buffalo, and how he alone, as medicine chief, could bring them back again.

Suddenly Cohill whispered, "I don't like any of it, sir.

He's covering up for time. This is an insolent attempt at reconnaissance, I believe."

"Stop it then." Thursday's voice was hard.

"It will have to run out—protocol requires it—you cannot stop him now until he is finished. That would be a grave insult."

"Is there anyone at Fort Starke who recognizes an order when it is given?"

Cohill rose to his feet. Stone Buffalo stopped talking in vibrant anger. Major Thursday leaned forward. "Cohill, no preliminary nonsense with him, no ceremonial phrasing. Straight from the shoulder as I tell you, do you hear me? They are recalcitrant swine. They must feel it."

Cohill stood there, white-faced. He said, "I hear you, sir. What shall I tell them?"

"Tell them I find them without honor or manhood. Tell them it is written on sacred paper that they will remain on their reservation. That they have broken this promise puts them beneath fighting men's contempt, makes them turkey-eating women. Tell them they are not talking to me, but to the United States. Tell them the United States orders them to leave here at once. They will break camp at dawn and return to the reservation, for I move in to their camp site at daylight," and Major Thursday turned his back and stalked off into the darkness, calling sharply for the officer of the guard.

Clay Sitterding, D'Arcy Topliff and Flint Cohill squatted in the white mists, gulping their steaming coffee. The morning was a gaunt old woman in the shadows, standing there wrapped in a shawl, seeing what she would not see again. A thin old woman with sadness in her face, and courage and the overpowering knowledge of life's inevitable defeat.

Ten years and better had passed under the bridges of Sitterding, Topliff and Cohill. Ten knowledgeable years of hard and bitter learning. They could have talked. "I told him not to receive them, not to smoke with them last night, and he shut me up." They could have said, "One hundred rounds of ammunition instead of three!" But you learn not to talk before you can ever learn other things. Behind them in the mists there was the movement of many men, but not enough men now, because the shock action of cavalry at one to three is suicidal madness without surprise. Who cares what you have commanded before, or what people think of you, or what other wars you have fought in? In war it is always what happens now! What happens next! Who commands here . . . now!

Sittering finished his bitter coffee and for one brief instant he could feel the harsh winds of March on his face—the winds that howl up the Hudson River Valley and cut across the parade ground at the Academy like canister fired at zero elevation. There had been a time when the melting heat of Starke had made him forget the chilled wine of those Eastern winds.

D'Arcy Topliff said, "I wish I'd married the one rich woman I ever met! I'd be a banker in St. Louis this morning, and still in bed.'

Cohill tried to laugh, but some ancient instinct within him had dried up the wells of his laughter. The curtain was down across the back of his mind, shutting him off from all he had been, so that he could only move forward. Some men are fortunate that way.

"Here we go," he said quietly, and with both hands he pressed briefly on the shoulders of the other two. "Just remember that the escort train is in mobile reserve, and if you get a fight, save me a piece."

You have seen it so often in the Jonathan Redfield print. The powder-blue trace of Crazy Man Creek against the burnt yellow grass on the rising ground behind. The dead of Company A stripped naked and scalped, their heads looking like faces screaming in beards. Major Thursday, empty gun in hand, dying gloriously with what is left of Company B, in an attempt to rally and save the colors, but this is how it happened. *This is how it happened:*

The column moved out with the mists of the morning still cold, moved out in a long breath of saddle soap on still-stiffened leather, rough wool, not yet sweat-damp, and the thin brown of gun oil. Dog-faced cavalry, the like of which has passed from the knowledge of the world. Up the gently sloping rise from the bivouac to the ridge line above Crazy Man Creek. Across the hogback ridge, outlined against the spreading yellow light that rimmed the eastern horizon. Guidons, booted carbine butts, hats creased fore and aft, backs arched and colors flying.

There are cowpokes who will tell you solemnly that some-times when a murderous thunderstorm howls down the valley, you can see them again crossing that ridge. That you can hear the brass scream of the charge echoing. But that is not so, for soldiers pass once only, and all that they ever leave behind is memory. "Close up the inter-vals! Close up!"

The point crossed the ridge first and wound on down the slope where the trail weaves onto high and rock-strewn ground before it reaches the ford. The point went on through and forded Crazy Man and signaled back from the other side to Lieutenant Sitterding at the head of A. All clear.

Sitterding gave the word, and A crossed the ridge and started down, with B, under D'Arcy Topliff, three hun-dred yards behind and echeloned three hundred yards to the left, west, rear. Which was by explicit order of Owen Thursday. So much for the creek side of the ridge. On the bivouac side, there was still Flintridge Cohill and the wagon train and the mounted guards from C. Flintridge Cohill was held up as soon as he started . . . by a broken linchpin.

Owen Thursday, sitting his horse high on the sky line, was the only man who could see the entire command. He sat there against the whitening dawn as if he had chosen that position to sit on and wait for it.

Company A rode on slowly down into the defile, break-fasts still warm in stomachs, saddles softening to the butt, muscles limbering up to the new day's work. Then unbe-lievably there was a sudden ring of fire in their faces and on both flanks. One hundred and eighty degrees of fire—half the horizon around—splintered around them like dry and rotted timber, tearing around them like grommets ripped from heavy cloth. Clay Sitterding and forty-two men were down. Half their mounts, reeling, galloping, were thrashing back over them, trying to get out and up the slope again.

Flint Cohill, blind to the sight of it because the ridge line masked it, knew it desperately for what it might be. He stared into his farrier sergeant's face.

He said, "Sergeant Magee, fix that pin and hold the train here on my order!"

And he spurred furiously toward the ridge top. Almost

it was as if Owen Thursday were trying to escape facing him. He seemed to wait until he could wait no longer, until Cohill was almost to him, then he sank his rowels into his horse and plunged him headlong down the opposite side toward the Valley of the Shadow. But not soon enough, for Cohill saw what he was going to do. Cohill saw it. With no further reconnaissance and no clear idea of what he was up against, with no brief withdrawal to reform, with all of A lying dead now in the defile for everyone to see, Thursday screamed to Topliff to deploy B and to hit the sides of the defile at the gallop as foragers.

Cohill turned his back. "Magee," he shouted through cupped hands, "get the wagons up here fast!"

Then Cohill turned again, and this time he saw that murderous ring of fire from the rocks, half a full circle round, and there were tears within him that would never, as long as he lived, quite leave him again. In that moment he knew that the train and the mounted guards were all that there was left; that he alone on an open ridge line was all that remained of the sovereign dignity of the United States for hundreds of miles around. But he was saying it this way—he was saying it out loud, "D'Arcy's gone . . . and Clay's gone . . . but no man gets off this ridge line . . . no man!"

"Sergeant Magee, take the wagon boxes from the beds! Put one here! . . . Put one twenty full paces to the left! . . . One down there where you're standing, and one here to the right! All hands turn to, to dig rifle pits between the boxes! Turn in all canteens! Corral all animals on the rope, down the backslope!"

It's not always in the book. It's a hundred thousand years. It's a heritage and a curse and the white man's burden. It's Cannae and Agincourt and Wagram and Princeton, and it's the shambles of Shiloh.

With Flint Cohill it was thirty-one men on a hog-back ridge and the thought in his angry mind that he'd never live now to be a general officer, but he'd die the best damned first lieutenant of cavalry that the world could find to do the job that morning!

Lying on the ridge top, searching the ghastly valley below with his glasses, Flint saw the last of it—an officer and three men and the colors on their broken staff. He couldn't swear to it, but it looked like Clay Sitterding and old Sergeant Shattuck and Aiken and Sergeant Ershick. Only for a minute before they went down under the final rush. Then Stone Buffalo's warriors were overrunning the dead of both A and B, pincushioning the bodies with arrows. Scalping. Lopping off a foot and the right hand, so that the spirits, too, would suffer mutilation and never fight again. Then the Indians withdrew to consider the ridge top, and, by the dust presently, they were commencing to ring it, to cut it off from water, to wither it for the kill.

Cohill called young Brailey over and squatted down with him. "Brailey, you're a show-off and a braggart, and I never thought I'd have the right job for you. But I have. Take the best horse on the picket line. Make Fort Starke. Tell 'em where we are, and tell 'em we may still be alive if they hurry. I'm making you corporal, but you'll never draw a dime of pay if we're dead when you get back. Move out and make it so."

Shortly after that, Cohill saw the tiny group far below, struggling painfully up the draw. Six men, crawling, dragging two, stumbling. Hatless and bleeding. Stopping exhausted, faces downward; starting up the slow way once again. Cohill finally got down to them. D'Arcy Topliff, hit four times and barely breathing. Glastonby of the red hair, from A. "Sir, we didn't have a chance!"—crying every time he tried to speak. Pointing back helplessly. Cursing, with the tears greasing the filth of his cheeks. "Get Mr. Topliff to the ridge top, Glastonby." And there were Moore and Stonesifer and Coyne, out of B, draging Bittendorfer with them. Shocked speechless. Bleeding. Obeying like whipped beasts. "Go on up, all of you, straight up the draw."

Cohill said that, because at that moment he saw the seventh man, still far below them. "And tell Sergeant Magee I'll be along in a few minutes . . . a few minutes behind you," and he scrambled on down the draw until he was crouched beside Owen Thursday.

"Cohill, sir."

Thursday turned and looked at him as if he had never seen him before in his life. The light was gone from his eyes and the pride was dead in him at last. All of his days the ghost of today had ridden with him, mocking his pride, pointing the finger of scorn at his personal ambition. General Thursday, of Clarke's Corps, of Cumberland Station, of Sudler's Mountain, with luck and the devil to help and a hero's crown for the snatching!

But today, the ghost was come alive at the cost of seventy-two men lying dead, through the ignorance that is pride's handmaiden, the stubborness that is ambition's mistress.

"I am dug in on the ridge top," Cohill said, "with the wagon boxes loopholed, and rifle pits. I have thirty-seven men, one officer and one man wounded. I have water and ammunition—"

"Get ready to move out at once," Thursday said. "We must try to cut back into Fort Starke." But his voice broke.

Flint Cohill shook his head. "Stone Buffalo is already ringing the position. We cannot leave that ridge top. If we try, we'll be cut to ribbons before we've gone ten miles."

"Get ready to move out, Mr. Cohill!" The voice was a high and broken whine.

"I've sent a courier to Starke, sir. I believe he'll get through. I believe Captain Joplyn can get here in five days. I can hold until then. Besides, we've no other choice! General—" Cohill said it deliberately, but there was no defiance in it, no indictment. He was almost pleading. "General, there are two dead companies down there—all the friends I've had in the world for years." He snagged his hand gun from his holster, spun it until it was butt first toward Thursday, then he thrust it out and held it. "You don't have to tell me again, but A and B are all present or accounted for, and so am I! I'll move out to your order, but only under arrest, sir! Only under arrest!"

Thursday rose slowly to his feet, Cohill's gun in hand. "I've had all I can have," he said softly; "this is where the road stops at last." His eyes were completely empty as Flint looked into them. The light was gone forever. "Mr. Cohill, your ridge top. I'm going back down. Good luck."

"Mr. Sitterding can't talk, sir, nor can Shattuck nor Ershick nor Aiken, and you have my word of honor that I won't . . . ever . . . for the good of the service." Flint whispered it almost.

And that is how they found Owen Thursday when the flying column from Starke relieved Cohill's party on the fifth day.

He was dead with the little group that had defended the colors—dead beside Sitterding, Shattuck, Ershick and Aiken—shot in the right ear, with the gun held so close that the contract surgeon couldn't have missed knowing that the major had squeezed off the trigger himself. But Flintridge Cohill got there first, for there are ways of living that are finer than the men who try to live them, and a regiment has honor that no man may usurp as his personal property. Glory is a jade of the streets who can be bought for a price by anyone who wants her. Thursday wanted her but his pockets were empty, so Cohill lent him the two dollars for posterity. Cohill took his own gun from Thursday's dead hand. He threw out the cylinder and jerked the five ball cartridges and the one empty case into his left hand. He spun the gun far out into Crazy Man Creek.

The five ball cartridges, he dropped one by one as he moved away, but the empty cartridge case he always carried with him for the rest of his life, for fingering it in his pocket always gave him courage in moments when he needed it—when the way was dark and decisions not easy.

And it was Cohill, years later, who reconstructed the scene for Jonathan Redfield to paint. "Major Thursday," he said, "was a very gallant officer. We found him dead with the little group that defended the colors—with Lieutenant Sitterding and Sergeant Shattuck and Ershick and Private Aiken. No man could have wished for more."

But even when he was very old, Cohill always looked sharply at anyone who said, "for the good of the service," and he always said, "What exactly does that mean to you, sir?"

TENNESSEE'S PARTNER

BY BRET HARTE
(Tennessee's Partner)

Once the highest paid short-story writer in America, Bret Harte (1836-1902) wrote perhaps the finest fictional accounts of the lusty and sometimes violent life in the mining camps and boomtowns during the great California gold rush of the 1850s—stories such as "The Luck of Roaring Camp" (filmed as a "B" picture under that title in 1937); "The Outcasts of Poker Flat" (filmed three times, once in 1919 as a silent, once in 1937 with Preston Foster and Van Heflin, and once in 1952 with Dale Robertson); and "Tennessee's Partner" (brought to the screen in 1955, with John Payne and Ronald Reagan). Somewhat lesser known than the other two stories mentioned, "Tennessee's Partner" (1869) is nonetheless a Bret Harte—and an Old West—classic.

I do not think that we ever knew his real name. Our ignorance of it certainly never gave us any social inconvenience, for at Sandy Bar in 1854 most men were christened anew. Sometimes these appellatives were derived from some distinctiveness of dress, as in the case of "Dungaree Jack"; or from some peculiarity of habit, as shown in "Saleratus Bill," so called from an undue proportion of that chemical in his daily bread; or from some unlucky slip, as exhibited in "The Iron Pirate," a mild, inoffensive man, who earned that baleful title by his unfortunate mispronunciation of the term "iron pyrites." Perhaps this may have been the beginning of a rude heraldry; but I am constrained to think that it was because a man's real name in that day rested solely upon his own unsupported statement. "Call yourself Clifford, do you?'' said Boston, addressing a timid newcomer with infinite scorn; "hell is full of such Cliffords!'' He then introduced the unfortunate man, whose name happened to be really Clifford, as "Jaybird Charley''—an unhallowed inspiration of the moment that clung to him ever after.

But to return to Tennessee's Partner, whom we never knew by any other than this relative title. That he had ever existed as a separate and distinct individuality we only learned later. It seems that in 1853 he left Poker Flat to go to San Francisco, ostensibly to procure a wife. He never got any farther than Stockton. At that place he was attracted by a young person who waited upon the table at the hotel where he took his meals. One morning he said something to her which caused her to smile not unkindly, to somewhat coquettishly break a plate of toast over his upturned, serious, simple face, and to retreat to the kitchen. He followed her, and emerged a few moments later, covered with more toast and victory. That day week they were married by a justice of the peace, and returned to Poker Flat. I am aware that something more might be made of this episode, but I prefer to tell it as it was current at Sandy Bar—in the gulches and barrooms—where all sentiment was modified by a strong sense of humor.

Of their married felicity but little is known, perhaps for the reason that Tennessee, then living with his partner, one day took occasion to say something to the bride on his own account, at which, it is said, she smiled not unkindly and chastely retreated—this time as far as Marysville, where Tennessee followed her, and where they went to housekeeping without the aid of a justice of the peace. Tennessee's Partner took the loss of his wife simply and seriously, as was his fashion. But to everybody's surprise, when Tennessee one day returned from Marysville, without his partner's wife—she having smiled and retreated with somebody else—Tennessee's Partner was the first man to shake his hand and greet him with affection. The boys who had gathered in the canyon to see the shooting were naturally indignant. Their indignation might have found vent in sarcasm but for a certain look in Tennessee's Partner's eye that indicated a lack of humorous appreciation. In fact, he was a grave man, with a steady application to practical detail which was unpleasant in a difficulty.

Meanwhile a popular feeling against Tennessee had grown up on the Bar. He was known to be a gambler; he was suspected to be a thief. In these suspicions Tennessee's Partner was equally compromised; his continued intimacy with Tennessee after the affair above quoted could only be accounted for on the hypothesis of a copartnership of crime. At last Tennessee's guilt became flagrant. One day he overtook a stranger on his way to Red Dog. The stranger afterward related that Tennessee beguiled the time with interesting anecdote and reminiscence, but illogically concluded the interview in the following words: "And now, young man, I'll trouble you for your knife, your pistols, and your money. You see your weppings might get you into trouble at Red Dog, and your money's a temptation to the evilly disposed. I think you said your address was San Francisco. I shall endeavor to call." It may be stated here that Tennessee had a fine flow of humor, which no business preoccupation could wholly subdue.

This exploit was his last. Red Dog and Sandy Bar made common cause against the highwayman. Tennessee was hunted in very much the same fashion as his prototype, the grizzly. As the toils closed around him, he made a desperate dash through the Bar, emptying his revolver at the crowd before the Arcade Saloon, and so on up Grizzly Canyon; but at its farther extremity he was stopped by a small man on a gray horse. The men looked at each other a moment in silence. Both were fearless, both self-possessed and independent, and both types of a civilization that in the seventeenth century would have been called heroic, but in the nineteenth simply "reckless."

"What have you got there?—I call," said Tennessee quietly.

"Two bowers and an ace," said the stranger as quietly, showing two revolvers and a bowie knife.

"That takes me," returned Tennessee; and with this gambler's epigram, he threw away his useless pistol and rode back with his captor.

It was a warm night. The cool breeze which usually sprang up with the going down of the sun behind the chaparral-crested mountain was that evening withheld from Sandy Bar. The little canyon was stifling with heated resinous odors, and the decaying driftwood on the Bar sent forth faint sickening exhalations. The feverishness of day and its fierce passions still filled the camp. Lights moved restlessly along the bank of the river, striking no answering reflection from its tawny current. Against the blackness of the pines the windows of the old loft above the express office stood out staringly bright; and through their curtainless panes the loungers below could see the forms of those who were even then deciding the fate of Tennessee. And above all this, etched on the dark firmament, rose the Sierra, remote and passionless, crowned with remoter passionless stars.

The trial of Tennessee was conducted as fairly as was consistent with a judge and jury who felt themselves to some extent obliged to justify, in their verdict, the previous irregularities of arrest and indictment. The law of Sandy Bar was implacable, but not vengeful. The excitement and personal feeling of the chase were over; with Tennessee safe in their hands, they were ready to listen patiently to any defense, which they were already satisfied was insufficient. There being no doubt in their own minds, they were willing to give the prisoner the benefit of any that might exist. Secure in the hypothesis that he ought to be hanged on general principles, they indulged him with more latitude of defense than his reckless hardihood seemed to ask. The Judge appeared to be more anxious than the prisoner, who, otherwise unconcerned, evidently took a grim pleasure in the responsibility he had created. "I don't take any hand in this yer game," had been his invariable but good-humored reply to all questions. The Judge—who was also his captor—for a moment vaguely regretted that he had not shot him "on sight" that morning, but presently dismissed this human weakness as unworthy of the judicial mind. Nevertheless, when there was a tap at the door, and it was said that Tennessee's Partner was there on behalf of the prisoner, he was admitted at once without question. Perhaps the younger members of the jury, to whom the proceedings were becoming irksomely thoughtful, hailed him as a relief.

For he was not, certainly, an imposing figure. Short and stout, with a square face, sunburned into a preternatural redness, clad in a loose duck "jumper" and trousers streaked and splashed with red soil, his aspect under any circumstances would have been quaint, and was now even ridiculous. As he stooped to deposit at his feet a heavy carpetbag he was carrying, it became obvious, from partially developed legends and inscriptions, that the material with which his trousers had been patched had been originally intended for a less ambitious covering. Yet he advanced with great gravity, and after shaking the hand of each person in the room with labored cordiality, he wiped his serious perplexed face on a red bandana handkerchief, a shade lighter than his complexion, laid his powerful hand upon the table to steady himself, and thus addressed the Judge:

"I was passin' by," he began, by way of apology, "and I thought I'd just step in and see how things was gittin' on with Tennessee thar—my pardner. It's a hot night. I disremember anysich weather before on the Bar."

He paused a moment, but nobody volunteering any other meteorological recollection, he again had recourse to his pocket handkerchief, and for some moments mopped his face diligently.

"Have you anything to say on behalf of the prisoner?" said the judge finally.

"Thet's it," said Tennessee's Partner, in a tone of relief. "I come yar as Tennessee's pardner—knowing him nigh on four year, off and on, wet and dry, in luck and out o' luck. His ways ain't aller my ways, but thar ain't any p'ints in that young man, thar ain't any liveliness as he's been up to, as I don't know. And you sez to me, sez you—confidentiallike, and between man and man—sez you, 'Do you know anything in his behalf?' and I sez to you, sez I—confidential-like, as between man and man—'What should a man know of his pardner?' "

"Is this all you have to say?" asked the Judge impatiently, feeling, perhaps, that a dangerous sympathy of humor was beginning to humanize the court.

"Thet's so," continued Tennessee's Partner. "It ain't for me to say anything agin' him. And now, what's the case? Here's Tennessee wants money, wants it bad, and doesn't like to ask it of his old pardner. Well, what does Tennessee do? He lays for a stranger, and he fetches that stranger; and you lays for *him* and you fetches *him;* and the honors is easy. And I put it to you, bein' a fa'r-minded man, and to you, gentlemen all, as fa'r-minded men, ef this isn't so."

"Prisoner," said the Judge, interrupting, "have you any questions to ask this man?"

"No! no!" continued Tennessee's Partner hastily. "I play this yer hand alone. To come down to the bedrock, it's just this: Tennessee thar has played it pretty rough and expensivelike on a stranger, and on this yer camp. And now, what's the fair thing? Some would say more, some would say less. Here's seventeen hundred dollars in coarse gold and a watch—it's about all my pile—and call it square!" And before a hand could be raised to prevent him, he had emptied the contents of the carpetbag upon the table.

For a moment his life was in jeopardy. One or two men sprang to their feet, several hands groped for hidden weapons, and a suggestion to "throw him from the window" was only overridden by a gesture from the Judge. Tennessee laughed. And apparently oblivious of the excitement, Tennessee's Partner improved the opportunity to mop his face again with his handkerchief.

When order was restored, and the man was made to understand by the use of forcible figures and rhetoric that Tennessee's offense could not be condoned by money, his face took a more serious and sanguinary hue, and those who were nearest to him noticed that his rough hand trembled slightly on the table. He hesitated a moment as he slowly returned the gold to the carpetbag, as if he had not yet entirely caught the elevated sense of justice which swayed the tribunal, and was perplexed with the belief that he had not offered enough. Then he turned to the Judge, and saying, "This yer is a lone hand, played alone, and without my pardner," he bowed to the jury and was about to withdraw, when the Judge called him back:

"If you have anything to say to Tennessee, you had better say it now."

For the first time that evening the eyes of the prisoner and his strange advocate met. Tennessee smiled, showed his white teeth, and saying, "Euchred, old man!" held out his hand. Tennessee's Partner took it in his own, and saying, "I just dropped in as I was passin' to see how things was gettin' on," let the hand passively fall, and adding that "it was a warm night," again mopped his face with his handkerchief, and without another word withdrew.

The two men never again met each other alive. For the unparalleled insult of a bribe offered to Judge Lynch—who, whether bigoted, weak, or narrow, was at least incorruptible—firmly fixed in the mind of that mythical personage any wavering determination of Tennessee's fate; and at the break of day he was marched, closely guarded, to meet it at the top of Marley's Hill.

How he met it, how cool he was, how he refused to say anything, how perfect were the arrangements of the committee, were all duly reported, with the addition of a warning moral and example to all future evildoers, in the *Red Dog Clarion* by its editor, who was present, and to whose vigorous English I cheerfully refer the reader. But the beauty of that midsummer morning, the blessed amity of earth and air and sky, the awakened life of the free woods and hills, the joyous renewal and promise of Nature, and above all, the infinite serenity that thrilled through each, was not reported, as not being a part of the social lesson. And yet, when the weak and foolish deed was done, and a life, with its possibilities and responsibilities, had passed out of the misshapen thing that dangled between earth and sky, the birds sang, the flowers bloomed, the sun shone, as cheerily as before; and possibly the *Red Dog Clarion* was right.

Tennessee's Partner was not in the group that surrounded the ominous tree. But as they turned to disperse, attention was drawn to the singular appearance of a motionless donkey cart halted at the side of the road. As they approached, they at once recognized the venerable Jenny and the two-wheeled cart as the property of Tennessee's Partner, used by him in carrying dirt from his claim; and a few paces distant the owner of the equipage himself, sitting under a buckeye tree, wiping the perspiration from his glowing face. In answer to an inquiry, he said he had come for the body of the "diseased," "if it was all the same to the committee." He didn't wish to "hurry anything;" he could "wait." He was not working that day; and when the gentlemen were done with the "diseased," he would take him. "Ef thar is any present," he added, in his simple, serious way, "as would care to jine in the fun'l, they kin come.'' Perhaps it was from a sense of humor, which I have already intimated was a feature of Sandy Bar—perhaps it was from something even better than that, but two thirds of the loungers accepted the invitation at once.

It was noon when the body of Tennessee was delivered into the hands of his partner. As the cart drew up to the fatal tree, we noticed that it contained a rough oblong box—apparently made from a section of sluicing—and half filled with bark and the tassels of pine. The cart was further decorated with slips of willow and made fragrant with buckeye blossoms. When the body was deposited in the box, Tennessee's Partner drew over it a piece of tarred canvas, and gravely mounting the narrow seat in front, with his feet upon the shafts, urged the little donkey forward. The equipage moved slowly on, at that decorous pace which was habitual with Jenny even under less solemn circumstances. The men—half curiously, half jestingly, but all goodhumoredly—strolled along beside the cart, some in advance, some a little in the rear of the homely catafalque. But whether from the narrowing of the road or some present sense of decorum, as the cart passed on, the company fell to the rear in couples, keeping step, and otherwise assuming the external show of a formal procession. Jack Folinsbee, who had at the outset played a funeral march in dumb show upon an imaginary trombone, desisted from a lack of sympathy and appreciation —not having, perhaps, your true humorist's capacity to be content with the enjoyment of his own fun.

The way led through Grizzly Canyon, by this time clothed in funereal drapery and shadows. The redwoods, burying their moccasined feet in the red soil, stood in Indian file along the track, trailing an uncouth benediction from their bending boughs upon the passing bier. A hare, surprised into helpless inactivity, sat upright and pulsating in the ferns by the roadside as the cortège went by. Squirrels hastened to gain a secure outlook from higher boughs; and the blue jays, spreading their wings, fluttered before them like outriders, until the outskirts of Sandy Bar were reached, and the solitary cabin of Tennessee's Partner.

Viewed under more favorable circumstances, it would not have been a cheerful place. The unpicturesque site, the rude and unlovely outlines, the unsavory details, which distinguish the nest-building of the California miner, were all here with the dreariness of decay superadded. A few paces from the cabin there was a rough enclosure, which, in the brief days of Tennessee's Partner's matrimonial felicity, had been used as a garden, but was now overgrown with fern. As we approached it, we were surprised to find that what we had taken for a recent attempt at cultivation was the broken soil about an open grave.

The cart was halted before the enclosure, and rejecting the offers of assistance with the same air of simple self-reliance he had displayed throughout, Tennessee's Partner lifted the rough coffin on his back, and deposited it unaided within the shallow grave. He then nailed down the board which served as a lid, and mounting the little mound of earth beside it, took off his hat and slowly mopped his face with his handkerchief. This the crowd felt was a preliminary to speech, and they disposed themselves variously on stumps and boulders, and sat expectant.

"When a man," began Tennessee's Partner slowly, "has been running free all day, what's the natural thing for him to do? Why, to come home. And if he ain't in a condition to go home, what can his best friend do? Why, bring him home. And here's Tennessee has been running free, and we brings him home from his wandering." He paused and picked up a fragment of quartz, rubbed it thoughtfully on his sleeve, and went on: "It ain't the first time that I've packed him on my back, as you see'd me now. It ain't the first time that I brought him to this yer cabin when he couldn't help himself; it ain't the first time that I and Jinny have waited for him on yon hill, and picked him up and so fetched him home, when he couldn't speak and didn't know me. And now that it's the last time, why"—he paused and rubbed the quartz gently on his sleeve—"you see it's sort of rough on his pardner. And now, gentlemen," he added abruptly, picking up his long-handled shovel, "the fun'l's over; and my thanks, and Tennessee's thanks, to you for your trouble."

Resisting any proffers of assistance, he began to fill in the grave, turning his back upon the crowd, that after a few moments' hesitation gradually withdrew. As they crossed the little ridge that hid Sandy Bar from view, some, looking back, thought they could see Tennessee's Partner, his work done, sitting upon the grave, his shovel between his knees, and his face buried in his red bandana handkerchief. But it was argued by others that you couldn't tell his face from his handkerchief at that distance, and this point remained undecided.

In the reaction that followed the feverish excitement of that day, Tennessee's Partner was not forgotten. A secret investigation had cleared him of any complicity in Tennessee's guilt, and left only a suspicion of his general sanity. Sandy Bar made a point of calling on him, and proffering various uncouth but well-meant kindnesses. But from that day his rude health and great strength seemed visibly to decline; and when the rainy season fairly set in, and the tiny grass blades were beginning to peep from the rocky mound above Tennessee's grave, he took to his bed.

One night, when the pines beside the cabin were swaying in the storm and trailing their slender fingers over the roof, and the roar and rush of the swollen river were heard below, Tennessee's Partner lifted his head from the pillow, saying, "It is time to go for Tennessee; I must put Jinny in the cart;" and would have risen from his bed but for the restraint of his attendant. Struggling, he still pursued his singular fancy: "There, now, steady, Jinny, steady, old girl. How dark it is! Look out for the ruts, and look out for him, too, old gal. Sometimes, you know, when he's blind drunk, he drops down right in the trail. Keep on straight up to the pine on the top of the hill. Thar! I told you so!—thar he is—coming this way, too—all by himself, sober, and his face ashining. Tennessee! Pardner!"

And so they met.

RAIDERS DIE HARD

BY JOHN M. CUNNINGHAM
(Day of the Bad Man)

High Noon (1951), winner of four Academy Awards and the hearts of film buffs everywhere, is widely considered to be the quintessential Western film. Not enough fans of High Noon know that it was based on a powerful short story by John M. Cunningham—"The Tin Star," first published in Collier's in 1947 (and included in The Best of the West). Two other Cunningham stories were also adapted for notable films: Day of the Bad Man, from the novelette which follows; and The Stranger Wore a Gun (1953), a 3-D Western featuring Randolph Scott and Claire Trevor and based on the story "Yankee Gold" (included in The Best of the West II).

Someone was standing at the window behind Judge Ogilvie. He straightened from his rosebush, and turned.

Sam Wyckoff was standing there, staring at the man he had served ever since he had met Ogilvie in the Army of the Republic.

The expression on Wyckoff's face surprised Judge Ogilvie. For the first time in their long career together, Wyckoff was gazing at his employer with poorly-hidden resentment, and with a kind of sadness.

"You going to santance this man today? This Hayes?" Wyckoff asked.

"Yes."

"To hang?"

"Yes. What else?"

"Is going to be trouble."

Ogilvie smiled a little. "There's always trouble when you try to hang a popular killer in this Territory. Only this time he's going to hang. Maybe it'll be the beginning of some real peace around these parts."

There was a pause. "You still going to sat the date for you wadding, too?" the burly man standing at the window demanded.

Ogilvie frowned. "I said I would. What's the court business got to do with that?"

"You ain't locky, Jodge. Better you wait to ask Miss Lampson."

"Keep your pagan superstitions to yourself."

"Don't cot no more rosses, Jodge. Miss Lampson will wait another day."

The judge bent over his rose bushes again. "She's waited two years already. I can't keep her bluffed forever. Wrap up that Bible I bought her and get out the horses. Court opens in fifteen minutes."

In some of the roses there was still a trace of dew, hidden deep inside, tiny silver specks, delicate and chill. The old pair of surgical scissors, U. S. Army, 1860, poked their blunt nib between the little green leaves and one by one the red roses fell, the long stems toppling aside into the palm of Ogilvie's crippled hand. He held the fingers of his withered arm like a little cup, laying the stems one by one in a newspaper.

He cut ten in the quiet garden above the creek, and then stopped to listen. There were horses in the creek bottom, hidden by the yellow cottonwoods, coming up the slope toward the garden. He could hear them blowing and grunting as they heaved, saddle-leather squeaking and groaning, the beasts panting loudly as they came up the steep bank.

The first rider was a plump, pleasant-looking man with a small, sharp, beak-like nose in a large, smooth, red face.

He smiled, his black eyes twinkling brightly. "Good morning, Judge. Picking flowers, I see."

The judge stood silent, straight and black. "Good morning, Charles. How are all the Hayes brothers?"

The three were armed according to custom; one pistol each, the usual accoutrement. Each also had, tucked under a knee, slanting down the saddle skirt, a rifle in a boot.

Charles touched his horse's mouth with the bit and it halted at the little picket fence at the rear of the garden. The other two ranged up alongside. One rolled a cigarette and struck a sulphur match, and behind a cloud of smoke which rose in the sun, he puffed and sighed. The other individual was like a shadow, slipping up on a lean dun jade.

The judge's shears relaxed open and he looked careless. "How are you, Jake? And you, Howard? I saw your kid brother, Rudy, in the jail last night, and he seemed splendid."

"We're all fine," Charles said. "It's a fine morning."

"Get to the point."

"All right, Ogilvie, I will," Charles said. "There ain't much to it. You been in our county about five years now. You've been a bright young man and a sharp lawyer with what law there is, I mean water rights and so on. But since you was appointed judge, there's been talk you're going to try to boss us people around. That you're going to make this county law-abiding, as you call it."

Ogilvie said, "Go on."

"We heard that you're saying you're going to make an example of Rudy. In fact, hang him."

"He's guilty of murder. The jury said so."

"Hell, yes, he's guilty! But that ain't the point. The point is, you can't just hang Rudy. Why, I wouldn't have even bothered to come here and bother you, Ogilvie, except for this talk, and you being a little different from them other judges. What they always done was order people out of the county, or give them a suspended sentence. Hell! Maybe six months in jail. But hanging's out around here. Understand?" He smiled and nodded at the roses. "Darn pretty flowers."

"They're called roses. Well, Charles, I know how you've been running things around here, one way or another, and I know it hurts your pride to have your brother hanged just for getting caught—but I say he's going to hang, Charles."

"I guess you don't understand, Judge," Charles said. "This ain't a case like in a lawbook."

The smoker blew out a long stream and said, profoundly, "Talk is cheap."

"Shut up, Jake. Judge—"

"Why don't we do it now?" Jake went on. "Why argue?"

"Shut up," the fat one said. "Judge, don't be ornery. That Pole of yours is a good man, but there's only one of him, and there's three of us."

"I guess you don't count me," the judge said.

The shadow on the dun plug laughed. "That Pole."

"I think he's a Hungarian," Ogilvie said. "A gentleman from Central Europe."

"How did you train him, Judge?" Howard asked. "With cheese?"

"A dirty coward," Jake said, puffing steadily. "A dirty coward sitting on a bench judging a real man."

"Shut up, I told you," the fat one said. "You and Howard keep quiet, now."

Howard—the shadow—said, "A lousy cripple."

The fat one turned sharply in the saddle and looked down at Howard. Howard's mouth dropped open like a gopher hole and he backed his horse away. "I'm sorry, Charles," he said in a small voice.

Charles turned back to the judge, "You don't have to hang Rudy, Judge. You can banish him. Banish him, Judge. I'm not ornery. I don't say let him go. Banish him."

The judge looked up. "Banish?"

"It's an old custom in this territory. The miners' courts started it. Banish. Get out. Don't come back. You can do it."

"Feudal," the judge said, smiling at the roses beside his feet. "Rudolph, thou hast forfeited thy fief. I banish thee forever from my realm. How long do they stay banished, Charles?"

"Beside the point," Charles said. "Often used in cases of doubt—or for other reasons."

"Reasons involving the judge's hide, I suspect."

Charles smiled again.

"But not involving the Federal law, which governs this territory, and to uphold which I am sworn. Charles, thou has forfeited thy fief. I banish thee forever from my garden."

Charles stopped smiling. "Listen. I never had to go this far before—for a long time. I'm warning you."

The screen door behind the judge twanged slowly open, the spring screeching and stretching in its rust.

"You don't have to took this, Jodge," Wyckoff said from the doorway. He held a Government .45-70 carbine, cocked, in his right hand, hip leveled, and held the screen door open with the other. He had a head like a chopping block and hair like that of an old badger. "If you say the word, you don't have to took this."

The three on their horses slumped a little, their right hands finding their way to resting places more convenient to their armament.

"I'm not 'taking' anything, in the sense you mean, Sam. Have you met these gentlemen? The Hayes brothers—those of them at liberty, that is. Since we are being feudal this morning, I shall introduce them as Charles the Fat, Jake the Slow and Howard the—what shall I say? Howard is the quaint young gentleman with the hare lip. Or is that an old shaving wound, Howard?"

Howard said, "Did you hear that, Charles? Did you hear what he said? He's talking about my moustache!"

"Got out," Wyckoff said. "Got out of here, you boms."

"Don't be so rough," the judge said quietly. "They are merely approaching me with a bribe."

"Not a bribe," Charles said. "You're not getting paid a dime. This is an order. You banish Rudy."

Ogilvie snipped the shears twice, examining the juncture of the cutting edges.

Charles gathered up his reins and lifted them. "Whoever has anything to do with hanging Rudy is going to get himself killed. That ain't in the Federal law either, but it'll work better."

"You should wear a rose behind your ear, Charles. Here, have a free rose."

Charles looked at him for a moment. He lifted his reins gracefully, swaying his plump horse around, and trotted away. The others lined out after him. The cottonwood trash rustled and cracked as they disappeared behind the yellowing foliage.

"What gall," the judge said, picking at a speck of rust on one blade of the scissors. "I expected they might try something, but hardly that they'd announce it."

Wyckoff spat off the end of the porch away from the

judge. "Why are we always fiding? Already we made free the Negroes. Who now?"

The judge looked down at the roses and smiled. He slipped the scissors back into his pocket, and stooping, began rolling the roses up in the damp newspaper. His right hand was nimble, his left hung idle, a withered little cup like a child's hand.

"Let's forget the Hayes boys and think of—love. Ah, Wyckoff, isn't it wonderful? You see, it is her gift, that I can love her freely, happily, without embarrassment, her particular genius. It is a wonderful thing."

Wyckoff looked down at him, his heavy mouth a crease among a field of heavy creases, and watched the judge wrap up the roses. "Wonnerful," he said. "You always riding poattry, everything for poattry. It is a wonderful thing, poattry."

"Don't be silly. This is no sentimental thing." The judge stood up, smiling, holding his sheaf of roses neatly wrapped. "I perceive her true beauty in the light of sound reason, Sam. Certainly her love is sound and real, if it can ignore such defects in a man. Such defects as—as I have. And who is a harder judge of a man than a woman? And so who on earth can be happier than I am? Who has a right to be? I have passed the judgment of a queen, I hold a heart more precious than the sun. Why shouldn't I be happy?"

"More poattry. You made up you mind you sat the date today?"

"That's it."

"Then I got some bad news fur you, Captain. I mean Jodge."

"What?"

"I wasn't going to tell you, but I got to now, if you going to sat the date today."

"Well, what is it?"

"She don't love you no more."

The judge looked at him in silence. "Is that a Hungarian joke? Why on earth would you say a thing like that?"

Wyckoff slowly blushed.

"What made you say a thing like that? Obviously, if she didn't, she would—oh, what am I talking about?"

Wyckoff stood frozen. "I'm sorry, Jodge."

The judge looked away. "Go get her presents—the book and the rings."

Wyckoff's right hand moved up and down in a kind of fumbled salute, and he turned abruptly. The judge followed, the roses like a child in the hollow of his crippled arm.

CHAPTER TWO
Before The Trial

There was a clump of yellow alders at the end of the deserted street of the town, where the saloons tapered off toward the creek. Wyckoff and the judge crossed the plank bridge, the hoofs of their horses rumbling, and turned up a short road toward the mountains. At the head of the road was a meadow crowded with horses and vehicles of all kinds, and in the middle, a white frame church with a log addition on the back.

Horses were tied everywhere; to the rail before the church, to the spokes of wheels, to the hanging limbs of trees. Wagons had been driven under the small windows of the church, and men stood on the sideboards, peering in. A few had brought ladders and boards, and had built trestles. A large group sat on the steps, ears turned toward the opened front doors.

There was a young woman on the side of the road, at the edge of the meadow, waiting under the yellow arch of leaves. Her firm, dark eyes peered from under a poke bonnet. Ogilvie saw her and a smile came up over his face. He swung down and walked forward, leading his horse. She was smiling back, standing with her hands held together, somewhat timidly.

He took off his hat, slipping the reins up his arm, and walked toward her, stopping a good five feet away. "Hello," he said gently. His eyes went over her face. "How are you? My God, you're lovely. I have something for you—to show you. The present I told you about." He grinned. "The time has come—we can set the date. I've bought the ranch. Will you come around in the back of the church, before I open the court? I'll show them to you."

"Scott—" she began, her smile gone, and her gaze dropping.

He waited. "Yes?" he asked gently.

She looked quickly at Wyckoff, appealingly.

"Yes?" the judge asked. "Well, what are you looking at Sam for? What's Sam done?"

She bent a little, one shoulder dropping, her hands still together. "Scott . . . I beg—"

"Why, what's the matter, darling?"

She shook her head.

"Come and tell me about it in the back, in two minutes," Ogilvie said. "Sam, come on. Bring the present." He led his horse past her. "You come and tell me all about it, darling."

She smiled at him again, stiffly. He turned and started to mount.

"Der rosses," Wyckoff said heavily.

Ogilvie stopped and looked down at the newspaper in the crook of his bad arm. He laughed. "I forgot." He tried to shove them at her with his bad arm, and caught himself, confused. He took them hurriedly in his right hand and extended them to her again, and the looped rein on his arm caught him back. He stood helpless, smiling stiffly at her with the roses extended.

She stepped forward and took them, and the paper fell away. The roses lay fresh and brilliant. "Oh," she said.

"Two years since I planted them," Ogilvie said. "Two years since we got engaged, and now they're ready, really good. And we're ready, finally. Come on back, darling. Just give me a minute to set up the exhibition."

She stood looking down at the roses, and he hurried away.

She looked up at Wyckoff, and said sadly, "You didn't tell him."

"I tried. Why would he believe me?"

The edges of her eyes shone with tears. "Yes, I know. I just thought maybe you could kind of—"

"Wait," Wyckoff said. "Don't tal him today. Not now. He got to santance this man Hayes. Since Hayes was caught Wiley is scared his brothers will break him out of jail, and they got to do something in a hurry."

"But he wants to set the date today! I'll have to tell him."

Wyckoff looked away. "Miss Lampson, this Wiley,

maybe he is only a passing thing. Wait a little more."

She looked down.

"I understand," he said. "Wiley is a big, handsome, pretty man, he is strong—got both arms. Big, fat arms to squeeze a woman. That's true, no?"

She flushed. "If you please."

"So is a bear got big arms. Look, I go to the woods, I got you a bear. Why don't you marry a bear? I tal you something, Miss Lampson—"

"You've said enough," she said in a small voice, her face red.

"Only this. The jodge, he will love you when you are old and full of wringles and your teeth you put in a glass-water. Ain't that something? But Wiley, even now he is always looking from the side of his eye."

"How dare you!" she said, her head up straight. "How dare you talk to me like that—you *peasant!*"

He smiled. "Yas, that's me, a peasant."

"Barney is big and strong and—capable. He can protect me."

"What makes you think," Wyckoff said. "The jodge can't protect you? Too skinny? Don't eat enoff? I suppose a woman got to prove it. And that's still poattry."

She looked down. "Nothing you will say will do any good."

"I know it. A woman got to prove everything. I must go to the jodge." He got down off the horse, led it around her, and when at a polite distance, took off his hat, bowed, and remounted. He crossed the meadow at a canter.

A voice called, "We going to hang him today, Scott?" The man was among the crowd on the front steps of the church. The judge rode on, face front, down the side of the building.

"Where's your bodyguard at, Ogilvie?" somebody else shouted from the top of a wagon.

"We're all waiting, Scott."

The prisoner was in a closely-covered wagon, which was backed up near the plank door to the little log addition in the rear of the church. There were half a dozen men loitering around the door, all heavily armed, and two sat on the high wagon seat in front. The team was neatly pegged out on the meadow nearby, grazing contentedly.

The sheriff was leaning against a wheel of the wagon.

"Your prisoner still there, Barney?" the judge asked.

Sheriff Wiley unhooked a high heel from a wagon spoke and smiled lazily, straightening up. "Where else? Or do you still think Sam should have won the election?"

"Not that, Barney. I never claimed you weren't good enough to be sheriff. I just said Sam would be better. More polite to put it that way." He looked in the back of the wagon. The tarp was white, and in the interior it was light and warm, trapping the heat of the weak sun. The man at the other end of the wagon bed drew on a cigarette as the judge looked in and spewed out a long stream of smoke in his direction. The smoke curled around Ogilvie's face.

"Going to sentence me today, Judge?" he asked, smiling gently. He flipped a little ash off the end of his smoke. "That's all right, Judge. You can go ahead and do it. I know the law's got to go through the motions." He smiled again, composed and friendly.

Wiley said, "Scott, I want to talk to you for a moment."

"Come inside," Ogilvie said, turning away from the wagon and ducking into the building. Wiley followed him in and shut the door. The place was half-dark, lighted by two bullseye windows, damp and smelling of rotting logs and the damp earth floor. On one side of the room were cupboards and a stack of old benches.

"Myra's coming here in a couple of minutes, so make it snappy. It's going to be kind of private."

Wiley looked at him carefully. The judge was smiling, dusting off the top of a table and the best of the chairs. "I saw you down there with her by the bridge."

"You sound a little critical. How come?"

"Nothing, nothing, Ogilvie." He cleared his throat. "Listen, Scott, I know you've had it in for me ever since I beat Sam in the election, but—" He stopped, looking away uncomfortably.

"Well, what is it? A favor? As it happens, the elections had no effect on my opinions. What do you want?"

Somebody knocked on the door and pushed it open. One of the guards stood there with his Winchester pointed politely down. "There's a few dozen people or so here to see you, Scott," he said. "The Hayes brothers. And Mrs. Quarry."

"How nice," Ogilvie said. "Will you ask them to wait? Tell the Hayes family I shall be busy for the next few years, and if they have anything important to do—Tell Mrs. Quarry to come in."

"No," Wiley said sharply.

Ogilvie turned. "Why not?"

"Not just yet."

Ogilvie swung to the door. "Ask her to wait, and shut the door. All right, what's the matter?"

"I just want to check," Wiley said in a low voice. "There's a little talk going around about—about you banishing Rudy instead of hanging him. I just wanted to make sure."

"Banishing?"

"Yeah. The old law. The one the vigilantes and the miners' courts used when they were up the creek. It was going around last night."

"Is that so? Last night."

Wiley looked at him steadily. "I just wanted to be sure. You know what it'll mean to me, if you do pull such a thing."

"What, exactly?"

"I'll get killed. Exactly."

"I'm not much up on the old customs. Tell me."

"If you banish him, he'll have to leave town by a certain time. If he hangs around I've got to enforce the sentence."

"Well, so what? You ran for the job."

"Listen, there'll be Rudy and the other three. Four of them, hanging around town. Four of them, Scott."

"What's the matter? Aren't you the people's hero? Can't you take care of a little thing like four bush-whackers?"

Wiley said nothing.

"What's the matter, Barney? Weren't you the best man after all? You're big and strong, Wiley. You're a pretty good shot. You won the turkey shoot last year, didn't you?"

"Turkey shoot," Wiley said.

"Why couldn't you just pretend that the Hayes brothers were a lot of turkeys?" Ogilvie said. "You could get one of the boys down in the saloon to make a gobbling noise. That would complete the illusion, and you'd be steady as a rock."

"Listen," Wiley said in the same low voice, "you can't cross me up like this. Just on account of that election."

"What do you think I am?" Ogilvie asked. "If I did cross you up, you could only blame yourself for giving me the idea. No, Blarney—I mean Barney, sorry—I won't cross you up. You know, there's another rumor that the Hayes boys are going to kill anybody that has anything to do with hanging Rudy, too. Well, I won't even ask you to hang him locally. I intend to sentence him to hang in the Territorial prison, where the job will be done anonymously. You can take your posse of stalwarts outside and drive Rudy up to the railroad by five this afternoon, and catch the train." He looked at Wiley's large, handsome face. "Your color is coming back, Barney. Can you go forward now with your head held high?"

"You think you're so damned smart," Wiley said, moving toward the door. "I have to ask you a favor and you rub it in. I'd like to see you hold down my job for a while." He let his eyes run down Ogilvie's bad arm to the wizened hand, smiled, and went out.

The judge looked down at the palm of his left hand. He could flex the biceps of the arm, and he could lift it toward the front a little. He made these movements tentatively, and then stood quiet, regarding the atrophied fingers. He tried to move one of them. Nothing happened.

The door opened, admitting a dark bulk, and closed again. Mrs. Quarry came into the dim light from the bullseye windows and stood with her arms folded, each hand nestled in the other sleeve, across her large stomach. She wore a black shawl around her shoulders, a man's blue shirt, and a long, full skirt of black cotton with small white dots. She looked used to work.

"Sit down, Mrs. Quarry," the judge said, turning a chair around for her with his good hand, holding the other one slightly behind him. "How are you getting along?"

"That's it," she said. "Just getting along. Our foreman's good. I mean mine. Thank God for that, he's a good man. I can't ride, but I can keep the branding irons hot, and that's a help. Besides, I'm learning to handle them. I don't like burning them animals. But then—"

The judge nodded and smiled. "Don't be too independent now, Mrs. Quarry. You know how it is, out here in the country. People'll feel hurt if you don't let 'em help you, even if you don't need it. You let 'em help you. You don't want to hurt anybody's feelings."

She sniffed and looked down and sniffed again, trying to keep her tears up her nose. "Judge," she croaked.

"Yes?"

"I want you to do me a favor."

"Every day I do at least one favor. What is it?"

"I want you to hang him. No mistake."

His eyebrows went up slightly.

"That's why I come. You won't let me down?"

"It'll all be taken care of properly. It's all taken care of in the law Mrs. Quarry. It isn't personal."

"It was personal when that weasel murdered Joe. That was personal."

"I know how you feel. You can depend on the law."

"That's it. I can't. We depended on the law, Joe did, from the beginning. And when them weasels stole our cows, where was it? Barney Wiley come out and looked for tracks just once in six months. As far as I know, the rest of the time he was down on main street—keeping the peace in the saloons. That's him. That's his job, Judge. Keeping the peace in town on Sunday morning."

The judge looked down. From beneath the edge of her full black skirt, one shoe-toe peeked out, a small, black, wrinkled toe. She probably had on high laced shoes under those petticoats. Morning after morning she would lace up those high shoes of hers and put on those tons of petticoats, when she was nearly too old to move. She wore modesty like the shield of her soul.

"We must uphold the law, Mrs. Quarry."

"You mean Barney Wiley? He shouldn't have even been sheriff, Judge. Sam Wyckoff should have been sheriff. Sam would have told Joe and the others what to do to surround them weasels, and nobody would have got kilt. Instead of Joe," she said bitterly, "trying to outshoot that pack of varmints, that shooting was all they knew. Well," she finished, "Joe's dead. And I'm going to hear that dog's neck pop, that Rudy Hayes, with my own two ears." A white fire leaped up in the back of her eye. "And if it don't, I'm going to shoot that no account sheriff myself, and nobody's going to blame me."

She looked down to see that her invisible toes did not trespass on anything unfitting. She got up and labored out on her flat feet.

CHAPTER THREE
To Kill a Sheriff . . .

Wiley and two guards came to the door and went through, leading the prisoner into the courtroom.

"You'd better put the rest of your men around in the courtroom," Ogilvie said.

Wyckoff came in with the wrapped-up book in his hand. The judge took it and went to the door.

Myra was sitting in a neat little buggy, the reins in her hands. Ogilvie put his hand in his coat pocket and took hold of something. "Come on, I've waited long enough, I'm free—the court can wait a minute."

She came through the door, brushing past Wyckoff. She shut the door on Wyckoff and faced the judge. "Scott—"

"That was beautiful. Say it again." He smiled at her and took a paper from his pocket. "Every time you say my name, I get dizzy. Am I still in love, Myra, after two years? Is that it?" He laid the paper on the table, and took a little box from another pocket.

"Scott, wait—"

"What for? All morning people have been asking me to do things for them, making me wait. I'm sick of waiting. You are too. We both are. We've waited so long, we've got the waiting habit."

He unwrapped the book and laid it on the table beside the paper and the box. "There it is. That's our future. Here's us, and the future. Forgive the drama," he said. "I had to celebrate it—announce it—legalize it? Anything so important as us, deserves a ceremony. Let me show you."

She was looking at the things on the table, her hands

tight together in front of her, the way she had been on the bridge.

"Here's your book. A white Bible," he said, smiling. "That's customary for the bride, isn't it? The box contains two wedding rings, one for you and one for me, and the paper is the deed to our ranch."

"No, Scott," she said.

He looked at her intently. "What do you mean, no?"

She stood up straight and took a deep breath. "All right," she said, "I didn't know it would be so difficult—"

He looked at her dumbly. "I'm beginning to get the idea," he said after a moment. "Something bad has happened. Good and bad. I mean about our marriage."

She swallowed.

"Do you mind if I sit down?" he asked. He sat in the clean chair and laid his good arm on the table. His wrist trembled. "What in God's name is it?" he broke out, his fist tightening against the tremble.

"Scott—we can't get married."

"We can't?" he asked tightly. "Why not? Are we first cousins or something?"

"I've fallen in love."

"What?"

"I'm sorry. I'm in love."

"Weren't we always in love?"

"I mean—with somebody else."

He sat quiet. "Somebody else. Not me? What are you talking about?"

"I'm sorry, Scott. Especially," she said, gesturing at the things on the table, "especially," she said, beginning to cry and putting her hand over her eyes, "after you did all this—"

"Myra, for Heaven's sake, I beg you, do not cry, let's keep it rational," he said in the same, tight, small voice. "You mean," he asked carefully, like a lawyer approaching an exceedingly subtle point, "you mean to say, you do *not* love me—after all. You mean that it was a delusion."

After a moment, he went on. "It's peculiar, I had no notion of this till today. God knows you're not deceitful. How could I be so stupid?" He closed his hand around the ring-box, hiding it. "Tell me," he said. "Was there a time when you did love me? In the beginning? A little while?"

"Scott," she said, "Scott, why couldn't I have been some other woman? Scott, I do love you—in a way—I don't want to hurt you. . . . You are so dear, so kind, so loving—have been so kind to me, why, every day there has been some little thing; the flowers, the unexpected things, all this time, you have made all my days so sweet. Scott, how can I repay you? It's so difficult. I do love you, in a way—but something has come up—"

"It's the long wait," he said, looking at the window. "The long wait." He smiled. "Who is the honored gentleman who has taken my place? Or shall I say, who has taken that which I pre-empted so long, hardly mine—presuming on a young girl's ignorance of men, let us say. Working on the young girl's sensibilities to make gratitude—"

"Please, Scott—"

"—to make gratitude and sentiment a substitute for love. Shall we say?" He stood up. "Who is the worthy gentleman? He must be a hero, a stalwart, a perfection of a man—Or why? Maybe he is just a man, a whole man, with two arms. Why should he, after all, have to be more than that? Just one, ordinary man— why would it take any more to wake up a young girl's heart? After all, who was I—after all."

She stood looking at him across the table. "It's Barney. Barney Wiley."

He looked up, above her head. "Wiley?" His eyes moved around as though he were trying to assemble a composition, making up a picture. "You mean the sheriff?"

"Yes. Barney Wiley."

"That's odd," he said quietly. "That I should have had no hint of it at all. Why, surely this thing must have had some kind of beginning. But he knew we were engaged. Surely you don't mean to say, he approached you—that you permitted him to approach. . . . No, hardly you."

"It was an accident He helped me one day, out riding. An accidental meeting." She looked sadly at the dirt floor. "A kind of friendship. You have been so busy, Scott—riding around all over the country on your circuit, hunting up our ranch—the ranch."

"That was my job, of course. I could hardly be accused of neglecting you. Unless it could be argued that a two-year engagement is, in fact, a kind of neglect of nature. I have presumed too much upon the human element."

She stood alone in the dim light, humble.

"So you want to go," he said.

"Yes," she said faintly.

"How funny. This was to be the occasion, a celebration. How funny, that it should turn out this way. All right. Good-bye."

She turned toward the door, and when she had reached it, turned again and smiled at him. "Good-bye, Scott."

"There's a man in there waiting for his sentence. I really shouldn't keep him waiting."

"Scott, I wish—I wish I had never met Barney. If I had not, we would have been happy."

"You mean," he said, smiling, *"I* would have been happy. Good-bye."

She turned and disappeared from the bright doorway.

Wyckoff came in, heavily and humbly. "You better go in there. They think you scared to hang him."

Ogilvie had the ring box in his hand.

"Did you hear her? What she said?"

"A liddle. She told me before."

Ogilvie flung the box in the corner.

Wiley opened the courtroom door and stuck his head in. "What's the matter? Everybody's waiting."

Ogilvie looked at him for a moment. "I hear there is a kind of an understanding between you and Myra."

Wiley stood silent for a moment, his hand on the edge of the door. He tried a smile. "I'm glad she told you. There isn't any understanding between us. There couldn't be, as long as she was engaged."

"Exactly. That was the understanding—that nothing would be understood until she had broken the engagement. The essence of an understanding is that nothing is said. But enough was said to reach the understanding. How did you do it? You must be pretty clever along some lines, Barney. It's pretty hard to make advances to a woman without their being advances."

Wiley said nothing. He stood blinking slowly in the doorway. "What do you mean?"

"I mean you have been courting her behind my back. It has dawned upon me slowly. In fact, you are a thief, and she does not know that she's been stolen."

"That's a lie."

"You are the liar."

They stood silent, their eyes locked.

"Or do you," the judge said, advancing slowly, "take me for a fool? Any first-year law student could read this back to the facts. I know the kind of underhanded play it was—you were so friendly and helpful, such a cheerful companion, you helped fill the dull hours when I was away on circuit, riding with her. Nothing open, nothing to make an issue, always just a friend, working on her. And now you've got the gall to stand there and try to look hurt."

Wiley smiled. He said, "All right, Scott, whatever it was, it's happened. As far as I'm concerned you can go climb the old elm tree. I've got her."

Ogilvie moved forward a step, his head sinking and his jaw sticking out a little. "Don't underestimate me, Wiley. I'm legal only just so far."

Wiley smiled openly. "You and Wyckoff. The almighty pair. What have you got now? I've got his job and your girl and from now on, as far as I'm concerned, I don't see why I even have to look friendly." He started to shut the door.

"Wait," the judge said.

Wiley watched him carefully. "You think you've got her," Ogilvie said. "You think I'm going to let you break her heart? Go on in there and call the court to order."

"What do you mean?"

"Do as you're told."

Wiley shut the door slowly and Ogilvie smiled at Wyckoff.

"What's the matter with you?" Wyckoff said. "Why you looking so happy?"

"Helena is too far. There's too much chance of Rudy's getting away. Don't you think? Besides, a local hanging would have a better effect as a public example. I'll set it for a week from today. He'll have to do it alone. They'll be laying for him. Maybe they'll kill him first and bust the jail. That's more likely."

"Supposing they get you first?"

"Supposing I take a long vacation? Beginning this afternoon."

Wyckoff looked at him carefully. "I think this is murder."

"It's the duty of the county sheriff to carry out the sentences, isn't it?"

"You can't get away with it," Wyckoff said softly. "Not inside you. It's legal, but it's murder. You got to take the chance. Wiley don't got to, unless you make him."

"It's his duty," Ogilvie said.

"What hoppened to you?"

The judge's head gave a spasmodic, trembling shake. "You think I'm going to let him get away with this? I'll kill him. I'll kill him from the bench."

"Is that what she wants?"

"He deserves it," Ogilvie said.

"By whose law?" Wyckoff nodded at the little white Bible. "You giving her a Bible, and then this. That's a laugh."

Ogilvie grabbed the book in his good hand.

"Put it down," Wyckoff said. "No matter who you are, you throw that book, you're finished."

Ogilvie dropped it on the table. "Get out," he said.

"Listen," Wyckoff said. "You think she wouldn't know? Who would you be fooling? You'd be a murderer. They hear about you engagement broking—then this. Everybody would know the truth. You think she love you then? The dogs would not even bite you— you would stink so."

"Get out," Ogilvie said. "Why should I take it? All my life I've been taking it. Then I find her, and now this dirty—this devil twists her mind. Why should I take it? Let him take it!"

Wyckoff said. "Some people is made to take it. Maybe you got to take it."

"Not any more. This time I'll write my own damn law." He smiled slowly. "It's going to be good, too. That slob. He looks so big and fine, and underneath he's such a sneaking little baby. Wait 'til they pull down on him. They'll make him cry first, he'll blubber and cry, like those little rebel troopers we caught that time."

"You're the devil. You're so sweet on top. Rosses. Flowers. I thought she got you gentled. But you still a devil underneath. I seen it before, you remember. I stop you once before. You remember the rebel troopers we took with the sharpened sabers, and you were going to cot them to pieces with them, for chopping up your arm."

"Get out of here."

Wyckoff took a step toward him. "Maybe I knock you out," he said in a low voice. "Knock you cold and break up the trial and go to jail. It would be better."

Ogilvie's arm flicked out and he flipped the gun out of Wyckoff's holster. He held it steadily on Wyckoff's chest. "Get out," he said.

Wyckoff looked down at the gun, and then at the face above it. "Please."

"I'd as soon kill you as not. Get out of here and keep out of my way."

Wyckoff's hand dropped. "All right. All right, Captain. I know. I understand." He turned away.

Ogilvie laid the gun on the table and went toward the court room door.

"Listen," Wyckoff said.

Ogilvie turned with his hand on the latch.

"If you going to do it," Wyckoff said, "don't be a fool about it. You lose her for good, this way, I would rather shoot Wiley myself, for you."

"You heard what I said," Ogilvie said coldly. "I'll do as I please and I'll do it my own way. I said this morning I'd set the date of my wedding today, hanging or no hanging. What makes you think I won't?"

"But now," Wyckoff said, "you are no good. No—good."

CHAPTER FOUR
The Judgment

She was sitting on the middle aisle seven rows back from the sanctuary rail, upon which Charles and Jake Hayes were resting their heels, their spurs dangling on the court side. Her face was the first thing Ogilvie saw in all that small sea of faces, his eyes going home there at once. She was smiling, looking toward one of the south windows, through which the sun was coming, full of the golden light of alder leaves outside.

She was smiling at Wiley, who was standing with his deputies in back of the prisoner's chair, leaning against the wall next to the window, his arms folded, one heel tucked up behind him against the wall.

It was a pair of smiles, intimate and tender on her part, and on his, pleased, confident and amused. Ogilvie looked away.

Mrs. Quarry was sitting in the front row across the aisle from the Hayes brothers.

Ogilvie walked across the low platform in the front of the church. The crowd hushed and then began to buzz louder than ever. They had taken the pulpit out and put a small table in instead. He sat down at it. Jake Hayes saw him and took his feet down, and Charles touched his arm. Jake slowly put his feet back up.

Ogilvie rapped sharply on the table with a carpenter's hammer. The crowd shut up the way a flock of birds suddenly freezes in a tree. Ogilvie opened the drawer of the table and adjusted the pistol which was lying inside so that it was convenient to his right hand.

He addressed the courtroom at large. "Yesterday, you heard the jury return a verdict of guilty. There never was any doubt of this. Rudy Hayes killed Joe Quarry in the sight of half a dozen men. That is, Quarry's riders, while they were surrounding Hayes, who was then in the act of stealing some of Quarry's cattle. This was murder in the first degree. I will now sentence the prisoner. Hayes, have you got anything to say?"

Rudy Hayes sat with his arms folded, not looking at the judge. He was smiling at his brother. Charles Hayes' little owl-beak nose was sharp as a talon in the middle of his fat pink face.

"Hell, no," Rudy Hayes said casually, "why should I say anything?"

"In that case I—"

"Your honor," Charles Hayes said, standing up, "may I plead with the court," he said gently, "in consideration of the youth of the prisoner, to banish him, rather than hang him?"

Somebody outside the windows began clapping and

shouted, "Hurray!" A small chorus took up the cheer and kept at it for a few seconds.

"Your honor is a man with a kind heart," Hayes said gently. "I beg you to banish my brother from the territory, and I guarantee that he will start a new life elsewhere. He is young and rash, your honor. You are a generous man, a big man, a kind man. You won't hang him. You'll show him mercy." The same number of hands began clapping, and precisely the same number of voices shouted with mechanical zeal, "Hurray, hurray, hurray!"

"You hear what the local citizens want, your honor."

"Sit down," Ogilvie said. "I never heard of anything more preposterous."

"Your honor," Mrs. Quarry said from her seat just beyond the rail, "I ask you to banish him too. For pity's sake. It was my husband he killed, after all. I was the one hurt most of all." A woman in the back of the court began to sob and gulp. Ogilvie started to rap with the hammer, and another woman began to blubber. He sat quiet.

"I don't understand this, Mrs. Quarry," he said. "I would rather expect you to insist on the full sentence."

Mrs. Quarry said, quietly and calmly, "No, Mr. Ogilvie, not so. It would be better to banish him. The poor young feller."

The clapping and cheering began again, and this time was joined by many more hands. Charles Hayes smiled at the judge.

"After all, Judge," Mrs. Quarry went on in her quiet, clear voice, "if I am willing to forgive Rudy Hayes his awful deed, why ain't you? If anybody has rights here, ain't it me? Your honor, *I* forgive him, and I plead with you, to leave him go."

A whole chorus of sobbing broke out in the rear of the church.

"Banish him!" the organized voices yelled from outside. And then hands in the courtroom began clapping, breaking out here and there, and rising to a roar. Cheers rose, and men began stomping their feet.

Ogilvie sat impassively, waiting. Charles Hayes smiled pleasantly at him. The cheering and the sobbing continued. Mrs. Quarry, looking pleased with herself, sat down.

The clapping began to die out and Ogilvie rapped moderately.

"A recess," he said. "For a few minutes only. Mrs. Quarry, I would like to speak to you privately in the back room—if you will be so kind." He stood up, shutting the table drawer, and went out.

They came around together, Charles Hayes and Mrs. Quarry, dignified and self-possessed. Hayes let her in, past Wyckoff, and shut the door behind himself. Ogilvie held a chair for her. She didn't take it.

"Congratulations, Charles," Ogilvie said. "You have an able pupil, but what is that without a gifted teacher? You were most appealing, Mrs. Quarry."

Mrs. Quarry looked modestly at her toes. "Mr. Hayes is a sincere man. I'm sure he is a sincere man. He asked me to forgive his brother." She looked up, smiling.

"Let's cut out the lying," Ogilvie said quietly.

Mrs. Quarry looked blank.

"Come, Mrs. Quarry. I know you want Rudy dead."

Mrs. Quarry sniffed. "Wiley said you was going to send that Hayes to Helena to hang next month and give Wiley a vacation for a while. I told you I wanted him hanged here, Judge. I told you why. I can't make no trip to Helena next month." Her eyes opened wide. "But it ain't that so much. Mr. Hayes here give me the idea, to banish him, and I see the point. Not Mr. Hayes's point, exactly. I want you to banish him, you set the time and then let them fight it out, and I hope they're both killed. That Hayes and Wiley both."

She swung around on Charles. "So there!" she spat. "You and your, 'Have mercy. Please!' says you, 'Forgive my brother, banish him.' All right, banish him, and let him and Wiley fight it out down town. Let them have mercy on each other. I'll be around and I think I'll bring a gun to the ball too." She smiled and her eyes were full of tears. "I'll teach them hounds for killing my Joe, them stinking dogs."

Wiley open the courtroom door and stood looking in. "What's going on?" he asked suspiciously. "Ogilvie, what are you doing?"

"Him," Mrs. Quarry said, jerking an elbow at Wiley.

"Look at him. He's the one at fault. *He* let the rustling go on and on."

Wiley came down slowly into the room.

"They want me to banish Rudy," Ogilvie said to him. "It'll be up to you to expel him from town, if he doesn't leave properly. How do you like that, Barney?"

Wiley looked at Hayes' gentle smile, and then at Ogilvie. "You're going to throw it all onto me. Is that it? Is that your revenge?"

"My apologies for Mr. Wiley," Ogilvie said, smiling at Barney, "he's a trifle upset. What revenge, Barney? Don't be silly. Nobody wants revenge. I'm a judge of the law. Mrs. Quarry has asked for mercy, and so has Rudy's brother. Aren't they entitled to consideration? Am I above mercy? Should I not show mercy? Why should *you* object to a show of mercy?"

"Mercy!" Wiley said. "It's a dirty murder, that's what it is, I can see it in your faces. Why don't you do what you should?"

They stood silent. A woodrat rustled in one of the corners. Hayes said, "I told the judge, he would be unhappy later if he hanged Rudy. He'd feel remorse. You see, Wiley, it's in everybody's interest to show mercy this way."

"Indeed it is," Ogilvie said. "And I know you'll do a good job, Barney. Nobody likes a coward. Not even a woman, a woman in love. They like cowards least of all. Do you suppose, Charles, Rudy would put a fight?"

"Well," Charles said, "Rudy likes it around here."

Wiley looked bitterly at the three of them. "Wait'll I tell about this."

"Tell what?" Ogilvie asked. "That we're showing mercy? Go on, you lousy coward, and watch your charge."

They watched Wiley go back through the door, moving heavily and slowly.

"Thank you, Judge," Mrs. Quarry said. She went out.

Hayes said, "You're a smart man, Judge. I always knew you were. You can get Wyckoff elected —in fact, you can appoint him to take Wiley's place, can't you? I mean, well, if things don't work out right for him. And besides, why can't you and I be friends, anyway? We can do each other a lot of good." He smiled. "All you have to do is sentence Rudy to banishment, like I said—

remember—and you'll be the best-liked man in the county."

"Really?" Ogilvie said. "Already I'm beginning to have a dirty feeling in my mouth. There's no point in this. What does it do? To kill that fool. If I could keep on killing him, and see him die forever—but once he's dead, what's left? Just plain nothing. Nothing but you, and Mrs. Quarry—oh, she and I would have a great time grieving together, muttering and mumbling over our woes. Nothing left but her and you and murder in my mouth to suck on till I slid into the pit. Get out, you fat slob, get out."

"Remember!" Charles said loudly warningly. "I'll take your cussing—but remember."

He went out. Ogilvie stood in the dim room. "Mercy," he said to himself. He looked at the white Bible.

She came in without knocking, soft in the dim light, a small figure slipping in and standing there, looking up at him.

"I heard some people talking," she said. "They said that man will never leave town. They said Barney would have to fight him, and Barney would be killed. They said that man's brothers would help him, and together they'd all kill Barney. Did you know that?"

"It's funny, when you come near, how everything changes—the light brightens, everything grows clear. Without you, there is—nothing, darkness, confusion. But now you're here," he said, looking down at her and smiling. "Yes. I know what they'll do to Barney."

"I ask you—knowing how you feel—but Scott. I depend on your generosity—your nobility. You wouldn't let anything happen to Barney, would you? You'll send him away with that prisoner, up to Helena, won't you? The way he said you would? We planned—he planned to take me with him, on the train. We would get married in Helena."

"In Helena?" he asked blankly. "Married? You and him?"

"You'll do what you said, won't you?"

"What would you do if I refused?" he asked, looking away from her.

"Would you refuse?" she asked gently.

He thought for a long moment. Then he said, smiling, "No, if you ask me, I will give it to you. I have to, anyway. It's my duty—a thing I never forgot until this afternoon."

"Thank you, Scott. I will always be grateful to you."

"That's something."

She turned to go. "I will always owe you my happiness, after all, won't I?"

"Accept it as a kind of gift; it is free. I'm not asking you for anything. To marry, and not to marry, to have you, or to be refused by you—what difference does it make? I still love you—you are still the same. Nothing that you ever did, caused me to love you, nothing you can do can cause me to stop loving you."

"Good-bye, Scott."

"Good-bye, darling. And don't worry about losing your precious Barney."

He took her to the door. He stood and watched her going back up along the side of the church.

Wyckoff leaned against the wagon wheel, watching him calmly. Ogilvie said, "I want your rifle. Not the Springfield. The Winchester. Leave it on the table in there."

"You want my pistol too, Judge?"

"The one in the drawer's enough."

"You want me, Jodge? Here I am. Here I am, Jodge."

"Watch after her."

He went back into the tiny courtroom, sat down at the table and pulled out the drawer again. He rapped on the table with the hammer and said in the silence, "I sentence you, Rudolph Hayes, to death by hanging in the Territorial Prison not later than thirty days from this date."

Nobody in the courtroom said anything. He ignored the fixed eyes of Charles Hayes and Mrs. Quarry, and said, matter-of-factly, "The request for banishment is denied, as an improbable and certainly outmoded solution to the worst problems of this territory. There cannot be any mercy until there has been justice, which begins with a respect for law. It is the duty of this court to assist in the firm establishment of justice in this territory. The court is dismissed."

Nobody moved.

He turned to Wiley and said in the same crisp, matter-of-fact voice, "Sheriff, you will take the prisoner and travel immediately to the railroad and board the five o'clock train eastbound to Helena."

"That's a hell of a thing," somebody shouted outside.

"That's all," Ogilvie said. "Go home."

They went, slowly and grudgingly at first, and then the courtroom was empty, except for three people, the two Hayes men and Mrs. Quarry, sitting in the front row, looking steadily at Ogilvie.

Wiley and his eight men herded the prisoner out through the back door into the shack behind.

Mrs. Quarry dropped her eyes and looked at her knees. A rattle of tug chains being hooked came faintly through open doors from the wagon outside. Voices rose and fell in brief argument. A faint breeze coming through the church swept down the aisle, lifting a piece of newspaper and coasting it down toward the door.

Mrs. Quarry took a corner of her shawl and held it to her eyes, hiding her face, and getting to her feet, went slowly down the aisle after the newspaper.

Howard Hayes appeared at the main door. "Charles," he said down the length of the aisle, "they're getting ready to pull out. They got Rudy tied up in there. Charles, what's going to happen to Rudy?"

Charles stood up. "So long, Judge," he said. "We'll be seeing you later."

Ogilvie took the pistol out of the drawer and pointed it at Charles' chest. "It would convenience me greatly if you gave me occasion to kill you now, Charles." Charles sat down. "But I guess you won't. We'll wait here a while."

CHAPTER FIVE
One Less for Helena

Howard ducked out of view beyond the door. They heard the short shout of the driver and the crack of a whip. Wheels groaned and harness clicked. The creak of hubs went past below the windows, and the rapid pummel of ridden horses. Dust rose in a thick cloud, and the sounds quickly faded. Distantly, the trotting horses pounded across the wooden bridge, and silence came back.

"Charles?" Howard called from outside somewhere. "You want me to chase them?"

"No," Charles said calmly.

"You want me to try a shot through the window, Charles?" Howard asked again.

"No, Howard," Charles said patiently. "Just wait a while."

They sat in silence. The shadows moved across the floor.

"You going anywhere this afternoon, Judge?" Charles asked casually. "Anywhere special?"

"Yes," Ogilvie said. "I'm going up to my ranch. I bought the old Bar WX, you know, Charles. You know the way? Up the bench, then straight up toward the mountains. You can't miss it."

Charles said, "Those sure were pretty roses you had down in your garden, Ogilvie. You remember? I keep remembering them, somehow."

The judge sat silent for a little while. "Yes," he said, looking down the long aisle, "I remember."

After a while, Ogilvie said, "All right, beat it."

They got up under the gun and went out, unhurried. He watched them go, and waited till the sound of their horses' hoofs had died. Then he closed the table drawer, shoved the pistol into his pants and went out the back door.

He took the rifle lying on the table in his good hand and clutching the stock with his elbow, awkwardly worked the lever, partly opening the breech. There was a cartridge already in the chamber.

He went out and stopped, seeing Sam Wyckoff sitting on the ground with the reins of his horse drooping handy. Myra was sitting in her buggy nearby.

"What are you here for, Myra?" Ogilvie asked.

"Barney," she said. "He said he'd get them started, and then come back for me, and we'll go in the buggy."

"Such is devotion to duty," Ogilvie said. He got his horse and mounted it, carrying the rifle across his pommel Indian style.

"Where you going, Jodge?" Wyckoff asked.

"For a little ride, Sam."

"Can I come?"

"I told you once," Ogilvie said. "Watch out for her." He rode on.

Wyckoff stood up and slowly slapped the dust off the seat of his pants. "Good thing I listen at the winder sometimes, or I'd never know nothink. Miss Lampson, I'm going to tal you a things. Something is going to happen very soon. I prove to you, a woman, that your Barney is a big coward. I do it so you don't make no mistakes."

She looked at him quietly, as though she were tired. "If you mean you're going to try to beat him up, don't bother. I know you're bigger. Nothing you could do would make any difference. I love him."

"You love him," Wyckoff said. "What you know about love? For you it is all guitars and grape juice, dancing in the moon. Why don't you young women ever learn that love is giffing things up? Love is a fighter, she is harder than nails, she is old, she got a face like a ham sandwich, she smiles when she hurts, she is loyal, she is *good*, she bears lots and lots children. She loves a real man, not a pritty one. Look, here comes your pritty one right now, young woman."

He pointed his chin across the meadow. Wiley loped his horse toward them. He pulled up, ignoring Wyckoff. "Come on, darling."

"Listen," Wyckoff said. "All these Hayes boms are laying for the jodge. Now. He is got to fight them. Why? For you, Miss Lampson, so you will be happy with prittyboy here? More poattry." He grinned. "Prittyboy, you come and help me in this fight."

"Cut it out," Wiley said heavily. "Come on, Myra. I'll leave my horse in town and—"

"Wait, Wiley," she said. "Sam, are you making this up?"

"Myra, darling. I said, come on—"

"Shot opp, young fellow," Sam said. "Miss Lampson, this morning they told the jodge they kill him and everybody that helped with hanging their brother. Why you think the jodge sent prittyboy here up to Helena, instead of hanging Rudy here? Now the jodge is staying here—he got to taking it for all of you."

He looked at Wiley. "I say to you, prittyboy, come on with me and help him. I took a chance in waiting this long."

"I don't believe it," Wiley said. "It's some kind of trick of his, some kind of lawyer sneak trick. Nobody ever fights three to one. They run."

"You don't coming?"

"No. I've got to go take care of my prisoner."

Wyckoff smiled. "He won't shoot you, anyway." He turned his horse. "Miss Lampson, I hope you are very happy with this dirty coward, all your life. Good-bye."

She put down her reins. "I think you'd better go with Sam, Barney."

He looked at her and said, "I'm sure it's just a story."

"Please go. Isn't it your duty?"

"My first duty," he said, looking away, "is to my prisoner. Come on, we have to make the train." He added, "I hope you won't make it necessary for me to drive you."

She looked at him in silence.

He said, dismounting and tying his horse to the back of the buggy, "Move over, Myra. I see I'll have to take over." He climbed in and took the reins. "So long, Wyckoff," he said.

"I'm sorry," she said. She climbed out and mounted his horse, untying it from the buggy. "Good-bye, Barney. Have a good time in Helena."

She turned her horse toward Wyckoff. "Sam, please, where are the rings? The ones he bought for us? I know there isn't much time—but please—*our* rings?"

The first shot was careful and deliberate, as Ogilvie had supposed it would be, but it came sooner than he had expected, at the moment when he was sighing with relief at emerging from the thickets of the canyon that ran up the bench onto the rough plateau above. It came—the sharp crack of the bullet passing, much like the pop of a whip, then the crack of the rifle itself, from behind, down the canyon.

He dropped forward over the horn and stabbed the mare with his spurs. She jumped out like a jackrabbit and made three bounds into a dead run.

He heard the second bullet whack into her head and as

she slid forward and he went down, he saw the blue smoke above a boulder ahead and to the left.

He went off over her head and landed flat on his belly, sliding in the gravel. The pistol fell out of his pants. He left it and ran to the right, into the cover of the boulders, away from the rifle ahead.

A third one opened up ahead, a little to the left of his new direction, and even as he ducked and began crabbing through the boulders he knew he was being simply herded back toward the first rifle.

He went back to the edge of the bench, fifty yards from where the road came up out of the canyon, and waited behind a rock. Howard came up on foot, his rifle in his hand. He stood looking around. Charles called something to him.

Ogilvie steadied his rifle against the rock and dropped Howard neatly in the road.

He left his rock and found three others, making a kind of nest, protected on two sides. He cranked another cartridge into his rifle and as he got into his rock nest, he saw Jake stand up from behind a boulder and aim. He threw his rifle up and squeezed off just as Jake's bullet hit him in the left forearm, breaking one of the bones. He looked up from the hole in his coat sleeve and saw Jake lying face down across his boulder, arms hanging down, like an empty shirt drying in the sun. His rifle lay in the open, thrown ten feet away.

He could hear Charles calling to Jake, the voice moving around among the boulders. He sat, dizzy, and as the pain in his arm grew and the sweat began to come out hard, Charles began to curse, the sound coming from behind Jake's boulder.

Charles stuck his head up like a prairie dog. Ogilvie swung his rifle, slowly, the weight of it seeming to drag. Charles saw him and snapped a shot at him. He cursed and as Ogilvie threw himself sideways, down behind one of his rocks, he snapped two more at him.

Charles cursed him slowly in the silence from behind his dead brother. He began firing deliberately against Ogilvie's side rock. The ricochets splattered down, pellets of broken lead stinging into Ogilvie's face, drops of blood forming up.

"Come out," Charles said, his voice choked with fury.

"Come out." He fired fast, bouncing bullets down into Ogilvie's hole, and Ogilvie lay still, his arm over his face. He heard the dry snapping of Charles' hammer fall on the empty gun, and threw himself up out of the hole onto his feet.

Charles stared at him openmouthed, a fresh cartridge in one hand, the opened rifle in the other. Ogilvie said, "Drop it," and held his rifle on him.

Charles dropped it, and made a leap across his boulder for Jake's rifle, lying on the ground. He got it, but not before Ogilvie was on him, holding his own gun on Charles' back as Charles knelt over the full gun.

"Get up, Charles," Ogilvie said. "I dislike all this bloodshed intensely. Just get up and be quiet. You're under arrest."

Charles stood up slowly, his fists clenched, his fat face bursting. He looked from side to side desperately, and suddenly turned and ran. Ogilvie swung up his rifle, one-armed, trying to line him up.

Another rifle fired, a deeper, heavier, shorter blast, and Charles fell, still running. Wyckoff came up over the edge of the bench, the Government carbine smoking. Charles lay still, panting.

"I heard what you said, Captain," Wyckoff said. "I mean, Jodge. He ain't dead. Only upsat a little."

"I'm obliged," Ogilvie said, lowering the Winchester. "In Barney's absence, do you think you could take him into your gracious custody, Sam?"

"I think," Myra said, looking over the edge of the bench, "Barney's absence will last for quite a while. Please, Scott, will you forgive me? Oh, my God, you're hurt." She scrambled up the bank and ran toward him, her hair awry, her dress rumpled and mussed. She stood looking up at his face.

"A few old shaving wounds," he said. "They always reopen when I smile too wide."

"Oh, Scott, why was I such a fool? Rub it in. I deserve it, rub it in. My head was full of foolishness."

Ogilvie sat down on a stone. He looked at Charles, groaning and wiggling.

"Sam," he said wearily, "remove that. And kindly dump Jake behind some rock out of sight. I want to welcome home my wife in a fitting manner, and these people are ruining the setting. A kiss is what I need, one simple kiss to make it well."

"Am I hearing poattry again? Jodge, you brains is foggy. I think you need a drink. Why don't you just take you wife and ride home with her to the rose garden? I stay here and clean up the robbish."

Myra smiled. "I brought the rings. Our rings," she said.

"That's all I want to hear," he said. "The way you say that. *Our* rings."

He took her arm and led her to the road.

A DOUBLE-DYED DECEIVER

BY O. HENRY
(The Texan)

O. Henry (William Sydney Porter, 1862–1910), the master of the surprise-ending short story, created two memorable Western desperadoes: the Cisco kid, who underwent a metamorphosis in the 1950s television series starring Duncan Renaldo and Leo Carrillo and became a dashing "Robin Hood of the Old West"; and the Llano Kid, the "villainous hero" of both the story "A Double-Dyed Deceiver" (1905) and the early Gary Cooper screen adaptation of it, The Texan (1930). Curiously, there is even a blending of the two characters in an obscure 1939 film with Tito Guizar and Alan Mowbray: its title is The Llano Kid, but it is loosely based on the exploits of the Cisco Kid.

The trouble began in Laredo. It was the Llano Kid's fault, for he should have confined his habit of manslaughter to Mexicans. But the Kid was past twenty; and to have only Mexicans to one's credit at twenty is to blush unseen on the Rio Grande border.

It happened in old Justo Valdo's gambling house. There was a poker game at which sat players who were not all friends, as happens often where men ride in from afar to shoot Folly as she gallops. There was a row over so small a matter as a pair of queens; and when the smoke had cleared away it was found that the Kid had committed an indiscretion, and his adversary had been guilty of a blunder. For, the unfortunate combatant, instead of being a Greaser, was a high-blooded youth from the cow ranches, of about the Kid's own age and possessed of friends and champions. His blunder in missing the Kid's right ear only a sixteenth of an inch when he pulled his gun did not lessen the indiscretion of the better marksman.

The Kid, not being equipped with a retinue, nor bountifully supplied with personal admirers and supporters—on account of a rather umbrageous reputation, even for the border—considered it not incompatible with his indisputable gameness to perform that judicious tractional act known as "pulling his freight."

Quickly the avengers gathered and sought him. Three of them overtook him within a rod of the station. The Kid turned and showed his teeth in that brilliant but mirthless smile that usually preceded his deeds of insolence and violence, and his pursuers fell back without making it necessary for him even to reach for his weapon.

But in this affair the Kid had not felt the grim thirst for encounter that usually urged him on to battle. It had been a purely chance row, born of the cards and certain epithets impossible for a gentleman to brook that had passed between the two. The Kid had rather liked the slim, haughty, brown-faced young chap whom his bullet had cut off in the first pride of manhood. And now he wanted no more blood. He wanted to get away and have a good long sleep somewhere in the sun on the mesquit grass with his handkerchief over his face. Even a Mexican might have crossed his path in safety while he was in this mood.

The Kid openly boarded the north-bound passenger train that departed five minutes later. But at Webb, a few miles out, where it was flagged to take on a traveller, he abandoned that manner of escape. There were telegraph stations ahead; and the Kid looked askance at electricity and steam. Saddle and spur were his rocks of safety.

The man whom he had shot was a stranger to him. But the Kid knew that he was of the Coralitos outfit from Hidalgo; and that the punchers from that ranch were more relentless and vengeful than Kentucky feudists when wrong or harm was done to one of them. So, with the wisdom that has characterized many great fighters, the Kid decided to pile up as many leagues as possible of chaparral and pear between himself and the retaliation of the Coralitos bunch.

Near the station was a store; and near the store, scattered among the mesquits and elms, stood the saddled horses of the customers. Most of them waited, half asleep, with sagging limbs and drooping heads. But one, a long-legged roan with a curved neck, snorted and pawed the turf. Him the Kid mounted, gripped with his knees, and slapped gently with the owner's own quirt.

If the slaying of the temerarious card-player had cast a cloud over the Kid's standing as a good and true citizen, this last act of his veiled his figure in the darkest shadows of disrepute. On the Rio Grande border if you take a man's life you sometimes take trash; but if you take his horse, you take a thing the loss of which renders him poor, indeed, and which enriches you not—if you are caught. For the Kid there was no turning back now.

With the springing roan under him he felt little care or uneasiness. After a five-mile gallop he drew in to the plainsman's jogging trot, and rode northeastward toward the Nueces River bottoms. He knew the country well—its most tortuous and obscure trails through the great wilderness of brush and pear, and its camps and lonesome ranches where one might find safe entertainment. Always he bore to the east; for the Kid had never seen the ocean, and he had a fancy to lay his hand upon the mane of the great gulf, the gamesome colt of the greater waters.

So after three days he stood on the shore at Corpus Christi, and looked out across the gentle ripples of a quiet sea.

Captain Boone, of the schooner *Flyaway*, stood near his skiff, which one of his crew was guarding in the surf. When ready to sail he had discovered that one of the necessaries of life, in the parallelogrammatic shape of plug tobacco, had been forgotten. A sailor had been dispatched for the missing cargo. Meanwhile the captain paced the sands, chewing profanely at his pocket store.

A slim, wiry youth in high-heeled boots came down to the water's edge. His face was boyish, but with a premature severity that hinted at a man's experience. His complexion was naturally dark; and the sun and wind of an outdoor life had burned it to a coffee brown. His hair was as black and straight as an Indian's; his face had not yet been upturned to the humiliation of a razor; his eyes were a cold and steady blue. He carried his left arm somewhat away from his body, for pearlhandled .45s are frowned upon by town marshals, and are a little bulky when packed in the left armhole of one's vest. He looked beyond Captain Boone at the gulf with the impersonal and expressionless dignity of a Chinese emperor.

"Thinkin' of buyin' that'ar gulf, buddy?" asked the captain, made sarcastic by his narrow escape from the tobaccoless voyage.

"Why, no," said the Kid gently, "I reckon not. I never saw it before. I was just looking at it. Not thinking of selling it, are you?"

"Not this trip," said the captain. "I'll send it to you C.O.D. when I get back to Buenas Tierras. Here comes that capstanfooted lubber with the chewin'. I ought to've weighed anchor an hour ago."

"Is that your ship out there?" asked the Kid.

"Why, yes," answered the captain, "if you want to call a schooner a ship, and I don't mind lyin'. But you better say Miller and Gonzales, owners, and ordinary plain, Billy-be-damned old Samuel K. Boone, skipper."

"Where are you going to?" asked the refugee.

"Buenas Tierras, coast of South America—I forgot what they called the country the last time I was there. Cargo—lumber, corrugated iron, and machetes."

"What kind of a country is it?" asked the Kid, "—hot or cold?"

"Warmish, buddy," said the captain. "But a regular Paradise Lost for elegance of scenery and be-yooty of geography. Ye're wakened every morning by the sweet singin' of red birds with seven purple tails, and the sighin' of breezes in the posies and roses. And the inhabitants never work, for they can reach out and pick steamer baskets of the choicest hothouse fruit without gettin' out of bed. And there's no Sunday and no ice and no rent and no troubles and no use and no nothin'. It's a great country for a man to go to sleep with, and wait for somethin' to turn up. The bananys and oranges and hurricanes and pineapples that ye eat comes from there."

"That sounds to me!" said the Kid, at last betraying interest. "What'll the expressage be to take me out there with you?"

"Twenty-four dollars," said Captain Boone; "grub and transportation. Second cabin. I haven't got a first cabin."

"You've got my company," said the Kid, pulling out a buckskin bag.

With three hundred dollars he had gone to Laredo for his regular "blowout." The duel in Valdos's had cut short his season of hilarity, but it had left him with nearly two hundred dollars for aid in the fight that it had made necessary.

"All right, buddy," said the captain. "I hope your ma won't blame me for this little childish escapade of yours." He beckoned to one of the boat's crew. "Let Sanchez lift you out to the skiff so you won't get your feet wet."

Thacker, the United States consul at Buenas Tierras, was not yet drunk. It was only eleven o'clock; and he never arrived at his desired state of beatitude—a state where he sang ancient maudlin vaudeville songs and pelted his screaming parrot with banana peels— until the middle of the afternoon. So, when he looked up from his hammock at the sound of a slight cough, and saw the Kid standing in the door of the consulate, he was still in a condition to extend the hospitality and courtesy due from the representative of a great nation. "Don't disturb yourself," said the Kid easily. "I just dropped in. They told me it was customary to light at your camp before starting in to round up the town. I just came in on a ship from Texas."

"Glad to see you, Mr.—," said the consul.

The Kid laughed.

"Sprague Dalton," he said. "It sounds funny to me to hear it. I'm called the Llano Kid in the Rio Grande country."

"I'm Thacker," said the consul. "Take that cane-bottom chair. Now if you've come to invest, you want somebody to advise you. These dingies will cheat you out of the gold in your teeth if you don't understand their ways. Try a cigar?"

"Much obliged," said the Kid, "but if it wasn't for my corn shucks and the little bag in my back pocket I couldn't live a minute." He took out his "makings," and rolled a cigarette.

"They speak Spanish here," said the consul. "You'll need an interpreter. If there's anything I can do, why, I'd be delighted. If you're buying fruit lands or looking for a concession of any sort, you'll want somebody who knows the ropes to look out for you."

"I speak Spanish," said the Kid, "about nine times better than I do English. Everybody speaks it on the range where I come from. And I'm not in the market for anything."

"You speak Spanish?" said Thacker thoughtfully. He regarded the Kid absorbedly.

"You look like a Spaniard, too," he continued. "And you're from Texas. And you can't be more than twenty or twenty-one. I wonder if you've got any nerve."

"You got a deal of some kind to put through?" asked the Texan, with unexpected shrewdness.

"Are you open to a proposition?" said Thacker.

"What's the use to deny it?" said the Kid. "I got into a little gun frolic down in Laredo and plugged a white man. There wasn't any Mexican handy. And I come down to your parrot-and-monkey range just for to smell the morning-glories and marigolds. Now, do you *sabe?*"

Thacker got up and closed the door.

"Let me see your hand," he said.

He took the Kid's left hand, and examined the back of it closely.

"I can do it," he said excitedly. "Your flesh is as hard as wood and as healthy as a baby's. It will heal in a week."

"If it's a fist fight you want to back me for," said the Kid, "don't put your money up yet. Make it gun work, and I'll keep you company. But no barehanded scrapping, like ladies at a tea-party, for me."

"It's easier than that," said Thacker. "Just step here, will you?"

Through the window he pointed to a two-story white-stuccoed house with wide galleries rising amid the deep-green tropical foliage on a wooded hill that sloped gently from the sea.

"In that house," said Thacker, "a fine old Castilian gentleman and his wife are yearning to gather you into their arms and fill your pockets with money. Old Santos Urique lives there. He owns half the goldmines in the country."

"You haven't been eating loco weed, have you?" asked the Kid.

"Sit down again," said Thacker, "and I'll tell you. Twelve years ago they lost a kid. No, he didn't die—although most of 'em here do from drinking the surface water. He was a wild little devil, even if he wasn't but eight years old. Everybody knows about it. Some Americans who were through here prospecting for gold had letters to Señor Urique, and the boy was a favourite with them. They filled his head with big stories about the States; and about a month after they left, the kid disappeared, too. He was supposed to have stowed himself away among the banana bunches on a fruit steamer, and gone to New Orleans. He was seen once afterward in Texas, it was thought, but they never heard anything more of him. Old Urique has spent thousands of dollars having him looked for. The madam was broken up worst of all. The kid was her life. She wears mourning yet. But they say she believes he'll come back to her some day, and never gives up hope. On the back of the boy's left hand was tattooed a flying eagle carrying a spear in his claws. That's old Urique's coat of arms or something that he inherited in Spain."

The Kid raised his left hand slowly and gazed at it curiously.

"That's it," said Thacker, reaching behind the official desk for his bottle of smuggled brandy. "You're not so slow. I can do it. What was I consul at Sandakan for? I never knew till now. In a week I'll have the eagle bird with the frog-sticker blended in so you'd think you were born with it. I brought a set of the needles and ink just because I was sure you'd drop in some day, Mr. Dalton."

"Oh, hell," said the Kid. "I thought I told you my name!"

"All right, 'Kid,' then. It won't be that long. How does Señorito Urique sound, for a change?"

"I never played son any that I remember of," said the Kid. "If I had any parents to mention they went over the divide about the time I gave my first bleat. What is the plan of your round-up?"

Thacker leaned back against the wall and held his glass up to the light.

"We've come now," said he, "to the question of how far you're willing to go in a little matter of the sort."

"I told you why I came down here," said the Kid simply.

"A good answer," said the consul. "But you won't have to go that far. Here's the scheme. After I get the trademark tattooed on your hand I'll notify old Urique. In the meantime I'll furnish you with all of the family history I can find out, so you can be studying up points to talk about. You've got the looks, you speak the Spanish, you know the facts, you can tell about Texas, you've got the tattoo mark. When I notify them that the rightful heir has returned and is waiting to know whether he will be received and pardoned, what will happen? They'll simply rush down here and fall on your neck, and the curtain goes down for refreshments and a stroll in the lobby."

"I'm waiting," said the Kid. "I haven't had my saddle off in your camp long, pardner, and I never met you before; but if you intend to let it go at a parental blessing, why, I'm mistaken in my man, that's all."

"Thanks," said the consul. "I haven't met anybody in a long time that keeps up with an argument as well as you do. The rest of it is simple. If they take you in only for a while it's long enough. Don't give 'em time to hunt up the strawberry mark on your left shoulder. Old Urique keeps anywhere from $50,000 to $100,000 in his house all the time in a little safe that you could open with a shoe buttoner. Get it. My skill as a tattooer is worth half the boodle. We go halves and catch a tramp steamer for Rio Janeiro. Let the United States go to pieces if it can't get along without my services. *Que dice, señor?*"

"It sounds to me!" said the Kid, nodding his head. "I'm out for the dust."

"All right, then," said Thacker. "You'll have to keep close until we get the bird on you. You can live in the back room here. I do my own cooking, and I'll make you as comfortable as a parsimonious Government will allow me."

Thacker had set the time at a week, but it was two weeks before the design that he patiently tattooed upon the Kid's hand was to his notion. And then Thacker called a *muchacho*, and dispatched this note to the intended victim:

EL SEÑOR DON SANTOS URIQUE,
   La Casa Blanca,
MY DEAR SIR:
   I beg permission to inform you that there is in my

house as a temporary guest a young man who arrived in
Buenas Tierras from the United States some days ago.
Without wishing to excite any hopes that may not be
realized, I think there is a possibility of his being your
long-absent son. It might be well for you to call and see
him. If he is, it is my opinion that his intention was to
return to his home, but upon arriving here, his courage
failed him from doubts as to how he would be received.

Your true servant,

THOMPSON THACKER.

Half an hour afterward—quick time for Buenas Tierras—
Señor Urique's ancient landau drove to the consul's door,
with the barefooted coachman beating and shouting at
the team of fat, awkward horses.

A tall man with a white moustache alighted, and assisted
to the ground a lady who was dressed and veiled in
unrelieved black.

The two hastened inside, and were met by Thacker
with his best diplomatic bow. By his desk stood a slender
young man with clear-cut, sunbrowned features and
smoothly brushed black hair.

Señora Urique threw back her heavy veil with a quick
gesture. She was past middle age, and her hair was beginning to silver, but her full, proud figure and clear olive
skin retained traces of the beauty peculiar to the Basque
province. But, once you had seen her eyes, and compre-
hended the great sadness that was revealed in their deep
shadows and hopeless expression, you saw that the woman
lived only in some memory.

She bent upon the young man a long look of the most
agonized questioning. Then her great black eyes turned,
and her gaze rested upon his left hand. And then with a
sob, not loud, but seeming to shake the room, she cried
"*Hijo* mio!" and caught the Llano Kid to her heart.

A month afterward the Kid came to the consulate in
response to a message sent by Thacker.

He looked the young Spanish *caballero*. His clothes
were imported, and the wiles of the jewellers had not
been spent upon him in vain. A more than respectable
diamond shone on his finger as he rolled a shuck cigarette.

"What's doing?" asked Thacker.

"Nothing much," said the Kid calmly. "I eat my first

iguana steak today. They're them big lizards, you *sabe?* I reckon, though, that frijoles and side bacon would do me about as well. Do you care for iguanas, Thacker?"

"No, nor for some other kinds of reptiles," said Thacker.

It was three in the afternoon, and in another hour he would be in his state of beatitude.

"It's time you were making good, sonny," he went on, with an ugly look on his reddened face. "You're not playing up to me square. You've been the prodigal son for four weeks now, and you could have had veal for every meal on a gold dish if you'd wanted it. Now, Mr. Kid, do you think it's right to leave me out so long on a husk diet? What's the trouble? Don't you get your filial eyes on anything that looks like cash in the Casa Blanca? Don't tell me you don't. Everybody knows where old Urique keeps his stuff. It's U. S. currency, too; he don't accept anything else. What's doing? Don't say 'nothing' this time."

"Why, sure," said the Kid, admiring his diamond, "there's plenty of money up there. I'm no judge of collateral in bunches, but I will undertake for to say that I've seen the rise of $50,000 at a time in that tin grub box that my adopted father calls his safe. And he lets me carry the key sometimes just to show me that he knows I'm the real little Francisco that strayed from the herd a long time ago."

"Well, what are you waiting for?" asked Thacker angrily. "Don't you forget that I can upset your apple-cart any day I want to. If old Urique knew you were an impostor, what sort of things would happen to you? Oh, you don't know this country, Mr. Texas Kid. The laws here have got mustard spread between 'em. These people here'd stretch you out like a frog that had been stepped on, and give you about fifty sticks at every corner of the plaza. And they'd wear every stick out, too. What was left of you they'd feed to alligators."

"I might as well tell you now, pardner," said the Kid, sliding down low on his steamer chair, "that things are going to stay just as they are. They're about right now."

"What do you mean?" asked Thacker, rattling the bottom of his glass on his desk.

"The scheme's off," said the Kid. "And whenever you have the pleasure of speaking to me address me as Don

Francisco Urique. I'll guarantee I'll answer to it. We'll let Colonel Urique keep his money. His little tin safe is as good as the time-locker in the First National Bank of Laredo as far as you and me are concerned."

"You're going to throw me down, then, are you?" said the consul.

"Sure," said the Kid cheerfully. "Throw you down. That's it. And now I'll tell you why. The first night I was up at the colonel's house they introduced me to a bedroom. No blankets on the floor—a real room, with a bed and things in it. And before I was asleep, in comes this artificial mother of mine and tucks in the covers. 'Panchito,' she says, 'my little lost one, God has brought you back to me. I bless His name forever.' It was that, or some truck like that, she said. And down comes a drop or two of rain and hits me on the nose. And all that stuck by me, Mr. Thacker. And it's been that way ever since. And it's got to stay that way. Don't you think that it's for what's in it for me, either, that I say so. If you have any such ideas, keep 'em to yourself. I haven't had much truck with women in my life, and no mothers to speak of, but here's a lady that we've got to keep fooled. Once she stood it; twice she won't. I'm a low-down wolf, and the devil may have sent me on this trail instead of God, but I'll travel it to the end. And now, don't forget that I'm Don Francisco Urique whenever you happen to mention my name."

"I'll expose you to-day, you—you double-dyed traitor," stammered Thacker.

The Kid arose and, without violence, took Thacker by the throat with a hand of steel, and shoved him slowly into a corner. Then he drew from under his left arm his pearl-handled .45 and poked the cold muzzle of it against the consul's mouth.

"I told you why I come here," he said, with his old freezing smile. "If I leave here, you'll be the reason. Never forget it, pardner. Now, what is my name?"

"Er—Don Francisco Urique," gasped Thacker.

From outside came a sound of wheels, and the shouting of some one, and the sharp thwacks of a wooden whipstock upon the backs of fat horses.

The Kid put up his gun, and walked toward the door. But he turned again and came back to the trembling

Thacker, and held up his left hand with its back toward the consul.

"There's one more reason," he said slowly, "why things have got to stand as they are. The fellow I killed in Laredo had one of them same pictures on his left hand."

Outside, the ancient landau of Don Santos Urique rattled to the door. The coachman ceased his bellowing. Señora Urique, in a voluminous gay gown of white lace and flying ribbons, leaned forward with a happy look in her great soft eyes.

"Are you within, dear son?" she called, in the rippling Castilian.

"*Madre mía, yo vengo* [mother, I come]," answered the young Don Francisco Urique.

THE SINGING SANDS

BY STEVE FRAZEE
(Gold of the Seven Saints)

"The Singing Sands" is a first-rate tale of man's lust for gold, a popular theme in Western fiction (and in Western film). Steve Frazee's evocative, cinematic prose style has led Hollywood to transfer a number of his novels and short stories to the silver screen, in some cases not very well. The best of the films based on his fiction are probably Many Rivers to Cross *(1955) from the novel of the same title, which starred Robert Taylor, Eleanor Parker, and James Arness, and* Running Target *(1956), a very good low-budget "B" adapted from the novelized version of Frazee's prize-winning novelette "My Brother Down There" (included in* The Best of the West II). *Less successful adaptations are* Wild Heritage *(1958), taken from the novel* Smoke in the Valley, *and* High Hell, *produced that same year—an updated soap-opera version of the novel* High Cage.

There were three passes ahead and their names were like the rhythm of a chant, Mosca, Medano and Music. The alliteration kept running in Johnny Anderson's mind as his tired pony chopped through the rabbitbrush, across alkali flats where the dust rose thin and bitter in the windless air. Like magic words that would kill the trouble behind, the names chased each other; but every few moments Anderson looked across his shoulder at the long backtrail.

Jasper Lamb was doing the same thing, twisting wearily in the saddle, squinting his bloodshot eyes at the gray distance. He was a middle-aged man, slouching, leanly built. For a year Anderson had prowled the mountains

80

with him. They had never faced any severe test until now; and now Anderson was wondering if he had picked the right partner. Lamb was not showing the proper concern about things.

Anderson worked his lips and ran his tongue around his mouth to clear dust and the cottony feeling that had been in his mouth ever since he knew there were men on their trail. "Which pass, Lamb?"

"Medano, I know it best." Lamb glanced at the heavily loaded mule he was towing. The mule was the strongest of the three animals, but it would not be hurried.

Each mile seemed to bring them no closer to the mountains with their golden streaks of frost-touched aspens. Looking backward at the space they had crossed, Anderson was uneasy because of the very emptiness. He said hopefully, "Maybe we threw them off when we made that fake toward Poncha Pass early this morning."

"I figured on wind," Lamb said. "There ain't been any. We've left a trail like a single furrow ploughed across a field. The wind blows like old Scratch here sometimes, but today it didn't." He had come out during the Pike's Peak bust, cutting his teeth on the mountains and losing his illusions at the same time, so now he did not rail against luck or the weather. "They'll be along."

Johnny Anderson was young. He had passed his twenty-second birthday the week before when they were making their final cleanup on their placer claim in the San Juan. He wasted energy cursing the vagaries of the weather; but half his anger was fear as he saw how Lamb's buckskin was limping. The horse had thrown a shoe in the rocky foothills just north of the Rio Grande the night before. Anderson tried to weigh the limp against the distance yet to go; and then he turned to look behind.

There was no dust far back. Mosca, Medano and Music. . . . He studied immense buff foothills ahead. He had never seen their like before but he was not greatly interested.

Lamb did not waste motion in shrugging or any other gesture. "You saw some of the toughs there in Baker's Park when we stopped overnight. Pick any bunch of them."

"We made a mistake!" Anderson said. "We shouldn't have stopped there, and then we guarded the panniers on the mule too close. We should have dumped them on the ground like they didn't amount to nothing. We made another mistake when we slipped out of there by night. We—"

"Sure, we made mistakes." Lamb leaned ahead to feel the shoulder of his horse. "We come out of the San Juan with a loaded mule at the end of summer. Nobody had to be smart to know what we're carrying." He kept watching the buckskin's shoulder. "We made our pile in a hurry, boy. I mistrust too much good luck."

Anderson let the thought grind away for a while. "Is your horse going to make it?"

"I doubt it, not without he rests and I try to do something for that tender foot." Lamb looked at the unshod Indian pony under Anderson. It cut no figure at all beside the buckskin. It rode hard and its gait was uneven but the mustang mark was there and there were guts in the pony for many miles yet. Lamb watched it for a moment with no expression on his bearded, dusty features.

Slowly the great pale brown hills came closer. No trees, no rocks broke the rounding contours. The ridges were sharp on the spines, delicately molded. The shadings of the coloration flowed so subtly into each other that Anderson could not tell whether the hills were a quarter of a mile away or two miles. The whole mass of them seemed to pulse in the still heat. Anderson's sudden loss of distance judgment gave him a queer feeling.

When he looked behind once more and saw only lonely vastness, the claws of fear began to loosen and the hills began to capture his attention. A gentle incline led the two men among the pinon trees. The pitchy scent of them was warmly strong. Lamb swung his sorefooted horse into a broad gulch and soon they were riding on a brown carpet that flowed out from the skirts of the hills. Pure sand.

The pack mule balked the moment its hooves touched the silky softness. It sniffed and held back on the tow rope, but at last Lamb urged it on ahead. Riding in an eerie silence broken only by the gentle plopping of hooves, the two men struck a course to turn the shoulder of the dunes where they ended against the mountains.

"That's the biggest pile of sand I ever saw!" Anderson said.

In the strike of the afternoon sun the sweeping curves of the hills blended into a oneness that robbed Anderson of depth perception. There were moments when the dunes had only height and length. He estimated the highest ridge at seven hundred feet, but it seemed so far away he guessed that a man could not reach it in a day.

Staring at the dunes, he forgot for a time the threat behind him—until Lamb stopped the buckskin suddenly. The dust was out there now, standing like thin smoke above the rabbitbrush on the way that they had come. As they watched, the first wind of the day came out of the southwest. The claws hooked in again and the tightness returned to Anderson's stomach.

He rode to the rear of the pack mule, thinking to urge it into greater speed when they started. Lamb's calmness stopped him. With one eye almost closed so that the side of his mouth was raised in the semblance of a smile, Lamb was slouching in the saddle and studying the dust as if not sure of the cause of it. He scrubbed the scum from his teeth with his tongue.

"There were five of them before," he said. "Guess there's still that many. You know something, Andy? They swung away this morning to get fresh horses at Pascual's ranch." Lamb eyed Anderson's wiry scrub. He glanced to the right, past cotton woods and pinon trees, up to where Mosca Pass trail came down in a V of the mountains. "Medano is still best for us. Once we hit the Huerfano, I've got more friends among the Mexicans than a cur has fleas."

"Let's go!"

Lamb swung down. "My horse won't last two miles."

"He's got to! We'll get to the rocks and stand 'em off."

"We might do that with Indians, yes." Lamb lifted the buckskin's left forefoot and looked at the hoof. "These are white men, Andy." He let the hoof drop. "They know what we got." He walked to a cottonwood at the edge of the gulch.

"White men or not, by God—"

"I ain't aiming to die over no gold," Lamb said. "I've got along too many years without it. I ain't figuring to let them have it either." He grinned and his toughness was never more apparent. "Just wait a spell. The wind is coming."

"Out in the valley it would have helped, but here, when we hit the trees—"

"Wait," Lamb said.

The wind reached them after a while. Strong and warm it came out of the southwest. There was an odd rustling sound and the sand lay out in streamers from the ridges of the dunes. It was difficult to tell about the dust cloud, but Anderson knew it must be closer.

All at once Anderson realized that the tracks he and Lamb had made in the broad gulch were gone. Unbroken sand that lay in gentle waves like frozen brown water covered every mark they had made since entering the gulch.

Lamb led his buckskin and the mule toward the dunes. The idea ran then in Anderson's mind that they would lose their pursuers by circling through the hollows of the hills; but when the animals struck the first ridge and began to labor in the shifting, slippery sand, he knew his thought was wrong.

They ploughed over the ridge and dropped into a small basin where the ground was bare. All around the edges of the hollow the sand was skirling, running in tiny riffles, and up on the great hills above them it was whipping from the spines in two different directions.

Lamb took the mule close to the side of the bowl where the sand came down steeply. He began to take the gold from the panniers. It was in wheels, circular pieces of buckskin gathered from the outside edge and tied with thongs. When the first few sacks dropped at the edge of the sand Anderson cried a protest.

"I'd rather fight for it!"

"I'd rather live," Lamb said. "We're not going to get clear unless I ride the mule. We'll get a little fighting even then. Give me a hand."

Each sack that thudded down was a wrench at Anderson's heart. He could not remember how easily the gold had come to them from a rich pocket in the San Juan; he could only estimate the weight of each sack as it fell at the edge of the fine silt.

"Not all of it, for God's sake!" he cried.

Lamb kept dropping the buckskin sacks. "Take what you want but remember you're riding a tired horse. Even Indian nags play out, Andy." A few moments later when

Lamb saw his partner stuffing sacks under his shirt, he said, "It'll be here when we come back, son."

It was not the words, but sudden wild music, that brought Anderson's head up with a jerk. It was a weird and whining sound, the bow of the wind playing across the sand strings of the ridges high above. Anderson listened only long enough to recognize what the sound was. It was mocking, discordant. He stuffed more gold inside his shirt.

When the panniers that had held almost two hundred pounds of weight were flapping loosely against the mule, Lamb's voice snapped across the wind with the crack of urgency, "Rake the sand down on top of the stuff while I shift my saddle to the mule."

Soft and warm, the sand slid easily under Anderson's raking hands. When he had covered part of the long row of sacks the wind had already concealed the marks where he had clawed. They climbed from the hollow, pausing on the ridge to peer through a brown haze at the dust still coming toward them. Anderson turned then to look into the little basin. All marks were gone, but he did not trust the smooth quickness of the sand.

"Maybe we could stand them off here," he said.

"Maybe we could die of thirst here, too." Lamb pointed across the shallow sand to the edge of the gulch. "It was six hundred and ten long steps, Andy, from that cottonwood with the busted top. Sight above the tree to that patch of gray rocks on the mountains. You got it?"

Anderson tried to burn the marks into his mind. He stared until he found a third point of sighting, the smoke-gray deadness of a spruce tree between the cottonwood and the patch of rocks. Six hundred and ten paces from the cottonwood. He could never forget this place.

Out in the rabbitbrush the riders had dropped into a swale. Only the dust they had raised behind them was visible. Lamb swung up on the mule and the mule tried to pitch him off. "I hope we never have to eat this devil," he said, "as tough as he is." He rode down the slope and into the broad expanse of shallow sand, towing his limping buckskin.

Anderson had difficulty in mounting. His shirt bulged with weight and his boots were full of sand. The hills were singing their high, queer song. He rode away, twisted in the saddle to watch his tracks; and he saw them drifting into smoothness almost as quickly as he made them. The treasure was safe enough but he worried because there seemed to be a gloating tone in the singing sands.

Now the dust was much closer and the fear of men was greater than all other worries.

Beside the eastern shoulder of the hills they crossed ground where water had carried brown earth from the mountains. The earth was cracked and curled upward in little chips. They let the animals drink when they hit the first seep of Medano Creek.

"Now we got our work cut out," Lamb said.

Medano Pass was rocky. The wind was funneling through it cold and sharp. Now the pursuers gained in earnest, for Anderson's pony began to lag and the hobbling buckskin began to lay back stubbornly on the lead rope.

From a high switchback Anderson saw the riders for the first time. Five of them, the same as before. "Let's get rid of the damned buckskin, Lamb!"

"About another mile and then we will."

When they came to a place where the trail was very narrow above a booming creek, Lamb said, "Drop a sack of gold here, Andy. The lead man will have to get down to get it. Every minute will help."

"Drop one of your own."

"I got only one," Lamb said patiently.

The gold was a terrible weight around Anderson's middle but he would not drop a sack. Nor would he part with it when he had to dismount to lead his pony up steep pitches. The sides of the horses were pounding. They stopped to rest at the top of a brutal hill. They could hear the sounds of the men behind them. Anderson tried to pull off his boots but the sand had worked so tightly around his feet and ankles that he could not get the boots off, and he was afraid to spend too much time in trying.

On a ledge above a canyon Lamb stopped again. He took the panniers from the buckskin, dropped a heavy rock into each of them, and hurled them away. He stripped the packsaddle and threw it by the cinch strap. Anderson heard it crash somewhere in the rocks out of sight. In the next stand of aspens Lamb took the buckskin out of sight and turned it loose.

He seemed to be gone a long time. Anderson stood

beside his trembling pony with his rifle ready, watching the trail. Lamb returned. His face was grim with the first anger he had shown since the pursuit began. He took his rifle and walked down the trail. "Go on," he ordered. "I'll be along directly."

Anderson went ahead on foot. There were seven shots, flat reports that sent echoes through the rocks. Anderson stopped, waiting, afraid. Presently Lamb came trotting up the trail. Blood was dripping from his left hand and his shirt was ripped above the elbow. He whipped the blood off his hand and said, "Get on, don't wait for nothing. Not far ahead they got a chance to flank around us if we stop to pick flowers."

On the next steep, narrow pitch Anderson dropped a sack of gold. It was a place where horses would have to hold in a straining position against the grade while the lead man got down. It was not much, but maybe it would help. Four more times he picked his spots and dropped more sacks.

Twice more Anderson went back on foot with his rifle. There were fewer shots each time.

Sunset dripped its colors on the mountains and they flamed with the hue that gave them their name, *Sangre de Cristo,* Blood of Christ. The colors died and the cold dusk came. Again Lamb went back on the trail and his rifle made crimson flashes. They passed the place where a Spanish governor had camped an avenging army two centuries before. They went over the top and the necks of the animals slanted downward.

It was dark then. A wind that came from vastness was running up the mountain. To Anderson, the pass had been the obstacle, and now they were across it. He breathed relief. The magic words, Mosca, Medano and Music came again; but moments later he forgot that it was his life he had worried about, and he thought of the gold they had left in the sand, and of the sacks of gold they had dropped on the trail. At least he had not thrown away everything; there were two sacks yet inside his shirt.

A pale moon rose, throwing ghostly light on the rocks. Far below the timber was a black sea. It was still a long way to the Huerfano, and there were things like weariness and hunger.

Lamb said, "Hold up a second."

In the dead stillness they heard the sound of hoofs sliding on stones on the trail behind them. The men were still coming. Not knowing who they were made it worse for Anderson. Their persistence chilled him. Lamb was a dark form near the head of the mule. "One of those three knows this trail," he muttered.

There had been five men. Anderson did not comment on the difference.

Lamb listened a moment longer. "They're on a short-cut that I didn't care to try." For the first time he sounded worried. He mounted and sent the mule down the trail on the trot.

The clatter of stones came loudly on the higher benches of the mountain.

Lamb set a dangerous pace, cutting across the sharp angles of the switchbacks, sending rocks in wild flight down the slopes. They made a long turn to the left and entered timber on the edge of a canyon where a waterfall was splashing in the moonlight. At the head of the canyon the trail swung back to the right. They were then in dense timber where the needle mat took sharpness from the hoofbeats of the horses.

"Hold it," Lamb called back softly, and then he stopped.

Above the canyon they had skirted, where the trail lay in Z patterns against the mountain, Anderson heard the riders. Suddenly there was an eerie quietness.

Lamb said, "Just ahead of us the trail is open to the next point. They can reach us good from where they are." He led the mule aside. "Put your horse across first but don't follow him too close."

Anderson pulled his rifle free. From the edge of the timber the trail ahead lay against cliffs of white quartz. It seemed starkly exposed and lighted. He peered up the mountain. The shadows were tricky among the huge rocks and he could make out nothing. But then he heard a tired horse blow from somewhere up there in the rocks.

He prodded his pony into the open. It went a few slow paces and stopped. With savage force he bounced a rock off its rump. The animal jumped and started on at a half trot.

Anderson ran. He heard the crashing of the rifles and from the corner of his eye he saw their flame. They seemed to be a long way off but yet he heard the smack of lead against the cliffs beside him. The pony was almost to the point when its hind legs went down. It screamed in agony and pawed its way along the ledge. It reared halfway up, twisting. Anderson saw the glint of moonlight on steel where the leather was worn off the horn, and that was when the pony was going into the canyon.

A man on the mountainside yelled triumphantly, "We got the mule!"

Then Anderson was across. He fell behind the rocky point and shot toward the sound of the voice. The horses were moving up there in the rocks now and someone was cursing. Anderson rammed in another cartridge and fired.

The mule came with a rush, nearly trampling him before he could roll aside and leap up. He caught the bridle with a desperate lunge when the animal would have jogged on down the trail. Soon afterward Lamb skidded around the point. He knelt and fired. "No good," he muttered. "Two of them got into the timber on foot." He reloaded and stood up. "Now let *them* try that trail."

If there had been a taunt or a challenge from the black trees, Anderson would have been sure he was fighting men instead of some determined deadliness that would follow him forever. But the trees were silent.

"Take the mule," Lamb said. "He'll stay with the trail. By daylight you'll be seeing sheep. Ask the first herder you come to how to get to Luis Mendoza's place. Wait for me there."

"We'll both—"

"I was ramming around these mountains when you was still wearing didies," Lamb said. "Listen to what I say, boy. Get to hell out of here with that mule. That's what they're after. They think the gold is still on it. We *want* 'em to think so because one of these days we've got to go back after it. Go on now."

Anderson gave the mule its head and let it pick its way down the trail. He was a half hour away from the point when he heard the first shots rolling sullenly high above him. In the bleak, cold hours just before sunup, he heard more shooting. And then the mountain was silent.

The two sheepherders sitting on a rock beside their flock in a high meadow eyed the mule keenly. "Luis

Mendoza?" They looked at each other. One of them pointed toward the valley. It went like that all morning, whenever Anderson stopped at adobes on the Huerfano. The liquid eyes sized up the mule and him, and weighed a consideration; but when he asked the way to Luis Mendoza's place, there was another careful weighing and he was pointed on.

The hot sun pressed him lower in the saddle. Sweat streaked down through the dust on his face, burning his eyes. At noon on this bright late-fall day he came into the yard of an adobe somewhat larger than the others he had passed. Hens were taking dust baths in the shade. There was a green field near the river, and goats upon a hill.

From the gloom of the house a deep voice asked, "Who comes?"

In Spanish Anderson said, "I am the friend of Jasper Lamb."

A little man walked from the house. His hair and mustache were white. His legs were short and bowed. From a nest of wrinkles around his eyes his gaze was like sharp, black points. He said, "You are followed?"

"We *were* followed."

"And Lamb?"

"He is in the mountains yet. He will come." Anderson wondered if he ever would.

The little man said sharply, "I am Luis Mendoza. Lamb is like my son. Do not doubt that he will be here. And now, you are welcome."

Thereupon a half dozen Mexican men of various ages appeared. One of them said, "Yes, it is the mule of Jasper Lamb."

"I have eyes." Mendoza's Spanish flowed rapidly then as he gave orders. Four men rode away, going slowly, chattering, obliterating the marks of Anderson's coming. He knew that if any of the three pursuers got past Jasper Lamb and reached the Huerfano, there would be only shrugs and muteness, or lies, to answer their questions.

"Go back for Lamb," Anderson said.

"He will be well, that one," Mendoza answered.

"He's wounded."

"That has happened before, also. Now we will take off your boots."

*   *   *

One of the pursuers did come in late afternoon. Lying on a pile of blankets on a cool dirt floor, Anderson heard the man ride up. "I look for a stolen mule, Mendoza."

Anderson tried to judge the enemy by the voice. A young man, he thought; and he knew already that he was a dangerous, determined man.

"Of that I know nothing."

Anderson clutched his rifle and started to get up. A broad Mexican sitting across the room from him shook his head and made cautioning gestures with his hands, and all the time he was grinning. After a moment Anderson recognized the wisdom of silence. For one thing, his feet were so scraped and sore and swollen from the sand that had been in his boots that he doubted if he could get across the room.

The man outside said, "The mule came this way. It had a heavy load. The man was young, with sandy hair."

"A *gringo* perhaps," Mendoza said lazily. "They do not stop for long on the Huerfano. The climate sometimes makes them ill," his voice slurred on gently. "Very ill."

"He could be in your house."

"I do not think so. My sons do not think so. My nephews do not think so."

There was a long silence.

"This stealer of mules is gone toward the Arkansas long ago, I think, although I did not see him," Mendoza said. "It is a long ride, my friend, and you are late now."

"Many things are possible," the pursuer answered, fully as easily as Mendoza had spoken. There was no defeat in his tone, but a cold patience that made Anderson wish he could get him in the sights of a rifle for an instant. "It could be that he is gone toward the Arkansas, and it could be that he is in your house, in spite of what all your sons and nephews think. Since the vote is in your favor, Mendoza, I will go toward the Arkansas myself."

"May God go with you," Mendoza said politely.

The man rode away. After a time Anderson dozed and then he woke, clutching where the weight should have been inside his shirt.

"At the head of your bed, *señor*," the man across the room murmured.

Anderson found the sacks and dragged them against

him, and then he slept until sometime in the dead of night when he heard a terrible shout, soon followed by laughter.

Lamb had arrived. He was shouting for wine.

Anderson and Lamb stayed three weeks on the Huerfano. Lamb had married Mendoza's oldest daughter ten years before. She had died in childbirth a year later. These were facts Anderson had never known before.

It was a simple, easy life here in the hills. There were sheep in the upland country, with old men and young boys to watch them. Maize and squash grew in the fields. Anderson did not know where the wine came from but it was here, and every night there was dancing at Mendoza's place.

Quite easily Lamb fell into the routineless drift of the life. He slept when it was hot. He hunted when he was in the mood, ate when he was hungry, and during the long, cool evenings he danced with the best of them on the packed ground in front of Mendoza's house. He was no longer the cool, efficient man who had directed the running fight across Medano. He acted as if he had forgotten the gold lying at the foot of the great dunes.

"We can get it any time," he told Anderson. "What's the rush?" It seemed to Anderson that he was casting around for an excuse. "It's best not to go back there anyway until that last fellow gives up. Only a week ago one of Luis' cousins saw him heading back over the pass."

"Why didn't Luis' cousin shoot him?"

"Why should he? Why should anyone on the Huerfano ask for unnecessary trouble? They can scrape up family battles enough to keep 'em busy all their lives, if they want to." Lamb went away to take a nap.

The change in him puzzled Anderson. Or was it a change? Lamb would have a man believe that he didn't care about that gold. Suspicion narrowed Anderson's mind. He fretted over the delay. He brooded about Lamb's motives; and he worried about the cold-voiced man who had followed the mule even after his companions were dead.

One day he could bear impatience no longer. He told Lamb he was going alone to the dunes.

"Hold your horses. The big *baile* comes off day after tomorrow. We'll leave then." Lamb sighed.

They gave two sacks of gold to Luis Mendoza. It was too much, Anderson thought, but when Lamb parted with his sack carelessly, Anderson felt that he must match it. They rode away on good horses, towing the mule as before. Anderson was in his own saddle, brought down from the mountain by one of Mendoza's sons two days after the Indian pony had gone over the cliff. There were new elk hide panniers on the mule, and they surely must be advertising the purpose of the trip to every Mexican on the Huerfano, so Anderson thought.

"We'll go up the Arkansas and over Hayden Pass and then swing down to the sand hills," Lamb said. "It's possible that fellow caught on to the fact the mule was traveling light. He may have somebody waiting on Medano."

Anderson said, "I don't favor this running in circles."

"I don't favor trouble, particularly not over a bunch of damned metal that grows wild in the mountains."

"That's what brought you out here in the first place."

"Yeah. Well, it was different then," Lamb said. He was unusually silent, almost surly, during the first two days on the trail.

They watered the animals on San Luis Creek when they came down to the floor of the inland plateau. Thirty miles away the dunes were a pale brown mass. Once again they seemed to be no closer after hours of dusty traveling. As if in a stupor, Lamb stared at the sunset on the *Sangre de Cristo*.

Anderson wanted to travel as far into the night as it took to reach the dunes but Lamb overrode him. They camped. Anderson did not sleep well. He kept his rifle close and was sensitive to all of Lamb's small movements and sounds. During the night Lamb rose to go out to the animals when the mule fouled up his picket rope. He came back to the camp slowly, a lean, tall figure slouching through the night.

Anderson held back the trigger of his rifle and cocked the piece silently. Afterward, when Lamb walked past and settled into his blankets with a grunt, Anderson let the hammer down again, and lay with the tightness ebbing slowly out of him.

It seemed to Anderson that they lagged when they started down the valley the next day. At last he cried, "You're in no hurry, damn it!"

"I ain't for a fact." Lamb gave him an oblique glance. "There's kinds of grief that I don't care to hurry into."

"That last man, don't worry about him."

"I ain't," Lamb said. "I'm worrying some about the other four."

They approached the northern end of the dunes. After they encountered the first shallow drifting of sand out from the skirts, they rode for almost ten miles beside the hills before they reached the broad gulch at the mouth of Medano Creek.

Anderson felt a constriction of breath. He wanted to gallop ahead. Nothing was changed. He saw the narrow-leaf cottonwood with the broken top and from a wide angle the gray rocks on the mountain. Mosca, Medano and Music. . . . He wanted to shout.

They left the horses at the cottonwood. Lamb was silent, almost sullen, as if there were no pleasure in this. He stayed at the cottonwood while Anderson led the mule out to the ridge and then part way up the side. When Anderson stopped to look back, he was pleased to see that his trail lay straight behind him and that he was almost in direct line with the sighting marks. He had to shift only a few · feet until he had them lined up, the snag-topped cottonwood, the dead spruce and the gray rocks.

He called then to Lamb to start his pacing. Anderson counted the steps as his partner came toward him. Three hundred and fifty across the shallow sand, another hundred to where Anderson waited. The two men went together up the ridge. It seemed higher than before. The total was six hundred steps when Anderson whirled around to take another sighting. They were dead in line.

"Six hundred and ten?" he asked, and his voice cracked on the edge of panic.

"That's right," Lamb answered, and a man could read anything into his tone.

Anderson kept plunging on, but he knew already, and it made him savage. There was no ridge. He was climbing a slope that led on and on toward the deceptive hollows and troughs of the soft, pale sand. The basin was gone.

He was a hundred feet above the gold on sand that ran like water.

He sighted again and then he turned and ran up the dune until his lungs ached and his leg muscles became knots of fire. He fell, staring along the surface of the wind-etched slope. Far off to his left there was a hollow, swooping all the way down to natural ground, but the basin with the gold was deeply covered. There was trickery in this; he had known it when the hills sang their song to him.

Anderson got up and staggered back to where Lamb was standing by the mule. "It wasn't six hundred and ten steps, was it?"

Lamb shifted his rifle. "Just what I said, Andy."

"Tell me the truth!" Anderson cocked his rifle and swung the piece on Lamb.

"Our gold is covered up," Lamb said. His squint was at once understanding and dangerous. "We're standing smack on top of it. Lower that barrel. It's full of sand."

Anderson let the barrel of his rifle tip down. Sand poured out in a silent stream. He let the tension off the hammer. "You knew the wind would cover it up, Lamb!"

"No, I didn't. I never realized how much this sand moves."

"We'll dig it out!" Anderson cried. "I don't care how deep it is!"

Lamb sat down. "We'll play hell trying to dig it out." He scooped his hand into the dune. Not far under the surface the sand was dark from dampness. He watched the fine dry grains from the top slide back into the hole. "It took a million years for the wind to make these hills. I guess the wind has got a right to do with them as it pleases. We'll never be able to dig ten feet down."

"Oh yes we will! Underneath it's damp. It'll hold. We'll start at the toe of the hill and tunnel. We'll line the tunnel with boards. We'll—"

Lamb shook his head. "Let me show you something." He dug with his hands, gouging long furrows downslope. The dark sand under the surface was damp for a short time only before the air dried it, and then it sloughed away. "Your boards wouldn't help much, if we knew where to get them. They'd dry out brittle. They'd crack and the sand would pour through the cracks and knotholes. If we were lucky enough to make twenty feet, one day the whole works would cave in on us."

"You act like you don't want to get the gold," Anderson accused.

Lamb looked out on the valley, toward the blue mountains on the edge of the San Juan. He was silent for a long time, a dusty, stringy man with a sort of puzzlement in his eyes. He said, "This gold is sort of used now. It ain't like brand new stuff, somehow. Even so I guess I'd stay and try to get it back, if I thought there was any chance."

"What do you mean, it's used?"

"I killed four men because of it. I lost a good buckskin horse."

"It was our neck or theirs!" Anderson said.

"Sure. I know that." Lamb frowned. "I ain't saying gold is bad, you understand, but it can cause you a pile of grief. I take it as an omen that the wind covered this mess of it up." Lamb rose. He smoothed with his feet the furrows he had made. "Let's move on."

"And leave a fortune just a hundred feet away from us?"

"It's the longest hundred feet God ever created, Andy."

"You don't want the gold?" Anderson asked.

"Not that, exactly. If we could get it, I'd take my share of it, but I'm kind of relieved that we can't get it."

Anderson licked his lips. "Suppose I get it out by myself?"

"I give my share to you right this minute. Now, let's go. We'll have to hump to get a tight camp set up in the San Juan before winter." He started down the dune.

"Then it's mine!"

"Sure, it's yours forever, Andy. Come on."

"You won't come around claiming half of it after I get it out?"

Lamb stopped and swung around. "You don't mean you're going to try?"

"I'm not going to run away from a fortune."

"We'll find another one," Lamb said.

"No! I know where this one is."

An hour later Anderson was in the same place, sitting with his rifle across his knees. He allowed that an obstacle stood between him and the treasure but the proximity of the gold outweighed all other considerations. He watched the dust where Lamb was riding away. Lamb might be trying to trick him. Lamb could have lied about the number of steps from the cotton-wood.

Darkness came down on the great valley that had been a lake in ancient times. Purple shades ran in the hollows of the dunes, and the crests of the ridges looked like the black manes of horses struggling toward the sky. A mighty silence lay on the piles of sand that had been gathering here for eons.

Anderson was still sitting on the sand above the treasure. He rose at last, sticking his rifle barrel down into the dune. When he went across the shallow sand to where his horse was tied in the cottonwoods, the animal stamped and whinnied. It could wait. Anderson found a dead limb. He used it to replace his rifle as a marker. He counted his steps back to the cottonwood. They were a few less than Lamb had said.

That night he camped on Medano Creek, waking a dozen times to listen to small noises. The dunes were huge, taking pale light from the ice points of the stars. At dawn he was riding through the pinons, searching for a less exposed campsite. He found it near a spring in a narrow gulch that looked out on the dunes. From here he could see part of the mouth of Medano Gulch, and he could see the marker he had left on the dune. He built a bough hut near the spring, fretting because it seemed to be taking time from more important work.

That afternoon he killed a deer, standing for several moments after the shot, wondering how far the sound of his rifle had carried; and then he was in a fever to get back to where he could watch the dunes.

There had been wind that morning. The marker was standing above the sand by eighteen inches or more. Anderson experienced a quick leap of hope; the wind had built the dunes, the wind had hidden the gold, and the wind could also uncover it again. It was a great thought.

Before evening the marker was almost covered. At dawn it was gone.

Without eating breakfast Anderson hurried from the trees and paced across the sand, taking sightings. Scrabbling on his hands and knees, he found the limb a few inches below the surface of the dune. He knew that he could always locate the spot but the limb was a tangible mark that gave him more of a link with the treasure than anything he carried in his mind. He set another marker at the base of the dune, a huge rock, three hundred and fifty steps from the cottonwood.

Sitting in his camp that afternoon, he worried about the loss of landmarks. The gray rocks on the mountain might change or slide away, the cottonwood and the dead spruce might blow over. He returned quickly to the broad gulch and set a row of rocks fifty paces apart, burying them on solid ground below the sand, in a line which pointed toward the treasure.

Now he felt better. Rocks were solid and heavy; they would not blow away. Going back to his camp in the evening, a brand new doubt struck him: suppose the wind uncovered his line of rocks. Anyone riding past would wonder why they had been placed so. The extensions of the thought worried Anderson until late in the night. He rose and went down the hill to have a look.

He put his face close to the sand, sighting. The surface was gently rippled. He could not see any stones, not even the large one he had left exposed purposely. He felt that his presence protected the gold; he was loath to leave. For a long time he stood shivering in the night. When he finally started back to his camp, a light wind swept down through the pinons. It was a dawn wind, natural; it came every morning and had nothing to do with the great winds that had built the dunes. But Anderson felt that it was a deliberate betrayal, and so he went back to the edge of the sand and stayed there until the wind died away.

During the days and weeks that passed he grew hollow-eyed and gaunt. He begrudged the time it required to get meat when he was out of food. His rest was never unbroken, disturbed by dreams of a powerful wind that swept the sand away to the rocks, leaving his sacks of gold lying in a long row where anyone could see them. That happened over and over, and then he dreamed of running down the hill to find himself entrapped in waist-deep sand among the trees. He struggled there, while out on the flat men were riding without haste to pick up the sacks. And then he would waken, trembling and almost ill from frustration.

Light snows dusted the valley. Whiteness lay in the grim wrinkles of the *Sangre de Cristo* and the dunes sparkled in the frosty air of early morning; but the snow never lasted long upon the sand. A season of winds followed. They gathered out of the southwest, twisting into crazy patterns when they struck the dunes. Sometimes Anderson saw sand streaming in four directions on ridges that lay close to each other.

When the wind was at its strongest he never heard the singing. The sounds came only with diminishing winds or when the blow was first rising. High-pitched music skirling from the ridges, running clear and sharp, then clashing like sky demons fighting when the wind made sudden changes. Anderson heard the singing at times when he stood at the foot of the dunes in still air, sensing the powerful rush of currents far above.

Sometimes, crouched in the doorway of his hut, he watched the queer half daylight of the storms and read strange words into the music. There was something in the sounds that wailed of lostness and of madness, of the times after centuries of rain had ceased, when the earth was drying and man was unknown.

Each time the wind ceased, while his ears still held music that could never be named or written into notes, Anderson went down the hill to see what changes had been made.

The dunes were never the same and yet they were always the same, soft contours on the slopes, wind-sharpened ridges, hollows that went down to natural earth, white streaks where the heavier particles of sand gathered to themselves. A million tons of sand could shift in a few minutes but nothing was really changed.

The wind did as it pleased; it did not do Anderson's work for him. Sometimes his limb marker was buried twenty feet deep; sometimes he found it lying ten feet lower than it had been. He always put it upright.

Long snows fell upon the valley. Deer came down from the hills. On clear days Anderson saw smoke at distant farms where pioneers were toughing out the winter. He thought of Lamb, snug by now in some tight, red-rocked valley of the San Juan. Lamb probably was searching for gold again, not really caring whether he found it or not. The thought infuriated Anderson.

Anderson was on the dunes one day when a wind, running steadily along the surface of the ground, began to eat into the side of the slope that covered the sacks. Tense and choked-up, he watched it, first with suspicion, and then with hope. Faster than any tool man could ever create, the numberless hands of the wind scooped sand until a rounding cove appeared. Anderson's largest marker rock sat on bare ground now. The cove extended, an oval running deeper and deeper into the side of the dune where his gold lay.

Anderson followed the receding sand as a man would pace after a falling tide. He counted until he knew he was within fifteen steps of the gold. Whirling around the edges of the cove, digging, lifting, the wind took sand away until Anderson knew he stood no farther than ten feet from the first sack. He could not stand inactive any longer. He began to burrow like an animal, and the wind worked with him effortlessly. He shouted incoherently when his hand closed on soft buckskin. The first sack.

It became an evil moment. Somewhere on Mosca or Medano or Music, or perhaps all three, there was a sudden change. The wind now came from a different direction. Sand poured down the slope faster than Anderson could dig. It grew around his legs, covering them. Sand rippled down the surface of the dune. It fell directly from the air. Cursing, half blinded, Anderson dug furiously. He might as well have been scooping water from a lake with his hands.

He was forced back as slowly as he had come. The cove filled up again. He stood in the wide gulch at last, on shallow sand where there never seemed to be appreciable change.

Almost exhausted, he stumbled away, muttering like a man insane. The wind began to lessen and the dunes sang to him, singing him back to his miserable hut of boughs among the pinons. He threw the sack of gold inside and lay by the spring until he was trembling from cold.

That night there was no wind. He crouched over his fire, and his eyes were as red as the flames that blossomed from the pinon sticks. It was no use to wait on the wind, for the wind would only torture him. He must do everything by his own efforts.

The next day he rode to a farm in the valley. The snow lay unevenly where ground had been ploughed, a pitiful patch of accomplishment, considering the vastness, Anderson thought. There was a low log barn, unchinked. A black-bearded young man came to the doorway of a one-room cabin with a rifle in his hands.

"I'm a prospector," Anderson explained. "I'm looking for some boards to build me a place. Been living in a bough hut."

"Build a cabin." The farmer's dark eyes were watchful, but they were also lonely.

"I lost my packhorse and all my tools coming over Music."

The man shook his head. "I've got an axe and a plough—and that's about it. Come spring, my brothers will be back with some things we need—I hope." He studied the shaggy condition of Anderson's horse. "Come in and eat."

The cabin was primitive. A man must be a fool, Anderson thought, to try to make a farm in this valley. The farmer's name was George Linkman. His loneliness came out in talk and he wanted Anderson to stay the night. From him Anderson found out that there was a man about ten miles east who had hauled a load of lumber from New Mexico the fall before and hadn't got around to building with it yet.

Ten miles east. That put the place close to the dunes, somewhere against the mountains.

Anderson rode away with one suspicion cleared from his mind: Linkman was not the man who had followed him and Lamb to the Huerfano. Linkman's voice was much too deep. But who was this man against the hills close to the dunes? Anderson was uneasy when he found the place at the mouth of a small stream, and realized that it was not more than two miles from his own camp.

He was reassured somewhat by the fact that the log buildings were old. There had been more cultivation here than at Linkman's place. No one was at home. He saw the pile of lumber, already warping. He stared at it greedily.

The man came riding in from the valley side of the foothills. He was a stocky, middle-aged man, clean shaved, with gray in his hair. His faded mackinaw was ragged. He greeted Anderson heartily and asked him why he hadn't gone inside to warm up and help himself to food.

"Just got here," Anderson said. *The voice.* . . . No, it wasn't the voice of the man who had come to Mendoza's place. That man had been young.

The farmer's name was Burl Hollister. While he cooked a meal he kept bragging about the potatoes he had grown last summer. There was a little hillside cellar still half full of them to prove his boast. Nothing would do but Anderson must stay all night with him.

By candlelight Hollister talked of the new ground he would break next spring, of the settlers who would come to the valley in time. Anderson nodded, watching him narrowly. This place was too close to the dunes, but of course it had been here long before Anderson and Lamb made their terrible mistake in the hollow of the sand.

Anderson brought up the matter of lumber and tools, speaking guardedly of a streak of gold he had discovered on Mosca Pass.

"Tools I can spare," Hollister said slowly, "but that lumber—that's something else. I figured to build the old lady a lean-to kitchen with it before she comes back in the spring. I was aiming to surprise her. This place ain't much for a woman yet, but in time—"

"You could get more lumber before spring." Anderson drew a sack of gold from his shirt. There was not much in the sack, perhaps a pound and a half, for he had left most of it in the buckskin pouch he had recovered from the dunes.

After some hesitation Hollister untied the strings and dipped his fingers into the yellow grains. "Good Lord!" he breathed. "Is that all gold?"

"You could buy more lumber, Hollister."

"Tools, yes," the farmer murmured. "I can spare tools, but doggone, it's a long haul to get boards here." He kept pinching the gold between his thumb and two fingers. "Is this from your claim on Mosca?"

Anderson did not answer too hastily. "No, that came from the San Juan. I don't know yet what I have on Mosca."

"All of it for the lumber?"

Anderson nodded.

Not looking up, Hollister said, "All right."

He hauled the lumber and tools the next day to the bottom of the hill below Anderson's camp. Hollister brought also a bushel of potatoes. He spent most of the morning digging and lining a tiny cellar to keep them from freezing. When that was done he said, "I'll help you carry the boards up here."

"You've done enough," Anderson said. "I've got to level off a place here first."

"You're welcome to stay with me till spring."

"Thanks, but I'd rather be closer to my work."

Hollister nodded, staring across at the dunes. "Sort of pretty, ain't they?"

"Not to me. There's too much sand," Anderson said, and then he began to worry about the implications of his statement. He was glad when Hollister left.

Now that he had the lumber, Anderson began to doubt that it would serve his purpose. He had planned to work only at night but desperation was growing in him. In the spring riders would be coming to Medano and Mosca constantly. It was better to take a chance now on Linkman and Hollister, so far the only men who knew he was here.

But he retained caution. Until he knew how the lumber would serve, he would not try to tunnel directly toward the gold. He started a hundred yards away from his line of rocks, in a direction at a right angle to the treasure. He drove short boards into the sand, overhead and on the sides of his projected tunnel. Then he shoveled, framing more lumber to support the boards as soon as the sand fell away from them. Sand poured through the cracks and between the warped edges where the boards did not fit tightly. He nailed more lumber over the cracks. In a month of brutal labor he made ten feet. And then one day when he was shoveling back, he heard a cracking sound. He got clear just before the tunnel collapsed.

He was standing with a shovel in his hand, too spent to curse, when Linkman rode up. Anderson did not hear him until the farmer was quite close, but when he saw the long shadow of the horse upon the sand, he dropped his shovel and leaped to grab his rifle.

"Hey!" Linkman cried. "What's the matter?"

Anderson lowered his rifle, but he kept staring at the visitor, who was looking curiously at the ends of boards sticking from the sand.

"That's a funny place for a potato cellar." Linkman tried to smile but he was too uneasy to make it real. He fumbled on, "I thought your mine was up on Mosca."

Anderson did not say anything. He saw the slow breaking of something in Linkman's expression, a fear, a disturbed sensation that Linkman tried to conceal. The man could not have made himself more clear if he had put a forefinger to his temple and made a circular motion.

"I was just riding around," Linkman said vaguely. "I guess I'll be going. I was just scouting for a place to get some firewood." He rode away.

Anderson went back to his camp. When he knelt at the spring he knew why Linkman had thought him mad. His beard was matted, his eyes hollow and bloodshot, his lips tight against his teeth. He was jolted for a few moments, and then he drank and turned his mind once more to the problem of the treasure.

It struck him suddenly. He would build his tunnel in the open, where he could make the boards tight and the framing strong. He would build sections that would fit together snugly, large enough for a man to crawl through easily. The next time the wind gouged out a hole in the direction of his gold, he would have his sections ready to lay in place. Let the damned wind cover them. The tunnel would be there, even if it was under two hundred feet of sand.

There were omissions in his plan that he did not care to dwell on at the moment; overall, it was a beautiful idea and that was enough. He rose to cook a meal and was annoyed to find he had no meat.

He found the horse tracks when he was hunting deer in the pinons above his camp. He spent the whole afternoon chasing up and down the hills until he knew that someone had been watching him, not only recently but for a long time. Instead of fear, he felt an insane fury that made him grind his teeth.

That night another gale came out of the southwest,

coursing toward the high passes. Restless in his cold hut, Anderson heard the howling of it; and later, the singing of the sands when the wind began to decrease.

Clean morning sunlight on the great buff hills showed Anderson that they were unchanged. The ends of the boards from his collapsed tunnel were hidden now, and for the hundredth time his limb marker above the gold was covered. For several moments he was motionless.

There were forces here that he could never conquer, a challenge that would lead him to wreckage. Lamb had known what he was doing when he wasted not a moment, but rode away. For the first time Anderson felt an urge to leave, but he knew that the wind could undo what it had done; and if he went away, he might be haunted forever by the thought that what he had waited for happened one hour, a day, or a week, after he quit.

He went down the hill and began to build the sections of his tunnel lining. He piled them on the shallow sand. He built them so that one man could drag them into place when the time came. It was not heavy work but it tired him more each day. He went at it with desperate urgency, thinking that the wind might choose a time to dig toward his treasure when he was unprepared.

Dizzy spells began to bother him during the three days it took to build the boxes. He had been eating scraps, or very little; and his mind had been burning up the resources of his body. This he realized, but time might run away from him, and so he staggered on at his work, resting only when his vision darkened.

Utterly spent, he finished the boxes one afternoon when there was no wind. He slumped down behind a pile of them, letting his hands fall limply into the fine sand.

Sleep struck him like a maul. He dreamed of the running fight across Medano, of the easy life on the Huerfano. He trembled in his sleep, a young man who was old and gaunt. A voice roused him slowly.

"Anderson! Anderson! Where are you?"

Groggily, Anderson tried to come out of his exhaustion. He thought he was back on the floor of Mendoza's house, with his feet swollen and scratched. The last pursuer had come across the pass and was inquiring about him and the mule.

"Hey, Anderson! Don't tell me you've got lost in one of those sluice boxes."

Anderson stared at his boots. There was no doubt of it: the voice was that of the man who had survived the chase, the same cool voice of a young man who would not give up. Anderson's rifle was in one of the boxes. He could not remember which one.

His muscles dragged wearily when he rose. He could not believe the man sitting there on the horse was Hollister.

"Sleeping in the middle of daylight!" Hollister grinned. His clean shaved face was bright. His gray hair showed below the frayed edges of his scotch cap. He frowned at the boxes. "You're a long ways from water with those sluices, Anderson."

Hollister was the man. Now that Anderson could separate his voice from his appearance, he was able to get rid of the inaccurate picture he had built of Hollister. Anderson moved around the boxes until he found his rifle. He remembered the flight across Medano long ago. It was Hollister's fault and his fault that the gold was here.

Hollister said, "You've worked yourself plumb string-haltered, Ander—" He stopped, staring into the muzzle of Anderson's rifle. "What's the matter?"

"You're the man that followed me and Lamb to the Huerfano! You're no farmer. You've been watching me ever since I've been here."

Hollister kept his hands on the saddle horn. He looked at Anderson gravely. "The farm belongs to a man who wanted to go back to Kansas for the winter. I'm the man, all right. Now there's just two of us. The wind got your gold, didn't it, Anderson?"

Anderson stepped away from the boxes, edging to the side so that if Hollister made his horse rear the act would not interfere with the shot. Anderson was ready to kill the man. He wanted to. All he lacked was some small puff of provocation.

Hollister gave him none. He sat quietly, moving only his head. "When I came back over the pass, I found the panniers and the packsaddle you threw away. There was only one place where you two could have covered your tracks that day—here. I knew you'd come back.

"There's two of us, Anderson. You're as well off as you were before. I'm much better off, thanks to your partner." He gave the thought time to grow. "You left the gold here. The wind covered it. Your partner should have known better, but of course we were pushing you hard and you didn't have much choice. There's ways to get at it, Anderson. How deep is it?"

Anderson did not answer. He still wanted to kill Hollister but he knew he could not do it.

"The two of us can get it out of there," Hollister said. "I know a way." He looked at the boxes. "That won't work. You figure to make a tunnel of them, don't you? The sand will blow in one end and pour into the other. I know a better way, Anderson."

He was bargaining only because the rifle was on him, Anderson thought. But no, Hollister must not be sure of where the treasure lay.

"I've got every ounce of every sack you dropped on Medano," Hollister said. "That goes in the split too. You know where the rest is. I'm not sure. You can't get it out. I know a way. I could have killed you, Anderson, months ago. If I had been sure of where the sacks were, maybe I would have." He smiled. "That's all in the past now. There's gold enough for ten men."

Anderson grounded his rifle. "You know a way to get it out?"

"Yes."

That was the bait, Anderson thought, the bait that would bring the deadfall crashing down on his neck. But belief began to grow in him. The thought that he could trust Hollister became more important than any idea the man had about recovering the treasure.

"Think about it," Hollister said. "You've no one to ask about me. I'm an odd man inside. When I give my word, Anderson, before God, it's good." He turned his horse and rode away. The faded mackinaw covering his broad back was an easy target all the way to the cottonwoods.

Anderson had believed him while he was here, but now the worms of suspicion began to twist and turn again. For a week Anderson did not go down upon the sands. He stayed in camp or hunted, and he saw no more fresh horse tracks on the hills. The winds came, piling sand in a long, curving ramp against his boxes, and the wind uncovered the boards where he had experimented with a tunnel. There was something ancient and ghostly in the look of the lumber sticking from the dune.

He knew with a dreary certainty that men could not defy the work of a million years of wind. The caprice of the gales would expose the treasure when the time came, but that might be a century from now.

There was also the thought that it could be tomorrow, and that was what held Anderson, gnawed with the fear of defeat only, no longer dreaming of what gold could buy. It struck him that if he could transfer the burden of worry, which in a way was exactly what Lamb had done, then he might be free.

He rode to see Hollister.

The man was sitting by a warm fire, smoking his pipe. "Out of potatoes, Anderson? The darned things are beginning to sprout. It must be getting near spring."

Near spring. Months of Anderson's life had flowed into the sands. He had lived like a brute.

"You look some better," Hollister said. He spoke like a neighbor being pleasant but knowing that there was bargaining to come.

"This way of yours to move the sand. . . ." Anderson let it trail off. There was no way to move the sand. His own ideas had been sure and clear about that once, but now he knew better.

"Yeah?" Hollister's eyes tightened.

"You've got the sacks I threw away on Medano?"

Hollister nodded.

"For them I'll tell you where the rest is, and you can have it all—if you can dig it out."

Hollister cocked his head. "I'd rather have you working with me—for half of everything."

"You're afraid I won't tell the truth? I thought Lamb had lied to me too, Hollister. He didn't. He paced the distance. I recovered one sack of gold, right where it was supposed to be."

Hollister rubbed his lips together slowly.

"One sack is all. The wind will break your heart, Hollister."

"I can beat it."

"Give me what I left behind on the pass. The rest is yours."

Hollister's eyes were bright. "Let's go up and take a look at the dunes."

The hooves of the horses made soft sounds in the broad gulch. The full weight of the hills bore on Anderson and he wondered how he had ever been fool enough to think he could outwit the dunes. He knew better now and he had learned before his mind broke on the problem.

"They're yours, Hollister."

The older man's satisfied expression threw a jet of worry into Anderson. Maybe he was selling out too cheaply. It was an effort to stick with his decision.

Hollister said, "Your sacks are buried just inside the door of the potato cellar."

Anderson pointed to the limb on the dune. He told Hollister about the rocks under the sand and the sighting marks and the number of steps from the tree.

"I knew most of that from watching you," Hollister said, "but I wasn't sure. Why'd you start the tunnel over there?" His gaze was sharp and hard.

"I did that after I knew you were spying."

Hollister knew the truth when he heard it. "It would have saved me gold if I had killed you, wouldn't it?" In the same conversational tone he went on, "I'm going to bring a ditch down from Medano. I'll flume it through the sand and let the water wash away what I want moved."

Water would seep into the sand. It would run out of cracks in the flume, causing the sections to buckle. The eternal wind would work easily while Hollister was floundering and cursing his broken plan. Anderson had never felt sorry for himself. Now he had sympathy for Hollister.

"Don't come back," Hollister said. "We've made our bargain. I'll kill you if you hang around or come back."

Anderson went up the hill to his camp. The first signs of spring were breaking on the edges of the valley. He hadn't noticed them before. He stared for a while at the bough hut. It was a hovel unworthy of a Digger Indian. *I stayed in that all winter.*

He took his camping gear and kicked the hut apart.

Out on the sand, Hollister was walking slowly. He had found the line of rocks. He turned and sighted, and then he looked at the boards where the wrecked tunnel had been. There would always be in his mind, Anderson knew, doubt that Anderson had told the truth. The sand would defy him, the winds would mock him, and the singing on the ridges would jeer him.

When Anderson rode away, he saw Hollister dragging the boxes with his horse, dragging them up to where he would build a flume that would break his heart. The struggle of the horse and man against the sand was a picture that Anderson would never forget.

He found the sacks in the potato cellar where Hollister had said. He opened each one and ran his hand inside and afterward looked at the grains of gold clinging to his cracked and roughened skin. The sand had done that too.

He stuffed the sacks inside his shirt. At once the weight was intolerable. Perhaps somewhere out on the floor of the valley where there was no sand to blow over it. . . . No, gold was not to be buried. He would put it inside the pack on his horse. Half of it was Lamb's.

Anderson hesitated and then he dropped one bag on the floor. He thought it was a small enough price to pay for transferring a crushing burden. He rode away, going toward the purple mountains of the San Juan Basin. For a while the tug of the treasure of the dunes was still strong, but he kept going until at last he knew beyond doubt that he had made a good decision.

At sunset he turned to look back. Against the high range the buff hills were small, pale, beautiful, changeless. Anderson raised his eyes to the crimson glory flaming on the summits of the Blood of Christ Mountains, watching quietly until the color seeped away; and then he rode on, knowing that tonight he would sleep as he had not slept for months.

The winds still sing across the dark manes of the sand dunes, wailing, if the ear can understand, of the man who lived for thirty years in a little hut among the pinons. He dressed in cast-off garments that ranchers brought him. He raised dogs that ran wild, eating them when times were lean. He was crazy as a bedbug, for he talked of gold he was going to wash from the sands. The wind alternately covered and uncovered the rotting sections of a flume he had tried to build around the shoulder of the dune.

He said that the wind knew a great secret and that four times the wind had almost showed him the secret; and then in the next breath he would curse the wind with such insane vehemence that people were glad to get away from him. There was something vicious about the old man, but there also was something pitiful and lost in the record of his life.

On a bright fall day when the aspens on Medano were golden streaks against the mountains he died on the sand with a shovel in his hands. George Linkman, a pioneer rancher, found him there with the hungry dogs whining and edging closer to him. Linkman shot the dogs. One yellow cur went howling across the sand almost to the rotting trunk of a huge, fallen cottonwood before it died.

There had been a strong wind the night before. When Linkman carried the old man toward the trees to bury him, he saw a line of rocks, a solid line of them, running from where the dead dog lay to the base of the first dune. It appeared that the crazy old devil had tried at one time to build a dam to catch the floodwaters of Medano Creek in the spring.

The next time Linkman came by the dunes—he was an old man and his riding days were numbered—he observed that the wind had covered the rocks once more.

SERGEANT HOUCK

BY JACK SCHAEFER
(Trooper Hook)

Jack Schaefer's short novel Shane *is an indisputable Western classic; the same is true of the 1953 film version
featuring Alan Ladd and Van Heflin. Another Schaefer
novel,* Monte Walsh, *which many critics and aficionados
feel is his best work and one of the finest Western novels
ever written, was filmed in 1970 with Lee Marvin and Jack
Palance in the starring roles. Except for "Sergeant Houck,"
the masterful tale of a man and a woman overcoming
racial prejudice on the Western frontier, the only other
Schaefer short story to be filmed was "Jeremy Rodock"
which became an excellent 1956 vehicle for the talents of
James Cagney, entitled* Tribute to a Bad Man.

Sergeant Houck stopped his horse just below the top of
the ridge ahead. The upper part of his body was silhouetted against the skyline as he rose in his stirrups to peer
over the crest. He urged the horse on up and the two of
them, the man and the horse, were sharp and distinct
against the copper sky. After a moment he turned and
rode down to the small troop waiting. He reined beside
Lieutenant Imler.

"It's there, sir. Alongside a creek in the next hollow.
Maybe a third of a mile."

Lieutenant Imler regarded him coldly. "You took your
time, Sergeant. Smack on the top too."

"Couldn't see plain, sir. Sun was in my eyes."

"Wanted them to spot you, eh, Sergeant?"

"No, sir. Sun was bothering me. I don't think——"

"Forget it, Sergeant. I don't like this either."

Lieutenant Imler was in no hurry. He led the troop

112

slowly up the hill. He waited until the men were spread in a reasonably straight line just below the ridge top. He sighed softly to himself. The real fuss was fifty-some miles away. Captain McKay was hogging the honors there. Here he was tied to this disgusting sideline detail. Twenty men. Ten would have been enough. Ten, and an old hand like Sergeant Houck with no officer to curb his style. Thank the War Department for sergeants, the pickled-in-salt variety. They could do what no commissioned officer could do. They could forget orders and follow their own thoughts and show themselves on the top of a hill.

Lieutenant Imler sighed again. Even Sergeant Houck must think this had been time enough. He lifted his drawn saber. "All right, men. If we had a bugler, he'd be snorting air into it right now."

Saber pointing forward, Lieutenant Imler led the charge up and over the crest and down the long slope to the Indian village. There were some scattered shots from bushes by the creek, ragged pops indicating poor powder and poorer weapons, probably fired by the last of the old men left behind when the young braves departed in war-paint ten days before. A few of the squaws and children, their dogs tagging, could still be seen running into the brush. They reached cover and faded from sight, disappeared into the surrounding emptiness. The village was silent and deserted and dust settled in the afternoon sun.

Lieutenant Imler surveyed the ground taken. "Spectacular achievement," he muttered to himself. He beckoned Sergeant Houck to him.

"Your redskin friend was right, Sergeant. This is it."

"Knew he could be trusted, sir."

"Our orders are to destroy the village. Send a squad out to round up any stock. There might be some horses around. We're to take them in." Lieutenant Imler waved an arm at the thirty-odd skin-and-pole huts. "Set the others to pulling those down. Burn what you can and smash everything else."

"Right, sir."

Lieutenant Imler rode into the slight shade of the cottonwoods along the creek. He wiped the dust from his face and set his campaign hat at a fresh angle to ease the crease made by the band on his forehead. Here he was, hot and tired and way out at the end of nowhere with another long ride ahead, while Captain McKay was having it out at last with Gray Otter and his renegade warriors somewhere between the Turkey Foot and the Washakie. He relaxed to wait in the saddle, beginning to frame his report in his mind.

"Pardon, sir."

Lieutenant Imler swung in the saddle to look around. Sergeant Houck was afoot, was standing near with something in his arms, something that squirmed and seemed to have dozens of legs and arms.

"What the devil is that, Sergeant?"

"A baby, sir. Or rather, a boy. Two years old, sir."

"How the devil do you know? By his teeth?"

"His mother told me, sir."

"His mother?"

"Certainly, sir. She's right here."

Lieutenant Imler saw her then, close to a neighboring tree, partially behind the trunk, shrinking into the shadow and staring at Sergeant Houck and his squirming burden. He leaned to look closer. She was not young. She might have been any age in the middle years. She was shapeless in the sacklike skin covering with slit-holes for her arms and head. She was sun-and windburned dark, yet not as dark as he expected. And there was no mistaking her hair. It was light brown and long and braided, and the braid was coiled around on her head.

"Sergeant! It's a white woman!"

"Right, sir. Her name's Cora Sutliff. The wagon train she was with was wiped out by a raiding party. She and another woman were taken along. The other woman died. She didn't. The village here bought her. She's been in Gray Otter's lodge." Sergeant Houck smacked the squirming boy briskly and tucked him under one arm. He looked straight at Lieutenant Imler. "That was three years ago, sir."

"Three years? Then that boy—"

"That's right, sir."

Captain McKay looked up from his desk to see Sergeant Houck stiff at attention before him. It always gave him a feeling of satisfaction to see this big slab of cross-grained granite that Nature had hewed into the shape of a man. The replacements they were sending these days, raw and unseasoned, were enough to shake his faith in the Service. But as long as there remained a sprinkling of these case-hardened oldtime regulars, the Army would still be the Army.

"At ease, Sergeant."

"Thank you, sir."

Captain McKay drummed his fingers on the desk. This was a ridiculous proposition. There was something incongruous about it and the solid, impassive bulk of Sergeant Houck made it seem even more so.

"That woman, Sergeant. She's married. The husband's alive, wasn't with the train when it was attacked. He's been located, has a place about twenty miles out of Laramie. The name's right and everything checks. You're to take her there and turn her over with the troop's compliments."

"Me, sir?"

"She asked for you. The big man who found her. Lieutenant Imler says that's you."

Sergeant Houck considered this behind the rock mask of his weather-carved face. "And about the boy, sir?"

"He goes with her." Captain McKay drummed on the desk again. "Speaking frankly, Sergeant, I think she's making a mistake. I suggested she let us see the boy got back to the tribe. Gray Otter's dead, and after that affair two weeks ago there's not many of the men left. But they'll be on the reservation now and he'd be taken care of. She wouldn't hear of it, said if he had to go she would too." Captain McKay felt his former indignation rising again. "I say she's playing the fool. You agree with me, of course."

"No, sir. I don't."

"And why the devil not?"

"He's her son, sir."

"But he's—— Well, that's neither here nor there, Sergeant. It's not our affair. We deliver her and there's an end to it. You'll draw expense money and start within the hour. If you push along, you can make the stage at the settlement. Two days going and two coming. That makes four. If you stretch it another coming back, I'll be too busy to notice. If you stretch it past that, I'll have your stripes. That's all."

"Right, sir." Sergeant Houck straightened and swung about and started for the door.

"Houck."

"Yes, sir."

"Take good care of her—and that damn kid."

"Right, sir."

Captain McKay stood by the window and watched the small cavalcade go past toward the post gateway. Lucky that his wife had come with him, even on this last assignment to this Godforsaken station lost in the prairie wasteland. Without her they would have been in a fix with the woman. As it was the woman looked like a woman now. And why shouldn't she, wearing his wife's third-best crinoline dress? It was a bit large, but it gave her a proper feminine appearance. His wife had enjoyed fitting her, from the skin out, everything except shoes. Those were too small. The woman seemed to prefer her worn moccasins anyway. And she was uncomfortable in the clothes. But she was decently grateful for them, insisting she would have them returned or would pay for them somehow. She was riding past the window, side-saddle on his wife's horse, still with that strange shrinking air about her, not so much frightened as remote, as if she could not quite connect with what was happening to her, what was going on around her.

Behind her was Private Lakin, neat and spruce in his uniform, with the boy in front of him on the horse. The boy's legs stuck out on each side of the small improvised pillow tied to the forward arch of the saddle to give him a better seat. He looked like a weird, black-haired doll bobbing with the movements of the horse.

And there beside the woman, shadowing her in the mid-morning sun, was that extra incongruous touch, the great granite hulk of Sergeant Houck, straight in his saddle with the military erectness that was so much a part of him that it would never leave him, solid, impassive, taking this as he took everything, with no excitement and no show of any emotion, a job to be done.

They went past, and Captain McKay watched them ride out through the gateway. It was not quite so incongruous after all. As he had discovered on many a tight occasion, there was something comforting in the presence of that big, angular slab of a man. Nothing ever shook him. He had a knack of knowing what needed to be done whatever the shifting circumstances. You might never know exactly what went on inside his close-cropped, hard-pan skull, but you could be certain that what needed to be done he would do.

Captain McKay turned back to his desk. He would wait for the report, terse and almost illegible in crabbed handwriting, but he could write off this detail as of this moment. Sergeant Houck had it in hand.

They were scarcely out of sight of the post when the boy began his squirming. Private Lakin clamped him to the pillow with a capable right hand. The squirming persisted. The boy seemed determined to escape from what he regarded as an alien captor. Silent, intent, he writhed on the pillow. Private Lakin's hand and arm grew weary. He tickled his horse forward with his heels until he was close behind the others.

"Beg pardon."

Sergeant Houck shifted in his saddle and looked around. "Yes?"

"He's trying to get away. It'd be easier if I tied him down. Could I use my belt?"

Sergeant Houck held in his horse to drop back alongside Private Lakin. "Kids don't need tying," he said. He reached out and plucked the boy from in front of Private Lakin and laid him, face down, across the withers of his own horse and smacked him sharply. He picked the boy up again and reached out and set him again on the pillow. The boy sat still, very still, making no movement except that caused by the sliding motion of the horse's foreshoulders. Sergeant Houck pushed his left hand into his left side pocket and it came forth with a fistful of small hard biscuits. He passed these to Private Lakin. "Stick one of these in his mouth when he gets restless."

Sergeant Houck urged his horse forward until he was beside the woman once more. She had turned her head to watch, and she stared sidewise at him for a long moment, then looked straight forward again along the wagon trace before them.

They came to the settlement in the same order, the woman and Sergeant Houck side by side in the lead, Private Lakin and the boy tagging at a respectful distance. Sergeant Houck dismounted and helped the woman down and plucked the boy from the pillow and handed him to the woman. He unfastened one rein from his horse's bridle and knotted it to the other, making them into a lead strap. He did the same to the reins of the woman's horse. He noted Private Lakin looking wistfully at the painted front of the settlement's one saloon and tapped him on one knee and handed him the ends of the two straps. "Scat," he said, and watched Private Lakin turn his horse and ride off leading the other two horses. He took the boy from the woman and tucked him under one arm and led the way into the squat frame building that served as general store and post-office and stage stop. He settled the woman on a preserved-goods box and set the boy in her lap and went to the counter to arrange for their fares. When he returned to sit on another box near her, the entire permanent male population of the settlement had assembled just inside the door, all eleven of them staring at the woman.

" . . . that's the one . . ."

" . . . an Indian had her . . ."

" . . . shows in the kid . . ."

Sergeant Houck looked at the woman. She was staring at the floor. The blood was retreating from beneath the skin of her face, making it appear old and leathery. He started to rise and felt her hand on his arm. She had leaned over quickly and clutched his sleeve.

"Please," she said. "Don't make trouble account of me."

"Trouble?" said Sergeant Houck. "No trouble." He rose and confronted the fidgeting men by the door. "I've seen kids around this place. Some of them small. This one now needs decent clothes and the store here doesn't stock them."

The men stared at him, startled, and then at the wide-eyed boy in his clean but patched skimpy cloth covering. Five or six of them went out through the door and disappeared in various directions. The others scattered through the store, finding little businesses to excuse their presence. Sergeant Houck stood sentinel, relaxed and quiet, by his box, and those who had gone out straggled back, several embarrassed and empty-handed, the rest proud with their offerings.

Sergeant Houck took the boy from the woman's lap

and stood him on his box. He measured the offerings against the small body and chose a small red flannel shirt and a small pair of faded overalls. He peeled the boy with one quick motion, ripping away the old cloth, and put the shirt and overalls on him. He set the one pair of small scuffed shoes aside. "Kids don't need shoes," he said. "Only in winter." He heard the sound of hooves and stepped to the door to watch the stage approach and creak to a stop, the wheels sliding in the dust. He looked back to see the men inspecting the boy to that small individual's evident satisfaction and urging their other offerings upon the woman. He strode among them and scooped the boy under one arm and beckoned the woman to follow and went out the door to the waiting old Concord coach. He deposited the boy on the rear seat inside and turned to watch the woman come out of the store escorted by the male population of the settlement. He helped her into the coach and nodded up at the driver on his high box seat and swung himself in. The rear seat groaned and sagged as he sank into it beside the woman with the boy between them. The woman peered out the window by her, and suddenly, in a shrinking, experimental gesture, she waved at the men outside. The driver's whip cracked and the horses lunged into the harness and the coach rolled forward, and a faint suggestion of warm color showed through the tan of the woman's cheeks.

They had the coach to themselves for the first hours. Dust drifted steadily through the windows and the silence inside was a persistent thing. The woman did not want to talk. She had lost all liking for it and would speak only when necessary, and there was no need. And Sergeant Houck used words with a natural and unswerving economy, for the sole simple purpose of conveying or obtaining information that he regarded as pertinent to the business immediately in hand. Only once did he speak during these hours and then only to set a fact straight in his mind. He kept his eyes fixed on the dusty scenery outside as he spoke.

"Did he treat you all right?"

The woman made no pretense of misunderstanding him. Her thoughts leaped back and came forward through three years and she pushed straight to the point with the single word. "Yes," she said.

The coach rolled on and the dust drifted. "He beat me once," she said, and the coach rolled on, and four full minutes passed before she finished this in her own mind and in the words: "Maybe it was right. I wouldn't work."

Sergeant Houck nodded. He put his right hand in his right pocket and fumbled there to find one of the short straight straws and bring it forth. He put one end of this in his mouth and chewed slowly on it and watched the dust whirls drift past.

They stopped for a quick meal at a lonely ranchhouse and ate in silence while the man there helped the driver change horses. Then the coach rolled forward and the sun began to drop overhead. It was two mail stops later, at the next change, that another passenger climbed in and plopped his battered suitcase and himself on the front seat opposite them. He was of medium height and plump. He wore city clothes and had quick eyes and features small in the plumpness of his face. He took out a handkerchief and wiped his face and removed his hat to wipe all the way up his forehead. He laid the hat on top of the suitcase and moved restlessly on the seat, trying to find a comfortable position. His movements were quick and nervous. There was no quietness in him.

"You three together?"

"Yes," said Sergeant Houck.

"Your wife, then?"

"No," said Sergeant Houck. He looked out the window on his side and studied the far horizon. The coach rolled on, and the man's quick eyes examined the three of them and came to brief rest on the woman's feet.

"Begging your pardon, lady, but why do you wear those things? Moccasins, aren't they?. They more comfortable?"

She looked at him and down again at the floor and shrank back farther in the seat and the blood began to retreat from her face.

"No offense, lady," said the man. "I just wondered—" He stopped. Sergeant Houck was looking at him.

"Dust's bad," said Sergeant Houck. "And the flies this time of year. Best to keep your mouth closed."

He looked again out the window and the coach rolled on, and the only sounds were the running beat of the hooves and the creakings of the old coach.

A front wheel struck a stone and the coach jolted up at an angle and lurched sideways and the boy gave a small whisper. The woman pulled him to her and onto her lap.

"Say," said the man, "where'd you ever pick up that kid? Looks like——" He stopped.

Sergeant Houck was reaching up and rapping a rock fist against the top of the coach. The driver's voice could be heard shouting at the horses and the coach slowed and the brakes bit on the wheels and the coach stopped. One of the doors opened and the driver peered in. Instinctively he picked Sergeant Houck.

"What's the trouble, soldier?"

"No trouble," said Sergeant Houck. "Our friend here wants to ride up on the box with you." He looked at the plump man. "Less dust up there. It's healthy and gives a good view."

"Now, wait a minute," said the man. "Where'd you get the idea——"

"Healthy," said Sergeant Houck.

The driver looked at the bleak, impassive hardness of Sergeant Houck and at the twitching softness of the plump man. "Reckon it would be," he said. "Come along. I'll boost you up."

The coach rolled forward and the dust drifted and the miles went under the wheels. They rolled along the false-fronted one street of a mushroom town and stopped before a frame building tagged "Hotel." One of the coach doors opened and the plump man retrieved his hat and suitcase and scuttled away and across the porch and into the building. The driver appeared at the coach door. "Last meal here before the night run," he said, and wandered off around the building. Sergeant Houck stepped to the ground and helped the woman out and reached back in and scooped up the boy, tucked him under an arm, and led the way into the building.

When they came out, the shadows were long and fresh horses had been harnessed and a bent, footsore old man was applying grease to the axles. When they were settled again on the rear seat, two men emerged from the building lugging a small but heavy chest and hoisted it into the compartment under the high driving seat. Another man, wearing a close-buttoned suitcoat and curled-brim hat and carrying a shotgun in the crook of one elbow, am-bled into sight around the corner of the building and climbed to the high seat. A moment later a new driver, whip in hand, followed and joined him on the seat and gathered the reins into his left hand. The whip cracked and the coach lurched forward and a young man ran out of the low building across the street carrying a saddle by the two stirrup straps swinging and bouncing against his thigh. He ran alongside and heaved the saddle up to fall thumping on the roof inside the guard-rail. He pulled at the door and managed to scramble in as the coach picked up speed. He dropped onto the front seat, puffing deeply.

"Evening, ma'am," he said between puffs. "And you, General." He leaned forward to slap the boy gently along the jaw. "And you too, bub."

Sergeant Houck looked at the lean length of the young man, at the faded levis tucked into short high-heeled boots, the plaid shirt, the brown handkerchief knotted around the tanned neck, the amiable, competent young face. He grunted a greeting, unintelligible but a pleasant sound.

"A man's legs ain't made for running," said the young man. "Just to fork a horse. That last drink was near too long."

"The Army'd put some starch in those legs," said Sergeant Houck.

"Maybe. Maybe that's why I ain't in the Army." The young man sat quietly, relaxed to the jolting of the coach. "Is there some other topic of genteel conversation you folks'd want to worry some?"

"No," said Sergeant Houck.

"Then maybe you'll pardon me," said the young man. "I hoofed it a lot of miles today." He worked hard at his boots and at last got them off and tucked them out of the way on the floor. He hitched himself up and over on the seat until he was resting on one hip. He put an arm on the window sill and cradled his head on it. His eyes closed. They opened and his head rose a few inches. "If I start sliding, just raise a foot and give me a shove." His head dropped down and the dust whirls outside melted into the dusk and he was asleep.

Sergeant Houck felt a small bump on his left side. The boy had toppled against him and was struggling back to sitting position, fighting silently to defeat the drowsiness overcoming him. Sergeant Houck scooped him up and set the small body across his lap with the head nestled into the crook of his right arm. He leaned his head down and heard the soft little last sigh as the drowsiness won. The coach rolled on, and he looked out into the dropping darkness and saw the deeper black of hills far off on the horizon. He looked sidewise at the woman and dimly made out the outline of her head falling forward and jerking back up, and he reached his left arm along the top of the seat until the hand touched her far shoulder. Faintly he saw her eyes staring at him and felt her shoulder stiffen and then relax as she moved closer and leaned toward him. He slipped down lower in the seat so that her head could reach his shoulder and he felt the gentle touch of the topmost strands of the braided coil of brown hair on his neck above his shirt collar. He waited patiently, and at last he could tell by her steady deep breathing that all fright had left her and all her thoughts were stilled.

The coach rolled on and reached a rutted stretch and began to sway and the young man stirred and began to slide on the smooth leather of his seat. Sergeant Houck put up a foot and braced it against the seat edge and the young man's body came to rest against it and was still. Sergeant Houck leaned his head back on the top of the seat and against the wall of the coach. The stars emerged in the clear sky and the coach rolled on, and the running beat of the hooves had the rhythm of a cavalry squad at a steady trot and gradually the great granite slab of Sergeant Houck softened slightly into sleep.

Sergeant Houck awoke as always all at once and aware. The coach had stopped. From the sounds outside fresh horses were being buckled into the traces. The first light of dawn was creeping into the coach. He raised his head and the bones of his neck cracked and he realized that he was stiff in various places, not only his neck but his right arm where the sleeping boy still nestled and his leg stretched out with the foot braced against the opposite seat.

The young man there was awake. He was still sprawled along the hard leather cushion, but he was pulled back from the braced foot and his eyes were open. He was inspecting the vast leather sole of Sergeant Houck's boot. His eyes flicked up and met Sergeant Houck's eyes, and he grinned.

"That's impressive footwear," he whispered. "You'd need starch in the legs with hooves like that." He sat up and stretched, long and reaching, like a lazy young animal. "Hell," he whispered again, "you must be stiff as a branding iron."

He took hold of Sergeant Houck's leg at the knee and hoisted it slightly so that Sergeant Houck could bend it and ease the foot down to the floor without disturbing the sleeping woman leaning against him. He stretched out both hands and gently lifted the sleeping boy from Sergeant Houck's lap and sat back with the boy in his arms.

Sergeant Houck began closing and unclosing his right hand to stimulate the blood circulation in the arm. The coach rolled forward and the first copper streak of sunlight found it and followed it.

The young man studied the boy's face. "Can't be yours," he whispered.

"No," whispered Sergeant Houck.

"Must have some Indian strain."

"Yes."

The young man whispered down at the sleeping boy. "You can't help that, can you, bub?"

"No," said Sergeant Houck suddenly, full voice, "he can't."

The woman jerked upright and pulled over to the window on her side, rubbing at her eyes. The boy awoke, wide awake on the instant, and saw the unfamiliar face above him and began to squirm violently.

The young man clamped his arms tighter. "Morning, ma'am," he said. "Looks like I ain't such a good nursemaid."

Sergeant Houck reached one hand and plucked up the boy by a grip on the small overalls and deposited him in sitting position on the seat beside the young man. The boy stared at Sergeant Houck and sat still, very still.

The sun climbed into plain view and the coach rolled on. It was stirring the dust of a well-worn road now. It stopped where another crossed and the driver jumped down to deposit a little packet of mail in a box on a short post.

The young man inside pulled on his boots. He bobbed his head in the direction of a group of low buildings up the side road. "Think I'll try it there. They'll be peeling broncs about now and the foreman knows I can sit a saddle." He opened a door and jumped to the ground and whirled to poke his head in. "Hope you make it right," he said, "wherever you're heading."

The door closed and he could be heard scrambling up the back of the coach to get his saddle. There was a thump as he and the saddle hit the ground and then voices began outside, rising in tone.

Sergeant Houck pushed his head through the window beside him. The young man and the driver were facing each other over the saddle. The young man was pulling the pockets of his levis inside out.

"Lookahere, Will," he said, "you can see they're empty. You know I'll kick in soon as I have some cash. Hell, I've hooked rides with you before."

"Not now no more," said the driver. "The company's sore. They hear of this they'd have my job. I'll have to hold the saddle."

The young man's voice had a sudden bite. "You touch that saddle and they'll pick you up in pieces from here to breakfast."

Sergeant Houck fumbled for his inside jacket pocket. This was difficult with his head through the window, but he succeeded in finding it. He whistled sharply. The two men swung to see him. His eyes drilled the young man. "There's something on the seat in here. Must have slipped out of your pocket." He saw the young man stare, puzzled, and start toward the door. He pulled his head back and was sitting quietly in place when the door opened.

The young man leaned in and saw the two silver dollars on the hard seat and swiveled his head to look up at Sergeant Houck. Anger blazed in his eyes and he looked at the impassive rock of Sergeant Houck's face and the anger faded.

"You've been in spots yourself," he said.

"Yes," said Sergeant Houck.

"And maybe were helped out of them."

"When I was a young squirt with more energy than brains," said Sergeant Houck. "Yes."

The young man grinned. He picked up the two coins in

one hand and swung the other to slap Sergeant Houck's leg, sharp and stinging and grateful. "Age ain't hurting you any, General," he said, and closed the door.

The coach rolled on, and the woman looked at Sergeant Houck and the minutes passed and still she looked at him. He stirred on the seat.

"If I'd had brains enough to get married," he said, "might be I'd have had a son. Might have been one like that."

The woman looked away, out her window. She reached up to pat at her hair and the firm line of her lips softened in the tiny imperceptible beginnings of a smile. The dust drifted and the minutes passed and Sergeant Houck stirred again.

"It's the upbringing that counts," he said, and settled into silent immobility, watching the miles go by.

Fifteen minutes for breakfast at a change stop and the coach rolled on. It was near noon when they stopped in Laramie and Sergeant Houck handed the woman out and tucked the boy under one arm and led the way to the waiting room. He stationed the woman and the boy in two chairs and strode away. He was back in five minutes with sandwiches and a pitcher of milk and two cups. He strode away again and was gone longer and returned driving a light buckboard wagon drawn by a pair of deep-barreled bays. The front part of the wagon bed was well padded with layers of empty burlap bags. He went into the waiting room and scooped up the boy and beckoned to the woman to follow. He deposited the boy on the burlap bags and helped the woman up on the driving seat.

"Straight out the road, they tell me," he said. "About fifteen miles. Then right along the creek. Can't miss it."

He stood by the wagon, staring along the length of the street and the road leading on beyond. The woman leaned from the seat and clutched at his shoulder. Her voice broke and climbed. "You're going with me?" Her fingers clung to the cloth of his service jacket. "Please! You've got to!"

Sergeant Houck put a hand over hers on his shoulder and released her fingers. "Yes, I'm going."

He walked around the wagon and stepped to the seat and took the reins and clucked to the team. The wagon moved forward and curious people along the street stopped to watch, and neither Sergeant Houck nor the woman was aware of them. The wheels rolled silently in the thick dust, and on the open road there was no sound except the small creakings of the wagon body and the muffled rhythm of the horses' hooves. A road-runner appeared from nowhere and raced ahead of them, its feet spatting little spurts of dust, and Sergeant Houck watched it running, effortlessly, always the same distance ahead.

"You're afraid," he said.

The wheels rolled silently in the thick dust and the road-runner swung contemptuously aside in a big arc and disappeared in the low bushes.

"They haven't told him," she said, "about the boy."

Sergeant Houck's hands tightened on the reins and the horses slowed to a walk. He clucked sharply to them and slapped the reins on their backs and they quickened again into a trot, and the wheels unwound their thin tracks endlessly into the dust and the high bright sun overhead crept over and down the sky on the left. The wagon topped a slight rise and the road sloped downward for a long stretch to where the green of trees and tall bushes showed in the distance. A jackrabbit started from the scrub growth by the roadside and leaped high in a spy-hop and leveled out, a gray-brown streak. The horses shied and broke rhythm and quieted to a walk under the firm pressure of the reins. Sergeant Houck kept them at a walk, easing the heat out of their muscles down the long slope to the trees. He let them step into the creek up to their knees and dip muzzles in the clear running water. The front wheels of the wagon were into the current and he reached behind him to find a tin dipper tucked among the burlap bags and leaned far out and down to dip up water for the woman and the boy and himself. He backed the team out of the creek and swung them into the wagon cuts leading along the bank to the right.

The creek was on their left and the sun was behind them, warm on their backs, and the shadows of the horses pushed ahead, grotesque moving patterns always ahead, and Sergeant Houck watched them and looked beside him once and saw that the woman was watching them too. The shadows were longer, stretching farther ahead, when they rounded a bend along the creek and the buildings came in sight, the two-room cabin and the several lean-to sheds and the rickety pole corral.

A man was standing by one of the sheds, and when Sergeant Houck stopped the team, he came toward them and halted about twenty feet away. He was not young, perhaps in his middle thirties, but with the young look of a man on whom the years have made no mark except that of the simple passing of time. He was tall, soft, and loose-jointed in build, and indecisive in manner and movement. His eyes wavered and would not steady as he looked at the woman and the fingers of his hands hanging limp at his sides twitched as he waited for her to speak.

She climbed down her side of the wagon and faced him. She stood straight and the sun behind her shone on and through the escaping wisps of the coiled braid of her hair.

"Well, Fred," she said, "I'm here."

"Cora," he said. "It's been a long time, Cora. I didn't know you'd come so soon."

"Why didn't you come get me? Why didn't you, Fred?"

"I didn't rightly know what to do, Cora. It was all so mixed up. Thinking you were dead. Then hearing about you. And what happened. I had to think about things. And I couldn't get away easy. I was going to try maybe next week."

"I hoped you'd come. Right away when you heard."

His body twisted uneasily, a strange movement that stirred his whole length while his feet remained flat and motionless on the ground. "Your hair's still pretty," he said. "The way it used to be."

Something like a sob caught in her throat and she started toward him. Sergeant Houck stepped down on the other side of the wagon and strode off to the creek and kneeled to bend and wash the dust from his face. He stood, shaking the drops from his hands and drying his face with a handkerchief and watching the little eddies of the current around several stones in the creek. He heard the voices behind him and by the wagon.

"Wait, Fred. There's something you have to know—"

"That kid? What's it doing here with you?"

"It's mine, Fred."

"Yours? Where'd you get it?"

"It's my child. Mine."

Silence, and then the man's voice, bewildered, hurt. "So it's really true what they said. About that Indian."

"Yes. He bought me. By their rules I belonged to him."

Silence, and then the woman's voice again. "I wouldn't be alive and here now, any other way. I didn't have any say about it."

Silence, and then the man's voice with the faint beginning of self-pity creeping into the tone. "I didn't count on anything like this."

Sergeant Houck turned and strode back by the wagon. The woman seemed relieved at the interruption.

"This is Sergeant Houck," she said. "He brought me all the way."

The man nodded his head and raised a hand to shove back the sandy hair that kept falling forward on his forehead. "I suppose I ought to thank you, soldier. All that trouble."

"No trouble," said Sergeant Houck. "Unusual duty. But no trouble."

The man pushed at the ground in front of him with one shoe, poking the toe into the dirt and studying it. "It's silly, just standing around here. I suppose we ought to go inside. It's near suppertime. I guess you'll be taking a meal here, soldier. Before you start back to town."

"Right," said Sergeant Houck. "And I'm tired. I'll stay the night too. Start in the morning. Sleep in one of those sheds."

The man pushed at the ground more vigorously. The little dirt pile in front of his shoe seemed to interest him greatly. "All right, soldier. Sorry there're no quarters inside." He swung quickly and started for the cabin. The woman took the boy from the wagon and followed him. Sergeant Houck unharnessed the horses and led them to the creek for a drink and to the corral and led them through the gate. He walked quietly to the cabin doorway and stopped just outside. He could see the man sitting on a straight-backed chair by the table, turned away from him. The woman and the boy were out of sight to one side.

"For God's sake, Cora," the man was saying, "I don't see why you had to bring that kid with you. You could have told me about it. I didn't have to see him."

Her voice was sharp, startled. "What do you mean?"

"Why, now we've got the problem of how to get rid of him. Have to find a mission or some place that'll take him. Why didn't you leave him where he came from?"

"No! He's mine!"

"Good God, Cora! Are you crazy? Think you can foist off a thing like that on me?"

Sergeant Houck stepped through the doorway. "It's been a time since last eating," he said. "Thought I heard something about supper." He looked around the small room and brought his gaze to bear upon the man. "I see the makings on those shelves. Come along, Mr. Sutliff. She can do without our help. A woman doesn't want men cluttering about when getting a meal. Show me your place before it gets dark."

He stood, waiting, and the man scraped at the floor with one foot and slowly rose and went with him.

They were well beyond earshot of the cabin when Sergeant Houck spoke again. "How long were you married? Before it happened?"

"Six years," said the man. "No, seven. It was seven when we lost the last place and headed this way with the train."

"Seven years," said Sergeant Houck. "And no child."

"It just didn't happen. I don't know why." The man stopped and looked sharply at Sergeant Houck. "Oh! So that's the way you're looking at it."

"Yes," said Sergeant Houck. "Now you've got one. A son."

"Not mine," said the man. "You can talk. It's not your wife. It's bad enough thinking of taking an Indian's leavings." He wiped his lips on his sleeve and spat in disgust. "I'll be damned if I'll take his kid."

"Not his any more. He's dead."

"Look, man. Look how it'd be. A damned little half-breed. Around all the time to make me remember what she did."

"Could be a reminder that she had some mighty hard going. And maybe came through the better for it."

"She had hard going! What about me? Thinking she was dead. Getting used to that. Maybe thinking of another woman. Then she comes back—and an Indian kid with her. What does that make me?"

"Could make you a man," said Sergeant Houck. "Think it over."

He swung away and went to the corral and leaned on the rail, watching the horses roll the sweat-itches out on the dry sod. The man went slowly down by the creek and stood on the bank, pushing at the dirt with one shoe and kicking small pebbles into the water. The sun, holding to the horizon rim, dropped suddenly out of sight and dusk swept swiftly to blur the outlines of the buildings. A lamp was lit in the cabin, and the rectangle of light through the doorway made the dusk become darkness. The woman appeared in the doorway and called and the men came their ways and converged there and went in. There was simple food on the table and the woman stood beside it. "I've already fed him," she said, and moved her head toward the door to the inner room. She sat down and they did and the three of them were intent on the plates.

Sergeant Houck ate steadily and reached to refill his plate. The man picked briefly at the food before him and stopped and the woman ate nothing at all. The man put his hands on the table edge and pushed back and rose and went to a side shelf and took a bottle and two thick cups and returned to set these by his plate. He filled the cups a third full from the bottle and shoved one along the table boards toward Sergeant Houck. He lifted the other chin high. His voice was bitter. "Happy home-coming," he said. He waited and Sergeant Houck took the other cup and they drank. The man lifted the bottle and poured himself another cup-third.

The woman moved her chair and looked quickly at him and away.

"Please, Fred."

The man paid no attention to the words. He reached with the bottle toward the other cup.

"No," said Sergeant Houck.

The man shrugged. "You can think better on whiskey. Sharpens the mind." He set the bottle down and took his cup and drained it. He coughed and put it carefully on the table in front of him and pushed at it with one forefinger. Sergeant Houck fumbled in his right side pocket and found one of the short straight straws there and pulled it out and put one end in his mouth and chewed slowly on it. The man and the woman sat still, opposite each other at the table, and seemed to forget his quiet presence. They stared at the table, at the floor, at the cabin walls, everywhere except at each other. Yet their attention was plainly concentrated on each other across the table top. The man spoke first. His voice was restrained, carrying conscious patience.

"Look, Cora. You wouldn't want to do that to me. You can't mean what you said before."

Her voice was low, determined. "He's mine."

"Now, Cora. You don't want to push it too far. A man can take just so much. I didn't know what to do after I heard about you. But I remembered you had been a good wife, I was all ready to forgive you. And now you——"

"Forgive me!" She knocked against her chair rising to her feet. Hurt and bewilderment made her voice ragged as she repeated the words. "Forgive me?" She turned and fairly ran into the inner room. The handleless door banged shut and bounced open again inward a few inches and she leaned against it inside to close it tightly.

The man stared after her and shook his head a little and reached again for the bottle.

"Enough's enough," said Sergeant Houck.

The man became aware of him and shrugged in quick irritation. "For you, maybe," he said, and poured himself another cup-third. He thrust his head a little forward at Sergeant Houck. "Is there any reason you should be noseying in on this?"

"My orders," said Sergeant Houck, "were to deliver them safely. Both of them. Safely."

"You've done that," said the man. He lifted the cup and drained it and set it down carefully. "They're here."

"Yes," said Sergeant Houck, "they're here." He rose and stepped to the outside door and looked into the night. He waited a moment until his eyes were accustomed to the darkness and could distinguish objects faintly in the starlight. He stepped on out and went to the strawpile behind one of the sheds and took an armload and carried it back by the cabin and dropped it at the foot of a tree by one corner. He lowered his bulk to the straw and sat there, legs stretched out, shoulders against the tree, and broke off a straw stem and chewed slowly on it. After a while his jaws stopped their slow, slight movement and his head sank forward and his eyes closed.

Sergeant Houck awoke, completely, in the instant, and aware. The stars had swung perhaps an hour overhead. He was on his feet in the swift reflex, and listening. The straw rustled under his shoes and was still. He heard the faint sound of voices in the cabin, indistinct but rising as tension rose in them. He went toward the doorway and stopped just short of the rectangle of light from the still burning lamp.

"You're not going to have anything to do with me!" The woman's voice was harsh with stubborn anger. "Not until this has been settled right!"

"Aw, come on, Cora." The man's voice was fuzzy, slow-paced. "We'll talk about that in the morning."

"No!"

"All right!" Sudden fury shook the man's voice. "You want it settled now! Well, it's settled! We're getting rid of that damn kid first thing tomorrow!"

"No!"

"What gave you the idea you've got any say around here after what you did? I'm the one to say what's to be done. You don't be careful, maybe I won't take you back."

"Maybe I don't want you to take me back!"

"So damn finicky all of a sudden! After being with that Indian and maybe a lot more!"

Sergeant Houck stepped through the doorway. The man's back was to him and he put out his left hand and took hold of the man's shoulder and spun him around, and his right hand smacked against the side of the man's face and sent him staggering against the wall.

"Forgetting your manners won't help," said Sergeant Houck. He looked around and the woman had disappeared into the inner room. The man leaned against the wall rubbing his cheek, and she emerged, the boy in her arms, and ran toward the outer door.

"Cora!" the man shouted. "Cora!"

She stopped, a brief hesitation in flight. "I don't belong to you," she said, and was gone through the doorway. The man pushed out from the wall and started after her and the great bulk of Sergeant Houck blocked the way.

"You heard her," said Sergeant Houck. "She doesn't belong to anybody now. But that boy."

The man stared at him and some of the fury went out of the man's eyes and he stumbled to his chair at the table and reached for the nearly empty bottle. Sergeant Houck watched him a moment, then turned and quietly went outside. He walked toward the corral and as he passed the second shed she came out of the darker shadows and her voice, low and intense, whispered at him.

"I've got to go. I can't stay here."

Sergeant Houck nodded and went on to the corral and opened the gate and, stepping softly and chirruping a wordless little tune, approached the horses. They stirred uneasily and moved away and stopped and waited for him. He led them through the gate to the wagon and harnessed them quickly and with a minimum of sound. He finished buckling the traces and stood straight and looked toward the cabin. He walked steadily to the lighted rectangle of the doorway and stepped inside and over by the table. The man was leaning forward in his chair, elbows on the table, staring at the empty bottle.

"It's finished," said Sergeant Houck. "She's leaving now."

The man shook his head and pushed at the bottle with one forefinger. "She can't do that." He swung his head to look up at Sergeant Houck and the sudden fury began to heat his eyes. "She can't do that! She's my wife!"

"Not any more," said Sergeant Houck. "Best forget she ever came back." He started toward the door and heard the sharp sound of the chair scraping on the floor behind him. The man's voice rose, shrilling up almost into a shriek.

"Stop!" The man rushed to the wall rack and grabbed the rifle there and swung it at his hip, bringing the muzzle to bear on Sergeant Houck. "Stop!" He was breathing deeply and he fought for control of his voice. "You're not going to take her away!"

Sergeant Houck turned slowly. He stood still, a motionless granite shape in the lamplight.

"Threatening an Army man," said Sergeant Houck. "And with an empty gun."

The man wavered and his eyes flicked down at the rifle, and in the second of indecision Sergeant Houck plunged toward him and one huge hand grasped the gun barrel and pushed it aside and the shot thudded harmlessly into the cabin wall. He wrenched the gun from the man's grasp and his other hand took the man by the shirt front and shook him forward and back and pushed him over and down into the chair.

"No more of that," said Sergeant Houck. "Best sit quiet." His eyes swept the room and found the box of cartridges on a shelf and he took this with the rifle and went to the door. "Look around in the morning and you'll find these." He went outside and tossed the gun up on the roof of one of the sheds and dropped the little box by the strawpile and kicked straw over it. He went to the wagon and stood by it and the woman came out of the darkness of the trees by the creek, carrying the boy.

The wagon wheels rolled silently and the small creakings of the wagon body and the thudding rhythm of the horses' hooves were distinct, isolated sounds in the night. The creek was on their right and they followed the tracking of the road back the way they had come. The woman moved on the seat, shifting the boy's weight from one arm to the other, and Sergeant Houck took him by the overalls and lifted him and reached behind to lay him on the burlap bags.

"A good boy," he said. "Has the Indian way of taking things without yapping. A good way."

The thin new tracks in the dust unwound endlessly under the wheels and the late waning moon climbed out of the horizon and its light shone in pale, barely noticeable patches through the scattered bushes and trees along the creek.

"I have relatives in Missouri," said the woman. "I could go there."

Sergeant Houck fumbled in his side pocket and found a straw and put this in his mouth and chewed slowly on it. "Is that what you want?"

"No."

They came to the main road crossing and swung left and the dust thickened under the horses' hooves. The lean dark shape of a coyote slipped from the brush on one side and bounded along the road and disappeared on the other side.

"I'm forty-seven," said Sergeant Houck. "Nearly thirty of that in the Army. Makes a man rough."

The woman looked straight ahead at the far dwindling ribbon of the road and a small smile curled the corners of her mouth.

"Four months," said Sergeant Houck, "and this last hitch is done. I'm thinking of homesteading on out in the Territory." He chewed on the straw and took it between a thumb and forefinger and flipped it away. "You could get a room at the settlement."

"I could," said the woman. The horses slowed to a walk, breathing deeply, and he let them hold the steady, plodding pace. Far off a coyote howled and others caught the signal and the sounds echoed back and forth in the distance and died away into the night silence.

"Four months," said Sergeant Houck. "That's not so long."

"No," said the woman. "Not too long."

A breeze stirred across the brush and took the dust from the slow hooves in small whorls and the wheels rolled slowly and she put out a hand and touched his shoulder. The fingers moved down along his upper arm and curved over the big muscles there and the warmth of them sank through the cloth of his worn service jacket. She dropped the hand again in her lap and looked ahead along the ribbon of the road. He clucked to the horses and urged them again into a trot, and the small creakings of the wagon body and the dulled rhythm of the hooves were gentle sounds in the night.

The wheels rolled and the late moon climbed, and its pale light shone slantwise down on the moving wagon, on the sleeping boy, and on the woman looking straight ahead and the great granite slab of Sergeant Houck.

THE TWO-GUN MAN

BY STEWART EDWARD WHITE
(Under a Texas Moon)

Stewart Edward White (1873–1946) has been acclaimed as the first author to write of the West on its own terms from its own point of view; his body of work, more fully than that of any other writer, represents all phases of pioneer America—Indian fighting, cattle ranching, logging, early exploration, gold rushes, land booms, and the exploits of mountain men, trappers, outlaws, and lawmen. A number of films have been made from his novels and stories, all silents except for Under a Texas Moon *and* Mystery Ranch *(1932); the latter title is based on a long, tense novelette entitled "The Killer." The most notable of the silents is* The Westerners *(1919), which was developed from White's first novel of the same title, published in 1901.*

I   THE CATTLE RUSTLERS

Buck Johnson was American born, but with a black beard and a dignity of manner that had earned him the title of Señor. He had drifted into southeastern Arizona in the days of Cochise and Victorio and Geronimo. He had persisted, and so in time had come to control the water—and hence the grazing—of nearly all the Soda Springs Valley. His troubles were many, and his difficulties great. There were the ordinary problems of lean and dry years. There were also the extraordinary problems of devastating Apaches; rivals for early and ill-defined range rights—and cattle rustlers.

Señor Buck Johnson was a man of capacity, courage, directness of method, and perseverance. Especially the latter. Therefore he had survived to see the Apaches subdued, the range rights adjusted, his cattle increased to thousands, grazing the area of a principality. Now, all the energy and fire of his frontiersman's nature he had turned to wiping out the third uncertainty of an uncertain business. He found it a task of some magnitude.

For Señor Buck Johnson lived just north of that terra incognita filled with the mystery of a double chance of death from man or the flaming desert known as the Mexican border. There, by natural gravitation, gathered all the desperate characters of three States and two republics. He who rode into it took good care that no one should ride behind him, lived warily, slept light, and breathed deep when once he had again sighted the familiar peaks of Cochise's Stronghold. No one professed knowledge of those who dwelt therein. They moved, mysterious as the desert illusions that compassed them about. As you rode, the ranges of mountains visibly changed form, the monstrous, snaky, sealike growths of the cactus clutched at your stirrup, mock lakes sparkled and dissolved in the middle distance, the sun beat hot and merciless, the powdered dry alkali beat hotly and mercilessly back—and strange, grim men, swarthy, bearded, heavily armed, with red-rimmed unshifting eyes, rode silently out of the mists of illusion to look on you steadily, and then to ride silently back into the desert haze. They might be only the herders of the gaunt cattle, or again they might belong to the Lost Legion that peopled the country. All you could know was that of the men who entered in, but few returned.

Directly north of this unknown land you encountered parallel fences running across the country. They enclosed nothing, but offered a check to the cattle drifting toward the clutch of the renegades, and an obstacle to swift, dashing forays.

Of cattle-rustling there are various forms. The boldest consists quite simply of running off a bunch of stock, hustling it over the Mexican line, and there selling it to some of the big Sonora ranch owners. Generally this sort means war. Also are there subtler means, grading in skill from the rebranding through a wet blanket, through the crafty refashioning of a brand to the various methods of separating the cow from her unbranded calf. In the course of his task Señor Buck Johnson would have to do with them all, but at present he existed in a state of warfare, fighting an enemy who stole as the Indians used to steal.

Already he had fought two pitched battles, and had won them both. His cattle increased, and he became rich. Nevertheless he knew that constantly his resources were being drained. Time and again he and his new Texas foreman, Jed Parker, had followed the trail of a stampeded bunch of twenty or thirty, followed them on down through the Soda Springs Valley to the cut drift fences, there to abandon them. For, as yet, an armed force would be needed to penetrate the borderland. Once he and his men had experienced the glory of a night pursuit. Then, at the drift fences, he had fought one of his battles. But it was impossible adequately to patrol all parts of a range bigger than some Eastern States.

Buck Johnson did his best, but it was like stopping with sand the innumerable little leaks of a dam. Did his riders watch toward the Chiricahuas, then a score of beef steers disappeared from Grant's Pass forty miles away. Pursuit here meant leaving cattle unguarded there. It was useless, and the Señor soon perceived that sooner or later he must strike in offense.

For this purpose he began slowly to strengthen the forces of his riders. Men were coming in from Texas. They were good men, addicted to the grassrope, the double cinch, and the ox-bow stirrup. Señor Johnson wanted men who could shoot, and he got them.

"Jed," said Señor Johnson to his foreman, "the next son of a gun that rustles any of our cows is sure loading himself full of trouble. We'll hit his trail and will stay with it, and we'll reach his cattle-rustling conscience with a rope."

So it came about that a little army crossed the drift fences and entered the border country. Two days later it came out, and mighty pleased to be able to do so. The rope had not been used.

The reason for the defeat was quite simple. The thief had run his cattle through the lava beds where the trail at once became difficult to follow. This delayed the pursuing party; they ran out of water, and, as there was among them not one man well enough acquainted with the country to know where to find more, they had to return.

"No use, Buck," said Jed. "We'd any of us come in on

a gun play, but we can't buck the desert. We'll have to get someone who knows the country."

"That's all right—but where?" queried Johnson.

"There's Pereza," suggested Parker. "It's the only town down near that country."

"Might get someone there," agreed the Señor.

Next day he rode away in search of a guide. The third evening he was back again, much discouraged.

"The country's no good," he explained. "The regular inhabitants 're a set of Mexican bums and old soaks. The cowmen's all from north and don't know nothing more than we do. I found lots who claimed to know that country, but when I told 'em what I wanted they shied like a colt. I couldn't hire 'em, for no money, to go down in that country. They ain't got the nerve. I took two days to her, too, and rode out to a ranch where they said a man lived who knew all about it down there. Nary riffle. Man looked all right, but his tail went down like the rest when I told him what we wanted. Seemed plumb scairt to death. Says he lives too close to the gang. Says they'd wipe him out sure if he done it. Seemed plumb *scairt*." Buck Johnson grinned. "I told him so and he got hosstyle right off. Didn't seem no ways scairt of me. I don't know what's the matter with that outfit down there. They're plumb terrorized."

That night a bunch of steers was stolen from the very corrals of the home ranch. The home ranch was far north, near Fort Sherman itself, and so had always been considered immune from attack. Consequently these steers were very fine ones.

For the first time Buck Johnson lost his head and his dignity. He ordered the horses.

"I'm going to follow that —— —— into Sonora," he shouted to Jed Parker. "This thing's got to stop!"

"You can't make her, Buck," objected the foreman. "You'll get held up by the desert, and, if that don't finish you, they'll tangle you up in all those little mountains down there, and ambush you, and massacre you. You know it damn well."

"I don't give a ——," exploded Señor Johnson, "if they do. No man can slap my face and not get a run for it."

Jed Parker communed with himself.

"Señor," said he, at last, "it's no good; you can't do it. You got to have a guide. You wait three days and I'll get you one."

"You can't do it," insisted the Señor. "I tried every man in the district."

"Will you wait three days?" repeated the foreman.

Johnson pulled loose his latigo. His first anger had cooled.

"All right," he agreed, "and you can say for me that I'll pay five thousand dollars in gold and give all the men and horses he needs to the man who has the nerve to get back that bunch of cattle, and bring in the man who rustled them. I'll sure make this a test case."

So Jed Parker set out to discover his man with nerve.

II THE MAN WITH NERVE

At about ten o'clock of the Fourth of July a rider topped the summit of the last swell of land, and loped his animal down into the single street of Pereza. The buildings on either side were flat-roofed and coated with plaster. Over the sidewalks extended wooden awnings, beneath which opened very wide doors into the coolness of saloons. Each of these places ran a bar, and also games of roulette, faro, craps, and stud poker. Even this early in the morning every game was patronized.

The day was already hot with the dry, breathless, but exhilarating, heat of the desert. A throng of men idling at the edge of the sidewalks, jostling up and down their center, or eddying into the places of amusement, acknowledged the power of summer by loosening their collars, carrying their coats on their arms. They were as yet busily engaged in recognizing acquaintances. Later they would drink freely and gamble, and perhaps fight. Toward all but those whom they recognized they preserved an attitude of potential suspicion, for here were gathered the "bad men" of the border countries. A certain jealousy or touchy egotism lest the other man be considered quicker on the trigger, bolder, more aggressive than himself, kept each strung to tension. An occasional shot attracted little notice. Men in the cow-countries shoot as casually as we strike matches, and some subtle instinct told them that the reports were harmless.

As the rider entered the one street, however, a more definite cause of excitement drew the loose population toward the center of the road. Immediately their mass blotted out what had interested them. Curiosity attracted the saunterers; then in turn the frequenters of the bars and gambling games. In a very few moments the barkeepers, gamblers, and lookout men, held aloof only by the necessities of their calling, alone of all the population of Pereza were not included in the newly-formed ring.

The stranger pushed his horse resolutely to the outer edge of the crowd where, from his point of vantage, he could easily overlook their heads. He was a quiet-appearing young fellow, rather neatly dressed in the border costume, rode a "center fire," or single-cinch, saddle, and wore no chaps. He was what is known as a "two-gun man": that is to say, he wore a heavy Colt's revolver on either hip. The fact that the lower ends of his holsters were tied down, in order to facilitate the easy withdrawal of the revolvers, seemed to indicate that he expected to use them. He had furthermore a quiet grey eye, with the glint of steel that bore out the inference of the tied holsters.

The newcomer dropped his reins on his pony's neck, eased himself to an attitude of attention, and looked down gravely on what was taking place.

He saw over the heads of the bystanders a tall, muscular, wild-eyed man, hatless, his hair rumpled into staring confusion, his right sleeve rolled to his shoulder, a wicked-looking nine-inch knife in his hand, and a red bandana handkerchief hanging by one corner from his teeth.

"What's biting the locoed stranger?" the young man inquired of his neighbor.

The other frowned at him darkly.

"Dares anyone to take the other end of that handkerchief in his teeth, and fight it out without letting go."

"Nice joyful proposition," commented the young man.

He settled himself to closer attention. The wild-eyed man was talking rapidly. What he said cannot be printed here. Mainly was it derogatory of the southern countries. Shortly it became boastful of the northern, and then of the man who uttered it. He swaggered up and down, becoming always the more insolent as his challenge remained untaken.

"Why don't you take him up?" inquired the young man, after a moment.

"Not me!" negatived the other vigorously. "I'll go yore little old gunfight to a finish, but I don't want any cold steel in mine. Ugh! it gives me the shivers. It's a reg'lar Mexican trick! With a gun it's down and out, but this knife work is too slow and searchin'.'"

The newcomer said nothing, but fixed his eye again on the raging man with the knife.

"Don't you reckon he's bluffing?" he inquired.

"Not any!" denied the other with emphasis. "He's jest drunk enough to be crazy mad."

The newcomer shrugged his shoulders and cast his glance searchingly over the fringe of the crowd. It rested on a Mexican.

"Hi, Tony! come here," he called.

The Mexican approached, flashing his white teeth.

"Here," said the stranger, "lend me your knife a minute."

The Mexican, anticipating sport of his own peculiar kind, obeyed with alacrity.

"You fellows make me tired," observed the stranger, dismounting. "He's got the whole townful of you bluffed to a standstill. Damn if I don't try his little game."

He hung his coat on his saddle, shouldered his way through the press, which parted for him readily, and picked up the other corner of the handkerchief.

"Now, you mangy son of a gun," said he.

III   THE AGREEMENT

Jed Parker straightened his back, rolled up the bandana handkerchief, and thrust it into his pocket, hit flat with his hand the touselled mass of his hair, and thrust the long hunting knife into its sheath.

"You're the man I want," said he.

Instantly the two-gun man had jerked loose his weapons and was covering the foreman.

"*Am* I!" he snarled.

"Not jest that way," explained Parker. "My gun is on

my hoss, and you can have this old toadsticker if you want it. I been looking for you and took this way of finding you. Now, let's go talk."

The stranger looked him in the eye for nearly a half minute without lowering his revolvers.

"I go with you," said he briefly, at last.

But the crowd, missing the purport, and in fact the very occurrence of this colloquy, did not understand. It thought the bluff had been called, and naturally, finding harmless what had intimidated it, gave way to an exasperated impulse to get even.

"You —— —— bluffer!" shouted a voice, "don't you think you can run any such ranikaboo here!"

Jed Parker turned humorously to his companion.

"Do we get that talk?" he inquired gently.

For answer the two-gun man turned and walked steadily in the direction of the man who had shouted. The latter's hand strayed uncertainly toward his own weapon, but the movement paused when the stranger's clear, steel eye rested on it.

"This gentleman," pointed out the two-gun man softly, "is an old friend of mine. Don't you get to calling of him names."

His eye swept the bystanders calmly.

"Come on, Jack," said he, addressing Parker.

On the outskirts he encountered the Mexican from whom he had borrowed the knife.

"Here, Tony," said he with a slight laugh, "here's a *peso*. You'll find your knife back there where I had to drop her."

He entered a saloon, nodded to the proprietor, and led the way through it to a box-like room containing a board table and two chairs.

"Make good," he commanded briefly.

"I'm looking for a man with nerve," explained Parker, with equal succinctness. "You're the man."

"Well?"

"Do you know the country south of here?"

The stranger's eyes narrowed.

"Proceed," said he.

"I'm foreman of the Lazy Y of Soda Springs Valley range," explained Parker. "I'm looking for a man with sand enough and *sabe* of the country enough to lead a posse after cattle-rustlers into the border country."

"I live in this country," admitted the stranger.

"So do plenty of others, but their eyes stick out like two raw oysters when you mention the border country. Will you tackle it?"

"What's the proposition?"

"Come and see the old man. He'll put it to you."

They mounted their horses and rode the rest of the day. The desert compassed them about, marvellously changing shape and colour, and every character, with all the noiselessness of phantasmagoria. At evening the desert stars shone steady and unwinking, like the flames of candles. By moonrise they came to the home ranch.

The buildings and corrals lay dark and silent against the moonlight that made of the plain a sea of mist. The two men unsaddled their horses and turned them loose in the wire-fenced "pasture," the necessary noises of their movements sounding sharp and clear against the velvet hush of the night. After a moment they walked stiffly past the sheds and cook shanty, past the men's bunk houses, and the tall windmill silhouetted against the sky, to the main building of the home ranch under its great cottonwoods. There a light still burned, for this was the third day, and Buck Johnson awaited his foreman.

Jed Parker pushed in without ceremony.

"Here's your man, Buck," said he.

The stranger had stepped inside and carefully closed the door behind him. The lamplight threw into relief the bold, free lines of his face, the details of his costume powdered thick with alkali, the shiny butts of the two guns in their open holsters tied at the bottom. Equally it defined the resolute countenance of Buck Johnson turned up in inquiry. The two men examined each other—and liked each other at once.

"How are you," greeted the cattleman.

"Good-evening," responded the stranger.

"Sit down," invited Buck Johnson.

The stranger perched gingerly on the edge of a chair, with an appearance less of embarrassment than of habitual alertness.

"You'll take the job?" inquired the Señor.

"I haven't heard what it is," replied the stranger.

"Parker here——?"

"Said you'd explain."

"Very well," said Buck Johnson. He paused a moment, collecting his thoughts. "There's too much cattle-rustling here. I'm going to stop it. I've got good men here ready to take the job, but no one who knows the country south. Three days ago I had a bunch of cattle stolen right here from the home-ranch corrals, and by one man, at that. It wasn't much of a bunch—about twenty head—but I'm going to make a starter right here, and now. I'm going to get that bunch back, and the man who stole them, if I have to go to hell to do it. And I'm going to do the same with every case of rustling that comes up from now on. I don't care if it's only one cow, I'm going to get it back—every trip. Now, I want to know if you'll lead a posse down into the south country and bring out that last bunch, and the man who rustled them?"

"I don't know——" hesitated the stranger.

"I offer you five thousand dollars in gold if you'll bring back those cows and the man who stole 'em," repeated Buck Johnson. "And I'll give you all the horses and men you think you need."

"I'll do it," replied the two-gun man promptly.

"Good!" cried Buck Johnson, "and you better start tomorrow."

"I shall start to-night—right now."

"Better yet. How many men do you want, and grub for how long?"

"I'll play her a lone hand."

"Alone!" exclaimed Johnson, his confidence visibly cooling. "Alone! Do you think you can make her?"

"I'll be back with those cattle in not more than ten days."

"And the man," supplemented the Señor.

"And the man. What's more, I want that money here when I come in. I don't aim to stay in this country over night."

A grin overspread Buck Johnson's countenance. He understood.

"Climate not healthy for you?" he hazarded. "I guess you'd be safe enough all right with us. But suit yourself. The money will be here."

"That's agreed?" insisted the two-gun man.

"Sure."

"I want a fresh horse—I'll leave mine—he's a good one. I want a little grub."

"All right. Parker'll fit you out."

The stranger rose.

"I'll see you in about ten days."

"Good luck," Señor Buck Johnson wished him.

IV THE ACCOMPLISHMENT

The next morning Buck Johnson took a trip down into the "pasture" of five hundred wire-fenced acres.

"He means business," he confided to Jed Parker, on his return. "That cavallo of his is a heap sight better than the Shorty horse we let him take. Jed, you found your man with nerve, all right. How did you do it?"

The two settled down to wait, if not with confidence, at least with interest. Sometimes, remembering the desperate character of the outlaws, their fierce distrust of any intruder, the wildness of the country, Buck Johnson and his foreman inclined to the belief that the stranger had undertaken a task beyond the powers of any one man. Again, remembering the stranger's cool grey eye, the poise of his demeanor, the quickness of his movements, and the two guns with tied holsters to permit of easy withdrawal, they were almost persuaded that he might win.

"He's one of those long-chance fellows," surmised Jed. "He likes excitement. I see that by the way he takes up with my knife play. He'd rather leave his hide on the fence than stay in the corral."

"Well, he's all right," replied Señor Buck Johnson, "and if he ever gets back, which same I'm some doubtful of, his dinero'll be here for him."

In pursuance of this he rode in to Willets, where shortly the overland train brought him from Tucson the five thousand dollars in double eagles.

In the meantime the regular life of the ranch went on. Each morning Sang, the Chinese cook, rang the great bell, summoning the men. They ate, and then caught up the saddle horses for the day, turning those not wanted from the corral into the pasture. Shortly they jingled away in different directions, two by two, on the slow Spanish trot of the cow-puncher. All day long thus they would ride, without food or water for man or beast, looking the range, identifying the stock, branding the young calves, examining generally into the state of affairs, gazing always with grave eyes on the magnificent, flaming, changing, beautiful, dreadful desert of the Arizona plains. At evening, when the colored atmosphere, catching the last glow, threw across the Chiricahuas its veil of mystery, they jingled in again, two by two, untired, unhasting, the glory of the desert in their deep-set, steady eyes.

And all day long, while they were absent, the cattle, too, made their pilgrimage, straggling in singly, in pairs, in bunches, in long files, leisurely, ruminantly, without haste. There, at the long troughs filled by the windmill or the blindfolded pump mule, they drank, then filed away again into the mists of the desert. And Señor Buck Johnson, or his foreman, Parker, examined them for their condition, noting the increase, remarking the strays from another range. Later, perhaps, they, too, rode abroad. The same thing happened at nine other ranches from five to ten miles apart, where dwelt other fierce, silent men all under the authority of Buck Johnson.

And when night fell, and the topaz and violet and saffron and amethyst and mauve and lilac had faded suddenly from the Chiricahuas, like a veil that has been rent, and the ramparts had become slate-grey and then black—the soft-breathed night wandered here and there over the desert, and the land fell under an enchantment even stranger than the day's.

So the days went by, wonderful, fashioning the ways and the characters of men. Seven passed. Buck Johnson and his foreman began to look for the stranger. Eight, they began to speculate. Nine, they doubted. On the tenth they gave him up—and he came.

They knew him first by the soft lowing of cattle. Jed Parker, dazzled by the lamp, peered out from the door, and made him out dimly turning the animals into the corral. A moment later his pony's hoofs impacted softly on the baked earth, he dropped from the saddle and entered the room.

"I'm late," said he briefly, glancing at the clock, which indicated ten; "but I'm here."

His manner was quick and sharp, almost breathless, as though he had been running.

"Your cattle are in the corral: all of them. Have you the money?"

"I have the money here," replied Buck Johnson, laying his hand against a drawer, "and it's ready for you when you've earned it. I don't care so much for the cattle. What I wanted is the man who stole them. Did you bring him?"

"Yes, I brought him," said the stranger. "Let's see that money."

Buck Johnson threw open the drawer, and drew from it the heavy canvas sack.

"It's here. Now bring in your prisoner."

The two-gun man seemed suddenly to loom large in the doorway. The muzzles of his revolvers covered the two before him. His speech came short and sharp.

"I told you I'd bring back the cows and the one who rustled them," he snapped. "I've never lied to a man yet. Your stock is in the corral. I'll trouble you for that five thousand. I'm the man who stole your cattle!"

A MAN CALLED HORSE

BY DOROTHY M. JOHNSON
(A Man Called Horse)

One of the foremost writers of contemporary Western fiction, Dorothy M. Johnson (1905–1984) created novels and short stories of high literary merit that show her understanding of the forces that shaped the American West. She was the recipient of numerous awards from such organizations as the Western Writers of America and the Western Heritage Foundation and was revered by the native Americans who populate her home state of Montana. A Man Called Horse is one of three films made from her short fiction. The other two are the surprisingly good The Hanging Tree *(1959), with Gary Cooper, Maria Schell, and George C. Scott, based on the novella of the same title, (also included in this volume) and* The Man Who Shot Liberty Valance *(1962), featuring John Wayne, James Stewart, and Lee Marvin, from the short story of the same title (included in* The Best of the West).*

He was a young man of good family, as the phrase went in the New England of a hundred-odd years ago, and the reasons for his bitter discontent were unclear, even to himself. He grew up in the gracious old Boston home under his grandmother's care, for his mother had died in giving him birth; and all his life he had known every comfort and privilege his father's wealth could provide.

But still there was the discontent, which puzzled him because he could not even define it. He wanted to live among his equals—people who were no better than he and no worse either. That was as close as he could come to describing the source of his unhappiness in Boston and his restless desire to go somewhere else.

150

In the year 1845, he left home and went out West, far beyond the country's creeping frontier, where he hoped to find his equals. He had the idea that in Indian country, where there was danger, all white men were kings, and he wanted to be one of them. But he found, in the West as in Boston, that the men he respected were still his superiors, even if they could not read, and those he did not respect weren't worth talking to.

He did have money, however, and he could hire the men he respected. He hired four of them, to cook and hunt and guide and be his companions, but he found them not friendly.

They were apart from him and he was still alone. He still brooded about his status in the world, longing for his equals.

On a day in June, he learned what it was to have no status at all. He became a captive of a small raiding party of Crow Indians.

He heard gunfire and the brief shouts of his companions around the bend of the creek just before they died, but he never saw their bodies. He had no chance to fight, because he was naked and unarmed, bathing in the creek, when a Crow warrior seized and held him.

His captor let him go at last, let him run. Then the lot of them rode him down for sport, striking him with their coup sticks. They carried the dripping scalps of his companions, and one had skinned off Baptiste's black beard as well, for a trophy.

They took him along in a matter-of-fact way, as they took the captured horses. He was unshod and naked as the horses were, and like them he had a rawhide thong around his neck. So long as he didn't fall down, the Crows ignored him.

On the second day they gave him his breeches. His feet were too swollen for his boots, but one of the Indians threw him a pair of moccasins that had belonged to the halfbreed, Henri, who was dead back at the creek. The captive wore the moccasins gratefully. The third day they let him ride one of the spare horses so the party could move faster, and on that day they came in sight of their camp.

He thought of trying to escape, hoping he might be killed in flight rather than by slow torture in the camp, but he never had a chance to try. They were more familiar with escape than he was and, knowing what to expect, they forestalled it. The only other time he had tried to escape from anyone, he had succeeded. When he had left his home in Boston, his father had raged and his grandmother had cried, but they could not talk him out of his intention.

The men of the Crow raiding party didn't bother with talk.

Before riding into camp they stopped and dressed in their regalia, and in parts of their victims' clothing; they painted their faces black. Then, leading the white man by the rawhide around his neck as though he were a horse, they rode down toward the tepee circle, shouting and singing, brandishing their weapons. He was unconscious when they got there; he fell and was dragged.

He lay dazed and battered near a tepee while the noisy, busy life of the camp swarmed around him and Indians came to stare. Thirst consumed him, and when it rained he lapped rain water from the ground like a dog. A scrawny, shrieking, eternally busy old woman with ragged graying hair threw a chunk of meat on the grass, and he fought the dogs for it.

When his head cleared, he was angry, although anger was an emotion he knew he could not afford.

It was better when I was a horse, he thought—when they led me by the rawhide around my neck. I won't be a dog, no matter what!

The hag gave him stinking, rancid grease and let him figure out what it was for. He applied it gingerly to his bruised and sun-seared body.

Now, he thought, I smell like the rest of them.

While he was healing, he considered coldly the advantages of being a horse. A man would be humiliated, and sooner or later he would strike back and that would be the end of him. But a horse had only to be docile. Very well, he would learn to do without pride.

He understood that he was the property of the screaming old woman, a fine gift from her son, one that she liked to show off. She did more yelling at him than at anyone else, probably to impress the neighbors so they would not forget what a great and generous man her son was. She was bossy and proud, a dreadful sag of skin and bones, and she was a devilish hard worker.

The white man, who now thought of himself as a horse, forgot sometimes to worry about his danger. He kept making mental notes of things to tell his own people in Boston about this hideous adventure. He would go back a hero, and he would say, "Grandmother, let me fetch your shawl. I've been accustomed to doing little errands for another lady about your age."

Two girls lived in the tepee with the old hag and her warrior son. One of them, the white man concluded, was his captor's wife and the other was his little sister. The daughter-in-law was smug and spoiled. Being beloved, she did not have to be useful. The younger girl had bright, wandering eyes. Often enough they wandered to the white man who was pretending to be a horse.

The two girls worked when the old woman put them at it, but they were always running off to do something they enjoyed more. There were games and noisy contests, and there was much laughter. But not for the white man. He was finding out what loneliness could be.

That was a rich summer on the plains, with plenty of buffalo for meat and clothing and the making of tepees. The Crows were wealthy in horses, prosperous and contented. If their men had not been so avid for glory, the white man thought, there would have been a lot more of them. But they went out of their way to court death, and when one of them met it, the whole camp mourned extravagantly and cried to their God for vengeance.

The captive was a horse all summer, a docile bearer of burdens, careful and patient. He kept reminding himself that he had to be better-natured than other horses, because he could not lash out with hoofs or teeth. Helping the old woman load up the horses for travel, he yanked at a pack and said, "Whoa, brother. It goes easier when you don't fight."

The horse gave him a big-eyed stare as if it understood his language—a comforting thought, because nobody else did. But even among the horses he felt unequal. They were able to look out for themselves if they escaped. He would simply starve. He was envious still, even among the horses.

Humbly he fetched and carried. Sometimes he even offered to help, but he had not the skill for the endless work of the women, and he was not trusted to hunt with the men, the providers.

When the camp moved, he carried a pack trudging with the women. Even the dogs worked then, pulling small burdens on travois of sticks.

The Indian who had captured him lived like a lord, as he had a right to do. He hunted with his peers, attended long ceremonial meetings with much chanting and dancing, and lounged in the shade with his smug bride. He had only two responsibilities: to kill buffalo and to gain glory. The white man was so far beneath him in status that the Indian did not even think of envy.

One day several things happened that made the captive think he might sometime become a man again. That was the day when he began to understand their language. For four months he had heard it, day and night, the joy and the mourning, the ritual chanting and sung prayers, the squabbles and the deliberations. None of it meant anything to him at all.

But on that important day in early fall the two young women set out for the river, and one of them called over her shoulder to the old woman. The white man was startled. She had said she was going to bathe. His understanding was so sudden that he felt as if his ears had come unstopped. Listening to the racket of the camp, he heard fragments of meaning instead of gabble.

On that same important day the old woman brought a pair of new moccasins out of the tepee and tossed them on the ground before him. He could not believe she would do anything for him because of kindness, but giving him moccasins was one way of looking after her property.

In thanking her, he dared greatly. He picked a little handful of fading fall flowers and took them to her as she squatted in front of her tepee, scraping a buffalo hide with a tool made from a piece of iron tied to a bone. Her hands were hideous—most of the fingers had the first joint missing. He bowed solemnly and offered the flowers.

She glared at him from beneath the short, ragged tangle of her hair. She stared at the flowers, knocked them out of his hand and went running to the next tepee, squalling the story. He heard her and the other women screaming with laughter.

The white man squared his shoulders and walked boldly over to watch three small boys shooting arrows at a target. He said in English, "Show me how to do that, will you?"

They frowned, but he held out his hand as if there could be no doubt. One of them gave him a bow and one arrow, and they snickered when he missed.

The people were easily amused, except when they were angry. They were amused, at him, playing with the little boys. A few days later he asked the hag, with gestures, for a bow that her son had just discarded, a man-size bow of horn. He scavenged for old arrows. The old woman cackled at his marksmanship and called her neighbors to enjoy the fun.

When he could understand words, he could identify his people by their names. The old woman was Greasy Hand, and her daughter was Pretty Calf. The other young woman's name was not clear to him, for the words were not in his vocabulary. The man who had captured him was Yellow Robe.

Once he could understand, he could begin to talk a little, and then he was less lonely. Nobody had been able to see any reason for talking to him, since he would not understand anyway. He asked the old woman, "What is my name?" Until he knew it, he was incomplete. She shrugged to let him know he had none.

He told her in the Crow language, "My name is Horse." He repeated it, and she nodded. After that they called him Horse when they called him anything. Nobody cared except the white man himself.

They trusted him enough to let him stray out of camp, so that he might have got away and, by unimaginable good luck, might have reached a trading post or a fort, but winter was too close. He did not dare leave without a horse; he needed clothing and a better hunting weapon than he had, and more certain skill in using it. He did not dare steal, for then they would surely have pursued him, and just as certainly they would have caught him. Remembering the warmth of the home that was waiting in Boston, he settled down for the winter.

On a cold night he crept into the tepee after the others

had gone to bed. Even a horse might try to find shelter from the wind. The old woman grumbled, but without conviction. She did not put him out.

They tolerated him, back in the shadows, so long as he did not get in the way.

He began to understand how the family that owned him differed from the others. Fate had been cruel to them. In a short, sharp argument among the old women, one of them derided Greasy Hand by sneering, "You have no relatives!" and Greasy Hand raved for minutes of the deeds of her father and uncles and brothers. And she had had four sons, she reminded her detractor—who answered with scorn, "Where are they?"

Later the white man found her moaning and whimpering to herself, rocking back and forth on her haunches, staring at her mutilated hands. By that time he understood. A mourner often chopped off a finger joint. Old Greasy Hand had mourned often. For the first time he felt a twinge of pity, but he put it aside as another emotion, like anger, that he could not afford. He thought: What tales I will tell when I get home!

He wrinkled his nose in disdain. The camp stank of animals and meat and rancid grease. He looked down at his naked, shivering legs and was startled, remembering that he was still only a horse.

He could not trust the old woman. She fed him only because a starved slave would die and not be worth boasting about. Just how fitful her temper was he saw on the day when she got tired of stumbling over one of the hundred dogs that infested the camp. This was one of her own dogs, a large, strong one that pulled a baggage travois when the tribe moved camp.

Countless times he had seen her kick at the beast as it lay sleeping in front of the tepee, in her way. The dog always moved, with a yelp, but it always got in the way again. One day she gave the dog its usual kick and then stood scolding at it while the animal rolled its eyes sleepily. The old woman suddenly picked up her axe and cut the dog's head off with one blow. Looking well satisfied with herself, she beckoned her slave to remove the body.

It could have been me, he thought, if I were a dog. But I'm a horse.

His hope of life lay with the girl, Pretty Calf. He set

about courting her, realizing how desperately poor he was both in property and honor. He owned no horse, no weapon but the old bow and the battered arrows. He had nothing to give away, and he needed gifts, because he did not dare seduce the girl.

One of the customs of courtship involved sending a gift of horses to a girl's older brother and bestowing much buffalo meat upon her mother. The white man could not wait for some far-off time when he might have either horses or meat to give away. And his courtship had to be secret. It was not for him to stroll past the groups of watchful girls, blowing a flute made of an eagle's wing bone, as the flirtatious young bucks did.

He could not ride past Pretty Calf's tepee, painted and bedizened; he had no horse, no finery.

Back home, he remembered, I could marry just about any girl I'd want to. But he wasted little time thinking about that. A future was something to be earned.

The most he dared do was wink at Pretty Calf now and then, or state his admiration while she giggled and hid her facc. The least he dared do to win his bride was to elope with her, but he had to give her a horse to put the seal of tribal approval on that. And he had no horse until he killed a man to get one. . . .

His opportunity came in early spring. He was casually accepted by that time. He did not belong, but he was amusing to the Crows, like a strange pet, or they would not have fed him through the winter.

His chance came when he was hunting small game with three young boys who were his guards as well as his scornful companions. Rabbits and birds were of no account in a camp well fed on buffalo meat, but they made good targets.

His party walked far that day. All of them at once saw the two horses in a sheltered coulee. The boys and the man crawled forward on their bellies, and then they saw an Indian who lay on the ground, moaning, a lone traveler. From the way the boys inched eagerly forward, Horse knew the man was fair prey—a member of some enemy tribe.

This is the way the captive white man acquired wealth and honor to win a bride and save his life: He shot an arrow into the sick man, a split second ahead of one of his small companions, and dashed forward to strike the still-groaning man with his bow, to count first coup. Then he seized the hobbled horses.

By the time he had the horses secure, and with them his hope for freedom, the boys had followed, counting coup with gestures and shrieks they had practiced since boyhood, and one of them had the scalp. The white man was grimly amused to see the boy double up with sudden nausea when he had the thing in his hand. . . .

There was a hubbub in the camp when they rode in that evening, two of them on each horse. The captive was noticed. Indians who had ignored him as a slave stared at the brave man who had struck first coup and had stolen horses.

The hubbub lasted all night, as fathers boasted loudly of their young sons' exploits. The white man was called upon to settle an argument between two fierce boys as to which of them had struck second coup and which must be satisfied with third. After much talk that went over his head, he solemnly pointed at the nearest boy. He didn't know which boy it was and didn't care, but the boy did.

The white man had watched warriors in their triumph. He knew what to do. Modesty about achievements had no place among the Crow people. When a man did something big, he told about it.

The white man smeared his face with grease and charcoal. He walked inside the tepee circle, chanting and singing. He used his own language.

"You heathens, you savages," he shouted. "I'm going to get out of here someday! I am going to get away!" The Crow people listened respectfully. In the Crow tongue he shouted, "Horse! I am Horse!" and they nodded.

He had a right to boast, and he had two horses. Before dawn, the white man and his bride were sheltered beyond a far hill, and he was telling her, "I love you, little lady. I love you."

She looked at him with her great dark eyes, and he thought she understood his English words—or as much as she needed to understand.

"You are my treasure," he said, "more precious than jewels, better than fine gold. I am going to call you Freedom."

When they returned to camp two days later, he was bold but worried. His ace, he suspected, might not be high enough in the game he was playing without being sure of the rules. But it served.

Old Greasy Hand raged—but not at him. She complained loudly that her daughter had let herself go too cheap. But the marriage was as good as any Crow marriage. He had paid a horse.

He learned the language faster after that, from Pretty Calf, whom he sometimes called Freedom. He learned that his attentive, adoring bride was fourteen years old.

One thing he had not guessed was the difference that being Pretty Calf's husband would make in his relationship to her mother and brother. He had hoped only to make his position a little safer, but he had not expected to be treated with dignity. Greasy Hand no longer spoke to him at all. When the white man spoke to her, his bride murmured in dismay, explaining at great length that he must never do that. There could be no conversation between a man and his mother-in-law. He could not even mention a word that was part of her name.

Having improved his status so magnificently, he felt no need for hurry in getting away. Now that he had a woman, he had as good a chance to be rich as any man. Pretty Calf waited on him; she seldom ran off to play games with other young girls, but took pride in learning from her mother the many women's skills of tanning hides and making clothing and preparing food.

He was no more a horse but a kind of man, a half-Indian, still poor and unskilled but laden with honors, clinging to the buckskin fringes of Crow society.

Escape could wait until he could manage it in comfort, with fit clothing and a good horse, with hunting weapons. Escape could wait until the camp moved near some trading post. He did not plan how he would get home. He dreamed of being there all at once, and of telling stories nobody would believe. There was no hurry.

Pretty Calf delighted in educating him. He began to understand tribal arrangements, customs and why things were as they were. They were that way because they had always been so. His young wife giggled when she told him, in his ignorance, things she had always known. But she did not laugh when her brother's wife was taken by another warrior. She explained that solemnly with words and signs.

Yellow Robe belonged to a society called the Big Dogs. The wife stealer, Cut Neck, belonged to the Foxes. They were fellow tribesmen; they hunted together and fought side by side, but men of one society could take away wives from the other society if they wished, subject to certain limitations.

When Cut Neck rode up to the tepee, laughing and singing, and called to Yellow Robe's wife, "Come out! Come out!" she did as ordered, looking smug as usual, meek and entirely willing. Thereafter she rode beside him in ceremonial processions and carried his coup stick, while his other wife pretended not to care.

"But why?" the white man demanded of his wife, his Freedom. "Why did our brother let his woman go? He sits and smokes and does not speak."

Pretty Calf was shocked at the suggestion. Her brother could not possibly reclaim his woman, she explained. He could not even let her come back if she wanted to—and she probably would want to when Cut Neck tired of her. Yellow Robe could not even admit that his heart was sick. That was the way things were. Deviation meant dishonor.

The woman could have hidden from Cut Neck, she said. She could even have refused to go with him if she had been *ba-wurokee*—a really virtuous woman. But she had been his woman before, for a little while on a berrying expedition, and he had a right to claim her.

There was no sense in it, the white man insisted. He glared at his young wife. "If you go, I will bring you back!" he promised.

She laughed and buried her head against his shoulder. "I will not have to go," she said. "Horse is my first man. There is no hole in my moccasin."

He stroked her hair and said, "'*Ba-wurokee.*'"

With great daring, she murmured, "*Hayha,*" and when he did not answer, because he did not know what she meant, she drew away, hurt.

"A woman calls her man that if she thinks he will not leave her. Am I wrong?"

The white man held her closer and lied. "Pretty Calf is not wrong. Horse will not leave her. Horse will not take another woman, either." No, he certainly would not. Parting from this one was going to be harder than getting her had been. *"Hayha,"* he murmured. "Freedom."

His conscience irked him, but not very much. Pretty Calf could get another man easily enough when he was gone, and a better provider. His hunting skill was improving, but he was still awkward.

There was no hurry about leaving. He was used to most of the Crow ways and could stand the rest. He was becoming prosperous. He owned five horses. His place in the life of the tribe was secure, such as it was. Three or four young women, including the one who had belonged to Yellow Robe, made advances to him. Pretty Calf took pride in the fact that her man was so attractive.

By the time he had what he needed for a secret journey, the grass grew yellow on the plains and the long cold was close. He was enslaved by the girl he called Freedom and, before the winter ended, by the knowledge that she was carrying his child. . . .

The Big Dog society held a long ceremony in the spring. The white man strolled with his woman along the creek bank, thinking: When I get home I will tell them about the chants and the drumming. Sometime. Sometime.

Pretty Calf would not go to bed when they went back to the tepee.

"Wait and find out about my brother," she urged. "Something may happen."

So far as Horse could figure out, the Big Dogs were having some kind of election. He pampered his wife by staying up with her by the fire. Even the old woman, who was a great one for getting sleep when she was not working, prowled around restlessly.

The white man was yawning by the time the noise of the ceremony died down. When Yellow Robe strode in, garish and heathen in his paint and feathers and furs, the women cried out. There was conversation, too fast for Horse to follow, and the old woman wailed once, but her son silenced her with a gruff command.

When the white man went to sleep, he thought his wife was weeping beside him.

The next morning she explained.

"He wears the bearskin belt. Now he can never retreat in battle. He will always be in danger. He will die."

Maybe he wouldn't, the white man tried to convince her. Pretty Calf recalled that some few men had been honored by the bearskin belt, vowed to the highest daring, and had not died. If they lived through the summer, then they were free of it.

"My brother wants to die," she mourned. "His heart is bitter."

Yellow Robe lived through half a dozen clashes with small parties of raiders from hostile tribes. His honors were many. He captured horses in an enemy camp, led two successful raids, counted first coup and snatched a gun from the hand of an enemy tribesman. He wore wolf tails on his moccasins and ermine skins on his shirt, and he fringed his leggings with scalps in token of his glory.

When his mother ventured to suggest, as she did many times, "My son should take a new wife, I need another woman to help me," he ignored her. He spent much time in prayer, alone in the hills or in conference with a medicine man. He fasted and made vows and kept them. And before he could be free of the heavy honor of the bearskin belt, he went on his last raid.

The warriors were returning from the north just as the white man and two other hunters approached from the south, with buffalo and elk meat dripping from the bloody hides tied on their restive ponies. One of the hunters grunted, and they stopped to watch a rider on the hill north of the tepee circle.

The rider dismounted, held up a blanket and dropped it. He repeated the gesture.

The hunters murmured dismay. "Two! Two men dead!" They rode fast into the camp, where there was already wailing.

A messenger came down from the war party on the hill. The rest of the party delayed to paint their faces for mourning and for victory. One of the two dead men was Yellow Robe. They had put his body in a cave and walled it in with rocks. The other man died later, and his body was in a tree.

There was blood on the ground before the tepee to which Yellow Robe would return no more. His mother, with her hair chopped short, sat in the doorway, rocking back and forth on her haunches, wailing her heartbreak.

She cradled one mutilated hand in the other. She had cut off another finger joint.

Pretty Calf had cut off chunks of her long hair and was crying as she gashed her arms with a knife. The white man tried to take the knife away, but she protested so piteously that he let her do as she wished. He was sickened with the lot of them.

Savages! he thought. Now I will go back! I'll go hunting alone, and I'll keep on going.

But he did not go just yet, because he was the only hunter in the lodge of the two grieving women, one of them old and the other pregnant with his child.

In their mourning, they made him a pauper again. Everything that meant comfort, wealth and safety they sacrificed to the spirits because of the death of Yellow Robe. The tepee, made of seventeen fine buffalo hides, the furs that should have kept them warm, the white deerskin dress, trimmed with elk teeth, that Pretty Calf loved so well, even their tools and Yellow Robe's weapons—everything but his sacred medicine objects—they left there on the prairie, and the whole camp moved away. Two of his best horses were killed as a sacrifice, and the women gave away the rest.

They had no shelter. They would have no tepee of their own for two months at least of mourning, and then the women would have to tan hides to make it. Meanwhile they could live in temporary huts made of willows, covered with skins given them in pity by their friends. They could have lived with relatives, but Yellow Robe's women had no relatives.

The white man had not realized until then how terrible a thing it was for a Crow to have no kinfolk. No wonder old Greasy Hand had only stumps for fingers. She had mourned, from one year to the next, for everyone she had ever loved. She had no one left but her daughter, Pretty Calf.

Horse was furious at their foolishness. It had been bad enough for him, a captive, to be naked as a horse and poor as a slave, but that was because his captors had stripped him. These women had voluntarily given up everything they needed.

He was too angry at them to sleep in the willow hut. He lay under a sheltering tree. And on the third night of the mourning he made his plans. He had a knife and a bow. He would go after meat, taking two horses. And he would not come back. There were, he realized, many things he was not going to tell when he got back home.

In the willow hut, Pretty Calf cried out. He heard rustling there, and the old woman's querulous voice.

Some twenty hours later his son was born, two months early, in the tepee of a skilled medicine woman. The child was born without breath, and the mother died before the sun went down.

The white man was too shocked to think whether he should mourn, or how he should mourn. The old woman screamed until she was voiceless. Piteously she approached him, bent and trembling, blind with grief. She held out her knife and he took it.

She spread out her hands and shook her head. If she cut off any more finger joints, she could do no more work. She could not afford any more lasting signs of grief.

The white man said, "All right! All right!" between his teeth, He hacked his arms with the knife and stood watching the blood run down. It was little enough to do for Pretty Calf, for little Freedom.

Now there is nothing to keep me, he realized. When I get home, I must not let them see the scars.

He looked at Greasy Hand, hideous in her grief-burdened age, and thought: I really am free now! When a wife dies, her husband has no more duty toward her family. Pretty Calf had told him so, long ago, when he wondered why a certain man moved out of one tepee and into another.

The old woman, of course, would be a scavenger. There was one other with the tribe, an ancient crone who had no relatives, toward whom no one felt any responsibility. She lived on food thrown away by the more fortunate. She slept in shelters that she built with her own knotted hands. She plodded wearily at the end of the procession when the camp moved. When she stumbled, nobody cared. When she died, nobody would miss her.

Tomorrow morning, the white man decided, I will go.

His mother-in-law's sunken mouth quivered. She said one word, questioningly. She said, *"Eero-oshay?"* She said, "Son?"

Blinking, he remembered. When a wife died, her husband was free. But her mother, who had ignored him with dignity, might if she wished ask him to stay. She invited him by calling him Son, and he accepted by answering Mother.

Greasy Hand stood before him, bowed with years, withered with unceasing labor, loveless and childless, scarred with grief. But with all her burdens, she still loved life enough to beg it from him, the only person she had any right to ask. She was stripping herself of all she had left, her pride.

He looked eastward across the prairie. Two thousand miles away was home. The old woman would not live forever. He could afford to wait, for he was young. He could afford to be magnanimous, for he knew he was a man. He gave her the answer. *"Eegya,"* he said. "Mother."

He went home three years later. He explained no more than to say, "I lived with Crows for a while. It was some time before I could leave. They called me Horse."

He did not find it necessary either to apologize or to boast, because he was the equal of any man on earth.

THE HANGING TREE

BY DOROTHY M. JOHNSON

(The Hanging Tree)

"The Hanging Tree" was conceived and written as a novel, but when Dorothy M. Johnson (1905–1984) was rather astonishingly unable to find a publisher for it, she painstakingly whittled it down to its present novella size for publication in her 1957 collection The Hanging Tree and Other Stories. *The film version, with Gary Cooper and Maria Schell, was released two years later.*

I

Just before the road dipped down to the gold camp on Skull Creek, it crossed the brow of a barren hill and went under the out-thrust bough of a great cottonwood tree.

A short length of rope, newly cut, hung from the bough, swinging in the breeze, when Joe Frail walked that road for the first time, leading his laden horse. The camp was only a few months old, but someone had been strung up already, and no doubt for good cause. Gold miners were normally more interested in gold than in hangings. As Joe Frail glanced up at the rope, his muscles went tense, for he remembered that there was a curse on him.

Almost a year later, the boy who called himself Rune came into Skull Creek, driving a freight wagon. The dangling length of rope was weathered and raveled then. Rune stared at it and reflected, If they don't catch you, they can't hang you.

Two weeks after him, the lost lady passed under the tree, riding in a wagon filled with hay. She did not see

166

the bough or the raveled rope, because there was a bandage over her eyes.

Joe Frail looked like any prospector, ageless, anonymous and dusty, in a fading red shirt and shapeless jeans. His matted hair, hanging below his shoulders, would have been light brown if it had been clean. A long mustache framed his mouth, and he wore a beard because he had not shaved for two months.

The main difference between Joe Frail and any other newcomer to Skull Creek was that inside the pack on his plodding horse was a physician's satchel.

"Now I wonder who got strung up on that tree," remarked his partner. Wonder Russell was Joe Frail's age—thirty—but not of his disposition. Russell was never moody and he required little from the world he lived in. He wondered aloud about a thousand things but did not require answers to his questions.

"I wonder," he said, "how long it will take us to dig out a million dollars."

I wonder, Joe Frail thought, if that is the bough from which I'll hang. I wonder who the man is that I'll kill to earn it.

They spent that day examining the gulch, where five hundred men toiled already, hoping the colors that showed in the gravel they panned meant riches. They huddled that night in a brush wickiup, quickly thrown together to keep off the rain.

"I'm going to name my claim after me when I get one," said Wonder Russell. "Call it the Wonder Mine."

"Meaning you wonder if there's any pay dirt in it," Joe Frail answered. "I'll call mine after myself, too. The Frail Hope."

"Hell, that's unlucky," his partner objected.

"I'm usually unlucky," said Joe Frail.

He lay awake late that first night in the gulch, still shaken by the sight of the dangling rope. He remembered the new-made widow, six years ago, who had shrieked a prophecy that he would sometime hang.

Before that, he had been Doctor Joseph Alberts, young and unlucky, sometimes a prospector and sometimes a physician. He struck pay dirt, sold out and went back East to claim a girl called Sue, but she had tired of waiting and had married someone else. She sobbed when she told him, but her weeping was not because she had spoiled her life and his. She cried because she could not possess him now that he was rich.

So he lost some of his youth and all his love and even his faith in love. Before long he lost his riches, too, in a fever of gambling that burned him up because neither winning nor losing mattered.

Clean and new again, and newly named Frail—he chose that in a bitter moment—he dedicated himself to medicine for a winter. He was earnest and devoted, and when spring came he had a stake that would let him go prospecting again. He went north to Utah to meet a man named Harrigan, who would be his partner.

On the way, camped alone, he was held up and robbed of his money, his horse and his gun. The robbers, laughing, left him a lame pinto mare that a Digger Indian would have scorned.

Hidden in a slit in his belt for just such an emergency was a twenty-dollar gold piece. They didn't get that.

In Utah he met Harrigan—who was unlucky, too. Harrigan had sold his horse but still had his saddle and forty dollars.

"Will you trust me with your forty dollars?" Joe Frail asked. "I'll find a game and build it bigger."

"I wouldn't trust my own mother with that money," Harrigan objected as he dug into his pocket. "But my mother don't know how to play cards. What makes you think you do?"

"I was taught by an expert," Joe Frail said briefly.

In addition to two professions, doctor and miner, he had two great skills: he was an expert card player and a top hand with a pistol. But he played cards only when he did not care whether he won or lost. This time winning was necessary, and he knew what was going to happen—he would win, and then he would be shattered.

He found a game and watched the players—two cowboys, nothing to worry about; a town man, married, having a mildly devilish time; and an older man, probably an emigrant going back East with a good stake. The emigrant was stern and tense and had more chips before him than anyone else at the table.

When Doc sat in, he let the gray-haired man keep

winning for a while. When the emigrant started to lose, he could not pull out. He was caught in some entangling web of emotions that Doc Frail had never felt.

Doc lost a little, won a little, lost a very little, began to win. Only he knew how the sweat ran down inside his dusty shirt.

The emigrant was a heavy loser when he pulled out of the game.

"Got to find my wife," was his lame excuse. But he went only as far as the bar and was still there, staring into the mirror, when Doc cashed in his chips and went out with two hundred dollars in his pockets.

He got out to the side of the saloon before the shakes began.

"And what the hell ails you?" Harrigan inquired. "You won."

"What ails me," said Doc with his teeth chattering, "is that my father taught me to gamble and my mother taught me it was wicked. The rest of it is none of your business."

"You sound real unfriendly," Harrigan complained. "I was admiring your skill. It must be mighty handy. The way you play cards, I can't see why you waste your time doctoring."

"Neither can I," said Doc.

He steadied himself against the building. "We'll go someplace and divide the money. You might as well have yours in your pocket."

Harrigan warned, "The old fellow, the one you won from, is on the prod."

Doc said shortly, "The man's a fool."

Harrigan sounded irritated. "You think everybody's a fool."

"I'm convinced of it."

"If you weren't one, you'd clear out of here," the cowboy advised. "Standing here, you're courting trouble."

Doc took that as a challenge. "Trouble comes courting me, and I'm no shy lover."

He felt as sore as raw meat. Another shudder shook him. He detested Harrigan, the old man, himself, everybody.

The door swung open and the lamplight showed the gray-haired emigrant. The still night made his words clear:

"He cheated me, had them cards marked, I tell you!"

Salt stunk unbearably on raw meat. Doc Frail stepped forward.

"Are you talking about me?"

The man squinted. "Certainly I'm talking about you. Cheating, thieving tin horn—"

Young Doc Frail gasped and shot him.

Harrigan groaned, "My God, come on!" and ducked back into darkness.

But Doc ran forward, not back, and knelt beside the fallen man as the men inside the saloon came cautiously out.

Then there was a woman's keening cry, coming closer: "Ben! Ben! Let me by—he's shot my husband!"

He never saw her, he only heard her wailing voice: "You don't none of you care if a man's been killed, do you! You'll let him go scot free and nobody cares. But he'll hang for this, the one who did it! You'll burn in hell for this, the lot of you—"

Doc Frail and Harrigan left that place together— the pinto carried both saddles and the men walked. They parted company as soon as they could get decent horses, and Doc never saw Harrigan again.

A year or so later, heading for a gold camp, Doc met the man he called Wonder, and Wonder Russell, it seemed to him, was the only true friend he had ever had.

But seeing him for the first time, Joe Frail challenged him with a look that warned most men away, a slow, contemptuous look from hat to boots that seemed to ask, "Do you amount to anything?"

That was not really what it asked, though. The silent question Joe Frail had for every man he met was "Are you the man? The man for whom I'll hang?"

Wonder Russell's answer at their first meeting was as silent as the question. He smiled a greeting, and it was as if he said, "You're a man I could side with."

They were partners from then on, drifting through good luck and bad, and so finally they came to Skull Creek.

They built more than one wickiup in the weeks they spent prospecting there, moving out from the richest part of the strike, because that was already claimed.

By September they were close to broke.

"A man can go to work for wages," Wonder Russell suggested. "Same kind of labor as we're doing now, only we'd get paid for it. I wonder what it's like to eat."

"You'll never be a millionaire working someone else's mine," Doc warned.

"I wonder how a man could get a stake without working," his partner mused.

"I know how," Joe Frail admitted. "How much have we got between us?"

It added up to less than fifty dollars. By morning of the following day, Joe Frail had increased it to almost four hundred and was shuddering so that his teeth chattered.

"What talent!" Wonder Russell said in awe. He asked no questions.

Four days after they started over again with a new supply of provisions, they struck pay dirt. They staked two claims, and one was as good as the other.

"Hang on or sell out?" Joe Frail asked.

"I wonder what it's like to be dirty rich," Wonder mused. "On the other hand, I wonder what it's like to be married?"

Joe Frail stared. "Is this something you have in mind for the immediate future, or are you just dreaming in a general kind of way?"

Wonder Russell smiled contentedly. "Her name is Julie and she works at the Big Nugget."

And she already has a man who won't take kindly to losing her, Joe Frail recollected. Wonder Russell knew that as well as he did.

She was a slim young dancer, beautiful though haggard, this Julie at the Big Nugget. She had tawny hair in a great knot at the back of her neck, and a new red scar on one shoulder; it looked like a knife wound and showed when she wore a low-necked dress.

"Let's sell, and I'll dance at your wedding," Joe Frail promised.

They sold the Wonder and the Frail Hope on a Monday and split fifteen thousand dollars between them. They could have got more by waiting, but Wonder said, "Julie don't want to wait. We're going out on the next stage, Wednesday."

"There are horses for sale. Ride out, Wonder." Doc could not forget the pale, cadaverous man called Dusty

Smith who would not take kindly to losing Julie. "Get good horses and start before daylight."

"Anybody'd think it was you going to get married, you're in such a sweat about it," Wonder answered, grinning. "I guess I'll go tell her now."

A man should plan ahead more, Joe Frail told himself. I planned only to seek for gold, not what to do if I found it, and not what to do if my partner decided to team up with someone else.

He was suddenly tired of being one of the anonymous, bearded, sweating toilers along the creek. He was tired of being dirty. A physician could be clean and wear good clothes. He could have a roof over his head. Gold could buy anything—and he had it.

He had in mind a certain new cabin. He banged on the door until the owner shouted angrily and came with a gun in his hand.

"I'd like to buy this building," Joe Frail told him. "Right now."

A quarter of an hour later, he owned it by virtue of a note that could be cashed at the bank in the morning, and the recent owner was muttering to himself out in the street, with his possessions on the ground around him, wondering where to spend the rest of the night.

Joe Frail set his lantern on the bench that constituted all the cabin's furniture. He walked over to the wall and kicked it gently.

"A whim," he said aloud. "A very solid whim to keep the rain off."

Suddenly he felt younger than he had in many years, light-hearted, completely carefree, and all the wonderful world was his for the taking. He spent several minutes leaping into the air and trying to crack his heels together three times before he came down again. Then he threw back his head and laughed.

Lantern in hand, he set out to look for Wonder. When he met anyone, as he walked toward the Big Nugget, he lifted the lantern, peered into the man's face, and asked hopefully, "Are you an honest man?"

Evans, the banker, who happened to be out late, answered huffily, "Why, certainly!"

Wonder Russell was not in the saloon, but tawny-haired Julie was at the bar between two miners. She left them and came toward him smiling.

"I hear you sold out," she said. "Buy me a drink for luck?"

"I'll buy you champagne if they've got it," Joe Frail promised.

When their drinks were before them, she said, "Here's more luck of the same kind, Joe." Still smiling gaily, she whispered, "Go meet him at the livery stable." Then she laughed and slapped at him as if he had said something especially clever, and he observed that across the room Dusty Smith was playing cards and carefully not looking their way.

"I've got some more places to visit before morning," Joe Frail announced. "Got to find my partner and tell him we just bought a house."

He blew out the lantern just outside the door. It was better to stumble in the darkness than to have Dusty, if he was at all suspicious, be able to follow him conveniently.

Wonder was waiting at the livery stable corral.

"Got two horses in here, paid for and saddled," Wonder reported. "My war sack's on one of 'em, and Julie's stuff is on the other."

"I'll side you. What do you want done?"

"Take the horses out front of the Big Nugget. They're yours and mine, see? If anybody notices, we bought 'em because we made our pile and we've been drinking. Hell, nobody'll notice anyway."

"You're kind of fidgety," Joe Frail commented. "Then what?"

"Get the horses there and duck out of sight. That's all. I go in, buy Julie a drink, want her to come out front and look at the moon."

"There isn't any moon," Joe warned him.

"Is a drunk man going to be bothered by that?" Wonder answered. "I'll set 'em up for the boys and then go show Julie the moon while they're milling around. That's all."

"Good luck," Joe Frail said, and their hands gripped. "Good luck all the way for you and Julie."

"Thanks, partner," Wonder Russell said.

And where are you going, friend? Joe Frail wondered. Your future is none of my business, any more than your past.

He staggered as he led the horses down the gulch, in case anyone was watching. A fine performance, he told himself; too bad it is so completely wasted. Because who's going to care, except Dusty Smith, if Julie runs off and gets married?

He looped the lines over the hitch rail so that a single pull would dislodge them. Then he stepped aside and stood in the shadows, watching the door.

Wonder Russell came out, singing happily: "Oh, don't you remember sweet Betsy from Pike, who crossed the big desert with her lover Ike?"

Another good performance wasted, Joe Frail thought. The lucky miner with his claim sold, his pockets full of money, his belly full of whiskey—that was Wonder's role, and nobody would have guessed that he was cold sober.

Wonder capped his performance by falling on the steps and advising them to get out of the way and let a good man pass. Joe grinned and wished he could applaud.

Two men came out and, recognizing Russell, loudly implored him to let some golden luck rub off on them. He replied solemnly, "Dollar a rub, boys. Every little bit helps." They went away laughing as he stumbled through the lighted doorway.

Joe Frail loosened his guns in their holsters and was ready in the shadows. The best man helps the happy couple get away, he remembered, but this time not in a shower of rice with tin cans tied to the buggy and bunting on the team!

Wonder Russell was in the doorway with Julie beside him, laughing.

"Moon ain't that way," Russell objected. "It's over this way." He stepped toward the side of the platform where the saddled horses were.

Inside the lighted room a white-shirted gaunt man whirled with a gun in his hand, and Dusty Smith was a sure target in the light for three or four seconds while Joe Frail stood frozen with his guns untouched. Then the noise inside the saloon was blasted away by a gunshot, and Wonder Russell staggered and fell.

The target was still clear while Dusty Smith whirled and ran for the back door. A pistol was in Joe Frail's right hand, but the pistol and the hand might as well have been blocks of wood. He could not pull the trigger—until the miners roared their shock and anger and Dusty Smith had got away clean.

Joe Frail stood frozen, hearing Julie scream, seeing the men surge out the front door, knowing that some of them followed Dusty Smith out the back.

There were some shots out there, and then he was no longer frozen. His finger could pull the trigger for a useless shot into the dust. He ran to the platform where Julie was kneeling. He shouldered the men aside, shouting, "Let me by. I'm a doctor."

But Wonder Russell was dead.

"By God, Joe, I wish you'd have come a second sooner," moaned one of the men. "You could have got him from the street if you'd been a second sooner. It was Dusty Smith."

Someone came around the corner of the building and panted the news that Dusty had got clean away on a horse he must have had ready out back.

Joe Frail sat on his heels for a long time while Julie held Wonder's head in her arms and cried. One of the little group of miners still waiting asked, "You want some help, Joe? Where you want to take him?"

He looked down at Julie's bowed head.

My friend—but her lover, he remembered. She has a better right.

"Julie," he said. He stooped and helped her stand up. "Where do you want them to take him?"

"It doesn't matter," she said dully, "To my place, I guess."

Joe Frail commissioned the building of a coffin and bought burying clothes at the store—new suit and shirt that Wonder had not been rich long enough to buy for himself. Then, carrying a pick and shovel, he climbed the hill.

While he was digging, another friend of Wonder's came, then two more, carrying the tools of the same kind.

"I'd rather you didn't," Joe Frail told them. "This is something I want to do myself."

The men nodded and turned away.

When he stopped to rest, standing in the half-dug grave, he saw another man coming up. This one, on horseback, said without dismounting, "They got Dusty hiding about ten miles out. Left him for the wolves."

Joe Frail nodded. "Who shot him?"

"Stranger to me. Said his name was Frenchy Plante."

Joe went back to his digging. A stranger had done what he should have done, a stranger who could have no reason except that he liked killing.

Joe Frail put down his shovel and looked at his right hand. There was nothing wrong with it now. But when it should have pulled the trigger, there had been no power in it.

Because I shot a man in Utah, he thought, I can't shoot any more when it matters.

Julie climbed the hill before the grave was quite finished. She looked at the raw earth, shivering a little in the wind, and said, "He's ready."

Joe stood looking at her, but she kept her eyes down.

"Julie, you'll want to go away. You'll have money to go on—all the money for his claim. I'll ride with you as far as Elk Crossing, so you'll have someone to talk to if you want to talk. I'll go with you farther than that if you want."

"Maybe. Thanks. But I kind of think I'll stay in Skull Creek."

She turned away and walked down the hill.

Sometime that night, Julie cut her throat and died quietly and alone.

II

Elizabeth Armistead, the lost lady, came to Skull Creek the following summer.

About four o'clock one afternoon, a masked man rode out of the brush and held up a stage coach some forty miles south of the diggings. Just before this, the six persons aboard the stage were silently wrapped in their separate thoughts, except the stage line's itinerant blacksmith, who was uneasily asleep.

A tramp printer named Heffernan was dreaming of riches to be got by digging gold out of the ground. A whiskey salesman beside him was thinking vaguely of suicide, as he often did during a miserable journey.

The driver, alone on his high seat, squinted through

glaring light and swiped his sleeve across his face, where sand scratched the creases of his skin. He envied the passengers, protected from the sand-sharp wind, and was glad he was quitting the company. He was going back to Pennsylvania, get himself a little farm. Billy McGinnis was fifty-eight years old on that last day of his life.

The sick passenger, named Armistead, was five years older and was planning to begin a career of schoolteaching in Skull Creek. He had not intended to go there. He had thought he had a good thing in Elk Crossing, a more stable community with more children who needed a school. But another wandering scholar had got there ahead of him, and so he and his daughter Elizabeth traveled on toward the end of the world.

The world ended even before Skull Creek for Mr. Armistead.

His daughter Elizabeth, aged nineteen, sat beside him with her hands clasped and her eyes closed but her back straight. She was frightened, had been afraid for months, ever since people began to say that Papa was dishonest. This could not be, must not be, because Papa was all she had to look after and to look after her.

Papa was disgraced and she was going with him into exile. She took some comfort from her own stubborn, indignant loyalty. Papa had no choice, except of places to go. But Elizabeth had had a choice—she could have married Mr. Ellerby and lived as she had always lived, in comfort.

If Papa had told her to do so, or even suggested it, she would have married Mr. Ellerby. But he said it was for her to decide and she chose to go away with Papa. Now that she had an idea how harsh life could be for both of them, she was sick with guilt and felt that she had been selfish and willful. Mr. Ellerby had been willing to provide Papa with a small income, as long as he stayed away, and she had deprived him of it.

These two had no real idea about what the gold camp at Skull Creek would be like. The towns they had stopped in had been crude and rough, but they were at least towns, not camps. Some of the people in them intended to stay there, and so made an effort toward improvement.

Mr. Armistead was reasonably certain that there were enough children in Skull Creek for a small private school, and he took it for granted that their parents would be willing to pay for their education. He assumed, too, that he could teach them. He had never taught or done any other kind of work, but he had a gentleman's education.

He was bone-tired as well as sick and hot and dusty, but when he turned to Elizabeth and she opened her eyes, he smiled brightly. She smiled back, pretending that this endless, unendurable journey to an indescribable destination was a gay adventure.

He was a gentle, patient, hopeful man with good intentions and bad judgment. Until his financial affairs went wrong, he had known no buffeting. Catastrophe struck him before he acquired the protective calluses of the spirit that accustomed misfortune can produce.

All the capital they had left was in currency in a small silk bag that Elizabeth had sewed under her long, full traveling dress.

Elizabeth was wondering, just before the holdup, whether her father could stand it to travel the rest of the day and all night on the final lap of the journey. But the stage station would be dirty and the food would be horrible—travel experience had taught her to be pessimistic—and probably it would be better if they went on at once to Skull Creek where everything, surely, would be much, much pleasanter. Papa would see to that. She could not afford to doubt it.

Billy McGinnis, the driver, was already in imagination in Pennsylvania when a masked rider rode out of scanty timber at his right and shouted, "Stop there!"

Billy had been a hero more than once in his career, but he had no leanings that way any more. He cursed dutifully but hauled on the lines and stopped his four horses.

"Drop that shotgun," the holdup man told Billy. He obeyed, dropping the weapon carefully, making no startling movement.

"Everybody out!" yelled the masked man. "With your hands up."

The printer, as he half fell out of the coach (trying to keep his hands up but having to hang on with one of them), noted details about the bandit: tall from the waist up but sort of short-legged, dusty brown hat, dusty blue shirt, red bandanna over his face.

The whiskey salesman stumbled out hastily—he had

been through this a couple of times before and knew better than to argue—and wondered why a man would hold up a stage going into a gold camp. The sensible thing was to hold up one going out.

The blacksmith, suddenly wide awake, was the third to descend. He accepted the situation philosophically, having no money with him anyway, and not even a watch.

But Mr. Armistead tried to defend his daughter and all of them. He warned her, "Don't get out of the coach."

As he stepped down, he tried to fire a small pistol he had brought along for emergencies like this.

The bandit shot him.

Billy McGinnis, jerking on the lines to hold the frightened horses, startled the masked man into firing a second shot. As Billy pitched off the seat, the team lit out running, with Elizabeth Armistead screaming in the coach.

She was not in it any more when the three surviving men found it, overturned, with the frantic horses tangled in the lines, almost an hour later.

"Where the hell did the lady go to?" the blacksmith demanded. The other two agreed that they would have found her before then if she had jumped or fallen out during the runaway.

They did the best they could. They shouted and searched for another hour, but they found no sign of the lost lady. At the place where the coach had turned over, there was no more brush or scrubby timber by the road, only the empty space of the Dry Flats, dotted with greasewood.

One of the horses had a broken leg, so the whiskey salesman shot it. They unhitched the other three, mounted and searched diligently, squinting out across the flats, calling for the lost lady. But they saw nothing and heard no answering cry.

"The sensible thing," the printer recommended, "is to get on to the station and bring out more help."

"Take the canteen along?" suggested the whiskey salesman.

"If she gets back here, she'll need water," the blacksmith reminded him. "And she'll be scared. One of us better stay here and keep yelling."

They drew straws for that duty, each of them seeing himself as a hero if he won, the lady's rescuer and comforter. The blacksmith drew the short straw and stayed near the coach all night, with the canteen, but the lady did not come back.

He waited alone in the darkness, shouting until he grew hoarse and then voiceless. Back at the place of the holdup, Billy McGinnis and Mr. Armistead lay dead beside the road.

Doc Frail was shaving in his cabin, and the boy called Rune was sullenly preparing breakfast, when the news came about the lost lady.

Doc Frail was something of a dandy. In Skull Creek, cleanliness had no connection with godliness and neither did anything else. Water was mainly used for washing gold out of gravel, but Doc shaved every morning or had the barber do it.

Since he had Rune to slave for him, Doc had his boots blacked every morning and started out each day with most of the dried mud brushed off his coat and breeches. He was a little vain of his light brown curly hair, which he wore hanging below his shoulders. Nobody criticized this, because he had the reputation of having killed four men.

The reputation was unearned. He had killed only one, the man in Utah. He had failed to kill another, and so his best friend had died. These facts were nobody's business.

Doc Frail was quietly arrogant, and he was the loneliest man in the gold camp. He belonged to the aristocracy of Skull Creek, to the indispensable men like lawyers, the banker, the man who ran the assay office, and saloon owners. But these men walked in conscious rectitude and carried pistols decently concealed. Doc Frail wore two guns in visible holsters.

The other arrogant ones, who came and went, were the men of ill will, who dry-gulched miners on their way out with gold. They could afford to shoulder lesser men aside.

Doc Frail shouldered nobody except with a look. Where he walked, other men moved aside, greeting him respectfully: "Morning, Doc. . . . How are you, Doc? . . . Hear about the trouble down the gulch, Doc?"

He brandished no pistol (though he did considerable target practice, and it was impressively public) and said nothing very objectionable. But he challenged with a look.

His slow gaze on a stranger, from hat to boots, asked silently, "Do you amount to anything? Can you prove it?"

That was how they read it, and why they moved aside.

What he meant was, "Are you the man I'm waiting for, the man for whom I'll hang?" But nobody knew that except himself.

By Skull Creek standards, he lived like a king. His cabin was the most comfortable one in camp. It had a wood floor and a half partition to divide his living quarters from his consulting room.

The boy Rune, bent over the cookstove, said suddenly, "Somebody's hollering down the street."

"That's a fact," Doc answered, squinting in his shaving mirror.

Rune wanted, of course, to be told to investigate, but Doc wouldn't give him the satisfaction and Rune wouldn't give Doc the satisfaction of doing anything without command. The boy's slavery was Doc's good joke, and he hated it.

There was a pounding on the door and a man's voice shouting, "Doc Frail!"

Without looking away from his mirror, Doc said, "Well, open it," and Rune moved to obey.

A dusty man shouldered him out of the way and announced, "Stage was held up yestiddy, two men killed and a lady lost track of."

Doc wiped his razor and permitted his eyebrows to go up. "She's not here. One of us would have noticed."

The messenger growled. "The boys thought we better warn you. If they find her, you'll be needed."

"I'll keep it in mind," Doc said mildly.

"They're getting up a couple posses. I don't suppose you'd care to go?"

"Not unless there's a guarantee I'd find the lady. What's the other posse for?"

"To get the road agent. One of the passengers thinks he'd recognize him by the build. The driver, Billy McGinnis, was shot, and an old man, the father of the lost lady. Well, I'll be going."

The messenger turned away, but Doc could not quite let him go with questions still unasked.

"And how," he inquired, "would anybody be so careless as to lose a lady?"

"Team ran off with her in the coach," the man answered triumphantly. "When they caught up with it, she wasn't in it any more. She's lost somewheres on the Dry Flats."

The boy Rune spoke unwillingly, unable to remain silent and sullen: "Kin I go?"

"Sure," Doc said with seeming fondness. "Just saddle your horse."

The boy closed down into angry silence again. He had no horse; he had a healing wound in his shoulder and a debt to Doc for dressing it. Before he could have anything he wanted, he had to pay off in service his debt to Doc Frail—and the service would end only when Doc said so.

Doc Frail set out after breakfast to make his rounds—a couple of gunshot wounds, one man badly burned from falling into his own fire while drunk, a baby with colic, a miner groaning with rheumatism, and a dancehall girl with a broken leg resulting from a fall off a table.

The posses were setting out then with considerable confusion and some angry arguments over the last of the horses available at the livery stable.

"You can't have that bay!" the livery stable man was shouting. "That's a private mount and I dassent rent it!"

"You certainly dassent," Doc agreed. "The bay is mine," he explained to three scowling men. The explanation silenced them.

Doc had an amusing thought. Rune would sell his soul to go out with the searchers.

"Get the mare ready," Doc said, and turned back to his cabin.

"I've decided to rent you my horse," he told the sullen boy. "For your services for—let's see—one month in addition to whatever time I decide you have to work for me anyway."

It was a cruel offer, adding a month to a time that might be endless. But Rune, sixteen years old, was a gambler. He blinked and answered, "All right."

"Watch yourself," Doc warned, feeling guilty. "I don't want you crippled." The wound was two weeks old.

"I'll take good care of your property," the boy promised. "And the horse too," he added, to make his meaning clear. Doc Frail stood back, smiling a little, to see which crowd Rune would ride with. There was no organized law enforcement in the gravel gulches of Skull Creek, only occasional violent surges of emotion, with mob anger that usually dissolved before long.

If I were that kid, thought Doc, which posse would I choose, the road agent or the lady? He watched the boy ride to the milling group that was headed for the Dry Flats and was a little surprised. Doc himself would have chosen the road agent, he thought.

So would Rune, except that he planned to become a road agent himself if he ever got free of his bondage.

Rune dreamed, as he rode in the dust of other men's horses, of a bright, triumphant future. He dreamed of a time when he would swagger on any street in any town and other men would step aside. There would be whispers: "Look out for that fellow. That's Rune."

Doc Frail's passage in a group earned that kind of honor. Rune, hating him, longed to be like him.

Spitting dust, the boy dreamed of more immediate glory. He saw himself finding the lost lady out there on the Dry Flats in some place where less keen-eyed searchers had already looked. He saw himself comforting her, assuring her that she was safe now.

He was not alone in his dreaming. There were plenty of dreams in that bearded, ragged company of gold-seekers (ragged even if they were already rich, bedraggled with the dried mud of the creek along which sprawled the diggings). They were men who lived for tomorrow and the comforts they could find somewhere else when, at last, they pulled out of Skull Creek. They were rough and frantic seekers after fortune, stupendously hard workers, out now on an unaccustomed holiday.

Each man thought he was moved by compassion, by pity for the lost and lovely and mysterious lady whose name most of them did not yet know. If they went instead because of curiosity and because they needed change from the unending search and labor in the gravel gulches, no matter. Whatever logic moved them, they rode out to search, fifty motley, bearded men, each of whom might find the living prize.

Only half a dozen riders had gone over the sagebrush hills to look for the road agent who had killed two men. The miners of Skull Creek gambled for fortune but, except when drunk, seldom for their lives. About the worst that could happen in looking for the lost lady was that a man might get pretty thirsty. But go looking for an armed bandit—well, a fellow could get shot. Only the hardy adventurers went in that posse.

When the sun went down, nobody had found anybody, and four men were still missing when the rest of the lady's seekers gathered at the stage line's Station Three. The state company superintendent permitted a fire to be set to a pile of stovewood (freighted in at great expense, like the horse feed and water and everything else there) to make a beacon light. The missing men came in swearing just before midnight. Except for a few provident ones, most of the searchers shivered in their broken sleep, under inadequate and stinking saddle blankets.

They were in the saddle, angry and worried, before dawn of the day Elizabeth Armistead was found.

The sun was past noon when black-bearded Frenchy Plante stopped to tighten his cinch and stamp his booted feet. He pulled off a blue kerchief that protected his nose and mouth from the wind-borne grit, shook the kerchief and tied it on again. He squinted into the glare and, behind a clump of greasewood, glimpsed movement.

A rattler, maybe. Might as well smash it. Frenchy liked killing snakes. He had killed two men, too, before coming to Skull Creek, and one since—a man whose name he found out later was Dusty Smith.

He plodded toward the greasewood, leading his horse, and the movement was there—not a rattler but the wind-whipped edge of a blue skirt.

"Hey!" he shouted, and ran toward her.

She lay face down, with her long, curling hair, once glossy brown, dull and tangled in the sand. She lay flat and drained and lifeless, like a dead animal. Elizabeth Armistead was not moving. Only her skirt fluttered in the hot wind.

"Lady!" he said urgently. "Missus, here's water."

She did not hear. He yanked the canteen from his saddle and pulled out the stopper, knelt beside her and said again, "Lady, I got water."

When he touched her shoulder, she moved convulsively. Her shoulders jerked and her feet tried to run. She made a choking sound of fear.

But when he held the canteen to her swollen, broken lips, she had life enough to clutch at it, to knock it accidentally aside so that some of the water spilled on the thankless earth. Frenchy grabbed the canteen and set it again to her lips, staring at her face with distaste.

Dried blood smeared it, because sand cut into the membranes of the nose like an abrasive. Her face was bloated with the burn of two days of sun, and her anguished lips were shapeless.

Frenchy thought, I'd rather be dead. Aloud he said, "No more water now for a minute. Pretty soon you can have more, Missus."

The lost lady reached blindly for the canteen, for she was blind from the glaring sun, and had been even before she lost her bonnet.

"You gotta wait a minute," Frenchy warned. "Don't be scared, Missus. I'm going to fire this here gun for a signal, call the other boys in. We'll get you to the stage station in no time."

He fired twice into the air, then paused. Two shots meant "found dead." Then he fired the third that changed the pattern and told the other searchers, listening with their mouths open slightly, that the lady had been found living.

The first man to get there was tall, fair-haired Rune, aching with sunburn and the pain of his wound, which had pulled open. When Frenchy found the lady, Rune had been just beyond a little rise of barren ground, stubbornly dreaming as he rode.

I should have been the one, he thought with dull anger. I should have been the one, but it's always somebody else.

He looked at the lady, drained and half dead, dull with dust. He saw the frail and anxious hands groping for the canteen, clutching it as Frenchy guided it to her mouth. He saw the burned, blind face. He said, "Oh, God!"

Frenchy managed a friendly chuckle.

"You're going to be all right, Missus. Get you to a doctor right away. That's a promise, Missus. Frenchy Plante's promise."

He put his name on her, he staked his claim, Rune thought. Who cares? She's going to die anyway.

"I'll go for Doc," Rune said, turning his horse toward the stage station.

But he couldn't go for Doc, after all. He took the news to Station Three; he had that much triumph. Then there was vast confusion. The stage line superintendent ordered a bed made up for the lady, and it was done—that is, the stocktender took the blankets off his bunk and gave them a good shaking and put them back on again. Riders began to come in, shouting, "How is she? Who found her?"

By the time Frenchy Plante arrived, with the lady limp in his arms, and an escort of four other searchers who had gone in the direction of his signal shots, it was discovered that nobody at all had started for Skull Creek to get the doctor.

Rune sat on the ground in the scant shade of the station with his head bowed on his knees, as near exhausted as he had ever been in his life. His shoulder wound hurt like fury, and so did his stomach whenever he remembered how the lost lady looked.

Frenchy Plante was the hero again. He borrowed a fresher horse and rode on to Skull Creek.

He found Doc Frail at home but occupied with a patient, a consumptive dancer from the Big Nugget. With her was another woman who looked up scowling, as Doc did, when Frenchy came striding in.

"Found the lady, Doc," Frenchy announced. "Want you to come right away."

"I have a patient here," Doc said in controlled tones, "as you will see if you're observant. This lady also needs me."

The consumptive girl, who had seldom been called a lady, was utterly still, lying on Doc's own cot. Her friend was holding her hands, patting them gently.

"Come out a minute," Frenchy urged, "so I can tell you."

Doc closed the door behind him and faced Frenchy in the street.

Frenchy motioned toward the door. "What's Luella doing in your place?"

"Dying," Doc answered. "She didn't want to do it where she works."

"How soon can you come? The lost lady's real bad. Got her to the stage station, but she's mighty sick."

"If she's as sick as this one," Doc said, "it wouldn't do her any good for me to start out there anyway."

"Damned if you ain't a hard-hearted scoundrel," commented Frenchy, half shocked and half admiring. "You ain't doing Luella no good, are you?"

"No. Nobody ever has. But I'm not going to leave her now."

Frenchy shrugged. "How long'll it be?"

"Couple hours, maybe. Do you expect me to strangle her to hurry it along?"

Frenchy's eyes narrowed. "I don't expect nothing. Get out there when you feel like it. I done my duty anyhow."

Was that a reminder, Doc wondered as he watched Frenchy ride on to the Big Nugget, that once you did a duty that should have been mine? That you killed Dusty Smith—a man you didn't even know—after I failed?

Doc Frail went back into his cabin.

A few hours later, Luella released him by dying.

It was dawn when he flung himself off a rented horse at the station and stumbled over a couple of the men sleeping there on the ground.

The lost lady, her face glistening with grease that the stocktender had provided, was quiet on a bunk, with a flickering lamp above her on a shelf. Cramped and miserable on his knees by the bunk was Rune, whose wrist she clutched with one hand. Her other arm cradled Frenchy's canteen.

There was a spot of blood on Rune's shoulder, soaked through Doc's neat dressing, and he was almost too numb to move, but he looked up with hostile triumph.

"She let me be here," he said.

"Now you can go back to Skull Creek," Doc told him, stating a command, not permission. "I'll stay here until she can be moved."

Dispossessed, as he had often been before, but triumphant as he had longed to be, Rune moved away, to tell the sleepy, stirring men that Doc had come. He was amused, when he started back to the gold camp a little later, by the fact that he still rode Doc's mare and Doc would be furious when he discovered it.

The searchers who delayed at Station Three because of curiosity were relieved at the way Doc Frail took charge there. The lost lady seemed to be glad of his presence, too. He treated her burns and assured her in a purring, professional tone, "You'll get your sight back, madam.

The blindness is only temporary, I can promise you that."

To the clustering men, he roared like a lion: "Clean this place up—she's got to stay here a few days. Get something decent for her to eat, not this stage-line diet. That's enough to kill an ox. Clean it up, I say—with water. Don't raise a lot of dust."

The superintendent, feeling that he had done more than his duty by letting the stocktender feed the search posse, demurred about wasting water.

"Every drop has to be hauled clear from Skull Creek," he reminded Doc, who snapped back, "Then hitch up and start hauling!"

The stocktender was caught between Doc's anger and the superintendent's power to fire him. He said in a wheedling voice, "Gonna make her some good soup, Doc. I shot a jackrabbit and had him in the pot before he quit kicking."

"Get out of here," snarled Doc. He bent again to the burned, anguished lady.

"You will be able to see again," he promised her. "And your burns will heal."

But your father is dead and buried, and Skull Creek is no place for you, my dear.

III

Frenchy Plante was still around when Rune got back to Skull Creek. Frenchy swaggered, as he had a right to do, being the man who had found the lost lady. But he spent only half a day or so telling the details over. Then he went back to the diggings, far up the gulch, to toil again in the muck and gravel. He had colors there, he was making wages with a small sluice, he had high hopes of getting rich. It had happened before.

The curious of Skull Creek left their own labors to stand by and get the story. When Frenchy was out of the way, Rune became the belligerent center of attention. He had just finished applying a bunchy bandage to his painful shoulder when he jumped guiltily at a pounding on Doc's door. He finished putting his shirt on before he went to take the bar down.

"Doc ain't back yet?" the bearded caller asked.

Rune shook his head.

"Expecting him?" the man insisted.

"He don't tell me his plans."

The man looked anxious. "Look here, I got a boil on my neck needs lancing. Don't suppose you could do it?"

"Anybody could do it. Wrong, maybe. Doc could do it right—I guess."

The man sidled in. "Hell, you do it. Ain't he got some doctor knives around, maybe?"

Rune felt flattered to have someone show confidence in him.

"I'll find something," he offered. He did not know the name of the thing he found, but it was thin and sharp and surgical. He wiped it thoroughly on a piece of clean bandage and, after looking over the boil on the man's neck, opened it up with a quick cut.

The patient said, "Wow!" under his breath and shuddered. "Feels like you done a good job," he commented. "Now tie it up with something, eh?"

He stretched out his booted legs while he sat back in Doc's best chair and waited for Rune to find bandaging material that pleased him.

"You was right on the spot when they found her, I hear," he hinted.

"I was second man to get there," Rune answered, pretending that to be second was nothing at all, but knowing that it was something, knowing that the man's boil could have waited, or that anyone could have opened it.

"Heard she's a foreigner, don't talk no English," the man hinted.

"She didn't say nothing to me," Rune answered. "Couldn't talk any language. She's an awful sick lady."

The man touched his bandage and winced. "Well, I guess that fixes it. Your fee the same as Doc Frail's, I suppose?"

As coolly as if he were not a slave, Rune nodded, and the man hauled a poke from his pocket, looking around for the gold scales.

For a little while after he had gone, Rune still hated him, even with the man's payment of gold dust stowed away in his pocket. So easy to get a doctor—or somebody with a knife, anyway—when you had the dust to pay for it! So easy to enter servitude if you were penniless and had to have a shoulder wound dressed and thought you were going to die!

Before the morning was half done, another visitor came. This time it was a woman, and she was alone. The ladies of Skull Creek were few and circumspect, armored with virtue. Rune guessed that this one, wife of Flaunce the storekeeper, would not have visited Doc Frail's office without a companion if she had expected to find Doc there.

But she asked in her prissy way, "Is the doctor in?" and clucked when Rune shook his head.

"Well, I can see him another day," she decided. "It was about some more of that cough medicine he gave me for my little ones."

And what for do they need cough medicine in warm weather? Rune would have liked to ask her. He said only, "He ain't here."

"He's out at the stage station, I suppose, with the poor lady who was rescued. Have you heard how she's getting along?"

"She's alive but blind and pretty sick," he said. "She'll get her sight back afterwhile."

"I don't suppose anyone knows why she was coming here?" the woman probed.

"Was with her pa, that's all I know. He's dead and she can't talk yet," Rune reported, knowing that what Flaunce's wife really wanted to know was, Is she a lady or one of those others? Was he really her father?

"Dear me," she asked, "is that blood on your shirt?"

Another one, then, who did not know his shame.

"I shot a rabbit, ma'am," he lied. That satisfied her, even though a man would not normally carry a freshly killed rabbit over his shoulder.

The woman decided the cough medicine could wait and minced up the deep-rutted street of the gulch, carefully looking neither to the right nor left.

At the store, buying supplies for Doc's account, Rune inquired, "Any news of the other posse? Them that was after the road agent?"

"It's bigger'n it was, now they found the lost lady. Some of the men figure there's got to be a lesson taught."

"If they catch him, that is," Rune suggested, and the storekeeper nodded, sighing, "If they catch him."

In Doc's absence, Rune carried out a project he had in mind, now that there was no fear of interruption by Doc himself. He searched with scrupulous care for the place where Doc hid his gold.

There should be some in the cabin somewhere. Doc had much more than a physician's income, for he had grubstaked many miners, and a few of them had struck it rich. Doc could afford to be careless with his little leather pokes of nuggets and dust, but apparently he wasn't careless. Rune explored under every loose board and in every cranny between the logs, but he didn't find anything. He did not plan to take the gold yet anyway. It could wait until he was free to leave.

And why don't I pull out now? he wondered. Two men that morning had asked if he wanted to work for wages, and he had turned them down.

It was not honor that kept him there—he couldn't afford the luxury of honor. It was not his wound; he knew now he wasn't going to die of that. The reason he was going to stay, he thought, was just because Doc expected him to run out. He would not give his master that much satisfaction.

He was Rune, self-named, the world's enemy. The world owed him a debt that he had never had much luck in collecting.

He thought he was going to collect when he came to Skull Creek in triumph driving a freight team and carrying his whole fortune—eighty dollars in gold—inside a canvas belt next to his skin. He drew his pay, had a two-dollar meal, and set out for the barber shop.

There was music coming from the Big Nugget. He went in to see the source. Not for any other purpose; Rune spent no money that he didn't have to part with. He did not mean to gamble, but while he watched, a miner looked up and said, scowling, "This is a man's game."

He began to lose, and he could not lose, he must not lose, because if you did not have money you might as well be dead.

When he left the saloon, he was numb and desperate and dead.

Toward morning he tried to rob a sluice. He was not yet hungry, but he would be hungry sometime. He had been hungry before and he was afraid of it. He lurked in shadows, saw the sluice had no armed guard. He was scrabbling against the lower riffles, feeling for nuggets, when a shot came without warning. He fell, pulled himself up and ran, stumbling.

Twenty-four hours later he came out of hiding. He was hungry then, and his shoulder was still bleeding. By that time, he knew where the doctor lived, and he waited, huddling outside the door, while the sun came up.

Doc, in his underwear, opened the door at last to get his lungs full of fresh air and, seeing the tall boy crouching on the step, said, "Well!" Noticing the blood-stiffened shirt he stepped back, sighing, "Well, come in. I didn't hear you knock."

Rune stood up carefully, trying not to move the injured shoulder, holding it with his right hand.

"I didn't knock," he said, hating this man of whom he must ask charity. "I can't pay you. But I got hurt."

"Can't pay me, eh?" Doc Frail was amused. "Guess you haven't heard that the only patients who didn't pay me are buried up on the hill."

Rune believed his grim joke.

"You've been hiding out with this for quite a spell," Doc guessed, as he teased the shirt away from the wound, and the boy shuddered. "You wouldn't hide out without a reason, would you?"

He was gentle from habit, but Rune did not recognize gentleness. He was being baited and he was helpless. He gave a brazen answer:

"I got shot trying to rob a sluice."

Doc, working rapidly, commented with amusement, "So now I'm harboring a criminal! And doing it for nothing, too. How did you figure on paying me, young fellow?"

The patient was too belligerent, needed to be taken down a peg.

"If I could pay you, I wouldn't have tackled the sluice, would I?" the boy demanded. "I wouldn't have waited so long to see you, would I?"

"You ask too damn many questions," Doc grunted.

"Hold still. . . . Your wound will heal all right. But of course you'll starve first."

Sullen Rune made no answer.

Doc Frail surveyed him. "I can use a servant. A gentleman should have one. To black his boots and cook his meals—you can cook, I hope?—and swamp out the cabin."

Rune could not recognize kindness, could not believe it, could not accept it. But that the doctor should extract service for every cent of a debt not stated—that he could understand.

"For how long?" he bargained, growling.

Doc Frail could recognize what he thought was ingratitude.

"For just as long as I say," he snapped. "It may be a long time. It may be forever. If you bled to death, you'd be dead forever."

That was how they made the bargain. Rune got a home he needed but did not want to accept. Doc got a slave who alternately amused and annoyed him. He resolved not to let the kid go until he learned to act like a human being—or until Doc himself became too exasperated to endure him anymore. Rune would not ask for freedom, and Doc did not know when he would offer it.

There was one thing that Rune wanted from him: skill with a gun. Doc's reputation as a marksman trailed from him like a tattered banner. Men walked wide of him and gave him courtesy.

But I won't lower myself by asking him to teach me, Rune kept promising himself. There were depths to which even a slave did not sink.

A letter came from Doc Frail the day after Rune returned to Skull Creek. It was brought by a horseback rider who came in from Station Three ahead of the stage.

Rune had never before in his life received a letter, but he took it as casually as if he had had a thousand. He turned it over and said, "Well, thanks," and turned away, unwilling to let the messenger know he was excited and puzzled.

"Ain't you going to read it?" the man demanded. "Doc said it was mighty important."

"I suppose you read it already?" Rune suggested.

The man sighed. "I can't read writing. Not that writing, anyhow. Print, now, I can make out with print, but not writing. Never had much schooling."

"He writes a bad hand," Rune agreed, mightily relieved. "Maybe the store man, he could make it out."

So there was no need to admit that he could not read, either. Even Flaunce, the storekeeper, had a little trouble, tracing with his finger, squinting over his glasses.

Doc had no suspicion that his servant could not read. He had never thought about the matter. If he had known, he might not have begun the letter, "White Sambo."

Hearing that, his slave reddened with shame and anger, but the store man merely commented, "Nickname, eh? 'White Sambo: Miss Elizabeth Armistead will arrive in Skull Creek in three or four days. She is still weak and blind. She must have shelter and care. I will provide the care, and the shelter will have to be in the cabin of the admirable and respectable Ma Fisher across the street from my own mansion.

" 'Convey my regards to Mrs. Fisher and make all the necessary arrangements. Nothing will be required of Mrs. Fisher except a temporary home for Miss Armistead, who will of course pay for it.' "

The storekeeper and the messenger stared at Rune.

"I'm glad it ain't me that has to ask Ma Fisher a thing like that," the messenger remarked. "I'd as soon ask favors of a grizzly bear."

Flaunce was kinder. "I'll go with you, son. She wants a sack of flour anyhow, over to the restaurant. I'll kind of back you up—or pick up the pieces."

Ma Fisher served meals furiously in a tent restaurant to transients and miners who were tired of their own cooking in front of the wickiups along the gulch. She seldom had any hired help—too stingy and too hard to get along with, it was said. Her one luxury was her cabin, opposite Doc's, weather-tight and endurable even in cold weather. Most of the population, willing to live miserably today in the hope of a golden tomorrow, housed itself in shacks or lean-to's or caves dug into the earth, eked out with poles and rocks and sods.

Ma Fisher fumed a little when she was informed that the lost lady would be her guest, but she was flattered, and besides she was curious.

"I won't have time to wait on her, I want that understood," she warned. "And I won't stand for no foolishness, either."

"She's too sick for foolishness, I'd say," the store-keeper said soothingly. "Hasn't got her sight back yet. She mighty near died out there, you know."

"Well," Ma Fisher agreed without enthusiasm. "Well."

The first words Elizabeth Armistead spoke in the stage station were, faintly, "Where is Papa?"

"Your father is dead," Doc Frail answered gently. "He was shot during the holdup."

Why didn't she know that? She had seen it happen.

She answered with a sigh: "No." It was not an exclamation of shock or grief. It was a soft correction. She refused to believe, that was all.

"They buried him there by the road, along with the driver," Doc Frail said.

She said again, with more determination, "No!" And after a pause she pleaded, "Where is Papa?"

"He is dead," Doc repeated. "I am sorry to tell you this, Miss Armistead."

He might as well not have told her. She did not accept it.

She waited patiently in darkness for someone to give a reasonable explanation for her father's absence. She did not speak again for several hours because of her weakness and because of her swollen, broken lips.

Doc wished he could give her the comfort of a sponge bath, but he did not dare offend her by offering to do so himself, and she was not strong enough to move her arms. She lay limp, sometimes sleeping.

When he judged that the girl could better bear the trip to Skull Creek in a wagon than she could stand the stage station any longer, he explained that she would stay at Mrs. Fisher's—a very respectable woman, she would be perfectly safe there—until she could make plans for going back East.

"Thank you," the lost lady answered. "And Papa is in Skull Creek waiting?"

Doc frowned. The patient was beginning to worry him. "Your father is dead, you know. He was shot in the holdup."

She did not answer that.

"I will try again to comb your hair," Doc offered. "Tomorrow you can wash, if you want to try it. There will be a blanket over the window, and one over the door, and I will be outside to make sure no one tries to come in."

Her trunk was there, brought from the wrecked coach. He searched out clean clothes that she could put on, and carefully he combed her long, dark, curling hair. He braided it, not very neatly, and wound the two thick braids up over her head.

IV

The wagon was slow, but Doc Frail preferred it for his patient; she could ride easier than in the coach. He ordered the wagon bed well padded with hay, and she leaned back against hay covered with blankets. He had a canvas shade rigged to protect her from the sun. The stage-line superintendent himself was the driver—mightily relieved to be getting this woman to Skull Creek where she would be no more concern of his.

Doc Frail had not looked ahead far enough to expect the escort that accompanied them the last mile of the journey. He sat with the lost lady in the wagon bed, glaring at the curious, silent miners who came walking or riding or who stood waiting by the road.

None of them spoke, and there was no jostling. They only stared, seeing the lady in a blue dress, with a white cloth over her eyes. From time to time, the men nearest the wagon fell back to let the others have their turn.

Once, Doc got a glimpse of the boy, Rune, lanky and awkward, walking and staring with the rest. Doc scowled, and the boy looked away.

For a while, the doctor closed his eyes and knew how it must be for the girl who could hear but could not see. The creak of the wagon, the sound of the horses' hoofs—too many horses; she must know they were accompanied. The soft sound of many men's feet walking. Even the restless sound of their breathing.

The lady did not ask questions. She could not hide. Her hands were clasped tightly together in her lap.

"We have an escort," Doc murmured. "An escort of honor. They are glad to see that you are safe and well."

She murmured a response.

At the top of the hill, where the road dipped down to the camp, they lost their escort. The riders and the walkers stepped aside and did not follow. Doc Frail glanced up as the wagon passed under the great, outthrust bough of the gnarled tree and felt a chill tingle the skin along his spine.

Well, the fellow deserved the hanging he would get. Doc regretted, however, that the mob that would be coming in from the north would have to pass Ma Fisher's cabin to reach the hanging tree. He hoped they would pass in decent silence. But he knew they would not.

Rune waited near the tree with the other men, torn between wanting to help the lost lady into the cabin and wanting to see the road agent hang. Whichever thing he did, he would regret not having done the other. He looked up at the great bough, shivered, and decided to stay on the hill.

He could see Doc and the stage superintendent help Miss Armistead down from the wagon. As they took her into Ma Fisher's cabin, he could see something else: dust in the distance.

A man behind him said, "They're bringing him in."

Rune had two good looks at the road agent before he died and one brief, sickening glance afterward. The angry miners were divided among themselves about hanging the fellow. The men who had pursued him, caught him, and whipped him until his back was bloody were satisfied and tired. Four of them even tried to defend him, standing with rifles cocked, shouting, "Back! Get back! He's had enough."

He could not stand; men pulled him off his horse and held him up as his body dropped and his knees sagged.

But part of the crowd roared, "Hang him! Hang him!" and shoved on. The mob was in three parts—those for hanging, those against it, and those who had not made up their minds.

Rune glimpsed him again through the milling miners beneath the tree. The posse men had been pushed away from him, their guns unfired, and men who had not pursued him were bringing in a rope.

The black-bearded giant, Frenchy Plante, tied the noose and yanked the road agent to his feet. Frenchy's roar came over the rumbling of the mob: "It's his fault the lost lady pridnear died! Don't forget that, boys!"

That was all they needed. Order came out of chaos. Fifty men seized the rope and at Frenchy's signal "Pull!" jerked the drooping, bloody-backed road agent off the ground. Rune saw him then for the third time, dangling.

A man beside him said knowingly, "That's the most humane way, really—pull him up all standing."

"How do you know?" Rune sneered. "You ever get killed that way?"

With the other men, he walked slowly down the hill. He waited in Doc's cabin until Doc came in.

"You had to watch," Doc said. "You had to see a man die."

"I saw it," Rune growled.

"And the lost lady might as well have. She might as well have been looking, because Ma Fisher kindly told her what the noise was about. And was offended, mind you, when I tried to shut her up!"

Doc unbuckled his gun belt and tossed it on his cot.

"You're going to wait on Miss Armistead," he announced. "I told her you would do her errands, anything that will make her a little easier. Do you hear me, boy? She keeps asking for her father. She keeps saying, 'Where is Papa?' "

Rune stared. "Didn't you tell her he's dead?"

"Certainly I told her! She doesn't believe it. She doesn't remember the holdup or the team running away. All she can remember is that something happened so the coach stopped, and then she was lost, running somewhere, and after a long time a man gave her a drink of water and took the canteen away again."

"Did she say where she's going when she gets her sight back?" Rune asked.

Doc let out a gusty breath. "She has no place to go. She says she can't go back because she has to wait for Papa. He was going to start a school here, and she was going to keep house for him. She has no place to go, but she can't stay alone in Skull Creek. It's unthinkable."

Ma Fisher came flying over to get Doc.

"The girl's crying and it'll be bad for her eyes," she said.

Doc asked coolly, "And why is she crying?"

"I'm sure I don't know," Ma answered, obviously injured. "I wasn't even talking to her. She started to sob, and when I asked her what was the matter, she said, 'Papa must be dead, or he would have been waiting here to meet me.' "

"Progress," Doc growled. "We're making progress." He went out and left Ma Fisher to follow if she cared to do so.

Doc was up before daylight next morning.

"When Ma Fisher leaves that cabin," Doc told Rune, when he woke him, "you're going to be waiting outside the door. If the lady wants you inside for conversation, you will go in and be as decently sociable as possible. If she wants to be alone, you will stay outside. Is that all perfectly clear?"

It was as clear as it was hateful. Rune would have taken delight in being the lady's protector if he had had any choice. (And Doc would, too, except that he wanted to protect her reputation. It wouldn't look good for him to be in the cabin with her except on brief professional visits.)

"Nursemaid," Rune muttered sourly.

Ma Fisher scowled when she found him waiting outside her door, but Miss Armistead said she would be glad of his company.

The lost lady was timid, helpless, but gently friendly, sitting in the darkened cabin, groping now and then for the canteen that had been Frenchy's.

Rune asked, "You want a cup to drink out of?" and she smiled faintly.

"I guess it's silly," she answered, "but water tastes better from this canteen."

Rune kept silent, not knowing how to answer.

"Doctor Frail told me your first name," the lost lady said, "but not your last."

"Rune is all," he answered. He had made it up, wanting to be a man of mystery.

"But everybody has two names," she chided gently. "You must have another."

She was indeed ignorant of frontier custom or she would not make an issue of a man's name. Realizing that, he felt infinitely superior and therefore could be courteous.

"I made it up, ma'am," he told her. "There's lots of

men here go by names they wasn't born with. It ain't a good idea to ask questions about folks' names." Then, concerned lest he might have offended her, he struggled on to make conversation:

"There's a song about it. 'What was your name in the States? Was it Johnson or Olson or Bates?' Goes that way, sort of."

The lady said, "Oh, my goodness. Doctor Frail didn't make up his name, I'm sure of that. Because a man wouldn't take a name like that, would he?"

"A man like Doc might," Rune decided. The idea interested him. "Doc is a sarcastic fellow."

"Never to me," Miss Armistead contradicted softly. "He is the soul of kindness! Why, he even realized that I might wish for someone to talk to. And you are kind, too, Rune, because you came."

To get her off that subject, Rune asked, "Was there any errands you'd want done or anything?"

"Doctor Frail said he would send my meals in, but I am already so much obligated to him that I'd rather not. Could you cook for me, Rune, until I can see to do it myself?"

"Sure," he agreed. "But I cook for Doc anyhow. Just as easy to bring it across the street."

"No, I'd rather pay for my own provisions." She was firm about that, with the pathetic stubbornness of a woman who for the first time must make decisions and stick to them even if they are wrong.

"I have money," she insisted. "I can't tell what denomination the bills are, of course. But you can tell me."

Poor, silly lady, to trust a stranger so! But Rune honestly identified the bills she held out.

"Take the five dollars," she requested, "and buy me whatever you think would be nice to eat. That much money should last for several days, shouldn't it?"

Rune swallowed a protest and murmured, "Kind of depends on what you want. I'll see what they got at Flaunce's." He backed toward the door.

"I must be very businesslike," Miss Armistead said with determination. "I have no place to go, you know, so I must earn a living. I shall start a school here in Skull Creek."

Arguing about that was for Doc, not for his slave. Rune did not try.

"Doc's going in his cabin now," he reported, and fled across the street for instructions.

The storekeeper's inquisitive wife got in just ahead of him, and he found Doc explaining, "The lady is still too weak for the strain of entertaining callers, Mrs. Flaunce. The boy here is acting as amateur nurse, because she needs someone with her—she can't see, you know. But it would not be wise for anyone to visit her yet."

"I see," Mrs. Flaunce said with cold dignity. "Yes, I understand perfectly." She went out with her head high, not glancing at the cabin across the street.

Doc thus cut the lost lady off from all decent female companionship. The obvious conclusion to be drawn—which Mrs. Flaunce passed on to the other respectable women of the camp—was that the doctor was keeping the mysterious Miss Armistead. Ma Fisher's stern respectability was not enough to protect her, because Ma herself was strange. She chose to earn her living in a community where no sensible woman would stay if she wasn't married to a man who required it.

When Mrs. Flaunce was gone, Rune held out the greenback.

"She wants me to buy provisions with that. Enough for several days, she says."

Doc's eyebrows went up. "She does, eh? With five dollars? Why, that'd buy her three cans of fruit, wouldn't it? And how much is Flaunce getting for sugar, say?"

"Dollar a pound."

Doc scowled thoughtfully. "This is a delicate situation. We don't know how well fixed she is, but she doesn't know anything about the cost of grub in Skull Creek. And I don't want her to find out. Understand?"

Rune nodded. For once, he was in agreement with his master.

Doc reached into his coat pocket and brought out a leather poke of dust.

"Put that on deposit to her account at the store," he ordered.

"Lady coming in on the stage wouldn't have gold in a poke, would she?" Rune warned.

Doc said with approval, "Sometimes you sound real smart. Take it to the bank, get currency for it, and take the currency to Flaunce's. And just pray that Ma Fisher doesn't take a notion to talk about the price of grub. Let the lady keep her stake to use getting out of here as soon as she's able.''

A week passed before he realized that Elizabeth Armistead could not leave Skull Creek.

V

Elizabeth could find her way around the cabin, groping, stepping carefully so as not to fall over anything. She circled sometimes for exercise and to pass the long, dark time and because she did not feel strong enough to think about important matters.

The center of her safe, circumscribed world was the sagging double bed where she rested and the table beside it, on which was the water bucket. She still clung to Frenchy Plante's canteen and kept it beside her pillow but only when she was alone so that no one would guess her foolish fear about thirst. But every few minutes she fumbled for the dipper in the bucket. She was dependent on strangers for everything, of course, but most important of them was Rune, who filled the water bucket at the creek that he said was not far outside the back door.

She had explored the cabin until she knew it well, but its smallness and scanty furnishings still shocked her. Papa's house back East had had nine rooms, and until his money began to melt away, there had been a maid as well as a cook.

She moved cautiously from the table a few steps to the front door—rough planks with a strong wooden bar to lock it from the inside; around the wall to a bench that Rune had placed so she would not hurt herself on the tiny stove; then to the back door.

But the need for decision gnawed at her mind and made her head ache.

"You must go back East just as soon as you can travel," Doctor Frail had said—how many times?

But how could she travel again when she remembered the Dry Flats that had to be crossed? How could she go without Papa, who was dead, they kept telling her?

The cabin was uncomfortably warm, but she could not sit outside the back door, where there was grass, unless

Rune was there. And she must not open the door unless she knew for sure who was outside.

She could not go back East yet, no matter what they said. To stay in Skull Creek was, of course, an imposition on these kind people, but everything would work out all right after a while—except for Papa, who they said was dead.

She remembered what Papa had said when his investments were dwindling.

"We do what we must," he had told her with his gentle smile when he made the hard decision to go West. And so his daughter would do what she must.

I must find a place for the school, she reminded herself. Perhaps Mrs. Fisher will let me use this cabin. I must offer her pay, of course, very tactfully so she will not be offended.

It was a relief to keep her mind busy in the frightening darkness, safe in the cabin with an unknown, raucous settlement of noisy men just outside the door. There were women, too; she could hear their laughter and screaming sometimes from the saloon down the street. But ladies did not think about those women except to pity them.

They were very strange, these people who were looking after her—Doc, who sounded strained and cross; Rune, whose voice was sullen and doubtful; Mrs. Fisher, who talked very little and came to the cabin only to groan into bed. Elizabeth was a little afraid of all of them, but she reminded herself that they were really very kind.

There was cautious knocking on the door, and she called out, "Yes?" and turned. Suddenly she was lost in the room, not sure of the position of the door. Surely the knocking was at the back? And why should any of them come that way, where the little grassy plot went only down to the creek?

She stumbled against a bench, groping. The knocking sounded again as she reached the door. But she was cautious. "Who is it?" she called, with her hand on the bar.

A man's voice said, "Lady! Lady, just let me in."

Elizabeth stopped breathing. The voice was not Doc Frail's nor Rune's. But it was cordial, enticing: "Lady, you ever seen a poke of nuggets? I got a poke of gold right here. Lady, let me in.''

She trembled and sank down on the floor in her darkness, cowering. The voice coaxed, "Lady? Lady?"

She did not dare to answer. She did not dare to cry. After a long time the pounding and the coaxing stopped.

She could not escape any more by planning for the school. She was remembering the long horror of thirst, and the noise the mob had made, going past to hang a man on a tree at the top of the hill. She hid her burned face in her trembling hands, crouching by the barred door, until a familiar and welcome voice called from another direction, "It's me. Rune.''

She groped to the front door, reached for the bar. But was the voice familiar and therefore welcome? Or was this another importunate, lying stranger? With her hand on the unseen wooden bar, she froze, listening, until he called again. His voice sounded concerned: "Miss Armistead, are you all right in there?"

This was Rune. She could open the door. He was not offering a poke of nuggets, he was only worried about her welfare.

"I was frightened," she said as she opened the door.

"You're safer that way in Skull Creek," he said. "Anything you want done right now?"

"You are so kind," she said gently. "No, there is nothing. I have plenty of drinking water in the bucket. Oh—if you go to the store, perhaps there would be some potatoes and eggs?"

After a pause he said, "I'll ask 'em." (A month ago there had been a shipment of eggs; Doc had mentioned it. There had not been a potato in camp since Rune came there.)

"Doc says to tell you you'll have your unveiling this evening, get your eyes open. I got to go find him now, give him a message from the Crocodile.''

"The—what?"

"Ma Fisher, I mean." She could hear amusement in his voice.

"Why, it's not nice to speak of her so. She is very kind to me, letting me share her home!"

There was another pause. He said, "Glad to hear it," and "I'll go find Doc now. He went to get a haircut.''

Doc's haircut was important. He went often to the barbershop for a bath, because he could afford to be clean, but never before in Skull Creek had he let scissors touch his hair, hanging in glossy waves below his shoulders.

A miner might let his hair and whiskers grow, bushy and matted, but Doc Frail was different. His long hair was no accident, and it was clean. He wore it long as a challenge, a quiet swagger, as if to tell the camp, "You may make remarks about this if you want trouble." Nobody did in his presence.

Except the barber, who laughed and said, "I been wantin' to put scissors to that, Doc. You gettin' all fixed up for the lost lady to take a good look?"

Doc had dignity even in a barber's chair. "Shut up and tend to business," he advised. There was no more conversation even when the barber handed him a mirror.

Rune had too much sense to mention the reformation. The tall boy glanced at him, smiled tightly, and reported, "Ma Fisher wants to see you. She's tired of having the lost lady underfoot."

Doc snorted. "Ma has no weariness or distaste that a poke of dust won't soothe." He turned away, but Rune was not through talking.

"Can I come when you take the bandage off her eyes?"

"No. Yes. What do I care?" Doc strode away, trying to put his spirits into a suitably humble mood to talk business with Ma Fisher.

The girl was a disturbing influence for him, for Rune, for the whole buzzing camp. She must get out in a few days, but she must not be made any more miserable than she already was.

He did not wait for Ma Fisher to attack, from her side of the dirty wooden counter in her tent restaurant. He spoke first: "You would no doubt like to be paid for Miss Armistead's lodging. I will pay you. I don't want you to get the idea that I'm keeping her. My reason for wishing to pay is that I want her to keep thinking the world is kind and that you have welcomed her."

Ma Fisher shrugged. "You can afford it. It's an inconvenience to me to have her underfoot."

Doc put a poke on the counter. "You can heft that if you want to. That's dust you'll get for not letting her know she's unwelcome. You'll get it when she leaves, in a week or so."

Ma lifted the leather sack with an expert touch. "All right."

Doc swept it back again. "One compliment before I leave you, Mrs. Fisher: you're no hypocrite."

"Two-faced, you mean? One face like this is all a woman can stand." She cackled at her own wit. "Just the same, I'd like to know why you're willing to pay good clean dust to keep the girl from finding out the world is cruel."

"I wish I knew myself," he answered.

I'll take off the dressings now, he decided, and let her get a glimpse of daylight, let her see what she's eating for a change.

He crossed the street and knocked, calling, "Doc Frail here." Rune opened the door.

Elizabeth turned her face toward him. "Doctor? Now will you let me see again? I thought if you could take the dressings off now, you and Rune might be my guests for supper."

You and Rune. The leading citizen and the unsuccessful thief.

"I'll be honored," Doc replied. "And I suppose Rune realizes that it is an honor for him."

He removed the last dressings from her eyes and daubed the closed lids with liquid.

"Blink," he ordered. "Again. Now try opening them."

She saw him as a blurred face, close up, without distinguishing characteristics. The one who protected in the darkness, the one who had promised to bring light. The only dependable creature in the world. There was light again, she had regained her sight. She must trust him, and she could. He had not failed her in anything.

But he was a stranger in a world of terror and strangers. He was too young. A doctor should be old, with a gray chin beard.

"Hurts a little?" he said. "You can look around now."

He stepped aside and she was lost without him. She saw someone else, tall in the dimness; that was Rune, and he was important in her life. She tried to smile at him, but she could not tell whether he smiled back.

Doc said, "Don't look in a mirror yet. When your face

is all healed, you will be a pretty girl again. Don't worry about it."

Unsmiling, she answered, "I have other things to concern me."

Elizabeth tried to make conversation as they ate the supper Rune had cooked. But now that she could see them dimly, they were strangers and she was lost and afraid.

"It's like being let out of jail, to see again," she offered. "At least I suppose it is. When may I go outside to see what the town is like?"

"There is no town, only a rough camp," Doc told her. "It's not worth looking at, but you may see it tomorrow. After sunset, when the light won't hurt your eyes."

The following day, after supper, when she heard knocking on the front door, she ran to answer. Dr. Frail had changed his mind about waiting until later, she assumed. He must have come back sooner than he had expected from a professional call several miles away.

She swung the door wide—and looked up through a blur into the blackbearded, grinning face of a stranger. Then she could not shut it again. A lady could not do a thing so rude as that.

The man swept off his ragged hat and bowed awkwardly. "Frenchy Plante, ma'am. You ain't never seen me, but we sure enough met before. Out on the Dry Flats."

"Oh," she said faintly. He looked unkempt and she could smell whiskey. But he had saved her life. "Please come in," she said, because there was no choice. She hoped he did not notice that she left the door open. With this man in the cabin, she wanted no privacy.

He remembered to keep his hat in his hand but he sat down without waiting to be invited.

"Figure on doing a little prospecting, ma'am," he said jovially. "So I just dropped in to say good-by and see how you're making out."

Frenchy was well pleased with himself. He was wearing a clean red shirt, washed though not pressed, and he had combed his hair, wanting to make a good impression on the lost lady.

"I have so much to thank you for," Elizabeth said earnestly. "I am so very grateful."

He waved one hand. "It's nothing, lady. Somebody would of found you." Realizing that this detracted from his glory, he added, "But of course it might have been too late. You sure look different from the first time I seen you!"

Her hands went up to her face. "Doctor Frail says there won't be any scars. I wish I could offer you some refreshment, Mr. Plante. If you would care to wait until I build up the fire to make tea?"

Doc Frail remarked from the doorway, "Frenchy would miss his afternoon tea, I'm sure."

There were a few men in the camp who were not afraid of Doc Frail—the upright men, the leading citizens, and Frenchy Plante.

Frenchy had the effrontery to suggest, "Come on in, Doc," but the wisdom to add, "Guess I can't stay, ma'am. Going prospecting, like I told you."

Doc Frail stood aside so as not to bar his progress in leaving. "I thought your claim was paying fairly well."

Frenchy made an expansive gesture. "Sold it this morning. I want something richer."

Elizabeth said, "I hope you'll find a million dollars, Mr. Plante."

"With a pretty lady like you on my side, I can't fail, can I?" replied the giant, departing.

Elizabeth put on her bonnet. With her foot on the threshold, she murmured, "Everyone is so kind." She took Doc's arm as he offered it.

"To the left," he said. "The rougher part of the camp is to the right. You must never go that way. But this is the way you will go to the hotel, where the stage stops. Next week you will be able to leave Skull Creek."

She did not seem to hear him. She trembled. She was staring with aching eyes at the rutted road that led past Flaunce's store and the livery stable, the road that took a sudden sweep upward toward a cottonwood tree with one great out-thrust bough.

"You are perfectly safe," Doc reminded her. "We will not go far this time. Only past the store."

"No!" she moaned. "Oh, no!" and tried to turn back.

"Now what?" Doc demanded. "There is nothing here to hurt you."

But up there where she had to go sometime was the

hanging tree, and beyond was the desert. Back all that distance, back all alone—a safe, quiet place was what she must have now, at once.

Not here in the glaring sun with the men staring and the world so wide that no matter which way she turned she was lost, she was thirsty, burning, dying.

But there must be some way out, somewhere safe, the cool darkness of a cabin, if she could only run in the right direction and not give up too soon—

But someone tried to keep her there in the unendurable sun glare with the thirst and endless dizzying space—someone held her arms and said her name urgently from far away as she struggled.

She jerked away with all her strength because she knew the needs of her own anguished body and desperate spirit—she had to be free, she had to be able to hide.

And where was Papa, while this strange and angry man carried her back to the cabin that was a refuge from which she would not venture forth again?

And who was this angry boy who shouted, "Doc, if you've hurt her, I'll kill you!"

When she was through with her frantic crying and was quiet and ashamed, she was afraid of Doc Frail, who gripped her wrists as she lay on Ma Fisher's bed.

"What was it, Elizabeth?" he demanded. "Nothing is going to hurt you. What did you think you saw out there?"

"The Dry Flats," she whispered, knowing he would not believe it. "The glaring sun on the Dry Flats. And I was lost again and thirsty."

"It's thirty miles to the Dry Flats," he told her brusquely. "And the sun went down an hour ago. It's getting dark here in the gulch."

She shuddered.

"I'll give you something to make you sleep," he offered.

"I want Papa," she replied, beginning to cry again.

Back in his own cabin, Doc walked back and forth, back and forth across the rough floor boards, with Rune glaring at him from a corner.

Doc Frail was trying to remember a word and a mystery. Someone in France had reported something like this years ago. What was the word, and what could you do for the suffering patient?

He had three books in his private medical library, but they treated of physical ailments, not wounds of the mind. He could write to Philadelphia for advice, but—he calculated the weeks required for a letter to go East and a reply to come back to Skull Creek.

"Even if they know," he said angrily, "we'll be snowed in here before the answer comes. And maybe nobody knows, except in France, and he's probably dead now, whoever he was."

Rune spoke cuttingly. "You had to be in such a hurry to make her start back home!"

Doc said, "Shut your mouth."

What was the word for the mystery? Elizabeth remembered nothing about the runaway of the coach horses, nothing about the holdup that preceded it, only the horror that followed.

"Hysteria?" he said. "Is that the word? Hysteria? But if it is, what can you do for the patient?"

The lost lady would have to try again. She would have to cross the imaginary desert as well as the real one.

VI

I will not try to go out for a few days, Elizabeth told herself, comforted by the thought that nobody would expect her to try again after what had happened on her first attempt.

The desert was not outside the cabin, of course. It was only a dreadful illusion. She realized that, because she could look out and see that the street was in a ravine. Nothing like the Dry Flats.

Next time, she assured herself, it will be all right. I will not look up toward the tree where they—no, I will simply not think about the tree at all, nor about the Dry Flats. Other people go out by stage and nothing happens to them. But I can't go right away.

Doctor Frail did not understand at all. He came over the next morning, implacable and stern.

"I have a patient to see down at the diggings," he said, "but he can wait half an hour. First you will walk with me as far as Flaunce's store."

"Oh, I couldn't," she answered with gentle firmness.

"In a few days, but not now. I'm not strong enough."

He put his hat on the table and sat on one of the two benches.

"You will go now, Elizabeth. You have got to do it now. I am going to sit here until you are ready to start."

She stared at him in hurt surprise. Of course he was a doctor, and he could be expected to be always right. He was a determined man, and strength came from him. It was good, really, not to make a decision but to have him make it, even though carrying it out would be painful. Like the time Papa made her go to a dentist to have a tooth pulled.

"Very well," she replied with dignity. She put her bonnet on, not caring that there was no mirror.

"You are only going for a walk to the store," he told her, offering his arm at the door. "You will want to tell your friends back home what a store in a gold camp is like. You will have a great many things to tell your friends."

She managed a laugh as she walked with her eyes down, feeling the men staring.

"They would not believe the things I could tell them," she agreed.

The sun was not yet high over the gulch and the morning was not warm but she was burning and thirsty and could not see anything for the glare and could not breathe because she had been running, but he would not let her fall. He was speaking rapidly and urgently, telling her she must go on. He was not Papa because Papa was never angry; Papa would never have let her be afraid and alone in the glare and thirsty and going to die here, now, if he would only let her give up and fall. . . .

She was lying down—where? On the bed in the cabin? And turning her head away from something, the sharp odor of something the doctor held under her nose to revive her.

The men had seen her fall, then, the staring men of Skull Creek, and she had fainted, and they must think she was insane and maybe she was.

She was screaming and Doc Frail was slapping her cheek, saying, "Elizabeth! Stop that!"

Then she was crying with relief, because surely now nobody would make her go out again until she was ready.

The doctor was angry, a cruel man, a hateful stranger. Angry at a helpless girl who needed only to be let alone until she was stronger!

She said with tearful dignity, "Please go away."

He was sarcastic, too. He answered, "I do have other patients," and she heard the door close.

But she could not lie there and cry as she wanted to do, because she had to bar the door to keep out fear.

At noontime she was calmer and built a fire in the little stove and brewed some tea to eat with a cold biscuit of the kind Rune called bannock. Nobody came, and in the afternoon she slept for a while, exhausted, but restless because there was a great deal of racket from down the gulch.

Rune leaned against a building with his thumbs in his belt, watching two drunk miners trying to harness a mule that didn't want to be harnessed. Rune was amused, glad to have something to think about besides Doc Frail's cruelty to the lost lady.

"Leave her strictly alone till I tell you otherwise," Doc had commanded.

Rune was willing, for the time being. She had cold grub in the cabin and the water bucket was full. He didn't want to embarrass her by going there anyway. He had seen her stumble and struggle and fall. He had watched, from Doc's shack, as Doc carried her back to the cabin, had waited to be called and had been ignored.

The plunging mule kicked one of the miners over backward into the dust, while a scattering of grinning men gathered and cheered.

The other drunk man had a long stick, and as he struck out with it, the mule went bucking, tangled in the harness. A man standing beside Rune commented with awe and delight, "Right toward Ma Fisher's restaurant! Now I'd admire to see that mule tangle with her!"

He shouted, and Rune roared with him. A roar went up from all the onlookers as the far side of Ma Fisher's tent went down and Ma came running out on the near side, screaming. The mule emerged a few seconds behind her, but the drunk miner was still under the collapsed, smoke-stained canvas.

There was a frenzied yell of "Fire!" even before Rune

saw the smoke curl up and ran to the nearest saloon to grab a bucket.

They kept the flames from spreading to any buildings, although the lean-to behind the tent was badly charred and most of the canvas burned.

Ma Fisher was not in sight by the time they got the fire out. Rune slouched away, grinning.

Ma Fisher made only one stop on the way from her ruined restaurant to the cabin. She beat with her fist on the locked door of the bank until Mr. Evans opened it a few inches and peered cautiously out.

"I want to withdraw all I've got on deposit," she demanded. "I'm going to my daughter's in Idaho."

He unfastened the chain on the inside and swung the door open. "Leaving us, Mrs. Fisher!"

"Sink of iniquity," she growled. "Of course I'm leaving. They've burned my tent and ruined my stove, and now they can starve for all I care. I want to take out every dollar.

"But you needn't think I want to carry it with me on the stage," she warned. "I just want to make the arrangements now. Transfer it or whatever you do, so's I can draw on it in Idaho."

"Will you need some for travel expenses?" the banker asked, opening his ledger.

"I've got enough dust on hand for that. Just let me sign the papers and get started."

Rune, lounging in Doc's doorway, saw Ma Fisher jerk at her own door handle and then beat angrily with her fist, yelling, "Girl, you let me in! It's Ma Fisher."

She slammed the door behind her, and Rune grinned. He worried a little though, wondering how her anger would affect the gentle Miss Armistead. But he had his orders not to go over there. His own opinion was that the lost lady was being mighty stubborn, and maybe Doc Frail was right in prescribing the let-alone treatment till she got sensible.

Elizabeth listened with horror to Ma Fisher's description of the wrecking of her restaurant. Ma paced back and forth across the floor and she spat out the news.

"How dreadful!" Elizabeth sympathized. "What can I do to help you?"

Ma Fisher stopped pacing and stared at her. It was a

long time since anyone had offered sympathy. Having had little of it from anyone else, she had none to give.

"I don't need nothing done for me," she growled. "I'm one to look after myself. Oh, laws, the cabin. I've got to sell this cabin."

"But then you'll have no place to live!" Elizabeth cried out.

"I'm going to Idaho. But I got to get my investment out of the cabin. You'll have to leave, Miss. I'm going tomorrow on the stage."

She was pacing again, not looking to see how Elizabeth was affected by the news, not caring, either.

"Man offered me five hundred dollars in clean dust for it not long ago, but I turned it down. Had to have a place to live, didn't I? Now who was that? Well, it won't be hard to find a buyer. . . . You've got your things all over the place. You better start packing. Could come on the same stage with me if you're a mind to."

Out into the open, away from refuge? Out across the Dry Flats—and before that, under the hanging tree? When she could not even go as far as Flaunce's store!

There was no one to help her, no one who cared what became of her. The doctor was angry, the boy Rune had deserted her, and this hag, this witch, thought only of her own interests. Papa had said, "We do what we must."

"I will give you five hundred dollars for the cabin," Elizabeth said coolly.

Doc Frail did not learn of the transaction until noon the next day. He had been called to a gulch ten miles away to care for a man who was beyond help, dying of a self-inflicted gunshot wound. Crippled with rheumatism, the man had pulled the trigger of his rifle with his foot.

Doc rode up to his own door and yelled, "Rune! Take care of my horse."

Rune came around from the back with the wood-chopping axe in his hand.

"Hell's broke loose," he reported. "Old lady Fisher left on the stage this morning, and the girl must be still in the cabin, because she didn't go when Ma did."

Doc sighed.

"Fellow that came by said she's bought Ma's cabin," Rune said, watching to see how Doc Frail would take that news.

Doc disappointed him by answering, "I don't care what she did," and went into his own building.

But while Rune was taking the mare to the livery stable, Doc decided he did care. He cared enough to cross the road in long strides and pound on the door, shouting, "Elizabeth, let me in this instant."

She had been waiting for hours for him to come, to tell her she had done the right thing, the only thing possible.

But he said, "If what I hear is true, you're a fool. What are you going to do in Skull Creek?"

She stepped back before the gale of his anger. She drew herself up very straight.

"Why, I am going to start a school for the children," she replied. "I have been making plans for it all morning."

"You can't. You can't stay here," Doc insisted.

"But I must, until I am stronger."

Doc glared. "You'd better get stronger in a hurry then. You've got to get out of this camp. You can start by walking up to the store. And I'll go with you. Right now."

Elizabeth was angry too. "I thank you for your courtesy," she said. "I must look out for myself now, of course." Looking straight into his eyes, she added, "I will pay your fee now if you will tell me what I owe."

Doc flinched as if she had struck him.

"There is no charge, madam. Call on me at any time."

He bowed and strode out.

He told Rune, "The order to leave her alone still stands," and told him nothing else.

Rune endured it for twenty-four hours. The door across the street did not open. There was no smoke from the chimney.

She's got just about nothing in the way of grub over there now, Rune fretted to himself. Ain't even building a fire to make a cup of tea.

But when Rune crossed the street, he did not go for pity. He had convinced himself that his only reason for visiting Elizabeth was that Doc had forbidden him to go there.

He knocked on the slab door but no answer came. He pounded harder, calling, "Miss Armistead!" There was no sound from within, but there was a waiting silence that made his skin crawl.

"It's Rune!" he shouted. "Let me in!"

A miner, passing by, grinned and remarked, "Good luck, boy. Introduce me sometime."

Rune said, "Shut your foul mouth," over his shoulder just as the door opened a crack.

Elizabeth said coolly, "What is it?" Then, with a quick-drawn breath like a sob, "Rune, come in, come in."

As she stepped away from the entrance, her skirt swung and he saw her right hand with a little derringer in it.

"The gun—where'd you get it?" he demanded.

"It was Papa's. They brought it to me with his things after—" Remembering that she must look after herself, not depending on anyone else, she stopped confiding. "Won't you sit down?" she invited formally.

"I just come to see—to see how everything is. Like if you needed something."

She shook her head, but her eyes flooded with tears. "Need something? Oh, no. I don't need a thing. Nobody can do anything for me!"

Then she was sobbing, sitting on a bench with her face hidden in her hands, and the little gun forgotten on the floor.

"Listen, you won't starve," he promised. "I'll bring your grub. But have you got money to live on?" He abased himself, admitting, "I ain't got anything. Doc don't pay me. If I had, I'd help you out."

"Oh, no. I will look after myself." She wiped her eyes and became very self-possessed. "Except that for a while I should appreciate it if you will go to the store for me. Until I am strong enough to walk so far by myself."

But Doc had said she was strong enough, and Doc Frail was no liar. Rune scowled at Elizabeth. He did not want to be bound to her by pity. It was bad enough to be bound to Doc by debt.

This tie, at least, he could cut loose before it became a serious burden.

"You got to get out of Skull Creek," he said harshly. "Unless you've got a lot of money."

"I have sufficient," she said.

Now she was playing the great lady, he thought. She was being elegant and scornful.

"Maybe where you come from, folks don't talk about such things," he burst out with bitterness. "It ain't nice, you think. Don't think I'm asking you how much you got. But you don't know nothing about prices here. You ain't been paying full price for what you got, not by a long ways. You want to know?"

She was staring at him wide-eyed and shocked.

"Sugar's ninety cents a pound at Flaunce's," he told her. "It went down. Dried codfish—you're tired of it, I guess, and so's everybody—it's sixty cents. Dried apples— forty cents a pound last time they had any. Maybe you'd like a pound of tea? Two and a half, that costs you. Potatoes and eggs, there ain't been any in a long time. Fresh meat you can't get till another bunch of steers come in. Now how long will your money last you if you stay in Skull Creek?"

She had less than five hundred dollars left after buying the cabin. Stage fare—that was terribly high. She had never had to handle money, and only in the last year had she even had to be concerned about it, since Papa's affairs had gone so badly.

But she said coolly, "I have a substantial amount of money, thank you. And I am going to start a school. Now tell me, please, who paid for my supplies if I didn't?"

Rune gulped. "I can't tell you that."

"So it was Doctor Frail," Elizabeth said wearily. "I will pay him. Tell him that."

"He'd kill me," Rune said. "Remember, I never said it was him."

Between two dangers, the lesser one seemed to be telling Doc himself. He did so at the first opportunity.

Doc did not explode. He only sighed and remarked, "Now she hasn't even got her pride. How much money has she got to live on?"

"She didn't tell me. Won't tell you, either, I'll bet."

"And she thinks she can make a fortune teaching school!" Doc was thoughtful. "Maybe she can earn part of her living that way. How many children are there in camp, anyway?" He scrabbled for a sheet of paper and began writing the names of families, muttering to himself.

"Go to the livery stable," he said without looking up, "and get a string of bells. They've got some. Then figure out a way to hitch them over her door with a rope that she can pull from inside her cabin."

"What for?" Rune demanded.

"So she can signal for help next time somebody tries to break in," Doc explained with unusual patience.

And what will I do to protect her when the time comes? Doc Frail wondered. Look forbidding and let them see two guns holstered and ready? That will not always be enough.

The noted physician of Skull Creek can outshoot anyone within several hundred miles, but will he fire when the target is a man? Never again. Then his hand and his eye lose their cunning, and that is why Wonder Russell sleeps up on the hill. If I could not pull the trigger to save the life of my friend, how can I do it for Elizabeth? I must have a deputy.

Rune was on his way out when Doc asked, "Can you hit a target any better than you dodge bullets?"

Rune hesitated, torn between wanting to boast and wanting to be taught by a master. If he admitted he was no marksman, he was not a complete man. But a slave didn't have to be.

He answered humbly, "I never had much chance to try. Target practice costs money."

"Stop at the store and get a supply of ammunition," Doc ordered. "I'm going to give you the world's best chance to shoot me."

Rune shrugged and went out, admitting no excitement. He was going to have his chance to become the kind of man from whose path other men would quietly step aside.

Doc watched him go, thinking, Are you the one for whom I'll hang? Put a gun in your hand, and skill with it, and there's no telling. But your lessons start tomorrow.

"I wish the school didn't matter so much to her," Doc muttered. "I wish she wasn't so set on it."

He had made some calls early that morning and was back in his cabin, scowling across the street at Elizabeth's, with its door standing open to welcome the children of Skull Creek.

Her floor was scrubbed; the rough plank table was draped with an embroidered cloth, and her father's books were on it. She visualized the children: shy, adorable, anxious to learn. And their mothers: grateful for a school, full of admonitions about the little ones' welfare, but trusting the teacher.

Doc turned to Rune, saw the rifle across his knees.

"You planning to shoot the children when they come?" he demanded.

"Planning to shoot any miner that goes barging in there with her door open," Rune answered. "Because I don't think there's going to be any children coming to school."

Doc sighed. "I don't either. After all the notes she wrote their mothers, all the plans she made."

At eleven o'clock, they saw Elizabeth shut her door. No one had crossed the threshold.

Doc growled, "Bring my mare. I've got a patient up the gulch. Then go see about getting her dinner."

Rune muttered, "I'd rather be shot."

Elizabeth had the derringer in her hand, hidden in a fold of her skirt, when she unbarred the door. She did not look at him but simply stepped aside.

"I don't care for anything to eat," she said faintly.

"If you don't eat nothing, I don't either."

She sipped a cup of tea, but she set it down suddenly and began to cry.

"Why didn't anybody come?" she wailed.

"Because they're fools," he told her sturdily.

But he knew why. He had guessed from the way the women acted when he delivered the notes. Elizabeth Armistead, the lost lady, was not respectable. She had come under strange circumstances, and the protection of Doc Frail was like a dark shadow upon her.

"I thought I would teach the children," she said hopelessly. "I thought it would be pleasant."

Rune drew a deep breath and offered her all he had—his ignorance and his pride.

"You can teach me," he said. "I ain't never learned to read."

The look of shock on her face did not hurt quite so much as he had supposed it would.

VII

Early cold came to Skull Creek, and early snow. Halfway through one gloomy, endless morning, someone knocked at Elizabeth's door, but she had learned caution. She called, "Who is it?"

A voice she did not know said something about books. When she unbarred the door, the derringer was in her hand, but she kept it decently hidden in the folds of her skirt.

He was a big man with a beard. He swept off a fur cap and was apologetic.

"I didn't mean to frighten you, ma'am. Please don't be afraid. I came to see if you would rent out some of your books."

Elizabeth blinked two or three times, considering the matter. "But one doesn't rent books!" she objected. "I have never heard of renting books. . . . It's cold, won't you come in so I can close the door?"

The man hesitated. "If you're sure you will let me come in, ma'am. I swear I'll do you no harm. It's only for books that I came. Some of the boys are about to go crazy for lack of reading matter. We drew straws, and I got the short one. To come and ask you."

It's my house, Elizabeth told herself. And surely no rascal would care for books.

This man happened not to be a rascal, though he acted so fidgety about being in there that Elizabeth wondered who he thought might be chasing him.

"They call me Tall John, ma'am," he said in introduction, cap in hand. "Any book would do, just about. We've worn out the newspapers from the States and we're tired of reading the labels on canned goods. And the winter's only just begun."

He paid five dollars apiece for the privilege of keeping three books for a month. (His listeners, when he read aloud in a hut of poles and earth, were a horse thief, a half-breed Arapaho Indian and the younger son of an English nobleman.)

Doc scolded Elizabeth for letting a stranger in, although he admitted that Tall John was a decent fellow.

"He was a perfect gentleman," she insisted. What bothered her was that she had accepted money for lending books.

Rune complained bitterly because his book supply was cut by three.

"Listen, boy," Doc said, "you can read like a house

afire, but can you write? Your schooling isn't even well begun. Do you know arithmetic? If you sold me eight head of horses at seventy dollars a head, how much would I owe you?"

"I wouldn't trust nobody to owe me for 'em," Rune told him earnestly. "You'd pay cash on the barrel head, clean dust, or you wouldn't drive off no horses of mine."

But thereafter his daily lessons in Elizabeth's cabin included writing, spelling and arithmetic. When the only books she had left were readers through which he had already ploughed his impetuous way, he was reduced to sneaking a look at the three medical books in Doc's cabin—Doc's entire medical library.

When Rune boasted of how much he was learning in his classes at the lost lady's cabin, Doc listened and was pleased.

"Each week, you will take her a suitable amount of dust for tuition," Doc announced. "I will have to decide how much it's going to be."

"Dust? Where'm I going to get dust?" Rune was frantic; the only delight he had was being barred from him, as everything else was, by his poverty.

"From me, of course. I can properly pay for the education of my servant, surely?"

"The lady teaches me for nothing," Rune said in defense of his privilege. "She don't expect to get paid for it."

"She needs an income, and this will help a little." Doc felt lordly. He was doing a favor for both his charges, Rune and the pathetic girl across the street. "If you don't care to accept a favor from me," he told Rune, "you'd better get used to the idea." With a flash of insight, he explained, "It is necessary sometimes to let other people do something decent for you."

That is, he considered, it is necessary for everybody but me. And I have a sudden very excellent idea about the uses of gold.

He had an interest in several paying placer claims, which he visited often because the eye of the master fatteneth the cattle, and the eye of an experienced gold miner can make a shrewd guess about how many ounces there should be on the sluice riffles at the weekly cleanup. His various partners seldom tried to cheat him any more.

With the ground and the streams frozen, placer mining had come to a dead stop, but Dr. Frail's professional income had dwindled only a little, and there was so much dust to his credit with the bank that he had no financial problems anyway.

He strode up the street to visit Evans, the banker.

"Your dealings with your customers are strictly confidential, are they not?" he inquired.

"As confidential as yours," Evans replied stiffly.

"I want to make a withdrawal. The dust is to be put into leather pokes that can't be identified as the property of anyone around here. Old pokes, well worn."

"Very well," said Evans, as if it happened every day.

"Weigh it out in even pounds," Doc instructed, and Evans' eyebrows went up. "I want—oh, six of them. I'll be back for them this afternoon."

He sat with Elizabeth just before supper, drinking tea, listening to the sounds Rune made chopping firewood outside the back door. Rune had the bags of gold and orders to conceal them in the woodpile to be found accidentally.

"And remember, I know very well how much is in there," Doc had warned him. "I know how much she's supposed to find when she does find it."

Rune had glared at him in cold anger, replying, "Did you think I would steal from *her?*"

Tall John's shack burned when he built the fire too hot on a bitter cold day. The three men who shared it with him were away. He ran out, tried to smother the flames with snow, then ran back to save what he could, and the roof fell in on him.

When help came, he was shouting under the burning wreckage. His rescuers delivered him to Doc's office with a broken leg and serious burns on his shoulders and chest.

Doc grumbled, "You boys think I'm running a hospital?" and started to work on the patient.

"He's got no place to go; our wickiup burned," the horse thief apologized. "The rest of us, we can hole up someplace, but John can't hardly."

"He needs a roof over his head and conscientious nursing," Doc warned.

"I could sort of watch him," Rune suggested, wondering if they would sneer at the idea.

"Guess you'll have to," Doc agreed. "All right, he can have my bunk."

Then there was less company to help Elizabeth pass the time. Rune bought her supplies and carried in firewood, but he was always in a hurry. There were no more interesting evenings with Doc and Rune as her guests for supper, because Doc never stayed with her more than a few minutes.

Winter clamped down with teeth that did not let go. Elizabeth began to understand why Tall John had found it necessary to borrow books—she was reading her father's books over and over to pass the time. She began to understand, too, why a man of pride must pay for such borrowing.

She sewed and mended her own clothes until there was no more sewing to do. Doc commissioned her to make him a shirt and one for Rune. She finished them and was empty-handed again.

Then she peeled every sliver of bark from the logs that made her prison.

Rune came dutifully twice a day to bring supplies, and do her chores, but he no longer had lessons.

"Tall John's teaching me," he explained.

"And what are you studying?" she asked with some coolness.

"Latin. So I can figure out the big words in Doc's books."

"Now I wonder whether Papa brought his Latin grammar," she cried, running to look at the books she could not read.

"You ain't got one," Rune said. "I looked. We get along without. Sometimes we talk it."

"I didn't think anybody talked Latin," Elizabeth said doubtfully.

"Tall John can. He studied it in Rome. Told me where Rome is, too."

Elizabeth sighed. Her pupil had gone far beyond her.

She faced the bleak fact that nobody needed her at all any more. And Doc said there would be at least another month of winter.

"I don't want to impose on you, now that you're so

busy," she told Rune with hurt dignity. "Hereafter I will bring in my own firewood and snow to melt for water. It will give me something to do."

"Don't hurt yourself," he cautioned. He didn't seem to see anything remarkable in her resolve to do hard physical labor. Elizabeth had never known any woman who carried water or cut wood. She felt like an adventurer when she undertook it.

Rune told Doc what she was planning, and Doc smiled. "Good. Then you won't have to find what's in her woodpile. She can find it herself."

He visited her that evening, as he did once a day, briefly. She was a little sulky, he noticed, and he realized that she deserved an apology from him.

"I'm sorry not to spend more time in your company," he said abruptly. "There is no place I'd rather spend it. But for your own protection, to keep you from being talked about—do you understand why I'd rather not be here when Rune can't be here too?"

Elizabeth sniffed. "Have I any good name left to protect?"

The answer was No, but he would not say it.

"Rune says you're going to do your own chores," he remarked.

"Beginning tomorrow," she said proudly, expecting either a scolding or a compliment.

Doc disappointed her by saying heartily, "Good idea. You need some exercise."

Then he wondered why she was so unfriendly during the remainder of his visit.

Her venture into wood cutting lasted three days. Then, with a blister on one hand and a small axe cut in one shoe—harmless but frightening—she began to carry in wood that Rune had already chopped and piled earlier in the winter.

She was puzzled when she found a leather bag, very heavy for its size, and tightly tied. Unable to open the snow-wet drawstring with her mittened hands, she carried the bag into the house and teased the strings open with the point of a knife.

She glimpsed what was inside, ran to the shelf for a plate, and did not breathe again until the lovely yellow treasure was heaped upon it.

"Oh!" she said. "Oh, the pretty!" She ran her chilled fingers through the nuggets and the flakes that were like fish scales. "Maybe it belongs to Ma Fisher," she said angrily to the emptiness of the cabin. "But I bought the place and it's mine now. And maybe there's more out there!"

She found them all, the six heavy little bags, and completely demolished the neat woodpile.

Then she ran to the rope of the warning bells and pulled it for the first time, pulled it again and again, laughing and crying, and was still pulling it when Rune came shouting.

She hugged him, although he had a cocked pistol in his hand. She did not even notice that.

"Look!" she screamed. "Look what I found in the woodpile!"

Doc came to admire, later in the day, and stayed for supper, but Elizabeth was too excited to eat—or to cook, for that matter. The table was crowded, because all the golden treasure was on display in plates or cups. She kept touching it lovingly, gasping with delight.

"Now you know," Doc guessed, "why men search for that. And why they kill for it."

"I know," she crooned. "Yes, I understand."

He leaned across the table. "Elizabeth, with all that for a stake, you needn't be afraid to go out next spring, go home."

She caressed a pile of yellow gold. "I suppose so," she answered, and he knew she was not convinced.

The woodpile was a symbol after that. She restored the scattered sticks to make a neat heap, but did not burn any of them. She went back to chopping wood each day for the fire.

She was hacking at a stubborn, knotty log one afternoon, her skirts soggy with snow, when a man's voice not far behind her startled her into dropping the axe.

He was on the far side of the frozen creek, an anonymous big man bundled up in a huge and shapeless coat of fur.

"It's me, Frenchy," he shouted jovially. "Looks like you're working too hard for a young lady!"

Elizabeth picked up the axe. When the man who once saved your life speaks to you, you must answer, she decided. Especially when you had nobody to talk to any more.

"I like to be in the fresh air," she called.

He waded through the snow. "Let me do that work for you, little lady."

Elizabeth clung to the axe, and he did not come too close.

"Sure having a cold spell," he commented. "Been a bad winter."

This is my own house, Elizabeth told herself. This man saved my life on the Dry Flats.

"Won't you come in and thaw out by the stove?" she suggested. "Perhaps you'd like a cup of tea."

Frenchy was obviously pleased. "Well, now, a day like this, a man can sure use something hot to drink."

Elizabeth felt guilty, ushering him into her cabin by the back way, as if trying to hide her doings from her guardians across the street. But he had come the back way, and not until later did it occur to her that his choice of routes had been because he wanted to avoid being seen.

He sat across the table from her, affable and sociable, waiting for the tea to steep. When his clothing got warmed, he smelled, but a lady could not tell a guest that he should go home and take a bath.

Frenchy had in mind to tell a fine big lie and perhaps to get himself a stake. The lost lady, he guessed, had brought lots of money with her. For her Rune bought the very best supplies available. She was strange, of course, about staying in her cabin all the time, and he had seen her almost fall down in a kind of struggling fit when she went outside. But she was very pretty, and she was nice to him. Doc Frail was her protector, but Frenchy had a strong suspicion that Doc Frail was frail indeed.

Frenchy went into his lie.

"Just can't hardly wait for a warm spell. I got the prettiest little claim you ever seen—colors galore. I'm going to be the rich Mr. Plante, sure enough. That is," he sighed, "if I can just keep eating till the ground thaws."

He blew politely into his tea to cool it.

"Yes, sir," mused Frenchy, "all I need is a grubstake. And whoever stakes me is going to be mighty lucky. That's how Doc Frail made his pile, you know. Grub-staking prospectors."

He did not ask her for anything. He did not suggest that she stake him. She thought of it all by herself.

"Tell me more, Mr. Plante," she said. "Maybe I will stake you."

He argued a little—couldn't possibly accept a stake from a lady. She argued—he must, because she owed him her life, and she would like to get rich. How much did he need?

Anything, anything—but with prices so high—and he'd have to hire labor, and that came high, too—

She calculated wildly. Six pokes of gold, a pound in each one. She had no basis for computing how much a prospector needed.

"I will give you half of what I have," she offered. "And you will give me half of the gold you find. I think we should have some sort of written contract, too."

Frenchy was dazzled. He had nothing to lose. He did not expect to have any gold to divide. His luck had been bad for months, and he intended to leave Skull Creek as soon as the weather permitted travel.

He dictated the contract as Elizabeth wrote in her prettiest penmanship, and both of them signed.

"The contract's yours to keep," he told her. It was a valid grubstake contract—if the holder could enforce it.

"I'll name the mine after you," he promised, vastly cheerful. "A few weeks from now—next summer anyway— you'll have to get gold scales to keep track of your take. When you see me again, you can call me Solid Gold Frenchy!"

At the Big Nugget, Frenchy took care to stand at the end of the bar nearest the table where Doc Frail was killing time in a card game.

The bartender was polite to Frenchy because business was poor, but his tone was firm as he warned, "Now, Frenchy, you know you ain't got no more credit here."

Frenchy was jovial and loud in his answer: "Did I say a word about credit this time? Just one drink, and I'll pay for it." He pulled out a poke.

Doc Frail was paying no attention to Frenchy and not much to the game. He took care to be seen in public most evenings, in the vain hope of weakening the camp's conviction that the lost lady was his property. He succeeded only in confusing the men, who felt he was treating her badly by leaving her in solitude.

Frenchy held up his glass and said with a grin, "Here's to the gold that's there for the finding, and here's to my grubstake partner."

Doc could not help glancing up. Frenchy had worn out three or four stakes already. Doc himself had refused him and did not know of a single man in camp who was willing to give him another start.

He looked up to see Frenchy grinning directly at him.

A challenge? Doc wondered. What's he been up to?

A suspicion of what Frenchy had been up to was like a burning coal in his mind.

Are you the man? he thought. Are you, Frenchy Plante, the man for whom I'll hang?

He stayed on for half an hour, until Frenchy had gone. He found Elizabeth in a cheerful mood, mending one of his shirts.

"The tea's been standing and it's strong," she apologized, getting a cup ready for him.

Drinking it, he waited for her to say that Frenchy had been there, but she only asked about Tall John's health.

Finally Doc remarked, "Frenchy Plante has suddenly come into comparative riches. He's got a grubstake from somewhere."

Elizabeth said mildly, "Is that so?"

"He said so when he bought a drink just now," Doc added, and Elizabeth was indignant.

"Is that what he's doing with it—drinking it up? I declare, I don't approve. I grubstaked him, if that's what you're trying to find out. But that was so he wouldn't starve and could go on mining when the weather moderates."

Doc said sadly, "Oh, Elizabeth!"

"It was mine," she maintained. "I simply invested some of it. Because I have plenty—and I want more."

Frenchy went on a prolonged, riotous and dangerous drinking spree. He was so violent that Madame Dewey, who kept the rooms above the Big Nugget, had him thrown out of there—at some expense, because two men were injured in removing him.

When he was almost broke, he really did go prospecting.

Doc and Rune treated Elizabeth with distant courtesy, mentioning casually the less scandalous highlights of

Frenchy Plante's orgy. They did not scold, but their courtesy was painful. She had no friends any more, no alternately laughing and sarcastic friend named Joe Frail, no rude but faithful friend named Rune. They were only her physician and the boy who did her errands. She lived in a log-lined, lamplit cave, and sometimes wished she were dead.

There was a window by her front door; Rune had nailed stout wooden bars across it on the inside. For privacy, an old blanket was hung over the bars. She could peek through the small hole in the blanket for a narrow glimpse of the street, but nothing ever happened that was worth looking at. To let in daylight by taking the blanket off the window was to invite stares of men who happened to pass by—and sometimes the curious, yearning, snow-bound miners were too drunk to remember that Doc Frail was her protector, or if they remembered, too drunk to care.

One of them, who tried to get in one evening in mid-April, was cunning when he made his plans. He was sober enough to reconnoiter first.

He knew where Doc Frail was—playing cards at the Big Nugget, bored but not yet yawning. Rune was in Doc's cabin with a lamp on the table, bent over a book. Tall John was limping down the gulch with a lantern to visit friends. And Frenchy Plante, who had some right to the lady because he had found her, was somewhere out in the hills.

The intruder felt perfectly safe about the warning bells. If the lady pulled the rope, there would be no noise, because he had cut the rope.

Elizabeth was asleep on her bed, fully clothed—she slept a great deal, having nothing else to do—when knuckles rapped at the back door and a voice not quite like Doc's called, "Miss Armistead! Elizabeth!"

She sat up, frozen with fright. Then the pounding was louder, with the slow beats of an axe handle. She did not answer, and with senseless anger the man began to chop at the back door.

She ran and seized the bell rope. It slumped loose in her hands. She heard the dry wood crack and splinter. She did not even try to escape by the front door. She reached for the derringer that had been her father's, pointed it blindly and screamed as she pulled the trigger.

Then she was defenseless, but there was no more chopping, no sound at all, until she heard Rune's approaching shout. She was suddenly calm and guiltily triumphant. Making very sure that Rune was indeed Rune, she unbarred the front door and let him in.

"I fired the little gun!" she boasted.

"You didn't hurt anybody," Rune pointed out. The bullet had lodged in the splintered back door. "We'll just wait right here till Doc comes."

But Doc solved no problems when he came. He sat quietly and listened to Elizabeth's story.

"I don't know," Doc said hopelessly. "I don't know how to protect you." He motioned toward the shattered splintered door. "Rune, fix that. I'll repair the bell rope."

Rune nailed the back door solid again and was noisy outside at the woodpile for a few minutes. When he came back, he said briefly, "Nobody will try that entrance again tonight. I'm going to bring blankets and sleep on the woodpile."

In Doc Frail's cabin he bundled blankets together. He straightened up and blurted out a question: "How much time do I still owe you?"

"Time? That old nonsense. You don't owe me anything. I just wanted to cut you down to size."

"Maybe somebody will cut you down to size sometime," Rune said. "I suppose you were never licked in your life. The great Joe Frail, always on top of the heap. It's time you got off it."

Doc said, "Hey! What's this sudden insurrection?"

"All you do is boss Elizabeth around. Why don't you get down on your knees instead? Didn't it ever dawn on you that if you married her, you could take her out of here to some decent place?" Rune was working himself up to anger. "Sure, she'd say she couldn't go, but you could make her go—tie her up and take her out in a wagon if there's no other way. How do you know the only right way to get her out of Skull Creek is to make her decide it for herself? Do you know everything?"

Doc answered, "No, I don't know everything," with new humility. He was silent for a while. "Don't think the idea is new to me. I've considered it. But I don't think she'd have me."

Rune picked up his blankets. "That's what I mean," he said. "You won't gamble unless you're sure you'll win." He slammed the door behind him.

VIII

When Doc set out to court Elizabeth Armistead, he put his whole heart into it, since this was what he had been wanting to do for a long time anyway. He was deferential and suitably humble. He was gentle. He was kind. And Elizabeth, who had never had a suitor before (except old Mr. Ellerby, who had talked across her head to her father), understood at once what Doc's intentions were.

He crossed the street more often and stayed longer. He came at mealtime, uninvited, and said he enjoyed her cooking. He even cut and carried in firewood. He brought his socks to be mended. They sat in pleasant domesticity at the table, while Elizabeth sewed and sometimes glanced across at him.

In his own cabin, Rune studied with the patient, Tall John.

And fifteen miles away, Frenchy Plante panned gravel. The ground had thawed, and rain made his labors miserable, but Frenchy had a hunch. Ninety-nine times out of a hundred, his hunches didn't pan out, but he trusted them anyway.

On a slope by a stream there was a ragged old tree. Beside it he had a pit from which he had dug gravel that showed occasional colors. He groaned out of his blankets one gray dawn, in his ragged tent, to find that the tree was no longer visible. Its roots washed by rain, it had fallen headfirst into his pit.

Frenchy swore.

"A sign, that's what it is," he growled. "A sign there wasn't nothing there to dig for. Damn tree filled up my pit. Going to leave here, never go back to Skull Creek."

But he had left a bucket by the tree, and he went for the bucket. The tree's head was lower than its roots, and the roots were full of mud, slick with rain. Mud that shone, even in the gray light.

He tore at the mud with his hands. He shelled out chunks like peanuts, but peanuts never shone so richly yellow. He forgot breakfast, forgot to build a fire, scrabbled in the oozing mud among the roots.

He held in his hand a chunk the size of a small crabapple, but no crabapple was ever so heavy.

He stood in the pouring rain with a little golden apple in his muddy hands. He threw his head back so the rain came into his matted beard, and he howled like a wolf at the dripping sky.

He staked his claim and worked it from dawn to dusk for a week, until he was too exhausted by labor and starvation to wash gravel any more. He might have died there in the midst of his riches, because he was too weak to go back to Skull Creek for grub, but he shot an unwary deer and butchered it and fed. The discovery that even he could lose his strength—and thereby his life and his treasure—frightened him. He caught his horse, packed up, and plodded toward Skull Creek, grinning.

He slogged down the gulch at dusk, eager to break the news to Elizabeth Armistead, but he had another important plan. He shouted in front of a wickiup built into the side of the gulch: "Bill, you there? It's Frenchy."

The wickiup had been his until he sold it for two bottles of whiskey. Bill Scanlan looked out and said without enthusiasm, "Broke already? Well, we got beans."

A man known as Lame George, lying on a dirty blanket, grunted a greeting.

"Crowded here," he murmured. "But we can make room."

"Anything happening?" Frenchy asked, wolfing cold fried pork and boiled beans.

"Stages ain't running yet. This camp's played out. What'd you find?"

"Some good, some bad. Mostly bad." That was honest, not that honesty mattered much, and not that prospectors expected it even among friends. "I was thinking about that time the boys drove the mules through the old lady's tent. I bet there ain't been a funny joke like that for a long time."

Lame George said sadly, "There ain't, for a fact. Nothing much to do, nothing to laugh about. We been digging but couldn't raise a color."

"I got a good idea for a funny joke," Frenchy hinted. "On Doc Frail."

Lame George snorted. "Nobody jokes him."

"I'd make it worth a man's while," Frenchy said with great casualness, and Lame George sat up to demand, "What'll you do it with? You find something?"

"What you got, Frenchy?" Scanlan asked tensely.

"The joke," Frenchy reminded them. "What about the joke on Doc?"

"Hell, yes!" Lame George exploded. "Let us in on something good and we'll take our chances on Doc." He glanced at Scanlan, who nodded agreement.

"All I want," Frenchy explained, spreading his hands to show his innocent intentions, "is to make a social call on the lady, Miss Armistead, without getting my head blowed off. Is Tall John still living at Doc's?"

"He got better and moved to a shack. Rune still lives with Doc. But what," Lame George demanded with justifiable suspicion, "do you want with the lady?"

"Wouldn't hurt her for the world. Won't lay a hand on her. Just want to talk to her." Frenchy added with a grin, "Just want to show her something I found and brought back in my pocket."

They swarmed at him, grabbed his arms, their eyes eager. "You made a strike, Frenchy? Sure you did—and she grubstaked you!"

Elizabeth sat at the table, mending by lamplight. Doc was across from her, reading aloud to their mutual contentment. He sat in comfort, in his shirt sleeves, his coat and gun belt hanging on a nail by the front door. The fire in the cookstove crackled, and the teakettle purred.

Doc chose his reading carefully. In an hour and a half, he worked through portions of the works of Mr. Tennyson and Mr. Browning and, apparently by accident, looked into the love sonnets of William Shakespeare—exactly what he had been aiming at from the beginning.

"Why," Elizabeth asked, "are you suddenly so restless? Are you tired of reading to me?"

Doc discovered that he was no longer sitting. He was walking the floor, and the time had come to speak.

"My name," he said abruptly, "is not really Frail."

She was not shocked. "Why did you choose that one, then?"

"Because I was cynical. Because I thought it suited

me. Elizabeth, I have to talk about myself. I have to tell you some things."

She said, "Yes, Joe."

"I killed a man once."

She looked relieved. "I heard it was four men!"

He frowned. "Does it seem to you that one does not matter? It matters to me."

She said gently, "I'm sorry, Joe. It matters to me, too. But one is better than four."

And even four killings, he realized, she would have forgiven me!

He bent across the table.

"Elizabeth, I enjoy your company. I would like to have it the rest of my life. I want to protect you and work for you and love you and—make you happy, if I can."

"I shouldn't have let you say that," she answered quietly. Her eyes were closed, and there were tears on her cheeks. "I am going to marry a man named Ellerby. And I expect I'll make his life miserable."

He said teasingly, "Does a girl shed tears when she mentions the name of a man she really plans to marry? I've made you cry many a time, but—"

He was beside her, and she clung as his arms went around her. He kissed her until she fought for breath.

"Not Ellerby, whoever he is, my darling. But me. Because I love you. When the road are passable—soon, soon—I'll take you away and you'll not need to set foot on the ground or look at—anything."

"No, Joe, not you. Mr. Ellerby will come for me when I write him, and he will hate every mile of it. And I will marry him because he doesn't deserve any better."

"That's nonsense," Doc Frail said. "You will marry me."

Across the street, a man with a bad cold knocked at Doc's door. He kept a handkerchief to his face as he coughed out his message to Rune:

"Can Doc come, or you? Tall John's cut his leg with an axe, bleeding bad."

"I'll come," gasped Rune, and grabbed for Doc's bag. He knew pretty well what to do for an axe cut; he had been working with Doc all winter. "Tell Doc—he's right across the street."

"Go to Tall John's place," the coughing man managed

to advise. As far as Rune knew, he went across the street to call Doc. Rune did not look back; he was running to save his patient.

When he was out of sight, another man who had been standing in the shadows pounded on Elizabeth's door, calling frantically, "Doc, come quick! That kid Rune's been stabbed at the Big Nugget!"

He was out of sight when Doc Frail barged out, hesitated a moment, decided he could send someone for his bag, and ran toward the saloon.

He tripped and, as he fell, something hit him on the back of the head.

He did not lie in the mud very long. Two men solicitously carried him back in the opposite direction and laid him in the slush at the far side of Flaunce's store. They left him there and went stumbling down the street, obviously drunk.

Frenchy Plante did not use force in entering Elizabeth's cabin. He knocked and called out, "Miss Armistead, it's Frenchy." In a lower tone, he added, "I got good news for you!"

She opened the door and demanded, "Is Rune hurt badly? Oh, what happened?"

"The boy got hurt?" Frenchy was sympathetic.

"Someone called Dr. Frail to look after him—didn't you see him go?"

Frenchy said good-humoredly, "Miss, I'm too plumb damn excited. Listen, can I come in and show you what I brought?"

She hesitated, too concerned to care whether he came in or not.

"Remember," he whispered, "what I said once about Solid Gold Frenchy?"

She remembered and gasped. "Come in," she said.

Doc reeled along the street, cold, soaking wet, and with his head splitting. He would have stopped long enough to let his head stop spinning, but he was driven by cold fear that was like sickness.

What about Elizabeth alone in her cabin? Where was Rune and how badly was he hurt? Doc was bruised and aching, tricked and defeated. Who had conquered him was not very important. Skull Creek would know soon enough that someone had knocked the starch out of Doc Frail without a shot being fired.

Rune, wherever he was, would have to wait for help if he needed it.

At Elizabeth's door Doc listened and heard her voice between tears and laughter: "I don't believe it! I don't think it's really true!"

The door was not barred. He opened it and stood watching with narrowed eyes. Elizabeth was rolling something crookedly across the table, something yellow that looked like a small, misshapen apple. When it fell and boomed on the floor boards, he knew what it was.

He asked in a controlled voice, "Has the kid been here?"

Elizabeth glanced up and gasped. She ran to him, crying, "Joe, you're hurt—what happened? Come sit down. Oh, Joe!"

Frenchy Plante was all concern and sympathy. "My God, Doc, what hit you?"

Doc Frail brushed Elizabeth gently aside and repeated, "Has the kid been here?"

"Ain't seen him," Frenchy said earnestly. "Miss Armistead was saying you'd been called out, he was hurt, so we thought you was with him."

Doc turned away without answering. He ran, stumbling, toward the Big Nugget. He stood in the doorway of the saloon, mud-stained, bloody and arrogant. He asked in a voice that did not need to be loud, "Is the kid in here?"

Nobody answered that, but someone asked, "Well, now, what happened to you?" in a tone of grandfatherly indulgence.

They were watching him, straight-faced, without concern, without much interest, the way they would look at any other man in camp. But not the way they should have looked at Doc Frail. There was nothing unusual in their attitudes, except that they were not surprised. And they should have been. They expected this, he understood.

"I was informed," Doc said, "that Rune had been knifed in a fight here."

The bartender answered, "Hell, there ain't been a fight here. And Rune ain't been in since he came for you two-three days ago."

Doc was at bay, as harmless as an unarmed baby. He turned to the door—and heard laughter, instantly choked.

Outside, he leaned against the wall, sagging, waiting for his head to stop spinning, waiting for his stomach to settle down.

There was danger in the laughter he had heard. And there was nothing he could do. Frail, Frail, Frail.

He realized that he was standing on the spot where Wonder Russell stood when Dusty Smith shot him, long ago.

He began to run, lurching, toward Elizabeth's cabin.

She was waiting in the doorway. She called anxiously, "Joe! Joe!"

Frenchy said, "I kept telling her you'd be all right, but I figured it was best to stay here with her in case anything else happened."

Doc did not answer but sat down, staring at him, and waited for Elizabeth to bring a pan of water and towels.

"Is Rune all right?" she demanded.

"I presume so. It was only a joke, I guess."

Golden peas and beans were on the table with the little golden apple. When Doc would not let Elizabeth help him clean the blood off his face, she turned toward the table slowly as if she could not help it.

"He named the mine for me," she whispered. "He calls it the Lucky Lady." Her face puckered, but she did not cry. She laughed instead, choking.

Rune came in at that moment, puzzled and furious, with Doc's bag.

"They said Tall John was hurt," he blurted out, and stopped at sight of Doc Frail.

"The way I heard it," Doc said across the towel, "you were knifed at the saloon. And somebody hit me over the head."

Rune seemed not to hear him. Rune was staring at the nuggets, moving toward them, pulled by the same force that had pulled Elizabeth.

Frenchy chortled, "Meet the Lucky Lady, kid. I got a strike, and half of it is hers. I'll be leaving now. No, the nuggets are yours, Miss, and there'll be more. Sure hope you get over that crack on the head all right, Doc."

Doc's farewell to Elizabeth was a brief warning: "Bar the door. From now on, there'll be trouble."

He did not explain. He left her to think about it.

*   *   *

She did not go to bed at all that night. She sat at the table, fondling the misshapen golden apple and the golden peas and beans, rolling them, counting them. She held them in her cupped hands, smiling, staring, but not dreaming yet. Their value was unknown to her; there would be plenty of time to get them weighed. They were only a token, anyway. There would be more, lots more.

She hunted out, in its hiding place, a letter she had written to Mr. Ellerby, read it through once, and burned it in the stove.

The golden lumps would build a wall of safety between her and Mr. Ellerby, between her and everything she didn't want.

She sat all night, or stood sometimes by the front window, smiling, hearing the sounds she recognized although she had never heard the like before: the endless racket of a gold rush. Horses' hoofs and the slogging feet of men, forever passing, voices earnest or anxious or angry, the creak of wagons. She listened eagerly with the golden apple cupped in her hand.

Even when someone pounded on her door, she was not afraid. The walls are made of gold, she thought. Nobody can break them down. A man called anxiously, "Lucky Lady, wish me luck! That's all I want, lady, all in the world I want."

Elizabeth answered, "I wish you luck, whoever you are," and laughed.

But when, toward morning, she heard an angry racket outside the back door, she was frightened for Rune. She ran to listen.

"I've got a gun on you," he was raging. "Git going, now!" And men's voices mumbled angrily away.

She spoke to him through the closed back door.

"Rune, go and get Doc. I have been making plans"

The three of them sat at the table before dawn. Coffee was in three cups, but only Rune drank his.

Doc listened to Elizabeth and thought, This is some other woman, not the lost lady, the helpless prisoner. This is the Lucky Lady, an imprisoned queen. This is royalty. This is power. She has suddenly learned to command.

"I would like to hire you, Rune, to be my guard," she began.

Rune glanced at Doc, who nodded. Rune did not answer. Elizabeth did not expect him to answer.

"I would like you to buy me a gold scale as soon as possible," she continued. "And please find out from Mr. Flaunce what would be the cost of freighting in a small piano from the States."

Doc said wearily, "Elizabeth, that's defeat. If you order a piano and wait for it to get here, that means you're not even thinking of leaving Skull Creek."

"When I thought of it, thinking did me no good," she answered, and dismissed the argument.

"Rune, please ask Mr. Flaunce to bring over whatever bolts of dress material he has—satin, in a light gray. I shall have a new dress."

Rune put down his coffee cup. "You could build a lean-to on the back here. I'd ought to stay pretty close, and I don't hanker to sleep on that woodpile often."

She nodded approval. "And another thing: grubstaking Frenchy brought me luck. Other miners will think of the same thing, and I will grubstake them, to keep my luck."

Rune growled, "Nonsense. Hand out a stake to every one that asks for it, and you'll be broke in no time. Set a limit—say every seventh man that asks. But don't let anybody know it's the seventh that gets it."

Elizabeth frowned, then nodded. "Seven is a lucky number."

Doc picked up his cup of cool coffee.

A handful of gold has changed us all, he thought. Elizabeth is the queen—the golden Queen Elizabeth. Rune is seventeen years old, but he is a man of sound judgment—and he is the second best shot in the territory. And I, I am a shadow.

Doc said gently, "Elizabeth, there may not be very much more gold for Frenchy to divide with you. You are planning too much grandeur."

"There will be a great deal more," she contradicted, serenely. "I am going to be very rich. I am the Lucky Lady."

IX

At the end of a single week, the fragility of the Skull Creek gold camp was plain. The town was collapsing, moving to the new strike at Plante Gulch.

The streets swarmed and boomed with strangers—but they were only passing through. Flaunce's store was open day and night to serve prospectors replenishing grub supplies and going on to the new riches. Flaunce was desperately trying to hire men to freight some of his stock on to diggings to set up another store before someone beat him to it.

Doc Frail lounged in his own doorway waiting for Rune to come from Elizabeth's cabin, and watched the stream of men passing by—bearded, ragged, determined men on foot or on horseback, leading donkeys or mules, driving bull teams with laden wagons, slogging along with packs on their shoulders. Almost all of them were strangers.

Let's see if I'm what I used to be, Doc thought, before Frenchy tricked me and got me hit over the head.

He stepped forward into the path of a pack-laden man, who was walking fast and looking earnestly ahead. When they collided, Doc glared at him with his old arrogance, and the man said angrily, "Damn you, stay out of the way," shoved with his elbow, and went on.

No, I am not what I used to be, Doc admitted silently. The old power, which had worked even on strangers, was gone, the challenge in the stare that asked, Do you amount to anything?

Rune came weaving through the crowd, and Doc saw in him power that was new. Rune looked taller. He wore new, clean clothing and good boots, although the gun in his holster was one Doc had given him months before. Rune was no longer sullen. He wore a worried frown, but he was sure of himself.

Doc pointed with his thumb to a vacant lot, and Rune nodded. It was time for his daily target practice, purposely public. In the vacant space where nobody would get hurt, Doc tossed an empty can, and Rune punctured it with three shots before it fell. The steady stream of passing men became a whirlpool, then stopped, and the crowd grew.

Someone shouted, "Hey, kid," and tossed another can. Doc's pistol and Rune's thundered a duet, and the crowd was pleased.

When Rune's gun was empty, Doc kept firing, still with his right hand but with his second gun, tossed with a flashing movement from his left hand as the first weapon dropped to the ground. No more duet, but solo now, by the old master. He heard admiration among the men around them, and that was all to the good. It was necessary that strangers should know the Lucky Lady was well protected. The border shift, the trick of tossing a loaded gun into the hand that released an empty one, was impressive, but Rune had not yet perfected it enough for public demonstration.

That was all there was to the show. The crowd moved on.

"Go take yourself a walk or something," Doc suggested. "I'll watch Elizabeth's place for a while."

"There's a crazy man in town," Rune said. "Did you see him?"

"There are hundreds of crazy men in town. Do you mean that fanatical preacher with red whiskers? I've been on the edge of his congregation three or four times but never stopped to listen. I wouldn't be surprised if the camp lynched him just to shut him up."

"He scares me," Rune admitted, frowning. "They don't like him, but he gets everybody mad and growling. He don't preach the love of God. It's all hell fire and damnation."

Doc asked, suddenly suspicious, "Has he been to Elizabeth's?"

"He was. I wouldn't let him in. But when I said he was a preacher, she made me give him some dust. She'd like to talk to him, figuring she'd get some comfort. He's not the kind of preacher that ever comforted anybody. Go listen to him when you have time."

"I have more time than I used to," Doc Frail admitted. Two new doctors had come through Skull Creek, both heading for the booming new settlement at Plante Gulch.

Doc had an opportunity to listen to the preacher the next afternoon. The piano player at a dance hall far down the street threw his back out of kilter while trying to move the piano. Doc went down to his shack, gave him some pain killer and with a straight face prescribed bed rest and hot bricks.

The man squalled, "Who'll heat the bricks? And I can't stay in bed—we're moving this shebang to Plante Gulch soon as they finish laying a floor."

"They need a piano player when they get there," Doc reminded him. "I'll tell the boss to see to it you get the hot bricks. You are an important fellow, professor."

"Say, guess I am," the man agreed. "Unless they get a better piano player."

Doc left the proprietor tearing his hair because of the threatened delay, then went out to the street. It was crowded with men whose movement had been slowed by curiosity, for across the street on a packing box the red-haired man was preaching.

His eyes were wild, and so were his gestures, and his sermon was a disconnected series of uncompleted threats. He yelled and choked.

"Oh, ye of little faith! Behold I say unto you! Behold a pale horse: and his name that sat on him was Death, and Hell followed with him! Verily, brethren, do not forget hell—the eternal torment, the fire that never dieth. And I heard a great voice out of the temple saying to the seven angels, go your ways, and pour out the vials of the wrath of God upon the earth.

"Lo, there is a dragon that gives power unto the beast, and you worship the dragon and the beast, saying, 'Who is like unto the beast?' And the dragon is gold and the beast is gold, and lo, ye are eternally damned that seek the dragon or the beast."

The preacher was quoting snatches of Revelation, Doc realized, with changes of his own that were not exactly improvements. But gold may be a dragon and a beast, indeed.

A man in the crowd shouted, "Aw, shut up and go dig yourself some beast!" and there was a roar of approving laughter.

"Remember Sodom and Gomorrah!" screamed the red-haired man. "For their wickedness they were burned—yea, for their sin and evil! Lo, this camp is wicked like unto those two!"

Doc Frail was caught in an impatient eddy in the moving crowd, and someone growled, "Give that horse a

lick or we'll never get out of Sodom and on to Gomorrah
by dark!"

The preacher's ranting stirred a kind of futile anger in
Joe Frail. What makes him think he's so much better
than his congregation? Doc wondered. There's a kind of
hatred in him.

"A sinful nation," shouted the preacher. "A people
laden with iniquity, the seed of evildoers, children that
are corrupters. Hear the word of the Lord, ye rulers of
Sodom; give ear unto the law of our God, ye people of
Gomorrah!"

The Book of the Prophet Isaiah, reflected Joe Frail,
who was the son of a minister's daughter. Immediately
the red-haired man returned to Revelation:

"There is given unto me a mouth speaking great things,
and power is given unto me to continue forty and two
months!"

A man behind Joe Frail shouted, "We ain't going to
listen that long."

"If any man have an ear, let him hear! He that leadeth
into captivity shall go into captivity; he that killeth with
the sword must be killed with the sword."

Joe Frail shivered in spite of himself, thinking, And he
that killeth with a pistol?

In that moment a man's voice said behind him, *"That
is the man,"* and Doc went tense as if frozen, staring at
the red-haired madman.

"That's the man I told you about," the voice went on,
moving past him. "Crazy as a loon. His name is Grubb."

How could it be? Doc wondered. How could that be
the man for whom I'll hang?

After a few days, the madman went on to Plante
Gulch.

By August, Elizabeth Armistead was rich and getting
richer. The interior log walls of her cabin were draped
with yards of white muslin, her furniture was the finest
that could be bought in Skull Creek, her piano had been
ordered from the East, and she dressed in satin. But only
a few men ever saw her, only every seventh man who
came to beg a grubstake from the Lucky Lady, and
Frenchy Plante when he came to bring her half the cleanup
from the mine.

This is Saturday, Doc Frail remembered. Cleanup day at the sluices. Frenchy will be in with the gold. And I will spend the evening with Elizabeth, waiting for him to come. The Lucky Lady hides behind a golden wall.

He found Elizabeth indignantly arguing with Rune.

"Frenchy sent a man to say they have a big cleanup this time," she told Doc. "And they want a man with a reputation to help guard it on the way in. But Rune refuses to go!"

"I don't get paid to guard gold," Rune said. "I hired out to guard you."

"Half of it's mine," she argued.

"And half of it's Frenchy's. He'll look after it. The bank's going to open up whenever he comes. But I'm going to be right here."

Doc said without a smile, "Young lady, you seem to have a sensible fellow on your payroll," and was pleased to see Rune blush.

By George, he thought, that's probably the first decent thing I ever said to him!

"I'll be here, too," Doc promised. "Just making a social call."

He was too restless to sit down and wait. He stood in the doorway, looking out, thinking aloud: "The month is August, Elizabeth. The day is lovely, even in this barren cleft between barren hills. And you are young, and I am not decrepit. But you're a prisoner." He turned toward her and asked gently, "Come for a walk with me, Elizabeth?"

"No!" she whispered instantly. "Oh, no!"

He shrugged and turned away. "There was a time when you couldn't go because you didn't have any place to go or enough money. Now you can afford to go anywhere, but you've got a pile of nuggets to hide behind."

"Joe, that's not it at all! I can't go now for the same reason I couldn't go before."

"Have you tried, Elizabeth?"

She would not answer.

He saw that Rune was watching him with slitted eyes and cold anger in the set of his mouth.

"Maybe your partner will bring you some new and unusual nuggets," Doc remarked. "I wonder where he gets them from."

"From his mine, of course," Elizabeth answered. Her special nuggets were not in sight, but Doc knew they were in the covered sugar bowl on the table.

"Madam, I beg to differ. The Lucky Lady is a placer operation. Water is used to wash gold out of dirt and gravel. Most of your nuggets came from there, all right. But—spread them out and I'll show you."

Unwillingly, she tipped the sugar bowl. It was packed with gold; she had to pry it out with a spoon. And this was not her treasure, but her hobby, the private collection she kept just because it was so beautiful.

Doc touched a golden snarl of rigid strands. "That's wire gold, hardened when it cooled. It squeezed through crevices in rock. Rock, Elizabeth. That's hard-rock gold, not placer, and it never came from diggings within a couple of hundred miles from here. Neither did those sharp-edged nuggets with bits of quartz still on them. That gold never came from the mine Frenchy named for you."

Elizabeth stared, fascinated and frightened. "It was in with some other lumps he brought. Where did he get it?"

"He sent for it, to give you. Some men go courting with flowers. Frenchy gives his chosen one imported gold nuggets."

"Don't talk that way! I don't like it."

"I didn't suppose you would, but it was time to tell you."

Frenchy was cleverly succeeding in two purposes: to please Elizabeth and to taunt Joe Frail.

And we are harmless doves, both of us, Doc thought.

"I wish you'd keep those grubstake contracts at the bank," Doc remarked. Four of them were paying off, and some of the others might. "Why keep them in that red box right here in your cabin?"

"Because I like to look at them sometimes," she said stubbornly. "They're perfectly safe. I have Rune to guard me."

Doc smiled with one corner of his mouth, and she hastened to add, "And I have you, too."

"As long as I live, Elizabeth," he said gently.

Rune tried to clear the air by changing the subject. "I hear the preacher, Grubb, is back."

"Then I would like to talk to him," said Elizabeth. "If he comes to the door, please let him in."

"No!" Doc said quite loudly. "Rune, do not let him in. He's a lunatic."

Elizabeth said coolly, "Rune will let him in. Because I want to talk to him. And because I say so!"

Doc said, "Why, Elizabeth!" and looked at her in astonishment. She sat stiff-backed with her chin high, pale with anger, imperious—the queen behind the golden wall, the Lucky Lady, who had forgotten how vulnerable she was. Doc Frail, newly vulnerable, and afraid since the great joke Frenchy had played on him, could not stare her down.

"Rune," he began, but she interrupted, "Rune will let him in because I say so."

Rune looked down at them both "I will not let him in, and not because Doc says to keep him out. I won't let him in—because he shouldn't get in. And that's how it is."

Doc smiled. "The world has changed, Elizabeth. That's how it is. Rune holds all the winning cards—and nobody needs to tell him how to play them."

Rune guessed dimly in that moment that, no matter how long he lived or what he accomplished to win honor among men, he would never be paid any finer compliment.

"Guess I'll go see what's doing around town," he said, embarrassed.

"Both of you can go!" Elizabeth cried in fury.

To her surprise, Doc answered mildly, "All right," and she was left alone. The nuggets from the sugar bowl were scattered on the table. She touched them, fondled them, sorted them into heaps according to size and shape. She began to forget anger and imprisonment. She began to forget that she was young and far from home.

Doc Frail was only a hundred yards away from the cabin when a messenger on a mule hailed him: "Hey, Doc! My partner Frank's hurt up at our mine. There's three men trying to get him out, or hold up the timbering anyway."

He flung himself off the mule and Doc, who had his satchel, leaped into the saddle. He knew where the mine was.

"Send some more men up there," he urged, and started for it.

Rune, strolling, saw him go and turned at once back to

the Lucky Lady's cabin. He did not go in. He hunkered down by the front door and began to whittle.

Down beyond the Big Nugget, the red-haired man was preaching a new sermon, lashing himself to fury—and attracting a more favorably inclined audience than usual. His topic was the Lucky Lady. There was no more fascinating topic in Skull Creek, for she was young and desirable and mysterious, and she represented untold riches, even to men who had never seen her, who knew her only as a legend.

"Lo, there is sin in this camp, great sin!" Grubb was intoning. "The sin that locketh the door on deliverance, that keepeth a young woman prisoner against her will. There is a wicked man who shutteth her up in a cabin, that she escape not, and putteth a guard before her door that righteousness may not enter!"

His listeners were strangers. They believed him, because why not?

One nudged another and murmured, "Say, did you know that?" The other shook his head, frowning.

"She cannot be delivered from evil." intoned Grubb, "because evil encompasseth her round about. She has no comfort within those walls because the servant of the Lord is forbidden to enter."

Someone asked, "Did you try?"

Grubb had tried just once, weeks earlier. But he remembered it as today, and anger was renewed in him. He began to yell.

"Verily, the servant of the Lord tried to enter, to pray with her for deliverance, to win her from evil. But the guard at the door turned him away and bribed him with nuggets. Lo, the guard is as evil as the master, and both of them are damned!"

His audience saw what he saw, the arrogant doctor who would not let the Lucky Lady go, and the young man who idled at her doorway to keep rescuers away. His audience stirred and murmured, and someone said, "By damn, that's a bad thing!" His audience increased, and Grubb, for once delivering a message to which men listened without reviling him, went on screaming words that he convinced himself were true.

One man on the edge of the crowd walked away—the horse thief who was a friend of Tall John, and of Doc who had cured him, and of Rune who had nursed him. The horse thief passed the barbershop and observed that Frenchy Plante was inside, getting his hair cut. Frenchy's mule was hitched in front, and the gold from the weekly cleanup was no doubt in the pack on the mule. But Frenchy was watching from the barber chair with a rifle across his knees, so the horse thief did not linger.

Walking fast, but not running, he paused in front of the Lucky Lady's cabin and spoke quietly to Rune:

"The red-haired fellow is raising hell, working the men up. Saying the girl could get away if it wasn't Doc pays you to keep her locked up. Don't act excited, kid. We're just talking about the weather. I think there's going to be hell to pay, and I'll go tell Tall John. Where's Doc?"

"Went on a call, on Tim Morrison's mule—to Tim's mine, I guess. Thanks."

Unhurried, Rune entered the Lucky Lady's cabin and sat down.

The horse thief, who did not happen to possess a horse just then, went to the livery stable and rented one. At a trot, he rode to the place where Tall John was washing gravel. Tall John dropped his pick and said, "Go look for Doc." He himself started back toward Elizabeth's cabin at a brisk limp.

Tall John observed that a fairly large crowd had gathered down beyond the Big Nugget, and occasionally a shout came from it.

If they ever get into her cabin, he told himself, they'll have to kill the boy first—and if that happens, she won't care to live either. He and I, between us, will have to keep Frenchy out. Heaven forbid that he should be her rescuer!

Tall John knocked on Elizabeth's door and after he identified himself, Rune let him in. He sat down to chat as if he had come only for a friendly visit.

The horse thief met Doc Frail walking. The man trapped in the cave-in had died. He was still trapped.

"There's trouble," the horse thief said bluntly, and told him what the trouble was.

"I'll take that horse, please," Doc replied. He rode at a trot; he did not dare attract attention by going faster. And he did not know what he was going to do when he got to the cabin—if he got there.

It is too late to try to take her out of Skull Creek now, he realized. I wonder how much ammunition Rune has. I haven't much—and what can I do with it anyway, except to shoot through the roof and make a noise?

He heard Frenchy shout "Hey Doc!" from down the street, but he did not turn.

The crowd beyond the Big Nugget was beginning to stir and to scatter on the edges. Rune, watching from a peephole in the blanket on the window, let Doc in before he had a chance to knock.

The three inside the cabin were still as statues. Elizabeth said, "They've just told me. Joe, I'll go out when they come in and I'll tell Grubb it isn't so."

"You'll stay right here," Doc answered. "I hope you will not think I am being melodramatic, but I have to do something that I have been putting off for too long. Tall John, can I make a legal will by telling it to you? There's not time to write it. I want to watch that window."

Elizabeth gasped.

Tall John said, "Tell me. I will not forget."

"My name is Joseph Alberts. I am better known as Joseph Frail. I am of sound mind but in imminent danger of death. I bequeath two thousand dollars in clean gulch gold to—Rune, what's your name?"

Rune answered quietly, "Leonard Henderson."

"To Leonard Henderson, better known as Rune, to enable him to get a medical education if he wants it. Everything else I leave to Elizabeth Armistead, called the Lucky Lady."

"Oh, so lucky!" she choked.

He did not say that he wanted Rune to take her away from Skull Creek. It was not necessary.

"That mob is getting noisier," Doc commented. "Tall John, you'd better go out by the back door."

"I will not forget," Tall John promised. He left the cabin, not stopping even to shake hands.

Just outside the window, Frenchy shouted, "Lucky Lady! I got gold for you! Open the door for Frenchy, Lucky Lady."

No one inside the cabin moved. No one outside could see in.

Frenchy hiccuped and said, "Aw, hell, she ain't home."

He rode on, then shouted, "But she's always home, ain't she?"

Doc spoke rapidly. "If I go out this door, both of you stay inside—and bar it. Do you understand?"

"I get it," Rune replied. Elizabeth was crying quietly.

Frenchy's voice came back. "Doc, you in there? Hey, Doc Frail! Come on out. You ain't scared, are you?"

Joe Frail went tense and relaxed with an effort of will.

"You wouldn't shoot me, would you, Doc?" Frenchy teased. "You wouldn't shoot nobody, would you, Doc?" He laughed uproariously, and Doc Frail did not move a muscle.

He heard the muttering mob now, the deep, disturbed murmur that he had heard from the hill on the day the road agent swung from a bough of the great tree.

He heard a shrill scream from Grubb, who saw Frenchy coaxing at the window and had seen Frenchy enter the cabin before.

Grubb's topic did not change, but his theme did, as he led his congregation. His ranting voice reached them:

"Wicked woman! Wicked and damned! Will all your gold save you from hell fire? Wanton and damned—"

Doc forgot he was a coward. He forgot a man lying dead in Utah. He forgot Wonder Russell, sleeping in a grave on the hill. He slammed the bar upward from the door and stepped into the street.

His voice was thunder: "Grubb, get down on your knees!"

Grubb was blind to danger. He did not even recognize Doc Frail as an obstacle. Clawing the air, he came on, screaming, "Babylon and the wicked woman—"

Doc Frail gasped and shot him.

He did not see Grubb fall, for the mob's wrath downed him. The last thing he heard as he went down under the deluge was the sound he wanted to hear: the bar falling shut inside the cabin door.

X

The rabble. The rabble. The first emotion he felt was contempt. Fear would come later. But no; fear had come. His mouth was cotton-dry.

He was bruised and battered, had been unconscious. He could not see the men he heard and despised. He lay face down on dirty boards and could see the ground through a crack. On a platform? No, his legs were bent and cramped. He was in a cart. He could not move his arms. They were bound to his body with rope.

The rabble shouted and jeered, but not all the jeering was for him—they could not agree among themselves. He knew where he was; under the hanging tree.

A voice cried furiously, "A trial! You've got to give the man a trial!"

Another shout mounted: "Sure, try him—he shot the preacher!"

This is the place and this is the tree, Joe Frail understood, and the rope must be almost ready. Grubb was the man, and I hardly knew he existed.

There was nothing that required doing. Someone else would do it all. There was something monstrous to be concerned about—but not for long.

And there was Elizabeth.

Joe Frail groaned and strained at the rope that bound him, and he heard Frenchy laugh.

"Let the boys see you, Doc," Frenchy urged. "Let 'em have a last good look!"

Someone heaved him to his feet and he blinked through his hair, fallen down over his eyes. The mob turned quiet, staring at a man who was as good as dead.

There was no need for dignity now, no need for anything. If he swayed, someone supported him. If he fell, they would stand him on his feet again. Everything that was to be done would be done by someone else. Joe Frail had no responsibilities any more. (Except—Elizabeth? Elizabeth?)

"Hell, that's no decent way to do it," someone argued with authority, not asking for justice but only for a proper execution. "The end of the cart will catch his feet that way. Put a plank across it. Then he'll get a good drop."

There was a busy delay while men streamed down the hill to get planks.

Joe Frail threw back his head with the old arrogant gesture and could see better with his hair tossed away from his eyes. He could see Skull Creek better than he wanted to, as clearly as when he first walked under the tree with Wonder Russell.

Elizabeth, Elizabeth. He was shaken with anger. When a man is at his own hanging, he should not have to think of anyone but himself.

And still, he understood, even now Joe Frail must fret helplessly about Elizabeth. Who ever really died at peace except those who had nothing to live for?

Men were coming with planks—four or five men, four or five planks. They busied themselves laying planks across the cart to make a platform so they could take satisfaction in having hanged him decently and with compassion. And from the side, Frenchy was bringing up a team of horses to pull the cart away.

Someone behind him slipped a noose down over his head, then took it off again, testing the length of the rope. Above, someone climbed along the out-thrust bough of the tree to tie it shorter. Joe Frail stood steady, not looking up, not glancing sideways at the horses being urged into position.

The crowd was quieter now, waiting.

Just as the team came into position in front of the cart, he saw movement down in the street of Skull Creek and strained forward.

Elizabeth's door had opened and Rune had come out of her cabin.

No! No! You damn young fool, stay in there and do what you can to save her! By tomorrow, they'll slink off like dogs and you can get her away safely. You fool! You utter fool!

What's he carrying? A red box.

No, Elizabeth! Oh, God, not Elizabeth! Stay in the cabin! Stay out of sight!

But the Lucky Lady had emerged from her refuge and was walking beside Rune. Walking fast, half running, with her head bent. Don't look, Elizabeth! My darling, don't look up! Turn back, turn back to the cabin. Tomorrow you can leave it.

A man behind Doc remarked, "Well, would you look at that!" but nobody else seemed to notice.

Doc said sharply, "What the hell are you waiting for?" Suddenly he was in a hurry. If they finished this fast enough, she would go back—Rune would see to it.

She was leaning forward against the wind of the desert that was thirty miles away. She was stumbling. But she did not fall. She had got past Flaunce's store.

The red box Rune is carrying? The box she keeps her gold in. Go back. Go back.

Someone slipped the noose down over his head again and he groaned and was ashamed.

She was struggling up the first slope of the barren hill, fighting the desert. Her right arm was across her eyes. But Doc could see Rune's face. Rune was carrying the heavy box and could not help the Lucky Lady, but the look on his face was one Doc had seen there seldom. It was pity.

The team was ready, the platform was prepared, the noose was around the condemned man's neck. The Lucky Lady stopped halfway up the hill.

There was almost no sound from the rabble except their breathing. Some of them were watching Elizabeth. She lifted her right hand and fired a shot from the derringer into the air.

Then they all watched her. The silence was complete and vast. The men stared and waited.

Rune put the red box on the ground and opened it, handed something to Elizabeth—a poke, Doc thought. She emptied it into her hand and threw nuggets toward the silent mob.

No one moved. No one spoke or even murmured.

Why, Rune has no gun, Doc saw. It is a long time since I have seen him with no holster on his hip. And Elizabeth has fired into the air the one shot her pistol will hold. They are unarmed, helpless. As helpless as I am.

The voice he heard was his own, screaming, "Go back! Go back!"

A man behind him rested a hand on his shoulder without roughness, as if to say, Hush, hush, this is a time for silence.

Elizabeth stooped again to the box and took out something white—the sugar bowl. She flung the great, shining nuggets of her golden treasure, two and three at a time, toward the motionless men on the slope. Then they were not quite motionless, there was jerky movement among them, instantly ceasing, as they yearned toward the scattered treasure but would not yield.

Elizabeth stood for a while with her head bent and her hands hanging empty. Joe Frail saw her shoulders move as she gulped in great breaths of air. Rune stood watching her with that look of pity twisting his mouth.

She bent once more and took out a folded paper, held it high, and gave it to the wind. It sailed a little distance before it reached the ground. She waited with her head bowed, and the mob waited, stirring with the restless motion of puzzled men.

She tossed another paper and another. Someone asked the air a question: "Contracts? Grubstake contracts?"

And someone else said, "But which ones?"

Most of the contracts had no meaning any more, but a very few of them commanded for the Lucky Lady half the golden treasure that sifted out of paying mines.

Frenchy's voice roared with glee: "She's buying Doc Frail! The Lucky Lady is buying her man!"

Joe Frail quivered, thinking, This is the last indignity. She has gambled everything, and there will be nothing for her to remember except my shame.

All the contracts, one at a time, she offered to the mob, and the wind claimed each paper for a brief time. All the nuggets in the sugar bowl. All the pale dust in the little leather bags that made the red box heavy.

Elizabeth stood at last with her hands empty. She touched the box with her foot and Rune lifted it, turned it upside down to show that it held nothing more, and let it fall.

Frenchy's shout and Frenchy's forward rush broke the mob's indecision. He yelled, "Come and git it, boys! Git your share of the price she's paying for Doc Frail!"

Frenchy ran for the scattered papers, tossed away one after another, then held one up, roaring, and kissed it.

The rabble broke. Shouting and howling, the mob scattered, the men scrabbled for gold in the dust. They swarmed like vicious ants, fighting for the treasure.

A jeering voice behind Doc said, "Hell, if she wants you that bad!" and cut the rope that bound him. The knife slashed his wrist and he felt blood run.

The Lucky Lady was running up the slope to him, not stumbling, not hesitating, free of fear and treasure, up toward the hanging tree. Her face was pale, but her eyes were shining.

About the Author

Bill Pronzini has published more than 30 novels (including several Westerns), 275 short stories and articles, and 1 nonfiction work. He has edited or co-edited some 20 anthologies. **Martin H. Greenberg** has been the editor or co-editor of more than 100 anthologies covering a wide range of fiction and nonfiction, including *The Fantastic Saint* by Leslie Charteris (with Charles Waugh) and *100 Great Fantasy Stories* (with Isaac Asimov and Terry Carr). Together, Mr. Pronzini and Mr. Greenberg have edited *The Arbor House Treasury of Great Western Stories*.

BOLD NEW FRONTIERS

279022